REDACTED VICE

BOOK SIX OF RISE OF THE PEACEMAKERS

Kevin Ikenberry & Kevin Steverson

Seventh Seal Press
Coinjock, NC

Copyright © 2021 by Kevin Ikenberry & Kevin Steverson.

All rights reserved. No part of this publication may be reproduced, distributed or transmitted in any form or by any means, including photocopying, recording, or other electronic or mechanical methods, without the prior written permission of the publisher, except in the case of brief quotations embodied in critical reviews and certain other noncommercial uses permitted by copyright law. For permission requests, write to the publisher, addressed "Attention: Permissions Coordinator," at the address below.

Chris Kennedy/Seventh Seal Press
1097 Waterlily Rd.
Coinjock, NC 27923
http://chriskennedypublishing.com/

Publisher's Note: This is a work of fiction. Names, characters, places, and incidents are a product of the author's imagination. Locales and public names are sometimes used for atmospheric purposes. Any resemblance to actual people, living or dead, or to businesses, companies, events, institutions, or locales is completely coincidental.

Cover Art by Ricky Ryan
Cover Design by Brenda Mihalko

Ordering Information:
Quantity sales. Special discounts are available on quantity purchases by corporations, associations, and others. For details, contact the "Special Sales Department" at the address above.

Redacted Vice/Kevin Ikenberry & Kevin Steverson -- 1st ed.
ISBN: 978-1648551352

For My Girls.

– Kevin Ikenberry

I would like to dedicate this to my wife, Stacey. She selflessly gives up time with me in my retirement so I can write and give you, the reader, time away from reality. She says I may be retired from the military, but I am not really retired. She's right. She always is.

I would also like to say thank you. Yes, to you. The characters in this book heard your demands for more, so we wrote more. Kevin and I could do no other. You made this book possible…and there will be more.

– Kevin Steverson

Chapter One

Krifay

Larth had to admit grilled fish fresh from the vibrant, clean waters off Siphon Point was pretty damned tasty. His penchant for fish, usually in the form of a modified, chopped, breaded, and fried stick had taken quite a turn during their unintended mini vacation. Instead of moving forward to points unknown at the orders of the guild master, they'd limped to Krifay after one of the hyperspace shunts on *Against the Wind* failed. They'd had to use a gate pass just to get to Krifay, though the Blue Ridge Kin had plenty of credits to cover it.

As he gently flipped a steak of something called mahi-mahi on the hot grill's surface, Larth couldn't help but smile. He and his partner were less than a year out of the prestigious halls of the Peacemaker Academy and had already bagged their first mission and deputized their first mercenary company.

Not bad for a couple of "pranksters without a serious bone in their bodies."

"Hey, Larth. When's lunch?"

He turned and saw the pretty blonde Human bouncing up to him. Like the others, she wore a swimming garment, but it seemed far too small to both cover and provide any type of support to her body. "I'm just grilling the fish. Ricky and Keaton have lunch duty today."

"Oh, I know," May Bolton said with a smile. If she'd been a Zuparti—like him—there wouldn't have been a nanosecond of hesitation. More than once, he'd thought about a potential coupling all the way to the physical part before revulsion brought him back to normal. Besides, she was a mercenary officer and a deputized agent of the Peacemaker Guild. That made her off limits, even for Larth. "But they've sloughed it off onto Sergeant Squarlik and the others again."

"Stop making cookies." Larth grinned. "Those Goka go nuts every time you bake them. Ricky and Keaton know this, so they beg you to bake them and then use them for bartering the chores back to Squarlik and his squad. It's pretty comical."

"Except for them oatmeal raisin cookies Cora wanted that one time," May said with a laugh. "Nobody should put raisins in anything."

"Agreed. I walked in on a game of Tumble Gambit, and Squarlik had the red end of the stick pointed at him. The pot had hard credits *and* cookies in it. One of the Jivool, I think it was Mardram…but it could have been his brother, Rynard. Hard to tell those two apart when they're sitting down with their backs to you. Anyway, the Jivool demanded they agree the raisin cookies were worthless and could not go into the pot. Squarlik had to bet something else."

"Is that why Squarlik moped around, grumbling about losing his favorite knife on a sure thing?" she asked.

"Yeah," Larth answered with a grin. "Mardram had a Holder's Choice card in his paw, along with three Hexagons and a Linear. All in the same color."

"Bless his heart." May whistled and said, "Sure as I'm standing here, that right there's a pot dragger. I seen it before but ain't had nary a one in my hand."

"Me either," he admitted. Larth moved across the grill to the mahi-mahi filets and a massive hunk of tuna for Jyrall. "Hey, will you go ask Snarlyface if he wants his tuna rare or civilized?"

"Rare," a gruff, deep voice said from the deck of their beachside bungalow. Larth looked up and saw Jyrall's massive frame leaning over a railing far too rickety to possibly hold him. The Besquith smiled ominously. "Is that mahi-mahi, too?"

"Um, no," Larth lied. *Dammit! There goes the entire catch again.*

"That's mahi-mahi, Larth. I can smell it."

"You're mistaken. I mean, since Cora hit you in the face with a volleyball yesterday, your whole smelling thing has been off."

"It has not!" Jyrall's smile faded. "But I must learn spiking. That was exhilarating."

Larth chuckled. "A bloody nose is exhilarating? We really need to get you laid, buddy."

Jyrall laughed. His wide, long jaw curled in a smile. "Don't you worry about me, Little Buddy."

Larth heard a soft snicker at his side. May and the other ladies had mistakenly started talking about old television shows right after their arrival on Krifay. Of course, Ricky and Keaton knew exactly what they were talking about, but Jyrall and Larth had never been exposed to *Gilligan's Island.* It hadn't taken long for Jyrall to finally turn the nickname game back on Larth. He'd assumed Jyrall hadn't minded being called Snarlyface for the last several years. He was wrong.

"You know I hate that," Larth said with a frown. "I think Snarlyface is a perfectly justifiable nickname. I don't know why you have to get so—"

Both May and Jyrall were laughing now. On the upper deck of the beach house, a sliding door opened, and the Blue Ridge Kin's dark haired Human commander, Cora McCoy, appeared. She walked across the thin deck, stood next to Jyrall, and placed her hand casually on his large, furry arm. "I think Little Buddy works very well," she said with a smile.

"Nobody asked you, Cora," Larth barked. It didn't really matter. He was more concerned about the level of...well, affection he'd seen between Cora and Jyrall over the last ten days. He tried to ascribe it to the Human connection to canines. While Jyrall, as a Besquith, was certainly canine in nature, he was anything but a friendly companion. That he and Cora would become familiar and comfortable with one another surprised Larth more than it seemed to surprise everyone else. While he liked Cora immensely, he was still worried about what precedent it might set. He also tried to tell himself he wasn't worried about Jyrall having his feelings hurt or his heart broken.

"Well," Cora began, "nicknames are funny like that. If you can't take it, don't dish it out."

Larth flipped Jyrall's tuna steak with the long, metal spatula and stared up at Cora. "You know, there's a lot of Human sayings I like, and I've adopted them for my own use. That one is not one of my favorites."

"But it's true," Jyrall said. "You've called me Snarlyface for years. I haven't really minded. More importantly, I've let my coming up with a nickname for you slide. It's just the nature of things. Eventually, the right one was going to come along. It could've been Gatchup, but I let that go. You shouldn't be worried about it. Besides, outside of our little group of folks, you know I'm never going to call you Little Buddy."

"You're damned right you're not going to!" Larth pointed angrily at Jyrall with the spatula as his own laughter bubbled to the surface. Amid the laughter of the group, Larth had to admit it was pretty funny.

A new voice called from the entrance to the compound off the main thoroughfare. "Hey, y'all. What's for lunch?"

Larth turned and saw that the Pushtal twin brothers, Ricky and Keaton, were pushing through the laser gate and onto the property. They'd visited the shipyard that morning to check on the progress of the hyperspace shunt repair. They both had satisfied looks on their faces, which told Larth vacation was over and *Against the Wind* was ready for the next mission.

"How's the ship?" Jyrall asked. Cora still hadn't taken her hand off his arm.

"She's ready and raring to go," Ricky said. "So I hear."

Keaton leaned in. "First Sergeant Figgle and the others have started the load process. I figure we can be off the planet in two to three hours. Maybe less. We are set to get the final inspection on her in an hour. After lunch."

Larth locked eyes with Jyrall for a moment. "Better update the guild."

Jyrall nodded. "I was thinking the same thing. How long will it take us to get to Weqq?"

Keaton shrugged. It was comical to see such a ferocious looking creature take on a Human sign of indifference. "It's two jumps. We'll be there in fourteen days, plus travel to the stargate, if all goes well."

If all goes well. The standard Human response to spaceflight. Larth kept his face straight. Sometimes, it was hard to believe the brothers weren't fully Human.

"Too bad we can't wrangle us one a them Blue Flights," Ricky quipped.

Jyrall laughed. "Would certainly make things easier and faster."

"Easy isn't what we do," Cora said.

Since the end of the mission on Parmick, Cora McCoy had taken command of the new mercenary company, the Blue Ridge Kin. On Krifay, they'd fully registered with the Mercenary Guild, though no one in the guild's office had any official capacity, given their internal tumult. Still, Cora had seen to filing the paperwork and arranging their accounts in accordance with the regulations. From everything Larth could see, she was going to be a fantastic mercenary commander. Yet his eyes returned to her hand lingering on Jyrall's arm. There was no doubting the two seemed closer now than they had prior to their arrival. Was the gesture a simple matter of friendship? Was there more to it? Were they all headed into a gigantic fucking disaster?

May elbowed him gently in the side. "Hey, don't burn the fish there, chef."

Her simple gesture brought him back to the task at hand, cooking lunch. It also served to quiet the doubting voice in his head. Maybe Humans were just innately physical, and they liked to touch. Surely that was it.

"Might as well round up the others," Ricky said. "Y'all can start cleaning up the house and be ready to move as soon as we finish eating and get the ship inspected."

"That's a good plan," Cora said. "Why don't you two—" she nodded at Jyrall and Larth, "—go take care of your notification. We'll get everything settled here. Then we can eat and board. We've got two weeks of travel ahead of us; might as well enjoy our last few hours planetside."

"That sounds like a plan," Jyrall answered with a smile. His massive hand closed over Cora's on his arm and patted it gently twice.

Larth felt his stomach twist a little on itself, but the feeling didn't last long. His slate, the smaller version strapped to his wrist, dinged with an incoming message. He glanced up and saw Jyrall consulting his own slate. He turned and whispered something to Cora, and she moved away with a smile on her pretty Human face. Larth looked at the words and felt the knot is his abdomen double.

<<STORMWATCH—URGENT MESSAGE>>

By regulation, there were only a handful of reasons why the Peacemaker Guild would send an urgent message, by name, over the classified data network known as Stormwatch. Two of the reasons equated to personal emergencies with the family of a Peacemaker. Those were never the kind anyone wanted to receive. The other three related to specific actions performed in the line of duty. One was the replacement of a fallen Peacemaker. Another was the emergency deployment of Peacemakers to an area where one had fallen—what Humans in Tri-V shows tended to call "officer down" situations—to maintain civil proceedings during contentious negotiations. The third was a change of mission directed by the highest level of the guild, usually from the guild master. Given their history and what they had accomplished on Parmick, there was little doubt in Larth's mind the message was anything else.

He opened the message and let the slate read the print of his right index digit.

//Change of mission. Separate immediately from the Blue Ridge Kin and proceed at best possible speed and least number of jumps to

Cetla-Prime in the Zustram System, Tolo Region. Proceed under cover—previous identities are secure. Rendezvous with Captain Dreel on site for mission parameters. Support authorized, but only the pilots for the ship you utilize. Highly recommend your previous vessel. Acknowledge Key Seven X-ray Four Charlie Two.//

Larth typed the acknowledgment sequence and quickly pulled the tuna and mahi-mahi from the grill. All of it appeared to be slightly overdone. As an omen for the upcoming mission, it could have been better.

"Well, partner," Jyrall growled above him, "that's not good."

"The fish I almost ruined or this shit?" Larth pointed at his slate.

Jyrall's mouth twisted. "Both."

Larth could only agree.

* * *

Cora stood to the side while the project's manager inspected the work his technicians had completed just that morning. As they were on *Against the Wind*, panels and compartments were open in both *Blue Ridge* and *Kellie's Stand,* as well, awaiting final inspection. She had her arm across her stomach, holding the elbow of the hand covering her mouth. She tried to keep it together, and she was doing a pretty good job of hiding her smile.

The inspector was standing beside the two brothers in the cargo bay of *Against the Wind*, because it had been flagged while in the Krifay system. It wouldn't do for anyone to know it was also the ship *Night Moves*. Ricky was fit to be tied, and it was all Keaton could do to keep him calm. Others in the bay shifted nervously from foot to foot or pincer to pincer.

"Just what in the hell do you mean, 'who is your mechanic?'" Ricky demanded. The look on his face was dangerous, never mind that he was a Pushtal, a bipedal race resembling tigers from Earth, and actually very dangerous.

"I mean no disrespect, honored one," the Jeha said as he stepped back, intimidated, but resolved to hold his ground. "But see? Look at what my technicians removed before they could start new with the shunt repairs." He pointed with several arms at the pile of components in the center of the bay.

After a moment, the Jeha continued, "I say 'repairs,' but I must really use the term shunt build. I ask again, who was your mechanic?"

The four Maki standing near Ricky inhaled sharply. Good mechanics and technicians in their own right, they were appalled at the insinuation on Ricky's behalf. Their split tails, extended up behind their heads in agitation, waved slowly.

The Jeha was insulting someone they considered their kin, regardless of Ricky's race. Over the last few months, their unit had taken to heart the notion of kinship. Technically, the McCoy brothers were not part of Blue Ridge Kin, but in the eyes of every enlisted member of the unit, they were honorary members. One of the Maki cracked his little knuckles in anticipation as he eyed the other Jeha technicians standing with the inspector.

"Build!" Ricky said. "Looky here. I'm 'bout to get sideways on you right here in the bay. You can't go running down a fella's work and not expect him to go upside your head. Yer fixin' to start sumthin' with a McCoy you don't want no part of. I'll be on you like a skeeter in the springtime."

"Calm down," Keaton advised. "Listen to him. You know we built those shunts way off in a sector hardly no one goes. I mean, it's not like we had the latest technology there. We maybe could stand to learn a little something here."

"Bullshit!" Ricky exclaimed. "We worked hard on 'em. We made plenty of jumps with…"

Ricky didn't finish the sentence as the Jeha bent down and picked up a piece of a circuit board with four of his small pincers. He held it out to Ricky. Ricky slowly took it from him and looked at it.

"Is this..." Ricky asked, his voice calmer.

"Yes," the inspector said. "You fried the overlay board for the synchronization stabilizer to the relay adapter of the modulation override and juxtaposition relay."

"That means…" Ricky started to say.

"Yes. I will not bore everyone with how the shunts work and the science involved. It is very complicated. I will say this: You, this ship, and everyone aboard should now be stuck…in between, never to be seen or heard from again. I cannot understand how you are not, given your setup."

"Well," Ricky said, as he stared wide-eyed at the piece in his paw. "Hell fire." It came out sounding like the word "far."

"I mean, I did have a backup piece I sorta made out of a dohicky. I took several whatchamacallits off a thingy-bob, since there were three of them for security measures, and linked 'em with a double connection of whosits. I figured it could hold in a pinch. I mean…I guess it did hold. Once…anyway."

"I see," the Jeha said slowly. "Let me ask you, did you consider the variations possible should the bypass roll back and overload the board?"

"Not really," Ricky admitted. "But, hey, it worked."

"It did," agreed the Jeha reluctantly. "My compliments on the patch, but, again, I contest it should not have." The other Jeha standing behind him attempted to nod, resulting in a comical bending of the segments of their upper body.

"Sometimes, you have to fix shit with bailing wire and waterfowl adhesives," stated the Maki most ready to fight for his kin.

"You know it, Kylont," Ricky agreed. He whispered back to the Maki, "It's duck tape. *Duck tape.*"

"*Duct* tape," Keaton corrected. He paused a moment and said, "With a 't,' you dang hillbilly."

"Whatever," Ricky said dismissively, waving his paw about. "We did what we had to do. Sometimes, ya gotta. Long as y'all got it fixed, and it won't happen again is all that matters. And it better not, 'cause we're paying an arm and a hind leg for it." He crossed his arms, and the four Maki followed suit.

Cora stepped up before things could go on any longer. "You four, stand by your ships. Let the inspector finish here so he can check us off. We have places to be." She paused and then said, "First Sergeant Figgle is overseeing the load-in on both ships right now."

All four Maki eyes widened, and they scrambled out of the cargo bay, worried about where the unit members might move their tools, toolboxes, and gear without their supervision. Cora shook her head and grinned. *Mechanics.*

"Colonel McCoy," the inspector said. "This ship is now ready to traverse the galaxy. I am personally guaranteeing the work on it. *Blue Ridge* and *Kellie's Stand* are as well. The entire shunt system on them is of our company's design, and I can assure you the work is impeccable."

One of the technicians behind him passed a slate up for his imprint signature and Cora's, verifying she and her mercenary company were satisfied with the work. Once she made her imprint to pay the remainder of the bill, the Jeha and his companions bowed and made their way off the ship.

When they were well and truly gone, Jyrall and Larth stepped into the cargo hold from behind a hidden compartment panel. Jyrall held out his huge paw. "Pay up."

"Fine," Larth said with a sigh, as he pulled a credit piece from a pocket on his vest. "You never want to bet me, and when you finally do, you win one. I thought for sure they were going to scrap. I would have paid good credits to see those four Maki rolling with the Jeha. No way were they going to allow Ricky to fight by himself."

"Them boys woulda whupped ass, you can bet on that," Ricky said defiantly. He looked down at the piece he was still holding.

Cora noticed the look and placed a hand on his shoulder. "Don't let it bother you, cousin. You turn a good wrench."

"Yeah," Keaton agreed. "Come on. Let's make sure we're ready to move out."

"That was well done," Jyrall said after the brothers left the hold. "You let Ricky defend his work but did not let it elevate to anything more than a disagreement."

"Sometimes, you have to let them vent and then smooth it all out." Cora shrugged. "It's all part of it. I mean, I know Ricky is not a member of the Kin, but you asked me to handle it so the technicians wouldn't remember you two. I just did my thing, I guess."

"We will ensure the credits for the repairs to this ship are paid back to your company," Jyrall said.

"Thank you," Cora said, "but there is no hurry. We're still looking pretty good in the ol' bank account."

"Yeah," Larth added. "But we pay what we owe. Even if it is a sucker bet." He looked over to the credit Jyrall still held in his paw. "Well, what are we waiting for? We have places to be." He walked down the ramp and called back over his shoulder, "I think I'll go see what new names First Sergeant Figgle has come up with for his troops."

Cora shook her head. "He does have some good ones. It's funny; he calls them everything in the book, and they still love him."

"They know when they are being led by a good leader, one who cares," Jyrall said. "I understand it completely. I feel the same about Captain Dreel."

"He is a good 'un," agreed Cora. She nodded toward the ramp and looped her arm in his. "Come on. We're missing formation.

* * * * *

Chapter Two

Snowmass

There wasn't much to like about Snowmass. Granted, during the short summer months, Lieutenant Colonel Tirr believed it might be a nice planet and almost hospitable for MinSha like him at the equatorial region. But as winter surged forward, the global temperatures dropped, and all the new arrivals could smell the ice and snow readying to drop on them. From what the locals said, the first measurable snowfall would come suddenly and with a ferocity that would surprise them. To that end, Tirr decided his mission needed to unfold at near breakneck pace. Even if they merely gathered the necessary samples from the remnants of the Lake Pryce facility and analyzed them in a temperature-controlled environment, he would be happy. While the MinSha carapace provided natural armor and protection, it did little for cold.

Thankfully, his team only had one real site to check, and thanks to the recent operations of Force 25, they had their first opportunity to test a matched site from the Dream World Consortium's list of potential targets. What they wanted, or what they might be looking for, was still unknown. The DWC had only half-wrecked the facility; the quick actions of Force 25 had prevented its total destruction. Despite the clumsy attempts to get rid of any evidence, some had been found almost completely intact. The most important piece of evidence had actually been the large hatchery-like tanks of water left behind.

Some had been successfully emptied, and combined with the recent rains, anything left in the bottoms of those tanks had been contaminated to the point of inviability. Two tanks were still full of water, and after careful and precise analysis, he was certain of one thing: The Dream World Consortium had not simply been analyzing the water. They had been trying to chemically alter it.

His squad leader, Sezza, appeared at his shoulder and looked at one of the filled tanks. He glanced at her. "Found anything?"

She chittered, "We found a great many things. It is discerning which are important and which are not that is taking the most time."

"Time is not our ally." Tirr glanced up at the slate gray clouds swirling above them. Local meteorologists were calling for the first snowfall at any time. The unpredictability of Snowmass' weather patterns approached legendary. The arrival of the eight-month long winter not only made insertion and recovery difficult, but it would also make completing the investigation almost impossible.

"We need to take everything we can as evidence. Once we've secured it, we will need to move it to an alternate location for the analysis and reporting process."

Sezza's antennae twitched. "Where do you want to go?"

Tirr ground his lower jaw. He hadn't thought much further than grabbing whatever they could and getting back to *Victory Twelve*. There was a rudimentary lab onboard, courtesy of Honored Queen Taal. He wasn't sure whether it would be enough to analyze anything or whether the storms would prevent them from getting back to orbit. Eight months was far too long.

"We should look into temporary lodging," Tirr said. "I'm not certain where the nearest—"

"Why don't you come with us?"

Tirr whirled to his right and saw the familiar, smiling face of Jamie Ibson. The former commander of Victoria Forces had happily accepted a lower ranking position with Force 25. While he smiled warmly at the MinSha, it did not reach his eyes. Tirr couldn't help thinking his friend looked concerned…and sad.

"Jamie." Tirr nodded solemnly and pranced forward. He'd grown used to the awkward movement necessary to approximate a Human hug. "It is good to see you, my friend."

"And you, Honored Tirr." Ibson wrapped his arms around Tirr's upper thorax, and they gently embraced each other. "I wish you'd been here a few weeks ago."

They released each other. Tirr lowered his head to the short Human's level. "I haven't seen any reports, given our mission and lack of communication. What have I missed?"

"It's more like what haven't you missed." Ibson removed his black patrol cap and ran a hand across his clean-shaven scalp. There was something he wanted to say, in Tirr's reasoning, but would not.

"I've never seen you like this. What happened? Did you find Snowman?"

"No." Ibson snorted and shook his head. "We know where he is, and we're getting ready to deploy to get him. Managed to find one of the Haulers' caches here, and it's massive enough that we moved in with room to spare. Managed to pick up more mercs, at least the ones we didn't kill. But we took some…losses. It's been hard here, my friend. Harder than we imagined it could be."

"Colonel Mason is healthy and in command?"

"Oh. Yeah. Tara is fine." Ibson sighed. Tirr could see the pain in his friend's face. They'd been through a lot at Victoria Bravo, but whatever had occurred on Snowmass had stung him.

"Would you mind telling me what happened?"

"It's a long story. While we came out on top, it's the kind of victory that really hurts. Humans call it a pyrrhic victory. It's really hard to know if we won or not."

Tirrs' antennae bounced in frustration. "What is it, Jamie? Tell me what happened."

Ibson took another deep breath and exhaled while looking off into the distance, before turning his bright eyes back to Tirr. "We followed our first real lead for Snowman. Old audio files from the Intergalactic Haulers' database about how James Francis met his wife, Jessica's mother, here. We arrived and discovered our old friends, the Dream World Consortium, were at it again. That's what you're here looking into, I know. If that wasn't bad enough, the politicians were struggling for power and putting mercenaries in play to secure their own positions. The Deputy Mayor, in particular, was the first one to call in mercenaries when things started to go south. From what we gather, she was trying to play them off Force 25. But things were bad before that, if you really want to know. The civilians here have been struggling against the local government for some time. The complaints against the Dream World Consortium were mounting toward an avalanche of violence. There were efforts on the planet that can really only be classified as resistance. Frustrated farmers and workers, backed by a Veetanho elder who'd managed to hide on the planet for years, attacked the Dream World Consortium's machinery when the DWC decided they no longer wanted to negotiate."

Tirr nodded. "Not keeping their end of the bargain again, right? Sounds familiar."

"That's their *modus operandi.* Sorry, that's Latin for a familiar, standard way of doing things."

"I know Latin, Jamie. It's a wonderful language for MinSha. It's how we really first understood you Humans."

Ibson took another breath. "Anyway, with the resistance raising hell with the DWC, the Deputy Mayor, a Human named Sophie Pryce, decided it would be a good time to renegotiate the security contract for the mercenaries who were already here. The Trenta Knights had held the contract for something like thirty or forty years. She approached Captain Gray, who acted as our commander, about taking the contract outright. Of course, that automatically turned the Trenta Knights against us. Tara intended for them to do so, and we were ready for them. We had a minimal force on the ground and gave them an easy target. Their commander decided to come after us with everything he had. I'm still not really sure why he made that decision unless it was fear of losing their contract."

"Must've been worth a lot of credits," Tirr said.

"Yeah," Ibson replied. "A whole bunch of them. So, they attacked us while we still had the small force in garrison. We took some casualties. Lost some promising new folks. Drew Morris and a few others."

"That's unfortunate. He was good."

"He was," Ibson said. "Tara focused us north, based on intel she had, and we went. This time, we expected the Knights to follow us, and we were more than ready for them. Tara put the entire company in place, and we prepared the battlefield as much as we could. The Knights came in, swinging hard, and we hit them back. They gave us fits, but we took them down. What we didn't factor in was their commander being a crafty son of a bitch."

"What makes you say that?"

Ibson huffed. "He was on a flyer, commanding his troops from the air. When we shot him down, he ejected from the flyer and came down under parachute, pulled a rifle, and opened fire."

"Why did you not shoot him when he first came out under parachute? End his miserable life right there?"

Ibson shook his head. "It's a Human thing. The old rules of war dictated you didn't shoot someone under parachute, because they couldn't do anything to harm you, or they could be captured and interrogated. None of us opened fire. By the time we did—well, the Misfits did—it was too late. We'd taken our most serious casualty."

Tirr's antennae straightened in fear. "Lucille? Deathangel 25?"

"No," Ibson replied, his face suddenly sad and distant. "Peacemaker Vannix."

Tirr felt an icy chill race through his thorax. "Oh, no."

Vannix was the model Peacemaker. She possessed all the qualities one would expect from the members of her guild, but there was something else about her. Something he saw in only a few races of the galaxy, and not typically hers. Vannix truly cared—she cared more about the citizens involved than the actual rules. Her ideas of justice and equality were very similar to Jessica Francis'. Though the two of them couldn't have been any more different, Tirr believed they would've been great friends. The loss of Vannix struck him more deeply than he thought possible.

"Yeah," Ibson said, "it really sucks. There's no other way to describe it."

"My condolences hardly mask our shared pain," Tirr replied. He brought up one foreclaw to his thorax and tapped in salute. "Vannix was the best of us."

"The very best of us," Ibson replied.

"Where do things stand now?"

The focus returned to Ibson's face. He'd obviously wanted to talk with someone about the loss and his feelings. Tirr could relate. While traveling with a squad of MinSha female warriors as his protection for the mission gave him great security, his ability to discuss and decompress equated to nil.

Ibson began, "Force 25 is two weeks or so from deployment. What we found in Snowman's cache has certainly helped, but a lot of it needs serious maintenance work. We've gotten started on that and are working to resupply the older CASPers with fuel and ammunition, which is why it's gonna take us a little more time to get off the planet. I'm looking forward to that. Getting off the planet, I mean. We can't afford any more setbacks."

Tirr knew enough about Humans to understand there was something his friend had not shared. "What are you talking about?"

"We lost Peacemaker Vannix, and just yesterday, Peacemaker Rains left."

"Left?" Peacemakers typically needed orders to move from one place to the next. Orders meant some type of advance knowledge. One never simply left an assignment.

"Yeah, he up and left. Something happened, and he left. He borrowed *Ptolemy*, a couple of CASPer techs, and their mech."

Tirr shook his head, and his antennae bobbed from side to side. "That makes no sense. There's been nothing from Guild Master Rsach or anyone?"

Ibson shrugged. "It's too early to hear anything from them. Jackson left on Peacemaker business, but we don't know the full story. Tara sent the guild an urgent communication, asking for a detailed summary and status report. Hopefully, we'll get some type of response soon. Rains really took Vannix's death hard."

"Which is completely understandable," Tirr replied.

"We just don't know what's going on with him. It's got Tara worried." Ibson shook his head and waved a hand in front of his face. "Enough of that. Let's get back to business. How can we help you?"

"We're gathering samples and trying to find as much intelligence as we can. Your forecasters say the first snows are imminent. When that happens, we're going to need a place to conduct our research."

"Well, you have that, and we'd be happy to have you," Ibson replied with a more genuine smile. "I'll let the boss know to expect you and your party. What do you think you'll find?"

Tirr pointed at the shallow pool. "We've been tracking the DWC and their interest in certain water sources. Lake Pryce was one of their targets. This facility, whatever it was used for, was part of that. I have a feeling we're going to find what we're looking for in the water. I just hope it doesn't take us too much time."

* * *

Trindlark System

Planet Gondlo

Starport

Millzak stood and stretched, raising all four arms above his head. He felt, more than heard, the pops in all four of his shoulder sockets, though they did make sounds. These days, he tended to creak and pop more than ever. Decades of Peacemaker assignments tended to do that to any who earned the title. Suspects and prisoners were not always compliant. Often, they needed a little physical coercion to come quietly. He was pretty good at reading the ones he would have a problem with, but it didn't make it any easier on his body. Especially these days.

He twisted back and forth a few times to get the rest of the kinks out. He looked around at the small operating center of the shuttle. For the hundredth time, he wished it had more leg room. It had always been a tight fit for him. Then again, he suspected most ships were small for a Lumar. *I will not have to endure it much longer. After this last assignment, it is retirement for me. Another Peacemaker will be assigned my ship and its shuttle.*

He laughed out loud at the thought and said, "If they don't retire it, too." No one was there to hear him. Like him, the ship was an older model and most likely bound for the scrapyards. The newer models and those upgraded had crews. His was operated by one individual.

For nearly his entire career, Millzak had covered a sector of space consisting of planets and races behind most of the galaxy in technology. Places like Asparra, Fyligga, and here. They weren't so far behind they lacked for any of the comforts. Interstellar trade, modern science, and medical care were available. It was more like those who inhabited the systems preferred slow growth in all areas. It suited Millzak fine. He had always liked things simple.

The planet Gondlo was such a place. It was one of the two inhabited planets of this system. It was a mining planet, and everything on it was built to support it. Its sister planet, Trindlark, was the modern one in the area, more in line with the rest of the galaxy. He was glad the runner he was after had come here and not gone there.

Here, Millzak knew he would run him to ground. He was familiar with many on this planet, especially those running the lone starport. Geerlargum would not leave this planet unless he was cuffed and led away by Millzak.

Finding the Oogar who had escaped from the minimum-security prison and been running for three systems was going to be a welcome ending to his career. That the escapee had come to the system where Millzak had been assigned for his commissioning mission so many years ago was not lost on him. He wished Zerze were still alive to talk about it after he retired.

Millzak paused before exiting the shuttle, remembering his friend. Zerze, like most of his class, was gone. Different races had different lifespans, and Zerze had lived a long life for a SleSha, but he was gone now. Millzak had taken leave to visit with him before he passed. He had been grateful for the time.

Others in their class had not reached old age. It was a dangerous profession. Millzak had scars, aches, and pains to vouch for it. *This time, I'm not getting hurt. I don't want to spend the first part of my retirement healing.* He walked down the ramp.

He entered the terminal on the other side of the tarmac and was greeted by an old friend. "Peacemaker Millzak, welcome back. It has been a while since you stepped foot on Gondlo."

"Partrongal, how have you been, my friend?" Millzak asked.

The Caroon lifted his long snout in greeting and said, "I have been well. A little bored, if I am being honest. Other than the scheduled ore shipments leaving, not much happens around here."

Millzak leaned on the long counter with his two right elbows. "What about the transfer shuttles of new workers?"

"Oh, those come twice a month like always. New workers come, a few of the old leave. Most of them are family members of one tribe or another. It rarely varies."

Millzak raised his eyebrow at his old friend. "What about races other than Caroon? Have there been many of those?"

"Well, now that you mention it," Partrongal said. He leaned closer and said in a low voice, "The Pangtol Company have about ten percent of their workforce made up of other races. They like to hire big ones. There are a handful of Lumar, who you know, a few Jivool, who seem to run big in their clans...oh, and a new one. The first I have seen here."

"Let me guess, an Oogar."

Surprise evident on Partrongal's face, he said, "Yes. How did you know, Peacemaker?"

"It is my job to know things. The Pangtol Company. Thank you for the information. I will not stop in when I leave, but I will be back. I have decided to make Gondlo my home when I retire."

"Retire? Really? If you tire of retirement, there is the position of chief of security here in the starport. The job is yours if you desire."

"Thank you. That is good to know," Millzak said. "But I am in no hurry to make that type of decision."

* * *

Millzak stood watching Geerlargum lift huge boulders and toss them into a transport cart. The Oogar was strong. Very strong. He began to rethink his vow to not get injured on this assignment. He glanced down at his pistol, which was useless here. Some of the gases escaped the vacuum and ventilation system and remained this deep in the mine. Normal sparks from steel on rock wouldn't do it, but a blast from a laser pistol could be the end of him and all the miners in this tunnel. Millzak was a simple Lumar, but he knew this to be a fact.

Shit, Millzak thought. He liked the Human swear words. They were simple yet conveyed all he felt at the moment. These were the words he first learned in taking on the Human language. It took him years to learn it; other Peacemakers did it much faster.

Resolved, Millzak shook his head and said loudly, "Geerlargum, you have run far enough. I am taking you in."

Geerlargum, clearly surprised, looked up and saw Millzak. Millzak saw his eyes go straight to the Peacemaker's badge on his chest and then to the holstered pistol. The Oogar grinned and picked up two fist-sized rocks, held them tight in his paws as weapons and stepped forward.

"Peacemaker, is there a problem?" a voice asked behind Millzak.

Geerlargum stopped in his tracks and looked past the Peacemaker. Millzak recognized the voice. "Tivlang, my friend. How is the family?"

"They are good," answered a fellow Lumar. "The little ones grow strong. My oldest can almost best me in double-arm wrestling. I hesitate to wrestle him now."

"That is good," Millzak said. He pointed to Geerlargum with an upper hand. "It seems I will have to wrestle this one to arrest him."

"Really?" Tivlang stepped up beside the Peacemaker. Another Lumar moved to the far side of Tivlang. Two more eased up on the other side of Millzak.

"Is this something you would prefer to keep to the Lumar?" another voice asked from the other side of the tunnel behind Geerlargum. "Or can a Jivool or three aid the Peacemaker?"

Geerlargum dropped the rocks and stared down at his large feet.

* * * * *

Chapter Three

First Sergeant Figgle stood in front, facing the formation. The Kin were formed up by ship assignment, with the troops of *Blue Ridge* centered and those belonging to *Kellie's Stand* on his right. On the left was a small platoon consisting of two Humans who were computer and communications specialists, the pilots—both Miderall and SleSha—and the four Maki mechanics. In front of First and Second Platoons, both of mixed races, stood NCOs. They were Sergeant Gallyind, a Jivool, and Staff Sergeant Rhineder, a gray-haired Human, known as Nails among the troops.

One of the Makis, Corporal Kylont, was the senior trooper for the Headquarters Platoon, even though he was considered a junior NCO. First Sergeant Figgle eyed all the troops standing loosely, most with hands or appendages behind their backs. When he was satisfied with what he saw, he acted.

"Fall in!" Figgle shouted.

The Goka understood the command, and the few with pinplants heard the translations instantly in their minds. Others heard them closely thereafter through earpieces. All knew what to do from repetition, so most snapped to the closest proximity of attention the Humans in formation used as soon as they heard any sound from him—hands or limbs at their sides and legs together.

"Receive the report!" Figgle shouted.

After the platoon sergeants gathered the information from their squad leaders, they reported to Figgle. Everyone was present, but the formalities had to be adhered to. Figgle had studied how Human military units conducted drills and ceremonies and insisted the unit adhere to them, since it was a Human-owned and -commanded mercenary company. It was a great way to build cohesion.

He spun around and waited for Colonel McCoy as she quickly strode over from behind one of the ships. When she was in front of him, he snapped an appendage up, the small pincer closed, and said, "Ma'am, the company is formed."

Cora saluted in return, and as soon as she moved her hand down, the first sergeant did as well. Cora gave the command, "Post!"

He turned and moved off to get around to the back of the formation. The executive officer, Captain Nileah Sevier, and Captains May Bolton and Lisalle Jones moved into position in front of the platoons. His platoon sergeants were in place behind their respective platoons by the time he reached his place.

"Stand at…" Cora paused after giving the preparatory command, and she waited for her officers to repeat it. Once they had given it in unison, she said, "Ease!"

To First Sergeant Figgle's satisfaction, all eyes turned toward the company commander as they placed their limbs behind their backs. He knew it wasn't exactly like Human military units, but it was close, given the mixed races and translations needed. He felt confident all were learning enough of the others' languages to take rudimentary commands on the parade field and, more importantly, in battle. He took note of a particular Maki. Both of his tail tips were slowly rising and lowering in formation.

* * *

Jyrall and Larth stood in the shadows on the ramp of their ship and watched the proceedings with the McCoy brothers. Larth glanced at the others to see if they saw what he did. He hoped they did.

"I bet a credit First Sergeant Figgle chews that pilot a new one for waving his tail around," Larth announced.

"No bet," Jyrall answered, without hesitation.

"Nope," Keaton agreed.

"Oh, that's his ass," Ricky said, nodding. "Once the first sergeant is through hollerin' at him, Kylont will make him do pushups 'til he cain't no more. I ain't takin' a sucker bet."

"It was worth a shot," Larth said, with a shrug.

"Shh," Jyrall said. "I want to hear what she says."

* * *

"We are getting ready to embark on our first contract together," Cora said, her voice carrying across the formation so all could hear her plainly. As a prior NCO, she maintained the learned ability to speak "from the gut," as it was called. The volume was increased, yet there was no strain on her vocal chords and, consequently, no distortion; her words were plain.

"While we travel, we will be separated in the company's ships. This is unavoidable for the time being. Eventually, I intend to purchase a larger ship to encompass us all when traveling between star systems. Right now, we make do. The officers and I will continue to fine tune our planning, and, by the time we reach our destination, they will be ready to convey my intentions, given various battle scenarios. The NCOs will continue to determine the best improvements on our standard operating procedures for garrison time, physical training, accounting for the different capabilities of races, and weapons and equipment training. They will, of course, propose them to me for final approval."

She hesitated a moment and then continued in a more casual tone, "Over the last several months, we have all grown together, learned from each other. There is not one of you I wouldn't give my life to provide cover fire for. Not one." She paused to let it sink in.

"Where we are going, we will join other units and prepare to defend against an attack that will be coming. Let me say that again: We will be attacked. How we respond to that attack will determine the outcome. I am confident we will prevail, as I fully intend to leave that planet with each and every one of you…my kin."

Colonel Cora McCoy snapped to attention and shouted, "Company…" She paused as the platoon leaders repeated the preparatory command. On cue, they did, and the unit members' loosely held hands, paws, arms, and appendages came up into more defined positions behind their backs.

She shouted, "Atten-shun!" She applied the appropriate emphasis in the right places as she stretched the word slightly.

As one, the entire company snapped to attention and shouted the company's motto in a sing-song voice. Every member, regardless of race, screamed it in English, as it had been learned by all. "Finish the Mission!"

It echoed loudly across the airfield, and the sound and enthusiasm gripped Cora's heart like a vise. She was nearly overtaken by emotions she never knew she could feel. These were her soldiers…her kin. She managed to keep her compsure as she spoke in a command voice, "First Sergeant."

As he came running around the formation, the platoon sergeants did the same, while the officers beat a hasty retreat the opposite way behind the formation. Figgle stopped at attention in front of his commander, snapped up a salute, and held it.

Cora said quietly to him, "Take charge of the company. Get them loaded, and let's go whup somebody's ass."

"Roger that, ma'am," First Sergeant Figgle answered solemnly.

The colonel moved off, and First Sergeant Figgle waited until she was on the ramp of the Peacemaker's ship, with her officers following closely behind. They disappeared into the shadows of the cargo bay.

"At ease," he shouted.

He began to pace in front of the company. All eyes followed him, even though, technically, they were *at ease* and had not been given the command to *stand at ease*. They all knew better. Top was speaking, and they had best pay attention.

"Listen up, you shitbirds," he said in his own version of the command voice.

He glanced toward Headquarters Platoon and the two colorful avian-like Mideralls. He gave an approximation of shrugging, which was difficult for his race. Goka didn't necessarily have shoulders. The term wasn't really meant to be a racial insult to them. He was calling every member of the unit the name. All the members knew he didn't mean the names he called them personally. Well, unless they screwed up. Then, in that moment, he meant what he called them if only to drive home what he was reprimanding them for.

First Sergeant Figgle continued, "Listen up, Kin. We're getting ready to load up. You all know your assigned ships. Do not screw up the manifests. I will be on *Blue Ridge* and Staff Sergeant Rhineder will be the senior NCO on *Kellie's Stand*. I will have Sergeant Bailey with me. She will oversee those troops on board our ship, while I attend meetings with the command. I wouldn't advise any of you window lickers to piss her off."

He paused a moment and used the staff sergeant's nickname. "If Nails tells me of any bullshitery on his ship during our travel to our destination, I will have the biggest case of the ass you have ever seen."

The first sergeant let that sink in. "Now, I have no doubt he will handle it accordingly. He has my permission to fuck you frog turds up as his demonstration partner in any hip pocket training he decides upon. And we all know what he will decide to train in. The man has more belts in Human martial arts than the pilots of *Blue Ridge* have for their outfits." He stopped and considered, tilting his head slightly. "Maybe not scarves and capes...but definitely more belts." There was a snicker among the troops, even the two Mideralls.

"He is going to toss you around like a ballfoot, or football. Yes, that is the word...a football. Anyway"—he stretched out the word—"after he is done with you, I will have something for your sorry ass when we get to our destination. You will *never* come off meal preparation and clean-up detail. Ever."

He whirled on the unit and shouted, "If I hear of any of you assclowns not showing the officers of this unit the proper respect—including the pilots, since Colonel McCoy has not decided what she wants them to be ranked as yet—I will personally rectify the situation. When I get ahold of you, I will reach down your throat and squeeze your soul until it leaves your body!"

Over in the Headquarters' Platoon, Stew whispered to Monty, "I say, say that is. He called us an assclown. An assclown is what he said, don't you know."

Stew whispered back, perhaps too loudly, "I haven't an idea, no idea that is, of what that may be. I'm still wondering about frog turds. Turds, I say."

"What's a window licker?" a Maki mechanic asked, quietly. Several shrugged. One of the computer/communication specialists giggled. She was a short red head, who said she knew what it was.

The first sergeant paused in his tirade and looked around, trying to determine who dared to speak when he was talking. With a grunt, he continued, "Kin, I want you to know...to know I am proud of the unit we have become in such a short time. Proud of the way you all used your prior experiences to help each other learn new things, new weapons, new systems, old systems, all that shit. I'm proud of the way you push yourselves, even beyond what I do. I am proud to call you my...kin."

Every member of the unit knew it was hard for the Goka standing in front of their formation to say that. Not that he didn't mean it with every fiber of his being, they knew he did, despite the names he called them. It was hard for him to show his true feelings, and they loved him all the more for forcing himself to do it.

He snapped to attention once he was back in the proper spot. "On the command to fall out, board the ships. Company...Attention!"

The company motto bounced around the airfield, echoing the motto once again.

* * *

Cora, standing with the rest, hidden in the shadows of the Peacemakers' ship, shook her head and said, "Where in the world did he learn to talk like a drill sergeant? From a bygone era, even?" She looked over at the two likely suspects.

"Not me," Larth said, raising his hands. "I mean, I recognize the tone and cadence from some of the old videos from Earth, but even I never heard of a shitbird."

"Don't look at me," Ricky said. "I mean, calling someone a frog turd is pretty harsh. I don't reckon I could let a feller do that to me, iffen I'm being honest. I might have to take a swing on him."

"You take a swing on them old school drill sergeants, and you'd get your ass handed to you, that's fer sure," Keaton said with a toothy grin.

Keaton looked at Cora and said, "Guilty. I downloaded several videos of Humans going through training, both real and entertainment types, from as far back as the 1980s in Earth calendars. They were some of Pop's favorite movies, and I still like to watch 'em. And you know what? Just like in those movies, the troops love him, no matter what he calls them."

"True," Cora admitted, surprised at which brother had provided the information to the company's senior NCO. "I remember my first CASPer instructor. She was mean as a game rooster, but I would follow her into the gates of hell on a raid. She had more names for us than I can remember."

Changing the subject, Jyrall said, "Here is where we must part ways for a time. We have our instructions, and you have a mission. When you meet with the Enforcers on Weqq, you will receive your full briefing. Defending the TriRusk is not going to be an easy task. I cannot say when we will see you again, but I trust we will."

"Oh, we will," Cora assured him as she stepped in for a hug, surprising the large Besquith. "We will complete the mission and meet up again."

"That, I have no doubt of," Jyrall said as she moved away and let Lisalle give Jyrall a quick hug.

Larth didn't notice as he was too busy being smothered in hugs on both sides by teary eyed May and a somber faced Nileah. "Don't you go getting into too many fights as Switch," May admonished. "When you are him, you take too many chances, I think."

"Hey," Larth said, "sometimes you have to be something you are not."

"Yeah," May countered, "but I think, when you are Switch, you enjoy the fall. You're all badass, and you are just being who you really are."

"Okay," Larth said with a grin, "I'll give you that. I'm not afraid of a little scrap."

"That's 'cause you ain't afraid of nuthin'," Ricky said as he enveloped his cousin in a big hug. "You be careful out there, Cora McCoy. You still gotta introduce us to the rest of our kin in them mountains on Earth."

"Yeah," Keaton said. "I hope they are as accepting as you of a couple of adopted Pushtal in the family."

"They better be," Cora said as she wiped away a small tear. "Or there's some other cousins who will tote a whupping all over Appalachia as I pound it into their dang fool heads. A McCoy is a McCoy, no matter how they came to be one."

* * *

"When we meet up with Captain Dreel, we will get the details of our mission," Jyrall said as he settled into his seat. "I do not know if we are to infiltrate an organization as Varkell and his crew, or if we are to transport goods using the same identity."

"There they go," remarked Keaton. "The system indicates they made the jump."

"Good," Jyrall said from the co-pilot's seat. He adjusted the restraints to be as comfortable as possible for their transition using the shunts on their ship.

"I wonder how long before word gets around that the mercenary company Blue Ridge Kin has the capability to leave a system without using the gate?" Larth asked as he floated behind the two seats, a hand in the loop of a maneuvering strap affixed to the bulkhead.

"It ain't gonna be long, I can tell ya," Ricky stated, holding onto his own strap. "It ain't gonna come from them living on Krifay, neither. It'll come from that joker running the gate. Nosey sumbitches."

"Of course they are," Jyrall said, looking at Ricky in confusion. "The Sumatozou have long bifurcated trunks as a nose. It is common knowledge."

"You're killing me, Snarlyface. Killing me," Larth said. "It's a figure of speech."

"Actually," Keaton informed them, "nosey means being inquisitive to the point of being rude about it."

"All I know is thems that run the gates run their mouths," Ricky stated, as he pointed through the forward portal toward the gate, small in the distance, shining from the star's light gleaming off it.

"Agreed," Jyrall said. "It is something we Peacemakers are made aware of. It is always a factor to consider."

"We are one minute until transition," Keaton announced. "After we do, we can eat. I'm starving. What are you cooking anyway?"

"Fish sticks," Larth answered proudly. "And fries," he added.

Jyrall looked down and slowly shook his head.

"Nice!" Ricky said. "I'm going to go back to my workshop and finish the drone I been working on."

"Which one?" Keaton asked, keeping his eyes on the instruments and making a slight adjustment.

"The big one," Ricky answered. "I'm putting drop hooks on it and going to name it Scar. It's kinda ugly, even for my standards."

"Drop hooks?" Jyrall asked as he glanced back up.

"Oh yeah," Ricky said. "He'll be able to carry a few grenades and drop them on command. I rigged some up so they will explode upon impact, not by timed fuse."

"Well, I hope you have them stored right and packed tightly with plenty of padding, you dang fool," Keaton said. He checked his instruments again. "T-minus five seconds."

"I mean, well, yeah," Ricky said. "I was going to do that next."

Jyrall whipped his head around in horror and saw Larth's eyes widen as well. Before he could speak, they made the transition, and his stomach lurched.

* * * * *

Chapter Four

Blue Ridge

Cora looked around the conference room. May and Lisalle sat on one side of the table with Figgle. Nileah, Sergeant Bailey, and Sergeant Gallyind sat on the other. Two of the Maki mechanics stood near the hatch, content to just observe. If there were any questions about the ships or equipment, besides the mechs, they were ready to answer them.

Cora turned toward Sergeant Bailey. "Alice, what is the status on the last two Mk 7s?"

"We're good to go, ma'am," answered the unit's mech maintenance sergeant. Like Lisalle, not only could she fight a mech, she had worked on them her whole career. "Corporal Limker is a quick learner. Between me and him and Captain Jones, we were able to get the servo motors replaced in number eleven and the fuel tanks on the jets for number thirteen. That's the last of the major repairs needed."

Cora looked toward the open hatch and the senior Maki on *Blue Ridge*. "Limker, I know you've been busy helping with the mechs, but what are the ship's weapons systems looking like?"

The Maki held his hand out with his middle finger extended. May covered her mouth and giggled. Limker realized his mistake and closed his fist. He then put his thumb up, instead. "We're up, ma'am.

All the systems are ready for use. We even have some spare missiles that Ricky helped me locate and buy."

"You flip off the ol' lady again, and I'm going to whack you with one of those big wrenches you use," Figgle said. "What's wrong with you, anyway?"

"Sorry, ma'am," the Maki said meekly. "I get them confused. Ricky shows them both to us all the time, depending on what we are working on and its status."

Cora held her composure. It wasn't easy. She wanted to laugh along with May. "Sergeant Gallyind, is your squad ready with the hovercraft?"

"Yes, ma'am," the Jivool answered. "We have trained on the duel .50s until we can set the headspace and timing on them in our sleep. The way Ricky set up the feeders, we don't have to worry about them jamming. Now, our only concern is running out of ammo. But there are always the two shoulder-fired missile launchers and the ten rounds we carry."

"Plus, it makes for good shielding for the infantry," Figgle observed. "Especially with the additional armor."

"There is that, Top," agreed Gallyind. "It never hurts to advance behind a moving shield. I wish we had a tank or two, though."

"They are on the wish list," Niliah said. "Along with a bunch of other things. At least we have Nails and the section using the Mk 4s as mobile mortars. That was genius of Ricky."

"I agree," May said. "The Mk 4s could never hope to keep up with the 7s, or even the 6s. Having them in the rear, yet moving forward, launching artillery rounds, could be a game changer. They do have a lot of armor. I mean, we could have them with us in a defensive position but not so much assaulting a target."

"Speaking of which," Cora said, "I read through the preliminary guidance on our mission. We will be in defense. An attack on Weqq is expected. Whether it's Kre'et'Socae, the Veetanho, or something else, they really want to get to the TriRusk. We are going to be part of a larger force. The message said more information will be forthcoming. I'm not sure whether we will receive another message before we depart this system or when we arrive."

"It would be nice if we had the details before the jump," Lisalle observed. "Makes it a lot easier to plan. Hell, I want to know who is on my left and right, ya know? Maybe some information on the terrain, the defense plans, the layout of the base. I hate going in blind."

"I hear you," Cora agreed. "We can only work with what we know so far. Our own unit doctrine will have to suffice. You three lead the mechs—" she indicated May, Lisalle, and Niliah, "—and I'll stay central with Top, Sergeant Bailey, and the sniper team. Until I send them out, that is.

"Sergeant Gallyind, Sergeant Glonk, and Corporal Bweenkit have the infantry platoon. In defense, depending on the layout, I intend to split them on either side of the headquarters' area. May, you'll stay central with your mechs, and Lisalle and Niliah will cover our flanks. We'll keep the hovercraft to the rear of us with the mortar mechs in case we have to assault an enemy position with the infantry."

"We may be able to position Squarlik up high and take advantage of the sniper team from the beginning," suggested Figgle. "At least for observation, if nothing else."

"Good point," agreed Cora. "A Goka with a .50 caliber, its scope, and his spotter's scope will be useful."

"Not to mention the observation drones Ricky made for them," May added.

"Those drones will come in handy if we need to send someone over the wall and take out the enemy's leader with a quiet slice or two," First Sergeant Figgle said. In a flash, two wicked blades appeared in a couple of his small pincers. As quick as he took them out, he put them away.

"Top," Cora admonished, "I keep telling you, I can't risk you on those types of missions. We'll need to designate a couple others for that."

"Fine," Figgle said. "But if you want the best results, you have to send the best, ma'am."

"We have to train our juniors so they become better than we are, Top," Cora reminded him.

"Yeah, yeah," Top said, "I get it. Doesn't mean I have to like it. I move as quickly and quietly as I always have. My knives stay sharp, too. Whatever happened to rank has its privileges, or however you Humans say it?"

"It does…and it doesn't," Niliah said. "Training others to do what you can do is more important than just doing it yourself. There will come a time when you are a step too slow, and you'll be glad a younger soldier is there to take up your slack."

"Well, that shit is years away, I'm here to inform you, ma'am," Top argued. "But…I understand what you're saying. I still don't like it, though. Look at Nails. He just keeps going and going. You would never guess how old he is."

"That man defies explanation," Lisalle agreed. "Nobody in the company can match him on a long run. Must be genetics, 'cause he has the same enhancements to pilot a mech as we do. And don't tell me it's 'cause we're women. Hell, men who are twenty years younger than he is can't keep up with him."

"It has to be in his bloodline," Cora said. "I wonder where his people hail from?"

"Somebody mentioned the Alps," May answered.

"Sounds about right," Cora said. "He has that slight accent. Not that we can talk about folks' accents. Stands to reason he came outta the mountains." She stared off into the distance for a few seconds, thinking. "They say my Great Uncle Milton, Pops McCoy to everyone else, was like that. Tough as leather and piloted a mech in combat long after he should have retired. Some folks are just made that way, I reckon."

Changing the subject, Niliah said, "We should be good on supplies. We have a full load of ammunition and power cells for the laser rifles. The grenade stockpile looks good, as do the crates of missiles for the mechs. We have plenty of rations and emergency rations to last the expected duration of the mission. Water won't be an issue, though we will need to purify it to be safe."

"Good," Cora said. "We have it divided between the two ships in case of a mishap, I take it?"

"Roger that," Niliah answered, nodding. "They also have all the mortar rounds since the 4s are on their ship."

"The hell with rations and emergency rations," Figgle said. "I just want to know how much flour we have on board and if anyone is making cookies. I'm here for the cookies, you know."

Everyone laughed. Even Figgle's mouth turned up in the closest thing to a grin a Goka could achieve. Cora shook her head and started to ask a question when they were interrupted by the ship's computer and communications specialist.

The young redhead stood in the hatchway, hesitant to enter. "Sorry to intrude, ma'am."

"Come in Specialist Conner," Cora said. "What do you have for me?"

"Well, the pilots inform me we will make the jump into hyperspace in thirty minutes. They want to make sure there is plenty of space to transition. *Kellie's Stand* is ready, as well."

She looked down at the papers in her hand and added, "Oh, and I almost forgot, I printed another message from the Peacemaker Guild. I read through it as it printed, like you told me to, in case there is ever anything you need to know ASAP. There is nothing time essential, but there are some strange requests."

"Really?" Cora reached for the papers. "Thank you. We'll wrap this up and be prepared for the jump in less than thirty minutes. Tell Monty and Stew to proceed."

"Roger that, ma'am." Specialist Conner turned and left.

As Cora started reading, everyone in the room noticed a change in her demeanor, and a frown formed on her face. They glanced at each other, puzzled. Figgle attempted to shrug his shoulders. He was still learning all the mannerisms of Humans, so he wasn't as concerned as he should be.

Cora looked up after she read through the message. "They want me to inform the leader of the Crusaders of a list of things. Things I am not prepared to reveal to anyone."

"What things?" Figgle asked, now as concerned as the others.

"Our command-and-control frequencies."

"Nope," May argued. "They don't need to monitor our internal channels."

"The number of troops with pinplants."

"No way," Lisalle argued. "Our troops don't need that type of interference in battle."

"Our full weapons load reports."

"That's not happening," Niliah stated. "Period. What if the numbers get out?"

"And the maintenance records for the CASPers," Cora finished.

"Hell no!" Sergeant Bailey exclaimed. "Ma'am," she added.

"Limker, you can raise that other finger to that," First Sergeant Figgle deadpanned. "Sounds like bullshitery to me."

"All of you are right," Cora said. "I am not giving out that type of information until I have a full briefing, and even then, I don't think it is warranted. I don't like the way this mission is starting out, and we haven't even put boots on the ground.

"Top, call over to Staff Sergeant Rhineder and make sure they don't send any information to anyone outside this chain of command. I don't know if the message went to them, as well, but do it just to be sure."

"Roger that, ma'am," Figgle said. "Though I'm sure Nails will look at it like you do. He won't give up any information."

"Yeah," Cora agreed. "I think you're right. I wonder if I should make him an officer. It seems odd we don't have one on that ship right now."

"You know good and well that if you did that, Nails would retire," Figgle said. "No offense to you ladies, but an old school NCO doesn't want the restrictions that come with that type of rank."

"None taken," Niliah volunteered. "I understand completely. But, sometimes, you have to take the promotion."

Cora laughed. "I won't do it, though the look on his face would be priceless. I do, however, need to look at hiring officers for the ships, other than the pilots, that is."

"Please do," Lisalle said. "If you only make the pilots officers *and* commanders of the ships, Monty and Stew will have the crew members in the most brightly colored, mismatched uniforms to ever cross space."

* * *

Kellie's Stand

"Roger that, Top," Nails said. He shifted the headset as he looked at the screen. "I saw the message. It's straight bullshit, and I ain't telling them nothin'."

"Good," Figgle said, "that's the way the ol' lady wants it."

"Why would they request all that information, anyway?" Nails asked. "That's the kind of stuff you want to know about an enemy before you attack. Somethin' stinks about it."

"I agree," Figgle said. "How's it going over there? We won't be able to communicate once we go into hyperspace, you know."

"It's quiet over here," Staff Sergeant Rhineder said. "I got 'em saying 'yes sir' and 'no sir' to the pilots. I figure the commander is going to make 'em ensigns or lieutenants or sumthin'."

"Good," Figgle said. "I think she will, too. She mentioned warrant officers." He grinned in his own way.

"What are you grinnin' at?" Nails asked.

"Nothing," Figgle said. "We have five minutes before jump. See you when we get there."

"Out here," Nails said. He looked around the small communications room and said to the other occupant, "Wonder what all the smilin' was about?"

"Beats me, Staff Sergeant," the young specialist said.

* * * * *

Chapter Five

Fontraxx

Mertrad System

Sixteen hours after emergence in the Mertrad system, Ricky guided *Night Moves*, its registration changed back, onto the landing pad designated by approach control. The four of them looked around at the surroundings and tried to gain their bearings. The declared intent of their stop was resupply, but they also intended to meet with Captain Dreel. While Dreel's usual meeting places were barely more than shanties, this particular station, called Fontraxx, was something else entirely.

Ricky squinted at the cameras. "I gotta say, this ain't one of them places you wanna get caught alone and unarmed."

Jyrall nodded thoughtfully as he studied the screen. "It's certainly not a place to be alone or unarmed unless you're a mercenary. Fontraxx, and the whole Mertrad system, is a typical mercenary pit. Even Peacemakers avoid this place on a regular basis."

"It's not quite a typical pit, then, Snarlyface," Larth said. "Since the Mercenary Guild came apart at the seams, you are just as likely to get killed as to get a job in places like these."

Keaton pointed a long claw at the right side of the screen. "That's the main corridor. Dreel's meeting place should be about halfway down it on the right side according to the GalNet here."

"Then I guess it's time we get dressed up." Jyrall stood to his full height and stretched. The return of gravity, even as light as it was, was welcome. "I'll admit, putting on Varkell's outfit again will be a little weird."

"Are we really sure about this?" Keaton asked. "Seems to me that nothing like information is safe these days. I can make sure it's all covered on the GalNet but, surely, somebody will recognize that Varkell and Switch weren't what they said they were on Parmick. I can't erase and rewrite someone's memory. You guys are in danger."

"News has gotta travel," Ricky agreed. "Hell, we're in danger, too."

"I don't believe Captain Dreel would steer us wrong," Jyrall replied. "I won't pretend to know all the hidden mechanisms our guild uses to manage its information, but when the leadership says something is good, we can take them at their word."

"Besides," Larth added. "It's a lot easier to put on an old identity than it is to create a brand new one. Isn't that what you're supposed to do?"

Keaton removed his Jacksonville Generals ball cap and rubbed his scalp. "You guys talk about the different things you learned at the Peacemaker Academy, like method acting, and you're ready to just put back on this identity and act like nothing ever happened? Seems damned risky."

"It's not that nothing ever happened," Jyrall said with a frown. "We're aware of what happened on Parmick. Most of the galaxy has likely heard about it as well. The guild has released information regarding the operation as having been under the sole command of Peacemaker Nikki Sinclair. The official report mentions that she deputized local mercenaries, as well, but does not specifically mention Varkell and Switch. Nor does it really mention the two of you."

"But if somebody searches them videos?" Ricky asked. "I can see where somebody could get in there and identify all of us right fast."

"I can see if they have the capability, sure," Larth replied.

"It's still video, and that's been pretty damned easy to manipulate for the last couple hundred years," Keaton said.

"Even the so-called smart video systems aren't that smart. That uncertainty plays to our advantage. Y'all watch enough spy movies to know there are technicians who can alter all that stuff," Larth replied.

The two brothers guffawed. "I can't believe you just said y'all," Keaton said.

Larth shrugged. "When in Rome."

Jyrall whirled on his partner. "Rome? This place isn't Rome."

The two Pushtal brothers and the Zuparti Peacemaker howled with laughter, leaving the giant Besquith rubbing his long face with both hands.

"I swear, one of these days…" Jyrall muttered as he made his way to his quarters, laughter echoing off the passageways around him.

* * *

If the station Fontraxx wasn't bad enough, the local bar, called the Deadwood End, resembled something out of one of those old movies to Jyrall. Charles Eastwood? Clint Bronson? He couldn't remember. The dusty and disheveled roadside appearance of the bar ensured there would be some kind of action going on, and that was precisely what Captain Dreel would want. They would find a quiet table, likely in a dark corner, and spend a few minutes talking about nothing for any nearby eavesdroppers. Yet they would have an entire conversation about their needs and objectives. For Jyrall, this was one of the most fun aspects of his job.

Jyrall approached the bar and nodded to the female Sidar behind it. She was cleaning and drying glasses with a dirty towel. Her eyes swept over the room and back to him again.

"What can I get you? Something to slake your thirst after hyperspace, traveler?"

Jyrall pointed at the taps. "A beer and none of that Equiri piss from Earth."

The bartender laughed, a brittle cackle that made him think of Hak-Chet, whom he hadn't seen in quite some time. Jyrall wondered where the Selector had gone as he forced a smile onto his face.

"Yeah, that Weiser is pretty awful," the bartender said.

"Awful doesn't even begin to translate, sister." Jyrall smiled, and the female Sidar's eyes came up to his, glittering.

"You looking for trouble? Or a job?"

At that moment, Jyrall understood. The bartender was not merely the bartender. She was likely the local merc pit boss, too. The deals done in her establishment undoubtedly earned her some type of cut. Maybe even a security fee to keep things quiet.

Jyrall shrugged. "Neither, at the moment. Just a quiet drink. Maybe a chance to catch up with others of my kind. It's been far too long."

The bartender smiled. "My name's Korr. And if you're wanting to talk with someone who is your kind, check the back corner by the restrooms. Guy's been back there all day. He's probably drunk a fifth of Daniels by himself, speaking of shitty Earth drinks."

"Really?" Jyrall grinned. "Sounds like someone wants to part with his credits. I wonder if he plays Tumble Gambit?"

Korr cackled again. "I guess you'll want to find out for yourself, big guy." She moved toward the taps and pulled a glass out from underneath the counter. To his surprise, the glass appeared clean. She poured in an amber colored beer with a thick, foamy head and passed it to him. "I like you. What's your name?"

"Varkell." Korr's eyes widened almost imperceptibly, but he caught it. He'd learned in his classes at the Peacemaker Academy that there were certain things to look for when the different species of the galaxy communicated with others. Elements of surprise, confusion, and understanding all had specific tells based on the species. While the Sidar were not typically anxious or nervous, they tended to have emotive faces. Even the best ones, like Selector Hak-Chet, occasionally let things slip.

She's heard that name.

"Welcome to my pit, Varkell. Your beer is on me."

Jyrall forced a laugh and smiled. "Then you've just become my favorite establishment. I'll be certain to make it worth your while."

"You do that, Varkell. But remember, it's either a job or trouble. I don't think you want trouble."

He realized she had essentially just offered him a job. Depending upon what Captain Dreel had to say, he'd have to play the role and, at least, ask about terms and conditions. With any luck, they could use her offer of employment as an angle to accomplish their wider objectives.

Jyrall grabbed his beer and set off for the corner. The being in the back corner booth was unmistakably Dreel, and he did appear to be quite intoxicated.

"Greetings, venerable one, do you have room for a packmate?"

Captain Dreel's eyes struggled to focus on him. With his head sagging to one side, Dreel pointed toward the chair. "Sit, pup."

In that instant, with that simple exchange, Jyrall knew his mentor was not inebriated. Yet his act was so strong and genuine, it would be hard for anyone untrained to think differently.

Jyrall took his seat and set his slate on the table. "You play Tumble Gambit?"

"Games of chance are for the weak, little one."

"Where have your travels taken you?"

Dreel grinned. "From the scorpion pits of Karma to all points known. My crusade for gainful employment continues. Unable to find work now because of those damned Human CASPers."

"They are formidable and reckless."

Dreel laughed, his drunken act giving it volume, which caused heads to turn their way and just as quickly caused them to turn away in disgust. "You have no idea, brother."

Jyrall felt a flush of realization. In Besquith, the term brother was reserved for family or those close enough to share a bond. Dreel had never once said it to Jyrall, even in their coded clandestine conversations. It was the mark of a peer, and Jyrall pinched his own leg under the table to keep from emoting. Dreel wasn't talking in code, either. Something was going on at Karma, but what he did not understand was the comment about the Human CASPers. Something was missing, but he'd take his chances and research it rather than look stupid in front of his mentor. Jyrall took a long, slow draught from his mug. Dreel did not reciprocate.

Now what?

"Have you let anyone else go? Failed to achieve all requirements of your contracts again?"

Jyrall blinked. *He obviously means Nay-Thok.*

Getting into the game, Jyrall grunted. "No one ever gets away from me. We always get even."

Dreel laughed again. "I've traveled many places. Done many things. From Parmick to Springton. Taken many missions and taken many credits. I've never let anyone go. Sometimes, in life, all I do is follow the credits, but I get my revenge."

Jyrall took another drink of the passable beer and processed everything he had just learned. Dreel was headed to Parmick. He understood the earlier portion of the message—the scorpion pit referred to Nikki Sinclair, based on her family's now-disbanded mercenary company. He was going to link up with her, but the objective of their mission wasn't yet clear. He also deduced the new mission for him and Larth was Springton. Dreel wanted the two young Peacemakers to follow the credits from Parmick and locate Nay-Thok at the far-flung outpost.

But what does that have to do with CASPers?

Dreel continued his drunken act, pulsing into rage. "Nine times. Nine times, I found my mark. You do the same, young one."

Mk 9 CASPers? Gods. That's a critical intelligence requirement if I've ever heard one.

Jyrall pointed at him. "And you, old cur? Did you find that mark, the tenth one? Or does it still elude you, hence your drunkenness and disrespectful tone in this fine establishment?"

Jyrall let his voice ring, and he knew more eyes were turning their way. He decided to play up the role a little more. "And you dare disrespect Varkell?"

"You are an Equiri's ass, but not as smart," Dreel grunted and sloshed his way to a standing position. "I meant no disrespect, pup. This conversation is over. I hope you treat your elders with more respect in the future. Varkell or not, your actions border on a violent response."

"From you?" Jyrall laughed loudly. "Varkell is not afraid of violence. Tell the others they best not cross my crew again."

Dreel pushed past Jyrall's larger frame and shambled out of the bar before turning toward the docks. Jyrall watched him for a long moment, ensuring no one followed him. The brothers were stationed in the passageway, and they too would be watching over Captain Dreel. He would not need their assistance, but just in case any foolish mercenaries believed he might be carrying credits, or anything else of value, it was best to provide support. Jyrall and the others knew they always took care of their own.

While he hadn't understood the concept of kin until recently, he knew his duty to others well. While Captain Dreel was the Deputy Prime Enforcer, and more than capable of taking care of himself, Jyrall wasn't about to let anything happen to his mentor.

When Dreel's shambling figure passed from view, Jyrall sat down again in silence. He pretended to be tapping his slate while waiting for Korr to approach and get down to the business she'd proposed. While he waited, his mind raced.

The guild believes Nay-Thok and Kr'et'Socae are after a Mk 9 CASPer. I'm supposed to follow the credits and take Larth to apprehend Nay-Thok. By calling me an Equiri's ass, I can only assume he's going after Kr'et'Socae with Nikki Sinclair.

The realization struck him between the eyes, and Jyrall became more pensive than he would've liked. The consequences of failure, on either of their parts, were formidable. Failing to track down Nay-Thok and the forged credits, so successfully worked out of Parmick for so long, would set back the guild's investigation of Kr'et'Socae. The disgraced Enforcer was after something credits, even forged credits, weren't enough to buy. He was after something else.

A Mk 9 CASPer prototype could certainly be part of that, but it wasn't everything. Humans, after all, were only one species in the Mercenary Guild. There were thirty-six or so other races who would fight for money. And while he was closer to Humans than many of his kind, Jyrall didn't believe they, alone, were worthy of such concern. The prototype was certainly something Kr'et'Socae would use as leverage in the pursuit of something else.

But what? What would be the value of such a prototype?

There was no way of knowing, short of going to Earth, and that was impossible. While Humans appeared to be making great strides toward total inclusion in the Galactic Union, Humans were held at arm's length in the other guilds. As mercenaries, though, the Humans certainly demonstrated prowess.

What could they possibly be trying to leverage by stealing a Human prototype?

He was still deep in thought when Korr approached and slid into Dreel's vacated seat. "May I join you?" the Sidar asked.

"Certainly. You're not here for trouble, so you must be here for business."

She smiled and folded her hands diplomatically in front of her. Resting her chest against the table, she leaned forward, her voice low. "I do have some business, if you're willing to discuss it?"

"I am merely passing through on a contract, Korr." Jyrall matched her low tone. "However, I am always looking for the next one."

She tapped her glass of bubbling blue liquid to his raised beer glass. "To the next one, Varkell. And many more after that."

"Especially lucrative ones."

Korr chuckled. "Well, when your current contract is over, let me know. I have an… employer who could certainly make this worth your while."

* * *

Snowmass

The scope of the underground facility took Tirr's breath away. His stunned surprise at the size and breadth of the space paled in comparison to the amount of materiel and supplies complementing the unit's newfound strength. He looked at the wide hangar door as his team of warriors pranced in from the snow.

"It's really something, huh?"

Tirr whirled toward the familiar voice. "Jamie's description failed to accurately describe it. He says there are more of these?"

Tara Mason, the commander of Force 25, smiled as she closed the distance. "Several. We're not sure exactly how many, or where they're located, but Snowman had something up his sleeve, most certainly."

Tara opened her arms for the Human embrace, and Tirr moved forward one step to wrap his foreclaws gently around her shoulders. "It is good to see you, my friend."

"You, as well, Colonel Mason."

He felt her against his thorax. "It's been too long. Have you found anything useful?"

Tirr released his embrace and stepped back. His ruby compound eyes studied her for a long moment. "Let's discuss that later. I would imagine you'd like to give us a tour."

Tara's face broke into a smile. "I'll certainly do that. Have you heard anything from Jessica?"

"Only what you have. The comments and reports she shares and nothing further. I know she's very interested in what's going on here," Tirr replied.

"I'd hoped she'd know more about these facilities. Maybe have some kind of insight into what her father was up to."

Tirr shook his head in a very Human gesture. "From what I understand, Jessica's father hid much of his business from her. Purposefully. He did not want her to know certain things until she was of age. Even now, after their reunion and subsequent parting, I fear there is much she does not know."

"Which," Tara replied, "for people like us who like to know what's going on and don't appreciate being kept in the dark is difficult to manage, much less plan for."

The strained look on her face gave Tirr the opening he was hoping for. The news from Colonel Ibson had stunned him, and he was determined to dig deeper.

"I am sorry about the loss of Peacemaker Vannix." Tirr tapped his thorax with one foreclaw. "I am honored to have met her. I hope her memory is a blessing to us all."

"I do, too, Tirr." One side of Tara's mouth curled under, and her pain was palpable. He didn't want to ask the question but knew he must.

"Where is Jackson?"

Tara shook her head and looked down at the ground. In a voice tinged with disgust, she replied, "I'm concerned he's in trouble and won't tell anyone. He should be fine, and I sent good people with him to watch his back, but I wish he'd let us know what's happening."

"There's been nothing from the Peacemaker Guild? No guidance of any type?"

Tara laughed. "No, the whole damned guild is silent. With the high council in hiding, the general council tabling all meetings for another twelve or thirteen months of Earth time, and their operatives and principals spread all over the galaxy, it's no wonder they haven't said anything. I'm not even sure they know what's going on in all these different places. I mean, how could they? There's far too much going on at this point and not enough information being shared."

"What does that mean for your mission?" Tirr's antennae bobbed with curiosity.

Tara shrugged, and he could hear her sigh. "I wish I knew, Tirr. There's far too much at stake right now. My mission is simple. Get Force 25 ready to go get Snowman. I'm supposed to hear when that will be directly from the guild master. Yet repeated efforts to get in contact with him for guidance have fallen short. I can't tell if I'm expected to fail or not."

Tirr studied her for a long moment and wished his face could portray the concern he felt. He let his antennae sag. "I do not think you've been set up to fail, Tara. Nor do I think *I've* been set up to fail. We are being asked to perform our individual missions to the best of our abilities. At some point, these things will come together. We will find Snowman. We will determine the Peacemaker's role in the galaxy with the collapse of the Mercenary Guild. All of these things we do are little pieces of a much larger puzzle."

Tara snorted. "Let me tell you something; I hated puzzles as a kid. I'd much rather have things laid out in front of me."

"And you don't think the guild master knows that?"

"Gods, Tirr, you sound just like Jessica."

"Your Human saying is there are worse things in life, my friend."

Her smile was genuine, and there was a sense of relief in her expressive features. "I'm glad you're here. Sorry the weather has already turned cold. We'll have eight months of this unless the guild gets our collective asses moving."

"We certainly appreciate you offering us a place to stay and work. Why don't you show us where we will be working?"

"There's really no place better suited for you and your team. The facility at Lake Pryce was destroyed, and, while things on the planet are certainly in the process of healing, especially with the government's interest in having us perform their security mission, I still don't trust some of the local citizens not to blabber unnecessarily. Having you here makes all the difference. We have plenty of room and plenty of supplies. Our house is yours."

Tirr nodded. "In our language, we say a hive can be a hive only if the bond is true. While we are different species, I feel such a bond with you and Jessica and the others. I am honored to call you friends."

Tara nodded, and, in her face, there was determination in place of grief.

"That honor is mine."

A tiny speaker mounted in the cave above them came to life. "Colonel Mason? Colonel Mason? Please contact Nelson at your earliest opportunity."

Tirr's antennae waggled. "Who is Nelson? That is a name I do not recognize from your unit rolls."

"He's our resident Wrogul. Signed on with us right after the second battle of Victoria Bravo. While he's one hell of an addition to the team, he's also a boatload of mischief. I can only guess what my science consultant has gotten us into now."

*****

Chapter Six

Night Moves

"Springtonp?" asked Larth. "Isn't that a—"

"Yes," Jyrall interrupted, "it is a Sumatozou world."

"Them nosey sumbitches," Ricky added. "You mean to tell me, we gotta set down on a whole planet of them big-ass beings?"

"Dealing with one or two running a gate is bad enough," Keaton observed. "I can just imagine a bunch of them…all curious about this ship, us, everything."

Jyrall looked over at Larth and said, "There are going to be places on that planet where less than desirables go, where trade is made. Trade that is not necessarily aboveboard, shall we say. That is where we're headed."

Larth nodded. "Arms dealers. That's probably gonna be exactly what we need."

Ricky shrugged. "Well, I guess we have the best disguise for it. That's the kind of place these guys would go." He indicated the four of them, and they knew he meant their alter egos.

"I'll do some searching on the GalNet and see what I can find," Keaton said. "There's got to be some information out there about the best places for a crew like ours to find some business."

"Good idea," Larth agreed.

Jyrall's voice turned serious. "Just so everybody remembers, when we get there, we look, we observe, and we keep to ourselves until we learn who the players are. We're going to have to learn quick because we don't want Nay-Thok to discover we're there, but at the same time, we have to find him."

"All righty, then," Ricky said, as he reached for the rung behind him to leave the operations center. "I'm goin' back to make some more of those little sensor bugs. I gave all I had to the Kin. We may need 'em. Gimme a holler before we make the jump, case'n I'm workin' on something delicate."

"You mean like grenades that blow on impact?" Keaton asked, as he shook his head without looking back at his brother, but Ricky had already left. "There's something wrong with that greasy fingered brother of mine," he said.

Larth looked at Jyrall and grinned. "We have the best team ever!"

* * *

Springton System

As they approached the planet, Jyrall and Larth made their way up to the operations center. Keaton glanced at Jyrall as he strapped himself into his customary seat.

"You will not believe where I'm going to be setting this ship down," Keaton said.

Larth asked, "Where is it? Like…I don't know…Barter Town?"

"Where is Barter Town?" Jyrall asked. He reached his hand up and scratched the side of his jaw. "We studied a lot of systems, and I know it's impossible to know every town and city on the planets I am aware of, but you would think Barter Town would have made the list, especially if it has a reputation for arms dealings. I know a lot of places, but I've never heard of Barter Town."

Keaton shook his head and laughed. "He's been watching old movies again. Max Mad, I think it's called."

"Nope," Larth said. "He's the badass hero of the video. The guy that plays him is a great actor. He's great in all the entertainment videos he plays a part in. Real level-headed guy, like me. Well, except he's Human and everything."

Jyrall squinted and looked at his partner and best friend. "Level-headed? Like you?" He glanced at Keaton, who did his best to concentrate on the atmospheric entry and not voice his opinion. He thought Keaton knew many of the movies Larth was talking about.

"We are going right to the main spaceport in the capital city," Keaton explained. "From everything I learned, arms trade is not frowned upon here. Our ship may not be as suspicious as we thought."

"Mercenaries," Jyrall stated.

"What?" Larth asked. He looked over their shoulders at the screens. "I don't see anything to indicate mercenaries. Do we need to make a run for it? I say we fight. Bring up the weapons, Keaton."

"No," Jyrall explained. "Mercenaries. The Sumatozou are a mercenary race."

"Oh," Larth said, slightly disappointed there wasn't going to be a fight. "I tend to forget that. All everyone really thinks about is the fact that they practically run the Cartography Guild and the gates and all that."

"Stands to reason, a mercenary race would have no issues with arms trade," Keaton observed.

"Maybe," Ricky said from behind them. "But you reckon they cotton to anyone trying to trade in CASPers? And a Mk 9 at that? 'Cause that right there is a reason fer every Human merc left to come a runnin' and whup ass. They'd have fellers who hate the guy next to him here workin' as a team. Hell, there's cargo ships and trade captains that would have their security team here a-fightin'."

"He's right," Jyrall said. "As scattered as the few remaining mercs are, something like a rumored Mk 9 getting into the wrong hands would truly mean the end for humankind. If enough came to try and prevent it, then they would be in one place and would very likely be wiped out by overwhelming forces. I don't think I could talk Cora into not coming."

"Yeah," Larth agreed. "And every member of the Kin would be right here with her, regardless of race."

"Force 25 would be right on her heels," Jyrall said. "It would not be good. It would surely throw the guild master's plans into disarray."

"The technology advancements on a Mk 9, if they're ready for production, are far ahead of any CASPers other races have gotten their hands, claws, paws, tentacles—whatever—on. You know how mercs try and destroy all the Mk 8s that become inoperable in combat? Self-destruct, blow in place, etcetera? I wouldn't doubt a Mk 9 has a failsafe built in."

"Like if you don't exit or enter one the right way, it blows," Ricky said, rubbing his paws together. He started to float away from his rung and quickly grabbed it again. "Well, that's how I'd build it, anyway."

"More things blowing up," Keaton said. "Great. The truth is, we have no way of knowing what the advancements are in a Mk 9."

"I know this," Jyrall said, "we don't want anyone else finding out."

"Well, I reckon we'd better find it first, afore word gets out, then," Ricky stated. "What's the plan?"

* * *

Planet Springton
Starport Tarmac

The four of them stood outside the ship. All were wearing their "Varkell's Crew" disguises. The only difference was the brothers now had different rifles slung across their backs with the barrels down. The Jivool laser rifles were shorter than the .50 cal rifles they carried last time. One had been destroyed, the other was now Sergeant Squarlik's most prized possession. Ricky had even added a powerful Goka scope to it for him. It would truly reach out and touch someone with an accurate shooter wielding it.

Jyrall shifted his eyepatch slightly. Once it was comfortable, he said, "We stick to the plan. I will go to the local offices of the Cartography Guild. Larth, you go find a weapons dealer who deals in unusual stuff. It doesn't have to necessarily be illegal; exotic or hard to get weapons would be the key."

"Right," Larth said as he unbuttoned and buttoned back the top one on his vest. Though he wore two pistols on each hip, he wanted to be able to get to the other two hidden underneath it. "A dealer like that would know if something as rare as a CASPer was available, regardless of what type. I'm on it."

Jyrall looked over toward the brothers. "You two stay together and head over to the warehouse district. It's not far from here. See what you can find out. It shouldn't be an issue with you speaking English. If anyone asks, tell them you spent years working with Humans in a mining colony as hired security or something."

"Right," Keaton said. "If they question it too much, we'll say, 'What? You think Humans can't be…I'm not saying pirates, but you know…' How's that?"

"Perfect," Jyrall answered. "That should be enough to throw them off. They'll want to know about imperfect Humans."

"Hell," Ricky said, "I'll make up all kinds of shit. I'll tell 'em the outfit was a bunch of Hatfields. Everyone knows them no-good Hatfields ain't no better than pirates." He spit to the side.

"Must you do that?" Jyrall asked, disgusted.

"Yep," Ricky stated. "Gotta get that name outa my mouth. Iffin' I gotta say it, I'm spittin'."

Keaton nodded. "I'm afraid I have to agree with him on this one. The rat-bastards."

"Low life snakes," Ricky agreed.

"Mudfish in a dried-up cattle pond," Keaton added.

"Buncha bo-weevils," Ricky said with a nod.

"Damn right," Keaton agreed. "All in the flour."

"Stinkin'—"

"Someday, you will have to explain it to me," said Jyrall, interrupting their back and forth tirade with a shake of his large head. "I am aware of clan feuds among my own kind, but this seems extreme.

"Yeah," Larth agreed. "I want details."

"One day, Boss," Keaton said. "When we have a long evening and some cold beer. Right now, we have too much to do to get worked up over it." He nodded sideways toward his brother, widened his eyes, and raised his brows in warning.

"You are correct," Jyrall said. "We need to keep our head in the game, so to speak."

"Awww, you been watching more of the old Earth shows," Larth said. "I'm proud of you."

"Whatever," the big Besquith said. "Lock her up, Keaton. We'll meet back here at the planned time."

* * *

Larth read the screen located in the wall beside the sliding entry of the building. *Gartholonick Holdings*. He shrugged and pressed the touchscreen. A moment later, a face appeared in place of the company's logo.

"May I help you?" the Jivool asked. It was a feminine voice. Looking closely, Larth could tell she was a young adult Jivool.

"You could," Larth said. "But not until I take a look at your goods. I mean, I can't buy anti-tank weapons sight unseen, now can I?" He gave her his best smile.

Her image disappeared, and the entryway slid open. Larth had noticed earlier that it was a small door built into a much larger bay door. He nodded to himself, straightened his vest, shifted his holsters, and walked through. His eyes widened at what he saw.

The young Jivool walked over from a series of small offices built against the side wall of the large warehouse. Larth glanced at her and back to the rows and rows of weapons. There was everything from small individual rockets to large missile systems on hovercraft and tracked vehicles. In the distance, he saw the barrels of several tanks covered by tarps.

"Greetings," the Jivool said. "I am Lilhitar. And you are?"

"Switch," Larth said. "My name is Switch." He nodded in greeting.

"Now that you see the *goods*," Lilinitar said, sweeping her arm up to indicate the rest of the large warehouse, "tell me what type of anti-tank weapon you are interested in, and we can attempt to come to an agreement on terms for said weapon."

"Well, what if you don't have what I am looking for?" Larth asked, tilting his head slightly.

"Rest assured," the young weapons dealer said, "if I do not have it, I can get it, given time."

"Really?" Larth asked, folding his arms across his chest.

"Really," Lilnitar said. She shifted her feet slightly, and her ears perked up. The tips of her claws protruded slightly from their sheaths. From his lessons in different races' body language, Larth knew this Jivool was slightly insulted and prepared for a challenge.

"The KZ9004?" Larth asked.

"We have them," Lilnitar said. "Though why you would want an outdated KzSha anti-armor system is beyond me. I've been sitting on two of them for years. I'll sell them to you but offer no warranty on rounds that do not penetrate more than a hand's length of armor."

"The Dual L200?" Larth asked.

The Jivool laughed. "The upgraded Lumar weapon? Please. The Dual L200 is nothing more than two shoulder-fired rockets with a cargo strap fixed between them so they can be fired from both upper shoulders at the same time. The idiots did nothing more to it, then named it 'Dual,' *and* changed its nomenclature from 100 to 200. Besides, it takes four hands to use it."

"But do you have it?" Larth asked.

"I know someone," she stated. "I can get it."

"You know someone," Larth mused. "Interesting." He stared at her for a few moments, sizing her up.

"If I don't, someone in my clan does," she added.

"I see," Larth said as he rubbed his chin. "What about…rockets for a Mk 6 CASPer?"

This time it was Lilnitar's turn to size up Larth, or 'Switch,' as she knew him. Larth stared back and waited for her to decide if she should even answer the question. Inside his mind, he had his fingers crossed, like they said in the old shows.

"I have some," she finally answered. "They're no different than the ones used in most Mk 7s. Not that many of those are left. It would seem, there has been a purging of late."

"Yeah," Larth said. "Whatever the Humans did to cause the Mercenary Guild to come down on them is not my business. I couldn't care less. But, regardless, I have a client who needs the rockets. Who knows, maybe he ran across a few Mk 6s and wants to rebuild and rearm them. Not my business. The credits he is willing to pay are."

"Agreed," she said, though the word came out slowly, as if she didn't truly agree. "I have two hundred on hand. I can get more from my parents' warehouse on Ja-wool. It would take twenty-one days minimum. I would have to add the transportation fees into the bill."

"Two hundred?" Larth said. "I'll run it by my boss and see, but I think that will do. How much are we talking about?"

She quoted a price, and he scoffed. He countered, and she came back with another. After a few minutes of back and forth, they agreed upon the price.

"I'll run it by the boss and be back first thing in the morning," Larth said. "Shouldn't be an issue."

"Let me know what Varkell says," she mentioned causally.

Larth whipped his head around. "How do you know his name?"

"There is a small network of dealers here. We take turns monitoring incoming traffic for potential customers. There are some none of us will deal with. Period."

"Really?" Larth asked. "Like who?"

"I'm not discussing it. Just know Varkell and his crew are *not* on the list," she said and waved it off. "Now, don't get me wrong, there are a few dealers here on Springton that would sell to an admitted terrorist to their own systems. My clan is not one of them."

Larth looked at her in a new light. *Honorable,* he thought. "I understand. I will be here first thing in the morning, and we can make the transaction. I'll have a couple of my associates with me to load them on a transporter skiff. I should warn you, they are Pushtal."

"Pushtal," Lilnitar repeated, nodding. She looked toward the closed doors of the offices.

On cue, a door opened, and one of the largest Jivool Larth had ever seen walked out of the small room. Behind him, panels of screens showed all areas of the warehouse, including the area outside the front door.

"Before you go, let me introduce you to my mate," Lilnitar said. "Meet Wilgith. He is head of security for the warehouse."

Wilgith stepped to his mate's side, an unspoken way of saying, "Don't even think about it." Larth knew it was to show him the warehouse was guarded by more than technology. He understood completely. There was a lot of credits in inventory stacked in the warehouse. Attempting to rob arms dealers was not unheard of anywhere in the galaxy.

Larth noticed the military uniform Wilgith wore. He read the patch on his shoulder, and though it was written in Jivool, he had enough grasp of the language to make it out. "The Slow Killers, huh?" Larth asked. "I've heard of them. I thought they hired out for security work."

"You're informed," the big Jivool said, surprise evident on his face. "We do. My—*the* commander has us all on leave, so we found other jobs until he calls us back. Mine, and my platoon's, happens to be with family."

"Platoon?" Larth asked, chastising himself inside for not looking beyond all the stacked weapons for the security placed around the warehouse.

Idiot, he thought. *Who you calling idiot? You didn't notice them either.*

He looked around—really looked. He noticed two places in the corners of the ceiling where rung ladders led up into fortified emplacements. He also noticed the two Jivool in each position. He looked no further. There were probably two in the other corners, as well as roving guards near the rear.

"Meh," he dismissed. "I don't blame you. There are some unsavory types out there who try to skip the bill, you know? Varkell's Crew would never consider it. It's not always about the credits. There may be no honor among thieves, but we aren't thieves. We're smugglers, and we have a reputation to uphold. See you tomorrow."

* * *

Silently Wilgith watched the Zuparti leave. After he left, Lilnitar looked at him. "An honorable group of smugglers? I would not have guessed that. From what we learned of them, they deal harshly with whoever crosses them. Maybe we should look into why they did it. They may very well have had reasons for taking out those they did."

"Maybe," Wilgith said. "I wonder how he knew what my patch said. He asked for CASPer rockets. Do you think they are providing the few Human mercs left with armaments for their machines?"

"That's a good question," Lilnitar said. "They need it. We'll send what we can, but we can't be obvious. The last thing we need is the Mercenary Guild deciding to treat Jivool like Humans."

"Yes," Wilgith said. "We don't need that. It's why my father disbanded the Slow Killers…for the time being. So they wouldn't be hired to fight Humans. The commander of a small Human company on Krifay and he go way back. Pete Brentale is a good man. My father calls him an honorary member of our clan."

"I was happy when you told me," she agreed. "Even happier when you joined me here permanently. I wish all Jivool felt the way he does. He and my father both disagree with the treatment of humankind, but we all must be careful in how we aid them."

"They were teammates in the first mercenary company they joined as youngsters," the big Jivool said. "Of course, they always agree with each other. They are like brothers."

"Well," she said as she nuzzled her mate with her snout against his chest, "I'm glad they are not truly brothers, or I would not have you as a mate."

"True," he said as he reached a large paw up and slowly scratched her back, thinking of the Zuparti they had just met. *That Zuparti was not nervous around me. A merc. A rather large merc. Astounding.*

* * * * *

Chapter Seven

Keaton noticed the look on his brother's face. He smelled it too. *Phew!* This was definitely not the best part of the warehouse district. He wondered how the Sumatozou, with their two noses, could stand being this close to the sanitary treatment facilities. Maybe they didn't use them for smelling. He would have to look it up.

"What in the hell fahr is that smell?" Ricky asked. He waved a hand back and forth in front of his face. "My dang eyes are watering."

"Their waste treatment facilities," Keaton said. He nodded up the street. "This end of the warehouse district butts up against them."

"Dayum!" Ricky exclaimed. "Maybe we should look for another lead to a smuggler's pit."

"There isn't another," Keaton argued. "The Sumatozou we met earlier said this is where to go."

"Ah hell," Ricky said. "He was drunk, and it's still daytime. You sure we can trust him?"

"He knew Varkell's name," Keaton countered. "I planted the information all over the GalNet so only those looking for deliveries like our crew does would know what, or who, to look for. He's in the business. Or used to be, anyway."

"I guess," Ricky said. "He's too old and drunk to do it anymore, even if he did make runs."

"That doesn't mean he doesn't know where to go," Keaton countered. "Very few know there are smuggler pits like merc pits."

"True," Ricky said. He showed a little teeth to a Bakulu ambling in their path. It quickly shifted over, determined not to become dinner for the angry looking Pushtals.

"This may be a world inhabited mostly by Sumatozou," Ricky proclaimed. "But they got all types here."

"Bakulu make good pilots," Keaton said, with a shrug. "Makes sense to see one coming out of the local smuggler's pit."

They stopped at the nondescript door on an unremarkable building. "Okay, this is it," Keaton warned. "Look serious. Dangerous and serious. We go in here like we're some kind of tourist on the beach, and they will eat us alive and get rid of the bodies."

"Got it," Ricky said.

* * *

Weqq

Even before the shuttle *Dalton*'s thrusters cycled back to idle, Cora was moving toward the external hatch. On approach, the vibrant green equatorial continents and their moisture-shrouded jungles seemed to call to her. The incredibly lush and green planet was an anomaly in her travels across the galaxy. She hadn't seen a landscape like it on any alien world since leaving Earth. It reminded her of the rolling hills of the southern Appalachian Mountains. Of home.

She disengaged the locking mechanism for the external hatch, and an onslaught of warm, humid air smacked her in the face. Cora felt as if every pore in her body opened at once and drank in the atmospheric moisture for the first time in years. In an instant, the stale smell of hyperspace travel in the ship's enclosed spaces evaporated. She closed her eyes and breathed deeply through her nose. She could smell loam, petrichor, and a half dozen things she did not recognize. The smell of rain, alone, was enough to bring a smile to her face. Weqq was a world unlike anything she'd seen, short of the jungles of South America, but even then, that had only been on Tri-V screens in her intermediate schooling. Even the kudzu forests of South Georgia in summertime could not compare.

Dominating one side of the landing area was the shattered hulk of what appeared to be an atmosphere-capable freighter. Maybe something slightly larger. She knew it was the remains of *Satisfaction*, Raleigh Reilly's flagship, from their Peacemaker Guild intelligence briefings. Every detail of Jessica Francis' mission to the planet found its way into the Kin's databases. The crash site appeared consumed by all manner of vehicles and robots disassembling and cannibalizing the ship. Cora idly wondered if there were any components she and her company could use before turning to take in more of the scene.

There were several other small ships in the large marshland clearing that appeared to be resting on massive, floating platforms. There appeared to be at least two companies' worth of soldiers and equipment in the area. With the headquarters tucked away in the jungle several kilometers to the west, the sheer numbers indicated a serious threat must be en route.

Yet the one thing that surprised her most appeared to be the predominance of Humans in the area. She remembered from the intelligence briefing that the initial research station on the planet had been manned by the MinSha. Try as she might, Cora could not see one anywhere. Nor did she see any of the TriRusk. Aside from a few elSha and Maki moving around the maintenance areas, there were few alien lifeforms.

An older man with gray hair sticking out from underneath his patrol cap approached. On the shoulders of his black coveralls were patches resembling something she'd seen in school. The white patch with the large, stylized, red cross was indicative of the Knights Templar from ancient Earth history. He made eye contact with her just as he tucked away a set of guide wands he'd used to position the shuttle on the landing pad.

"Colonel McCoy? The Blue Ridge Kin?"

"That's me," Cora replied.

The man responded without a shred of emotion, "Welcome to Weqq. On behalf of Crusader Prime, welcome to our operation."

Crusader Prime?

Cora kept her face straight. "My orders are to report to Enforcer Tok. Can you direct me to his location?"

The man paused, and a troubled look crossed his weathered face. "Ma'am, I have orders to take you to Lieutenant Colonel Smith. He will conduct your unit's in-briefing and see to your indoctrination."

Smith? Cora almost flinched. *Surely it can't be the same bastard from Parmick, can it?*

Then-Major Sean Smith was one of the reasons she and the other women had been kicked out of the Ridge Runners. His continual unwanted advances had finally irritated her to the point where she'd smashed the side of the bastard's head with a beer mug. Her actions had left them stranded on Parmick. For a long time, she figured it'd been the biggest mistake of her career. Yet it had opened another door, and she and her new officers had stepped through it with a purpose. Now, they had their own mercenary company. The chances of it being the same son of a bitch she'd hit were low, but Cora realized this was another opportunity for the fickle finger of fate. Mercenary units never seemed to escape it for long.

"I don't think you understood me. My orders are to report to Enforcer Tok. My orders come from Guild Master Rsach himself."

"Ma'am, I'm not here to argue with you. I have my own orders. Your unit is task organized to the Crusaders for this mission, and—"

"The *hell* we are. Get me to Enforcer Tok, or I take my ships and my company, and we get the fuck out of here." She hadn't intended for the anger or the language to come screaming out, but based on the response from the man in front of her, it was the right thing. He took off as if he'd been shot in the ass. About two minutes later, a Jivool wearing the familiar blue vest of a Peacemaker ambled toward them. The look on his face was bemused.

"You must be Cora McCoy?" he called from the slope below.

"I'm hoping you're Enforcer Tok."

The Jivool chuckled. "That, I am. Welcome to Weqq."

Cora descended the ramp and walked up to him. She'd been up close and personal with Jivool and Oogar before, but not with an Enforcer. "Thank you for coming to meet us. The Blue Ridge Kin reports for duty."

The Enforcer nodded—a comical move of his ursine face, combined with an inhuman shrug of his shoulders. "We're glad to have you working with the Crusaders for this mission. Lieutenant Colonel Smith, their executive officer, has been summoned to provide you additional instructions."

Cora shook her head and waggled a finger. "Guild Master Rsach said we work specifically with you. No one else."

"Did you receive the information request from the Crusaders?"

"Yes, we did, and it's total horseshit. I'm not providing any of that information to someone I don't know, Peacemaker or Enforcer or who the hell ever, without a direct order from Guild Master Rsach."

Enforcer Tok screwed one side of his maw under and frowned. "You speak as if you've been deputized. I know that is not the case."

"We haven't been. But that doesn't change the fact that you're asking for things we equate to company secrets. According to the

Mercenary Guild, that line of inquiry is illegal, except in a legal dispute, as required for evidence to pursue some type of charges."

"You don't work for the Mercenary Guild. Your guild is in tatters, even as we speak," Tok said.

"This company was formed under the codicils of the Mercenary Guild's requirements and regulations. To that end, we will continue to operate as a mercenary organization. We will not become a member of the Crusaders. And, unless you're charging me with some sort of crime, I'm not handing over any company information without speaking with Guild Master Rsach."

"We'll see about that," Tok rumbled. He waved one big paw in front of his face. "Enough of that, we have bigger things to worry about. You are aware we are expecting an attack, yes?

"We're very aware. We understand that's why we're here. My combat forces are trained and ready to support you, Enforcer Tok."

Except, you're not really in charge here, and that's chapping your hide. Ain't it?

"We have a good working relationship with Human units. I believe you'll fit in well here."

Cora caught something in his words. "Enforcer Tok? Are you expecting my company to be fully Human?"

"Well, at least eighty percent Human is the goal of the Crusaders. You wouldn't have been contacted if—"

From behind her, Cora heard First Sergeant Figgle's voice. "Ma'am? Is there any trouble? I'd like to get the troops offloaded and bedded down as quickly as possible."

Cora watched the look on Tok's face slide from frustrated bemusement to absolute shock. "What in the name of Hr'ent are you playing at, Colonel McCoy?"

Cora wanted to laugh, but instead she added steel to her voice. "This is First Sergeant Figgle. He is the top NCO of the Blue Ridge Kin. If I am not around, he speaks for me."

She could tell the Enforcer's mind was racing. Humans and Goka were not supposed to have a good relationship. Yet everything about Figgle and his approach to her and their command was strikingly professional and respectful. She knew the Enforcer, and whoever Crusader Prime turned out to be, were going to have kittens before all was said and done.

A new voice called from down on the ground to her left. "Enforcer Tok, I see you've met *Colonel* McCoy? It's wonderful to see you again, *ma'am.*"

Dread hit Cora's stomach like an uppercut punch.

Of all the beer joints in all the world. Or whatever that line is.

Cora turned and looked down into the smiling face of *Lieutenant Colonel* Sean Smith. He now wore the silver leaves of a lieutenant colonel and the familiar smug expression she'd left him with on Parmick. Cora took a slight bit of pride in knowing that she outranked the son of a bitch this time around.

She nodded in his direction. "Smith. I understand I'm supposed to see you regarding placement of my people in quarters?"

Smith continued to grin at her as if she were once again a mark at the bar. "Oh, certainly, *ma'am.*"

The way he stressed the last word was anything but respectful. Cora resisted her first urge to draw her pistol from the holster on her right hip and shoot him between the eyes. "Fine, then let's get about it. First Sergeant Figgle will handle everything in that respect. I'll be meeting privately with Enforcer Tok to discuss deployment and—"

"Oh, no you won't. You're going to be meeting with Crusader Prime. He's on his way now and should arrive within the next six hours. Until then, you'll take all your orders from me."

Cora lowered one shoulder to him. She remembered Colonel Talmore from the Ridge Runners once doing something similar when she was a young mercenary. Cora tapped with one finger at the silver eagles on her shoulders. "Let's be clear about something, Smith. I command a mercenary company. I do not work for you. My mercenary company does not work for you. Therefore, you have no rank or authority over me. The next time you say something along those lines and disrespect me, or my people, you'll be the one explaining to the guild master and your Crusader Prime why the Blue Ridge Kin left or forewent their contract."

The asshole had the audacity to laugh. "I understand your concern about our methods, but you have to understand, Cora. We really all are in this together. Humans are going to be the saviors of the galaxy. We thought it was going to be through our mercenary forces. But we realized we needed something more. The Four Horsemen have proven to be more than a hindrance to our expanse of the galaxy. Our Crusaders will be the hallmark of the Peacemaker Guild. That's what will bring peace to the galaxy. You know just as well as anyone else that peace cannot be brokered. It has to be made."

Cora didn't immediately respond. Instead, she brought her eyes to the horizon and studied closely what she saw around her. The ability to make peace the Crusader way appeared to be through total annihilation. A sizable collection of Mk 7 and Mk 8 CASPers dominated the landing zone. State-of-the-art maintenance facilities stood ready to receive what looked like all of them at the same time. Pallets upon pallets of ammunition moved in an automated train toward the jungle. The more common elements of Human mercenary companies, armored vehicles and tanks, were absent. There were a few flyers, but none of the typical layout for a company. The Crusaders seemed intent on the firepower of the CASPer over everything else. None of it seemed right.

"What do you think? If you join us, we'll be sure to restock your troops with the best gear we have. It's all here if you want it. Only the best for those who commit to doing things the Crusader way." Smith leered at her.

Cora turned her gaze back to him and noticed he was older than she remembered. The morning sun glinted on his neck, and she saw there were two sets of pinplants. She'd never undergone the procedure herself and had encouraged as many of her troops as she could to rely on their own innate abilities and not maintain a hardwired connection. It wasn't uncommon for Humans to have multiple sets, and she wondered about the load of all that data as she studied the crinkles around Smith's eyes. She'd last seen him only two years before, and yet he seemed to have aged five, if not ten, years.

"I'll think about it. In the meantime, my company does things the way we do them. If you or anyone else has any problems with that, you can take it up with me or First Sergeant Figgle."

Smith smiled, but there wasn't any mirth on his face. "Oh, don't worry, Cora, we will certainly do that. I don't know how you managed to find work again, much less command of a fully equipped mercenary company. I'm impressed."

"I figured you were still smarting from a mug slap, Smith."

He laughed. "Oh, I forgave you for that a long time ago. Your judgment isn't going to be up to me at all."

Cora watched him walk away and realized the feeling in her stomach wasn't dread. It was abject fear, and she couldn't help wondering what her troops were walking into. Nothing seemed to make sense, and yet Guild Master Rsach had sent them here for a reason. Everything that the Crusaders appeared to be doing went against what she knew the Peacemaker Guild's leadership would want.

Does the guild master expect us to become Crusaders? Because it doesn't seem like they want peace at all. It seems like they want to dominate the galaxy. Is peace really worth that much to them?

Cora took a deep breath and again noticed the peculiar scents of the planet. One in the moist, heavy air reminded her of the sweet smell of death. As she turned back to the shuttle, she met the staring faces of May and Lisalle.

"Was that Major Smith?" Lisalle asked. "Kinda looked like him."

"Yeah," Cora said. "He's a light bird now. Kind of strange to see him here."

"Especially saying all them things he was spouting," May interjected. "This place smells funny, and I don't mean all the jungle shit."

Cora nodded first at May and Lisalle and then at First Sergeant Figgle as he approached. "Your orders, ma'am?"

Cora thought for a moment and decided the best course of action was to portray things as normally as possible. "Standard deployment. Get the CASPers in their racks but don't connect anything to any of their systems. Use our power generators. Use our networks. Don't allow the Crusaders to plug into anything."

"Closed loop for communications and operations, too?" Lisalle asked. "I'll get that set up."

"Do it, and make sure everybody in the company knows that if they see a Crusader messing around any of our gear, I want to know about it. I don't trust what's going on here. I'm damned sure they're going to eavesdrop on us or mess with our equipment. Post armed guards and automatic sentries. Have Ricky's drones on standby, too."

"Yes, ma'am. Standard deployment. What do we know about the threat?" Figgle asked. "Certainly the Enforcers and Crusaders are still preparing a defense."

"They're preparing all right, but I'm not sure exactly what they're preparing for, and that's what bothers me. I ain't sure our suspected enemy is any worse than what we've found here. My gut doesn't like this at all."

"We damned sure don't want to be worried about who's behind us," May said. "If we can't trust anybody, we can't trust that they're telling us the truth about the threat either, right?"

"What about the TriRusk? Any sight of them?" Lisalle asked.

"Nothing," Figgle replied. "If we are supposed to be protecting them, shouldn't they be a part of the mission?"

"Makes sense to me," May replied. "Unless these assholes are here for something else. Told y'all; this stinks."

Cora nodded. "You know how we say we don't trust anybody but kin? That goes double for this bullshit operation. Make sure everybody knows the score."

Figgle touched the top of his carapace near his eyes in a salute. "We complete the mission, ma'am. Even the shitty ones."

*****

Chapter Eight

Springton

The door slid shut behind the brothers, and they found themselves standing in a small waiting room. The signs on the wall indicated it was a warehouse for refreshment drinks of various types. There was a shelf in the corner with at least twenty different types in containers designed for many different races. There were also several examples of squeeze bulbs for near zero gravity use.

A Sumatozou was seated in a large chair behind a counter, visible from just above his waist. To one side of the counterspace, a wide door was closed and obviously electronically locked, as it had no doorknob or latch of any kind.

Ever curious, Ricky studied the door and the frame it was built into. Determined not to show surprise, he noticed a slight difference in texture about chest high. There were three small circles. He knew the door was built with kinetic weapons inside it, or someone from the other side could easily shoot through the small ports without fear of ricochets on the other side. He also knew it would be easy to build lasers into a wide door for the same use.

Another glance around the room showed him several spots that would be the best places to hide monitoring devices. Well, they would for him anyway. He knew they were in the right place. He turned back and watched as Keaton worked to get them through the door.

"Greetings," Keaton said. It didn't necessarily come across as a pleasant greeting. It was more or less a formality. It was to be expected. The entire galaxy knew Pushtal were not friendly or pleasant.

The Sumatozou tilted his head slightly in puzzlement and said, "Greetings. How may I help you this fine day?" Only one of his hands was visible.

"Fine?" asked Keaton. "I don't know about that. It'll be fine once I secure a load and the boss gets off my back about mounting operational costs and repair bills."

"I see," the big being said. "Pardon my inquisitiveness. My earpiece translates what you are saying into my language just fine, but in my other ear, I hear you speaking…a Human language… not Pushtal."

"So," Keaton said, "you got a problem?" This he hissed in Pushtal. It was one of the few phrases he and Ricky had learned recently.

"No," the Sumatozou said, raising one of his large hands in mock surrender. "I was just curious."

"We didn't know if you had access to Pushtal," Ricky said, speaking English, but doing his best to hide his southern accent.

"Not that it's any of your concern," Keaton said. "We spent a lot of time in areas Humans are attempting to colonize. Even making…deliveries, shall we say, to Earth."

"There are a lot of…*drinks*," Ricky added, indicating the shelf in the corner. "Ones Humans are willing to pay good credits for. Drinks made by other races. You know, stuff they can't make yet, but desperately need."

"Go on," the doorkeeper said. He waved his hand in a circle, indicating he wanted more information.

"Bah," Keaton dismissed. "The runs are drying up. The boss says there are not as many customers as there once were. Besides, it's bad business delivering to a losing side. That's a good way to get caught up in the wrong end of things. And you and I both know that is not the place to be."

"Agreed," the Sumatozou said.

One of his trunks idly reached up and scratched the top of the other with its flexible tip. Keaton knew from Jyrall's instructions that it was a sign the alien was relaxing. Letting down one's guard, so to speak. He further proved Keaton's observation by pulling his hidden hand from underneath the counter and leaning back in his chair with his fingers laced across his big stomach.

"So, you are interested in delivering *drinks*? There may be some work for you around here. My products are covered, but others may have need of reliable delivery. Maybe."

The big being leaned forward to a screen and looked up, hands ready. "Tell me, what is your boss' name and the name of your company so I may do a quick search? You know, to ensure I'm not recommending the wrong sort to others looking for deliveries."

Keaton glanced at his brother and showed a little teeth. He kept the same look when he turned back and said, "Varkell."

The doorkeeper squinted slightly at hearing just one word as a way of introducing the outfit the two Pushtal worked for but entered the information on the screen. A minute later, his eyes widened as he read quickly. He turned to Keaton with a pleased look on his face, almost one of relief.

"Highly recommended, I see," the Sumatozou said. "Forgive my earlier rudeness. I'm sure you understand. My name is Talnorgeth. This is my pit."

"It is understandable," Keaton admitted.

"Hell, I wouldn't trust a couple of Pushtal, either," Ricky said. "Bunch of pirates."

At this, Talnorgeth grinned in his race's smile. "Not until I find out they are Rylon and Zarr of One-Eyed Varkell's Crew."

He continued, "I say trust. It has a different kind of meaning in this business. Not that I'd trust you to back me in a bar fight…or with my sister…you understand. I would, however, trust you with a run of valuable cargo. By all indications, your outfit gets it where it needs to be on time, without adding to the shipping cost afterward."

"We do," Keaton confirmed.

"What's your sister look like?" Ricky asked as he leaned on the counter. "And can she cook?"

Talnorgeth shook his head with a grimace and pointed to the door. A loud *click* indicated it was now unlocked. The brothers walked over, and Keaton pushed it open. They both were surprised when they entered a brightly lit room.

Keaton stepped forward so his brother could close the door behind them. Instead of a dimly lit bar, like most merc pits, the large room was well furnished, with a brightly lit bar on one side. There were various groups of sitting areas, well away from each other. The expensive chairs were designed for multiple races.

Keaton led Ricky to the bar where they both ordered sparkling water as if they knew what they wanted before entering the place. The well-dressed Sumatozou was armed with a large pistol strapped to his hip. He completed their order quickly and asked if he could be of any other service. They declined.

They made their way toward a group of comfortable chairs, shifted their rifles to the side, and settled in. The small table between them had an inlaid screen with several job offers displayed. The screen was inset into the table so no one else in the room could see what the user was looking at.

Ricky glanced around while his brother switched from screen to screen, perusing the jobs listed. He nodded politely to a pair of Bakulu and a Jeha near their table, but a comfortable distance away. The Bakulu, who noticed him, dipped several eyes in greeting. No words were said.

Ricky nudged his brother's arm. Highlighted was a run from Springton to a location to be determined. The amount offered was ridiculous, even for smugglers. The contact listed a location to meet on the far side of the warehouse district, close to the starport tarmac, and a name. Captain Gimmold, Commander of the Eye Pokers.

Ricky was reaching for his slate to transfer the information when the job listing disappeared. At almost the same time, their sensitive ears heard the Jeha say out loud, "Gimmold agreed to our counteroffer. Let us go prepare the ship. We leave in two days."

* * *

Jyrall stepped to one side of the walkway to allow the muttering Sumatozou room for its ample body to walk by. The big being never looked up. He moved slowly, head down, as if he had received the worst news of his life. Jyrall glanced ahead and noticed two others. Judging by their uniforms, they were obviously security for the Cartography Guild. Or, at least, for the building where their offices were.

The two guards turned and entered the building the other came from. Jyrall glanced back at the downtrodden one and saw him turn into a combination restaurant and bar. He filed the information away in the back of his mind. Perhaps he should attempt to speak to the individual if he was still in the establishment.

He entered the large lobby of the building. Seated in opposite corners at small desks with several screens were the two guards he had seen moments earlier. He ignored them and moved to a long counter.

"May I help you?" asked the Sumatozou standing behind it. The sound of her voice and her choice of attire let Jyrall know she was female.

"Yes," Jyrall said. "I would like to speak to someone about a possible trace through gates."

"Trace?" asked the receptionist. "Do you mean to inquire about the location a ship or ships emerged upon exit?"

"Exactly," Jyrall said. "The system it came out in." He leaned on the counter, attempting to show this was something he had asked for in other places and that he expected to find the information he was searching for.

"I see," she said, without hesitation. "Are you a Peacemaker?"

Her question startled Jyrall. He rose to his full, imposing height. *How does she know?* "What? Why would I be a Peacemaker?"

She ignored his question. "All right, you are not a Peacemaker. Have you been deputized by a Peacemaker to conduct official Peacemaker business?"

Jyrall decided to bring a little more "Varkell" into the picture. "No, I have not been *deputized* by a Peacemaker. Enough with the Peacemaker questions," he said in a voice that allowed no hidden implications. He was getting angry. "I need to know where a ship went because they took someone with them. Someone that owes. The individual must be made to pay."

At hearing the rise in volume and tone of his words, both security guards stood and walked over. Jyrall could easily see the one guard with his uncovered eye. The patch over his covered eye greatly enhanced his peripheral vison, and he was able to keep track of the other one.

"You seem to be no help," he stated. "I want to speak to someone who can get me the information I need without playing 'Ask Varkell a hundred stupid questions.'"

The receptionist stared at Jyrall for a few seconds, then waved the security off. She pushed a corner of the screen facing her and said, "Wait a moment, please."

A minute later, a door slid open behind her. A well-dressed male stepped through. The larger Sumatozou took in the room and the situation in one glance. He stepped to the counter.

"What seems to be the issue here?" he asked, addressing his receptionist while looking Jyrall over.

She said, "Cartographer Lincol, this is Varkell, I believe. He insists on speaking to someone other than me without having answered the standard questions. He wants to know the exit location of a ship which used a gate. I have not been told which entry gate was used, yet."

"I see," Lincol said. He folded his thick arms in front of his chest. "It's obvious by your apparel, you are not associated with the

Peacemaker's Guild. Even if you were, you would have to be on proven official business for me to even begin to search for that information."

He paused for effect. "Now, it is possible for others to obtain this type of information, but it usually is associated with substantial donations to the Cartography Guild's Retirement Fund, you understand. Kind of a thank you, caring for those who have made it possible for others to traverse the galaxy." He gave an indication of his race's smile. "Which we, as a guild, feel is quite heartfelt and in no way something an individual or organization would ask…for anything other than noble reasons."

Jyrall was disgusted by his words. It seemed as if he were speaking with a used ship salesman. "I'm not *donating* anything until I know the information can be had." He folded his arms.

Starting the negotiation, Lincol said, "Perhaps if I had more information, I could tell you if a donation by you would be appropriate for our…members. Retirement can be difficult financially, you understand, and as for me, I intend to plan ahead."

He shooed the receptionist out of the way before he stepped in front of her system to enter information on the screen and said, "Move, Dear One." He glanced up at Jyrall. "What was this individual's race?"

"Jeha," Jyrall answered. "Why? Does it really matter?"

"Normally, no." Lincol said. "Buuut there have been some directives passed down to us as of late. They concern Humans, so they are of no issue here." He waved his trunk around to indicate they were irrelevant.

The big guild representative continued, "Which system gate did this ship enter?"

"Well..." Jyrall said. He reached up and scratched below the patch on his eye with a claw. "The system was Parmick, but the ship didn't use the gate. It was equipped with shunts."

"With shunts?" Lincol asked. He stepped back. "I am afraid we will not be able to help each other today. I would need the gate location and approximate time of entry to crosscheck recorded hyperspace exits into potential systems."

"There are rumors the Jeha came here...and left the same way. I wanted to verify the information. Are you saying you can't track it, even from within this system? Can't you just check all recorded system entries using the approximate time?" Jyrall asked.

"Near impossible," Lincol replied. "The possibilities are numerous. And, I am embarrassed to say, not everyone working on the many stargates do their jobs as required. There are some who fail to record every entry into their assigned system."

He gave Jyrall a serious look. "Just today, I was given the task of removing the guild membership of an individual who had been warned several times to adhere to guild regulations and additional instructions."

He shook his big head. "No aid to Human mercenaries means just that, you understand. Some things cannot be used to contribute to retirement. Even if it is only turning a blind eye for a few minutes." He looked directly at Jyrall's patch. "No disrespect intended, Varkell. I am sorry for your disability."

Sensing no animosity toward the remark, he continued. "In effect, I ended Argold's career. Or he did, I should say. I was merely the messenger. Still, I suppose it comes with the territory. As a Regional Administrator, my office is no longer in a stargate in a dead-end mining system, so there is that."

Before Jyrall could say anything else, double doors opened on one end of the lobby, and ten young adult Sumatozou shuffled out of a large room. Above their heads and through the doors behind them, Jyrall could see several mock stargate control stations. As a group, they turned and went out the front doors.

"Training for the day has ended early, I see," Lincol said.

"Yes," the receptionist confirmed. "It was scheduled. Tomorrow, they begin to learn the operation of fusion-powered gates and major gate traffic. The system needs to be reconfigured."

"Well? Where are the technicians?" asked Lincol, forgetting he had a guest.

"It is not scheduled until the morning," she explained. "I had to shift some things around and schedule transportation. It could not be done today." She raised both of her trunks in apology.

Lincol turned back to Jyrall. "It never ends around here."

"For your time," Jyrall said and held out a huge paw.

"Oh, why thank you for the donation." Lincol took the small stack of hard credits. They were 100-credit pieces. "Perhaps, next time, I can be of more assistance. I will ensure this is taken care of. I'm sure you would like it to be listed as anonymous?"

"Absolutely," Jyrall agreed. "Absolutely."

* * *

Night Moves

Springton Starport

"What do you mean you want me to get into the Regional Cartography Guild Offices?" Larth asked.

"There are several training centers there. I want you to get in tonight and download the files from one," Jyrall said.

Keaton leaned back in his seat in the small conference room on the ship and said, "I can provide a small drive with enough room to store it, no problem." He ran a paw over his head as if ruffling hair instead of short fur. "I have a few programs I can include to erase the fact that it was used. It won't take long to upload the files to it. There are several to choose from. I just need to do a little research to make sure I choose the right one."

"But why?" Larth asked. "I got us a deal on rockets. We can use it as an in to find out if any CASPers are being sold. Surely this outfit would know. The guys are in at the local smugglers' pit—even though they say it isn't really a pit. Who would have thought? Anyway, why? We need to track down Gimmold. He was on the ship with Nay-Thok when he escaped. He may know where he went."

"We will look into Gimmold, but I am sure he will not be at the warehouse tonight. We will go to the address in the morning and watch for him." Jyrall took a deep breath and said, "Look, as things progress, we may need to know whatever we can learn from the Cartography Guild. I am not sure what the directives are that Lincol mentioned, but he did say they involved Humans. If nothing else, we can pass the files to Cora and the Kin."

"True," Larth said as he rubbed his chin. "I guess."

"Besides," Jyrall said. "I have a hunch."

"Oh, hell naw!" Ricky said. "That's some movie cop shit right there."

"A hunch? I'm on it," Larth said, standing. "Keaton, hurry up with the research. I'm going to watch the replay from Jyrall's eye patch and case the joint. Come on, Ricky. Do some Ricky Shit and hook it up to a screen."

"What is a joint?" Jyrall asked Keaton after the other two left the room. "Stars! What is a case of them?"

* * * * *

Chapter Nine

Bartertown Spaceport

Karma IV

Like any quasi-military organization, the Peacemaker Guild had more than its fair share of near conspiracy theories, lies, and outright stories. Among them, several fictions dealt with the facilities at Karma. Home of the largest Peacemaker Guild penitentiary in the galaxy, the planet also had conveniently poor choices for other Peacemaker-centric facilities. For example, the primary landing pads for all Peacemakers sat at the far end of one spoke off the main terminal complex.

To get from the landing pads to the penitentiary complex, the Peacemakers had to escort their charges down the length of the spur before reaching a transfer point. From a security standpoint, it made little sense. After one hundred and seventy hours in hyperspace, the last thing anyone really wanted was a thousand-meter walk through a narrow, crowded spur teeming with all manner of species. The lights, sounds, and crowds of the spur could be disorienting and confusing at times.

On more than one occasion, Peacemakers had been forced to use squads of armed guards, sometimes five Peacemakers for every criminal, to get their charges from one place to another safely. They called the spur "the gauntlet." More than one Peacemaker knew of others who'd either lost their charge in the gauntlet or had been forced to draw their weapon and put their subject down during an escape attempt. No one wanted to escort a prisoner alone.

So far in his long career, Millzak had managed to avoid the gauntlet, at least for a solo transit. While his operations seldom tended to be clandestine, he had never had the opportunity to arrest and solely transport a prisoner to Karma before now. As luck would have it, his first solo prisoner transport through the gauntlet was an Oogar. And not just any Oogar. Geerlargum was a thousand kilograms of bad attitude and trouble. While he'd played soft, and even remorseful, for his crimes, Millzak believed there was much more going on inside his head which he had no way of knowing. He didn't trust the Oogar as far as his four arms could throw him. Which, for a Lumar versus an Oogar, was pretty far.

No sooner had *Tango Forte*'s shuttle *Allegro* touched down on the pad, than Millzak was moving to the security compartment in the rear of the shuttle. Geerlargum looked up from the multi-species bunk. He stood and stretched his massive frame. There were three types of restraints Millzak could use for the transport phase. Deliberating on which ones to apply took him a moment longer than other Peacemakers. As luck would have it, the normal restraints and the powered restraints were in working order. The maximum-security restraints appeared to have been either badly maintained or damaged.

"You can trust me, Peacemaker."

Millzak glanced up at Geerlargum and grunted. "The hell I can. You wait there. It's only going to take me a minute."

He retraced his steps through the shuttle's narrow passage and found his personal belongings neatly bagged along one side of the forward section. Millzak dug through the top bag and quickly found the set of powered restraints he'd brought for backup.

A Peacemaker is always prepared.

He made his way back to the containment cell and watched Geerlargum frown through the clear door.

"You didn't have to go to all that trouble for me."

Millzak smiled. "Yes, I did. Hands please."

Geerlargum knew the routine and stuck his hands through the portal, allowing Millzak to slip the powered restraints over his massive paws and onto his wrists. When both restraints were secure, a small green light illuminated on the central band to show Millzak the connections were tight and holding. After adjusting the strength of the bonds to their maximum setting, he stepped to the side of the cell, tapped the console, and opened the thick, clear door.

"Let's go."

He'd never seen an Oogar look so sad. It was almost comical the way Geerlargum had approached everything from the moment of his arrest. He'd promised to squeal and provide all the information Millzak wanted and had done so marvelously. He'd been exceptionally cooperative, likely in the hope that some type of deal could be made for a lighter sentence or even his freedom.

Confident they were ready, Millzak gestured toward the shuttle's ramp, and the two walked off together.

As they entered the bustling hangar bay, Millzak was surprised to see that there were no additional Peacemakers there to support him. He'd requested armed support several times en route from the emergence point. The Peacemaker office's assurances he would be met and escorted appeared to have been either forgotten or maliciously ignored. Given what he knew of operations on Karma, he couldn't help but wonder if it was intentional rather than incompetence or coincidence.

The pair made their way across the hangar bay and entered the spur. It was everything Millzak had ever heard it was, and worse. Through his career, he'd seen plenty of areas outside mercenary bases which seemed less than hospitable to the general public. Tiny restaurants that offered questionable menus, loads of cheap, unclean tattoo parlors, and establishments of all manner of ill repute lined the corridor's walls. There was a scent of something between rotten fish and death which threatened to take his breath away.

Beings of all species milled through the spur. Around them were Pushtal, MinSha, Zuul, and more than a dozen other species. From what he could see, Millzak was the only Lumar in the entire length of the spur. Instinctively, he lowered one right hand and kept it close to his sidearm.

As a trainee, he had had more than ample opportunities to participate in training exercises where he was the lone Lumar. He'd long been accustomed to the questioning looks and covered smiles of others in his presence. Far too many underestimated all Lumar. Yet, in the faces of those around him now, Millzak didn't see underestimation. He saw fear. In some, he saw abject hate.

At the halfway point of the spur, there was a security checkpoint. The checkpoint was unmanned, which did not surprise Millzak at all, given what he'd seen so far. For a planet with a sizable Peacemaker presence, almost everyone looked past the seedy underbellies of the community at large. Things on Karma always seemed a little bit sketchy, even with the large Peacemaker presence, but this was totally wrong for a guild checkpoint. There should have been some type of legal presence, unless the checkpoint was deemed too dangerous to occupy. His eyes studied the empty space and saw a fine layer of dust on a couple of the platforms nearby. No one had stood watch in quite some time.

Again, his hand grazed the handle of his pistol. For the second time in five hundred meters, he seriously considered drawing it, if only for a measure of safety and security. But such things were not allowed. When a Peacemaker drew their weapon, justice was to be served in the face of danger—a threat which must be honored. While he didn't believe he was in immediate danger, and the situation just didn't seem to be right, that wasn't cause enough to draw his weapon.

He turned his attention back to Geerlargum in time to see both of the Oogar's fists swinging toward him in a two-armed strike. Millzak instinctively ducked, and the blow missed, save for the top of his thick head, which took the brunt of one paw and the underside of the restraints. The impact was enough to spin him across the width of the corridor and slam him into the abandoned watch post. After tumbling over the counter, Millzak came up with his weapon drawn and saw Geerlargum racing down the corridor. He took aim, attempted to center himself with a quick breathing technique, and prepared to pull the trigger. Geerlargum darted to his right and into a sub-corridor.

Fuck!

Millzak gave chase, racing past stoned locals who seemed almost uncooperative in the way they refused to get out of his way.

He roared, "Peacemaker! Let me through!"

The crowd parted slightly, enough for him to get through and make the turn down the sub-corridor. After twenty paces, he ran into a wall of beings standing perfectly still as if watching something. He pushed his way through with sharp elbows and all four shoulders working against the crowd as far as he could before he stepped into an area where Geerlargum's massive body lay slumped under a massive Besquith in a blue vest.

"Did you see that?" someone in the crowd behind him whispered.

"Yeah. That Besquith beat the shit out of that Oogar."

"Entropy," another soft voice said. "How did the Peacemakers get so strong?"

Millzak met Captain Dreel's eyes. He smiled in return. "I think I found something of yours, Peacemaker."

"Looks like you did, sir."

Dreel chuckled. "And here I was lamenting my need for a workout. Anyway, glad to give you some assistance, Peacemaker."

Millzak holstered his sidearm and stepped fully into the circle, squarely onto one of Geerlargum's paws with his boot. There was no response, so he ground his heel into the sensitive space between two of the pads. Geerlargum groaned and rolled and finally gasped in pain.

"Ow."

"Get up," Millzak said. "You try anything like that again, and I'll drop you before you can sneeze."

The Oogar said nothing. After a moment, he rolled to his feet and stood slowly.

"I suppose attempted escape is going to be added to my charges?"

Millzak stepped into Geerlargum's space and looked up at him. He pointed with one of his four arms; the other three were balled in fists. "Hear me, Oogar. I meant what I said. You try that shit again, and I will drop you. Are we clear?"

"We're clear, Peacemaker Millzak."

There was a flurry of activity around them. The still crowd parted to reveal four security guards from the Peacemaker Guild, all Lumar, arriving to take charge of the prisoner. Millzak knew better than to say anything to them. While they were good enough handlers, they sometimes tended to not be able to reiterate the instructions they were given. Questions had confused more than one Lumar over the course of history. Him included.

"I'll be looking into what's going on here," Dreel said. "There's no reason you should not have been met at the hangar, much less met an escort at the checkpoint. Under no circumstances should the watch not be stood."

Millzak relaxed slightly. "Something about this place doesn't feel right."

Dreel laughed. "Karma never has. I despise this planet with my entire pelt."

After securing the prisoner and sending him on his way to the penitentiary for his sentencing, Dreel asked Millzak to follow him to a nearby office. He tapped on the control panel and produced a key card from his vest. The door slid open. To his surprise, it was not a Peacemaker office. It appeared to have belonged to a mercenary company that was long defunct. Inside, it was obvious the facility was still secure enough for them to have a private conversation with the presence of an anti-listening device. Dreel set one up on a small table between them and sat in one of the chairs. He gestured to another.

"This won't take long. But I need to know if you're with me on something."

Millzak squinted. "If I'm with you? You're a captain, and I'm just a Peacemaker. I am to retire. My orders have been cut, sir. What are you playing at?"

Dreel took a deep breath and exhaled slowly. His voice was low, but Millzak could sense excitement. "Millzak, old friend, I have solid intelligence about the whereabouts of Kr'et'Socae. One of my long-time contacts, whom I trust with my life, forwarded the information. I know where he is. Right now. I'm going after him. I need someone I can trust and someone unexpected. You are my first choice."

A surge of pride welled up in the Lumar's chest and almost made his eyes water. "Is this an official mission?"

Dreel shook his head. "No. This is me taking action on intelligence. The guild master does not know. This is not something found on the general reports through Stormwatch. This is credible information I came across, and I intend to exploit it and go after him. But I cannot do it alone. I need someone who can get close. Maybe closer than anyone's ever gotten. That is you, Peacemaker Millzak. Are you with me?"

Millzak smiled. "Damned right I am. Stand or fall."

"Stand or fall," Dreel said. He reached into his vest. He handed Millzak the distinctive rank insignia of a single silver tab. "And you aren't a Peacemaker anymore. They wanted to ensure you received this at your retirement. I thought you deserved to wear it on your last mission. Congratulations, Lieutenant."

* * *

Snowmass

Tirr had never been up close and personal with a Wrogul before, and after three days of sharing laboratory space, he wasn't sure he ever wanted to again. The generous offer from Tara Mason to house his squad while they conducted their analysis on the samples removed from Lake Pryce notwithstanding, Tirr was relatively certain the Wrogul was not only crazy, but borderline psychopathic. In all his dealings with the various species of the Galactic Union, he'd never come upon anything quite like the octopus. Nelson was at times funny and caustic. Other times he acted like a prima donna. Tirr's antennae bounced at the term—he particularly loved it. More often than not, Nelson acted like a child. When Tirr had spoken with Tara about it, the Human commander had merely smiled.

"Nelson certainly has his fits. But what child doesn't?"

"He is hardly a child, Tara."

"How do we really know that, Tirr?"

He'd given that some thought before responding. "If he is a child, why is he with you? With Force 25?"

Tara's smiled faded slightly. "He came to us after Victoria Bravo and offered his assistance with investigating our enemies. He's an intelligence specialist and a scientist. That's something I can't let go. Child or not."

Tirr didn't know if her comments really meant that Nelson was indeed a child, or if his inane behavior was normal. Either way, Tirr wasn't very happy with his laboratory partner.

They'd completed their initial testing of the Lake Pryce samples and found nothing new among the usual targets in pH, total dissolved solids, and a host of other, more common, attributional tests. Having found no differences in chemical balance, it was time to dig deeper. Together, they'd spent two days working to isolate certain compounds that appeared to be present. Further analysis showed similar amounts present in the different locations he and his squad had already tested.

While it wasn't entirely possible most of those combinations formed naturally, Tirr intended to look for what was being manipulated. Were there substances being added? Were the actual properties of the water itself being changed for some reason? Those were the answers he wanted to find. There was no doubt the Dream World Consortium was working on the water in these worlds. But because they weren't Dream Worlds, their actions meant they were either trying to replicate something in those water sources, or they were planning to manipulate them somehow.

This was problematic because many of the water sources were on planets far removed from the inner workings of Galactic Union politics. One of the sites was on Earth. Given the recent uprisings in the Mercenary Guild and the questionable behavior of the Four Horsemen, Tirr couldn't help but postulate a theory that the Dream World Consortium was after some measure of revenge, but directed at whom?

That appeared to be the million-credit question. If Tirr could answer that, or at least provide some additional information to the guilds for them to focus on in their collective decision-making processes, then he could call it a win. As it was, he and his squad were still clutching at straws.

Tirr ambled into the laboratory on the morning of the fourth day. Outside, the first winter storm of the season howled. MinSha were cold averse, and while he'd never seen snow, much less a blizzard, Tirr had no intentions of going outside until they boarded their shuttle for departure. Maybe then he'd see what all the fuss was about, but snow appeared to be cold, wet, and uncomfortable, which was enough to keep him inside.

"Good morning," Nelson quipped. His tank was located on the far side of the laboratory, mounted atop a wheeled movement device. Tirr didn't know if it was standard equipment for a Wrogul, but the motorized cart allowed the being to move its water tank wherever it needed to go. Rather than being stuck in one place forever for a long period of time, Nelson could effectively perform the water experiments and inquiries. It was quite the setup, but Tirr couldn't imagine being chained, literally, to one's environment.

"Good morning to you," Tirr replied.

"Are we mere mortals doomed to travail upon the same old things today?"

Tirr nodded as he approached his workstation and tried not to let his antennae droop with dread. "The same old things, yes."

"Splendid! You're early. You know, Humans colloquially state something about avians and…"

"I know. Worms."

"Be that as it may, it doesn't answer why you're here as early as I am." Nelson waggled a tentacle as if pointing at himself.

His statement sounded more like a challenge than another question. Tirr made eye contact with the Wrogul dangling over the side of its tank. "Sometimes it's a matter of just getting the work done. I notice you're here early as well."

"Oh, I never sleep. Well, I suppose there are some moments where I kinda drift off, but normally, I don't sleep all that much. I like to keep moving. And watching old holo shows and movies."

Tirr cocked his head to one side. "As in Human ones?"

Nelson waved a tentacle. "Oh no, all of them. They're all amazing. Even some of those Flatar things. Those devious little bastards. Their flicks are amazing. Better than any other horror movies I've ever watched." The laugh that emanated from the Wrogul's audio speaker made Tirr chuckle. A Wrogul who liked horror movies seemed as improbable as Human beings he could actually care about. Over the last few cycles, he'd seen and done things he'd never believed possible.

"Well, I guess we'll just keep working."

"All work and no play makes Nelson a dull boy."

"Let me guess, that's from a movie, too?"

"You know it. Human goes crazy trapped in a big place in a snowstorm." Nelson's raspy laugh echoed in the room. He turned away from Tirr to consult his own workstation. "Better watch out for our two-legged friends, Tirr."

Tirr wasn't listening. The motorized cart-tank thing was close enough he could touch it. He watched the water rippling from Nelson's movements for a moment and grabbed for a test tube even before he realized he was doing it. He reached out and dipped the tube into the water, filling it halfway. He withdrew his foreclaw and turned to his own station and placed the sample in a rack with the Lake Pryce samples and two from Cruxton Prime. If nothing else, he could calibrate the equipment, but one thought stuck with him.

The DWC is testing and, possibly, manipulating water sources. Almost every known race in the galaxy needs water in some form.

What do they know that we don't?

* * * * *

Chapter Ten

Springton

Larth stood low in the shadows across the street from the building. He was sure he could not be seen by the naked eye. Sensors concerned him, so he spent considerable time searching for them. He looked down at the small scrambler in his hand. It was lit up, indicating it was working. He patted the pocket on his vest to ensure the small drive was still there.

He glanced around one more time, stuck his hands in his pockets, and strolled into the lighted area on the corner. He whistled loudly, some unknown tune, like he didn't have a care in the world. When he reached the next patch of shadows, he ducked low and ran to the corner of the building.

All right, he thought. *Nobody saw me. I wonder why I had to walk like that and whistle?*

Because that's how it was done on the shows.

Oh, right.

Shhhh!

You shush. I'm about to give myself away, and if I do, I'm going to be pissed.

He noticed the set of windows but realized this was a modern building. There was no way he was going to get away with slipping a blade in and unlocking it. He opted to try some Ricky Shit. He reached in a different pocket and pulled out the tube, the little suction cup, and the small finger length laser cutter Ricky had devised.

He put the tip of the laser against the pane next to the framework in the middle and turned it on. It cut through the clear material. Larth didn't bother to see what exactly it was. It could have been a version of glass or clear polymer of some type. It didn't matter. The laser cut right through it. He stopped, put the little suction cup on it, and held it with his other paw.

After he cut all the way around, it popped out. He carefully set it against the building and crawled through the opening. He glanced around.

Stupid facilities. At least it doesn't stink.

He put his ear to the door and listened. After a moment, he heard the scrape of a chair. The night security. He patted the butts of the pistols on his hips for good measure.

He placed one of the small video bugs Ricky had given him under the door. He checked his slate, entered the code to break the scramble, and connected the two. The security guard was seated not thirty feet away. He was in luck; the Sumatozou faced away from him and was staring at his own slate. The scrambler didn't affect it.

He must have a downloaded show. Whatever he was watching, Larth didn't want to know. The sounds coming from it were…primal.

Ew!

Larth slid his slate back into its pocket and eased the door open. He carefully stepped over the bug, let the door close quietly, and turned right. He walked backward, watching the guard until he felt the double doors behind him. He eased one open and slipped inside. He pulled his slate back out and confirmed the guard was still in position.

He moved quickly to the first set of controls. All three were still on from the day's training. He slid the connector into a slot on the main screen and nodded to himself as the four green lights started blinking. After a moment, the first three glowed steadily. Larth recorded the control console while he waited. As far as he knew, there wasn't much to see, but Keaton wanted it, so he did it.

He stood up and wandered around the large room, sure the scrambler in his pocket would keep any monitoring system from working. Without the code, they would continue to restart, unlike his video bug. He checked on the guard again and was satisfied he wasn't moving from his position. One side of the room was set up for lectures. He noticed a slate on the instructor's podium.

It didn't take him long to access it. What he used wasn't as sophisticated as Keaton's personal programs, but the standard ones all Peacemakers learned were sufficient to get into a normal slate and erase any evidence he had been there.

His eyes widened when he read the latest in additional guidance to gate masters. Human merc companies were to be charged at least double the standard rates, and by no means were they to be given "credit" and allowed to use a gate without paying. This included the occasional donations that occurred within reason. The standard reporting procedures and revenue split with the guild were still in place for other races, along with the warning of excessive use of the privilege. There were to be no exceptions. Delaying any use by Humans was encouraged.

Interesting, he thought. *I wonder how many are stranded with no way to pay?*

The next instructions were to report all Human mercenary movement immediately, as well as any large shipments of goods to and from Human systems. The exceptions were Krifay and one other system used by many races for needed protein supplies.

Others can eat, but let's starve the Humans. Hypocrites. Still, basing from Krifay seems to be a great idea in hindsight…and having shunts on our ship and the Kin's sure helps.

Within minutes of all four lights glowing solid and showing a complete copy of the mock-up control system's files, Larth was outside the building. He opened the top of a small tube and squeezed a thin line of clear putty all the way around the cut portion of the window. He pushed the piece back into place and held it there with the suction cup for five minutes.

It was an eternity to the Zuparti. There had been no issues getting past the occupied security guard, retrieving the bug, and slipping back out of the building.

Maybe there will be more excitement tomorrow when we follow some real smugglers. Yeah…now be cool and whistle as I walk away.

* * *

Arms Dealer Facility

As soon as Larth approached the door, he heard the locks disengage. He grinned at Ricky and Keaton and opened it. Behind them, Jyrall shook his head. He had decided to come with them early this morning to get a feel for the Jivool. Arms dealers sympathetic to what was happening to humanity could come in very handy in the future. If they truly were.

"Switch. On time I see," Lilnitar said as she walked over. She gave the other three a cursory glance, seemingly unfazed by their size and weapons.

"We got places to be, things to do," Larth answered. He waved at the other three. "This is the boss and the two Pushtal I mentioned."

She tilted her head slightly and said, "Varkell, Rylon, Zarr."

Jyrall was surprised she knew their names. Larth hadn't mentioned telling her. Out of the corner of his patched eye, he noticed it didn't bother Keaton. Perhaps Keaton had included their assumed identities as part of the information on what could be found of them if the GalNet search was thorough enough.

A large Jivool pulled a transport sled around one of the rows of weapons. On it were four crates. They held the rockets Larth had purchased.

"The credit transfer came through, so I had Wilgith load them for me. You can transfer them to your lift, unless you want to buy the sled."

"Not necessary," Jyrall said. "Switch spent enough of my credits as it is."

"He agreed to the price," she said. "Is there going to be a problem?"

Jyrall noticed Wilgith's paw ease toward his holstered pistol. He recognized the model. It was a rapid shot laser. A deadly, expensive weapon.

"No," Jyrall dismissed. "It's for a good cause."

Jyrall could tell by her body language that Lilnitar was surprised. "A cause? Since when does a Besquith smuggler care about *causes*?"

Jyrall bent over and picked up two cases of the rockets, held one under each arm and turned to her. "Some things you can't find, no matter how deep you search." He walked out the door held by Larth. The brothers followed, each carrying a case of their own.

* * *

"Now what was that all about?" Lilnitar asked, still stunned by the conversation.

"I don't know," Wilgith said, "but even I can't just pick up two of those cases like they weigh nothing."

"There's more to him than physical strength," Lilnitar said. "More to all of them."

* * *

"There he is," whispered Keaton.

"Yep," Ricky confirmed. "That's the joker we saw in the pit. Them Bakulu ain't with him though. Their ass is prob'ly on the ship."

"They move too slow," Larth said. "I would have left them, too. This doesn't look like the best part of the warehouse district. I don't care how close we are to the tarmac."

"He went through the door," Jyrall said. "He's the only being we've seen here all morning. Let's move in."

"Right," Larth said. "I'm coming around the side now. There is no rear entrance. Only the large bay doors and the small one in them. There is no back door to watch. No windows either. What a stupid building design."

"You do realize, the builder never intended it to need those types of things," Jyrall said. He moved down the walkway with the brothers.

"I don't know," Ricky said. "Larth is right. I dang shore would have made sure I had a way to get out. I mean, it's the warehouse district. Every deal made down here cain't be aboveboard."

They met Larth at the door. Without hesitating, Jyrall opened it and walked inside. The Jeha whirled around and stared at the four of them. He was standing in front of a large crate, holding a slate with four pincers. There was no one else in the building. The door to the small office in the corner was open, and its lights were turned off.

The Jeha drew a small laser pistol surprisingly fast. "Do not move. Who are you?"

"I would advise you to put that away," Jyrall said. "Switch has you two to one."

The Jeha looked to the side and saw the two pistols in the Zupar-ti's hands. Both were aimed at his head. Slowly, he holstered the pis-tol. Larth kept his two on target.

"What is this?" he demanded. "Some kind of hijacking? I don't even have the cargo on my ship. Since when do pirates go to work before a ship is loaded?"

"Where's Gimmold?" Jyrall asked gruffly.

"I don't know," the Jeha said. "Hey, I recognize you two from the pit." He pointed at Ricky and Keaton. "You are not pirates; you would have never made it through the door there. This is my con-tract. What's going on here?"

Jyrall thought fast. "No, we're not pirates. Gimmold skipped out before paying his debt. We tracked him here."

"Skipped a payment?" the Jeha asked. "Entropy! I should have known his agreeing to my counteroffer without bartering was unusu-al. I am Ban-Tilk. You are?"

"Varkell," Jyrall answered. He waved at Larth to indicate he could put his weapons away. "We are in the same line of business, you and I."

"I see. Well, if Gimmold is in the habit of not paying for a run, I won't be wasting my time or F11 to take the cargo to its final destination. Not to mention gate fees. We were to depart tomorrow. He can forget about getting the down payment back, as well."

"If I catch up to him, he won't ever pay for another delivery," Jyrall said with menace. "He owes more than credits."

"Speaking of credits, Varkell, I want to thank you for saving me a lot of them. If you don't mind, I will be on my way. My crew and I will leave this system for a while. There are other pits in other systems. Systems far from this one. The down payment was enough to sustain our operation for a while."

He moved toward Jyrall and held the slate out. "Perhaps you can continue to track him with this. It is the instructions for the run and was left with this." He indicated the container with a slight twist to his segmented body and a wave of several pincers. "Oh, and if it were me, I'd take the cargo and see what I could get for it. Serves Gimmold right."

"I like the way you think," Jyrall said as he took the slate. "Profitable runs to you and yours."

"And to you," Ban-Tilk said with a slight dip of his upper segments. "I never saw you. You never saw me."

"Agreed," Jyrall said as he stepped to the side and allowed the Jeha access to the door.

* * *

"Do we try and catch Gimmold or do we see what's in the box?" Larth asked.

"Gimmold is not in the city," Jyrall said. He handed the slate to Keaton.

"No," Keaton agreed. "He's not on the planet. This says to take the crate to the Shaylin System. Gimmold will meet the transporter near the Springton gate and follow it through."

"The Shaylin System?" Larth asked. "Isn't it abandoned?"

"Pretty much," Keaton said. "Solar flares. The colony of Caroons abandoned the mines and left years ago. I think the last of the equipment and anything valuable have been removed from the system."

"Yeah," Ricky added. "Pops talked about going there several years ago and seeing what we could salvage but decided it wasn't worth the hassle."

"I would imagine one would need to be suited for protection, even on the surface of the planet," Jyrall said.

"Looks like we're headed there," Larth said. "Maybe we can catch Nay-Thok with Captain Gimmold."

"Let us hope," Jyrall said. "We'll load the cargo on *Night Moves* and go to Shaylin. Of course, we may need to change the identity of the ship in case they remember ours."

"Easy enough," Keaton said. "One good thing about it, it's only one jump to get there from here."

"Good," Jyrall said. "Grab that transport lift in the corner. Let's get this out of the warehouse and prepare to leave the planet before anyone questions us. We follow the credits."

"Now you're talkin', Snarlyface," Larth said, rubbing his paws together. "This time, I get to use a crowbar so we can see what's in the box. It's the right size for a CASPer. My bet is that's what it is."

"No bet," Jyrall said. "It has to be. We'll open it before we leave…on our ship."

* * *

Larth rubbed his stomach and belched. "I love king crab, but I hate fighting for the meat. Thanks, Ricky."

"No problem," Ricky said. "What good are claws if you can't cut right through king crab legs and pop them open like unfolding a hot dog bun?"

"What's a hot dog? Never mind. If you two are through playing with your food, we can go see to the crate. Then we can prepare to take off," Jyrall suggested. He wasn't serious. He and Keaton had gone through a substantial pile of legs themselves.

"Sounds good to me," Larth said, leaning back lazily. "I can't eat another bite."

"There are two cheese biscuits left," Ricky said.

Larth perked up. "Yeah? Gimme one."

* * *

After cleaning up and disposing of the shells in the waste disposal unit, the four of them made their way to the cargo hold. The large crate took up a sizable portion of the hold space, which was reduced because of the added bulkheads and hidden compartments. The four crates of CASPer rockets took up the rest.

Minutes later, Ricky elbowed his brother and grinned. Jyrall stood back with an arm across his chest, holding one elbow with a hand while covering his mouth with the other as he tried not to show his teeth in a smile. He had witnessed Cora strike the same pose.

Larth hung on the crowbar. One end was inserted in the edge of the container's front panel. Both his feet were against the box as he pulled for all he was worth. The panel wasn't budging. Jyrall had pried it open enough to get the crowbar in, but Larth demanded he be the one to actually crack it open.

"We'll never get this twice-cursed crate open," Larth called out, letting his feet dangle while he held on. "Never. It won't budge."

"Allow me," Jyrall said as he stepped over.

"Fine, big guy," Larth said, dropping to the deck. "Let's see you do it."

Jyrall gave a mighty pull on the crowbar, and the spot welds on that side broke free. He reached up and grabbed the edge and gave it several hard pulls. The remaining small welds broke.

"Show off," Larth said, his hands on his hips. "I could have done that. If I was as big as you…and as strong."

"I believe you, Little Buddy," Jyrall said. He nodded seriously.

"I was going to say that I had me a laser and could cut them real quick like," Ricky said. He shrugged.

"Now you tell me," Larth said. "You and me need to communicate better around here." He broke into a grin. He often found it hard to stay serious. "Anyway, pull that all the way off and let's see this Mk 9."

*****

Chapter Eleven

Weqq

Cora McCoy took a well-earned break from the leadership of her company to perform soldier-level maintenance on her own Mk 7 CASPer. The late afternoon sun beat down on everything, and stifling humidity rose from the soil in thick, awful waves. As she checked over the machine, from jump pedals to upper communications systems and cameras, Cora immediately felt more relaxed and at home than she had in quite some time. Not that leadership was a bad thing, but it often put so much mental pressure on a commander, it was difficult to separate out time to do the things they needed to remain a soldier. As such, Cora relished the opportunity to be in and around her CASPer, even for a short time.

Since leaving Parmick, she'd spent little more than an hour inside the suit. In their assembly area, the Crusaders appeared to have built a makeshift weapons range, and Cora considered taking her CASPer for a quick qualification and calibration run. Instead, she decided all CASPers needed to reach the same operational readiness level across the Blue Ridge Kin. Batteries checked, fuel systems topped off, and ammunition fully loaded were the items at the top of the checklist.

Cora tapped her slate and sent the order for all CASPers and other weapons systems to reach what they'd taken to calling Minuteman Status. The idea was that a Minuteman was ready to go, fully deployed and armed, in less than one minute. While it would take a little bit longer than a minute for the CASPers to fully initialize and start up, having everything ready to go would increase their ability as a unit to get into their mechs quickly and be ready to fight. Speed was life, as she'd learned in her initial CASPer training course years before. Cora had completed all the other checks and was waiting for ammunition loading when the first radio call came.

"Colonel McCoy?" The voice belonged to Specialist Conner, the communication specialist from *Blue Ridge* who'd taken over the command post comms on deployment. *We need combat callsigns.*

"This is Colonel McCoy. Go ahead."

"Ma'am, the Crusader command post just reached out to us. They're experiencing some type of communications issue, and there are three ships transitioning from the emergence point toward the planet. They have no radio contact or data transfer."

Cora wanted to roll her eyes. "Did they check their manifests and schedules? Surely they know who is supposed to be inbound."

Conner replied, "I asked them the same question. They say it's supposed to be their Prime with another unit."

"So, what's the problem? Just that they can't talk with them?"

"Yes, ma'am. That seems to be the trouble. But there is no information on the IFF for them, either." Conner paused. "I'm watching the radar now, and the vessels have successfully burned and dropped into orbit. None of them are broadcasting IFF of any type."

The IFF system was as old as modern war. The lightning-fast ability to identify friend or foe, based on transponders, was a valuable piece of intelligence which also served as force protection. Cora considered her options. She could direct her team to reach out via radio or via the information network to see if they could receive any type of signal from the inbound vessel's navigation systems. Or they could do nothing. The Crusaders' command-and-control issues were not her problem. And while she believed in being a team player, she also did not care to tip off a potential adversary and compromise the forces on the surface.

"Ma'am? They're hammering me for additional assistance. What should I tell them?"

Cora tapped open a communications channel to all of the Blue Ridge Kin. "All Kin, this is Colonel McCoy. Recall and stand-to. I want you ready for action in three minutes."

She knew, at that instant, all of her troopers, enlisted and officer alike, were mobilizing to action. Cora turned her attention to bringing her CASPer online as her ammunition handler, a Maki named Private Sreet, worked to load her MAC and other weapon systems.

Cora stabbed her slate with a finger and connected it to the CASPer's systems as she backed herself into the cockpit and strapped in. She pulled on a communications headset and said, "Crusader command, this is Blue Ridge Kin Actual. Recommend alert status. What is the status of those inbound ships?"

"Crusader command, unknown. Inbound ships are in orbit and appear to be deploying dropships." The radio operator sounded bored and uninterested, almost as if he didn't care.

Cora fought to contain her surprise and her rising anger. "What? You didn't bother to call us until they were right on top of us? What the hell are you guys thinking?"

She didn't wait for a response. Instead, she brought the CASPer's systems up and immediately concocted a plan to defend the Blue Ridge Kin's orbital and ground forces. Cora selected a different frequency and connected to her ships in orbit.

"*Blue Ridge* and *Kellie's Stand*, this is Colonel McCoy. Get yourselves to battle stations and watch for inbound, unknown vessels. Prepare your weapons. You are cleared to engage if fired upon."

One of the Midderalls—she guessed it was Monty—replied, "Roger, I say, roger, ma'am. We are looking for them now, right now, we'll find them. General quarters, yes, general quarters."

As comical as it was, Cora didn't smile or laugh. This was serious business. As far as she was concerned, the Crusaders had let them down. She transferred to the Kin ground forces' command channel. First Sergeant Figgle was calling her.

"Ma'am? We're seventy percent green. What's our plan?"

"Interior perimeter defense."

She heard a chuckle. "Then you're thinking what I'm thinking, ma'am. I've got everyone positioning themselves that way now. Posting air guards and deploying automated weapons platforms at the edge of the perimeter."

"Excellent," Cora replied. Her MAC, the CASPer's attached magnetic accelerator cannon, went green, and Sreet gave her a thumbs up from the ground. She triggered the Mk 7's hatch to close. "Have the CASPers form on me."

"Copy that."

As all her CASPer's systems came online, Cora routed all communications and sensor information to her main display. She could see the signatures for dropships descending into the atmosphere about a hundred klicks away. There was no doubt they were headed directly for the assembly area. There was still nothing from the Crusader command center regarding intent. Even though she was looking for as much information as possible, there was no way Cora was going to transmit anything to the inbound ships. The creepy, uncomfortable feeling in her stomach would not go away.

This ain't right.

She pushed the concern away and focused on getting her unit ready for combat. As a mercenary, you could either be unprepared and dead or prepared. Cora was set on being the latter. She adjusted frequencies and called her officers.

"All right, here's what we're going to do. Perimeter defense. CASPers are the maneuver element, but have our dropships spun up and ready to provide close air support. Have a couple of those Mk 4 CASPers target each ship for direct fire."

Nileah responded first. "I've got two Mk 4s moving to each dropship. Nails is in charge."

"Copy that," Cora replied, with a hint of a smile. As usual, Nileah was thinking ahead of her.

"I'm back with the infantry. A squad of Goka and a squad of Jivool," May said. "I'll take Sergeant Squarlik with me to back up Top and the others."

"Copy, May," Cora replied. As usual, her women were on top of things. First Sergeant Figgle would most certainly fight the infantry from the ground and having May in her Mk 7 CASPer and Squarlik manning the automated weapons console would provide them the necessary cover.

"Permission to push out reconnaissance?" Lisalle asked. "Based on the way the Crusaders are preparing to deploy, they're expecting the enemy to touch down outside their perimeter. They're orienting to the southwest."

Cora thought for a moment and decided it was a prudent course of action and not inherently risky. "Approved, Lisalle. Stay back as far as you can until the Crusaders engage if that's what this comes down to. Measure what the threat is and then be prepared to honor it."

"You sound like Larth." May laughed. *"Meep, meep!"*

"Meep, meep!" Cora laughed. The simple act took away the weight of command. Relaxed and confident, she realized her unit might not have all the kinks worked out, but they were ready to fight as one. "Let's just be ready. I don't think we're gonna have to wait long."

"Ma'am?" Conner called from their command post. "Crusader long-range cameras have the dropship. Based on what they've got here, in the assembly area, those aren't friendlies. They look like modified Cochkala dropships. I can't get any other information off their net, and they're not sharing. They say their systems are down."

I call bullshit.

"Roger, keep me informed." Irritated, Cora tweaked her displays to center on the descending dropship. She watched them for a moment, and after glancing down at the terrain map on one multifunction display, she determined roughly where they would be landing. Experience and analytics tended to correlate, as Colonel Talmore would have said. The dropships, three of them, appeared headed for a landing just to the southwest in the tree line. If true, their landing zone put them between the Crusader assembly area and the old MinSha science facility from Tara Mason's database. Cursing their luck, Cora changed frequencies.

"Crusader command post, this is Blue Ridge Kin Actual. Do you have combat forces at your facility inside the tree line?"

"Blue Ridge Kin Actual, this is Crusader Five," she heard Lieutenant Colonel Smith say. "You are not cleared for that information."

Cora took a breath and spoke slowly. "In case you haven't noticed, Smith, those dropships are headed for a point somewhere between this assembly area and that facility. You have two choices: answer my question or prepare to lose that facility while your people are playing around out here, trying to find their asses with both hands and a map."

"Your tone is unnecessary, Colonel McCoy."

"Answer my question!" Cora snapped. "You're about to lose good people if you can't arrange your forces to defend your positions."

She resisted the urge to ask him if he had learned anything from the Ridge Runners' last mission when indecision and the inability to respond to enemy maneuver cost them their company and Colonel Talmore's life. Even as she repressed that response, she was already formulating a plan. If the Crusaders didn't act, she would.

Damn their need to know and everything else in between.

"We have minimal forces in that area. I am pushing a platoon to defend."

Cora rolled her eyes. A platoon against three dropships were not odds she wanted to take. She tapped her frequency control to connect privately with First Sergeant Figgle.

"Top?"

Figgle's voice came back, "I am prepared to deploy three full squads of infantry, ma'am. We'll need a section of CASPers for fire support. Just tell us when."

"It's going to be sooner rather than later, I think. Once those dropships start their landing flares, and we confirm their intent, I want our forces moving. Do not, I say again, do not leave our internal perimeter compromised."

"Not a chance, ma'am."

"Ma'am," Conner called from the command post. "The Crusaders are asking for all that information again. They want everything from pinplants, sensor relays, and command-and-control frequencies."

"No," Cora replied. "You can tell them to pound sand."

"With pleasure, ma'am."

A thought snuck up on her, and Cora sucked in a quick breath. "First Sergeant, ensure our perimeter defense is monitoring every type of connection capability they have. I don't want them using this as a diversion to try to backdoor our systems."

"Understood, ma'am. Good thinking. I don't trust any of these fuckers."

"Neither do I."

"Ma'am? One of the dropships has released a load of bombs."

Cora looked at her display. "Plot the target and send it."

A red icon appeared. Cora's finger flew on her slate controls as she overlaid the intelligence mapping from Jessica Francis' database. However Jyrall and Larth had managed to acquire it, it was a godsend. The dropship appeared to be hitting the location of the TriRusk underground colony.

They're definitely hostiles.

"Kin, hostiles inbound. Prepare to engage." Cora paused. "First Sergeant, take your teams and go. Lisalle, all recon approved. All the way out to the TriRusk caverns—sending you the location now."

"Got it."

"May, take your section and follow Top," Cora added. "Weapons free on any hostile you can engage. Whoever these bastards are, let 'em have it!"

* * *

Werner Rhineder thought he'd seen everything. A mercenary for more than thirty-eight years, his experience told him everything so far on the planet was not only wrong and bordering on incompetence, but deadly. While being a mercenary was certainly a younger man's game, he'd known for quite some time this was his calling. Since the age of eighteen, when he joined his first outfit in the southern regions of Germany, Rhineder knew this was what he wanted to do.

His first deployments saw the three companies he bounced between lose more than sixty percent of their roster within the first minutes of combat. He knew from that moment forward, that war, especially the kind mercenaries were paid to engage in, was not a funny thing. It was serious business. Try as he might, he couldn't scrape away the crust that had been gently building over his personality ever since.

Now pushing sixty, Rhineder's dedication to the task at hand wasn't purely out of self-preservation. He knew his time in a mech was limited. Yet he'd seen far too many young mercenaries die because of how they had been trained. Or more specifically, how they hadn't been trained. He'd been thinking about retiring and heading back to Earth when the Blue Ridge Kin recruited him. Without a second thought, he'd signed on, and not for the pay. He realized it was the need to stop seeing young mercenaries needlessly dying. If he could get any part of his experience across to them, no matter their species, he would feel vindicated after a lifelong career. And his own survival.

He knew it hadn't been luck, but at the same time, he couldn't shake the feeling that his good fortune needed to be passed on. There was no replacement for training and experience. It was a self-appointed responsibility he took seriously. So much so that even taking orders from a Goka didn't bother him. This was all about the greater good. Of all the mercenary organizations he'd ever worked for, only the Blue Ridge Kin seemed to have that in mind from the get-go.

Given his orders, to deploy two sections of Mk 4 CASPers with the dropships for close air support, he couldn't help but think they were missing another opportunity. While the infantry was certainly more than capable of providing firepower and quick maneuvers, one section of CASPers was not going to be enough. There were two remaining Mk 4s, his mech and one belonging to Specialist Anderson.

Anderson was young, somewhere north of twenty-one, and completely outmatched when it came to CASPers. The pilots of Rhineder's old units had a phrase: being behind the aircraft. Anderson seemed to always be behind. There were always stories of "that guy" in a unit. From everything Rhineder had seen, Anderson was fast on his way to becoming "that guy."

"Sergeant Rhineder, I've got a problem."

Rhineder grunted. "I've told you to call me Nails. What's wrong?"

"Uh, I've got a fan overheat warning."

Rhineder gritted his teeth. "Which fan?"

"It's my auxiliary control panel fan."

"Switch it off. The only way you're going to need that is if your main fan fails. Otherwise, you're sitting there looking at a yellow light on your caution and warning panel, and that's going to be all you think about. Turn it off and disable the backup function."

"Got it," Anderson replied. "Thanks. I'm green for ops."

Green is a good word, but it doesn't necessarily mean you're ready, kid.

"Fall in on me." Rhineder started for the perimeter. As he walked the mech, he tapped the frequency controls and called up First Sergeant Figgle. For a Goka, he was a damned fine NCO and proof that leadership was species-immaterial. "Top, I'm moving your direction with Anderson on my wing. I've got two sections on the dropships, and you're gonna need more firepower in the jungle."

He imagined what the first sergeant was thinking. Two full sections of Rhineder's CASPers were loaded on dropships to provide close air support by hanging out the rear deck. With two more CASPers on the ground outside the separate perimeter defense, one of them being his own, Top was unlikely to be worried that the other two CASPer sections would know what to do.

"Understood. Form on us. We're moving toward the tree line now."

"We're moving," Rhineder called. He changed frequencies quickly. "Anderson, on the bounce."

"Right behind you, Nails."

Ahead of them, two of the Cochkala dropships flared and prepared to land. He was wondering if they were going to clear the area when he saw what looked like several boxes of bomblets fall from the dropship into the jungle below. The staccato crack of explosive devices loaded with flechettes rang through the speakers inside the CASPer's cockpit. Deforestation had come a long way over the course of his career.

"What was that?" Anderson asked.

"They're clearing a drop zone. Standard operating procedure. Those are deforestation pellets."

"Will they be able to clear out all those trees?"

"Not all of them, but enough. They're meant for small brush. That means their dropships are dropping infantry forces, and maybe skiffs."

"What kind of skiffs?"

"If I knew that, Anderson, we wouldn't be moving that direction to provide overwatch. Stay with me."

Rhineder pushed down on his pedals and max jumped the CASPer to the southwest. He didn't bother looking behind to see if Anderson was there; he trusted his instincts that the young man would actually shut up and focus on the battle at hand. At the apex of his jump, Rhineder figured it would take two more max jumps to get them in position to join up with the infantry as they penetrated the jungle. Any more than two jumps, and fuel would be an issue.

"Two more on the max, Anderson. Stay with me."

There was no response from the young man, which Rhineder thought was a good thing. Again, it proved that the young man might actually be listening and applying some of the experience and knowledge his senior NCO was trying to provide. With his feet lightly on the jump jets, Rhineder cushioned the landing of the CASPer and then jumped again to the southwest. After another leap, they fell in behind the Goka and Jivool heavy infantry as they penetrated the jungle.

"Top, this is Nails. We're with you on your six."

Figgle responded. "Roger. Take up rear security."

Rhineder clicked his radio transmit button. "Roger, rear security, and we'll pick up air guard, too."

"Good thinking. I have no idea what we're facing yet."

"I think we're about to find out, Top."

The company's operations network came to life, and Rhineder heard Specialist Conner's voice. "All Blue Ridge units, we've got skiffs. A half dozen armored skiffs have offloaded from the dropships and are heading into the jungle toward the old research facility."

Rhineder looked down at the stores aboard his CASPer. There hadn't been time to get a full load out of ammunition for both hand cannons, but there was a full load out for his MAC. It would have to be enough.

"Anderson, what is your weapons status?"

"I'm green, Nails. Full load out."

Rhineder hated the next thought that came to him. The younger pilot with the fully loaded CASPer should really be in the lead of their two-person element. Experience told him the more heavily armed CASPer would be the best one to take up a secure point if necessary. He also realized the young man would most likely shit himself when combat was actually engaged.

"Fall in behind me, Anderson. I've got the point."

"Right behind you, Nails."

No sooner had they joined the rear of the infantry formation, then what appeared to be the Cochkala opened fire. The amount of fire coming from their left flank was serious but did not appear to be dangerously targeted. Rhineder realized they couldn't see who they were shooting at yet. While the enemy had managed to clear their landing zone in the jungle, the thick vegetation gave a measure of concealment to his forces. They needed to use that against the enemy.

"Top, Nails. I'm thinking a flanking maneuver."

Figgle chuckled. "You or me?"

"Me," Rhineder replied. "I'll take Anderson with me and cut directly toward them. When they engage us, you should be able to swarm them from their left side. Depending upon how they're rolling out their skiffs, you might even be able to separate and envelope them."

"Excellent thinking," the First Sergeant said. "Let me know when you're ready to move."

Rhineder replied, "We're ready. Moving now."

"What's our plan, Nails?" Anderson called.

With an audible sigh, Rhineder adjusted his radio and transmitted directly to Anderson. "Stay right behind me. When I tell you, get up on line with me because we're gonna cut through the Cochkala line of skiffs. If we do it fast enough, the little badgers won't know what's hit them. We'll be able to separate their forces."

"I've got two targets at ten and eleven o'clock. Go to the right of them? That larger gap?"

Rhineder studied his display for a second and realized the young man had not only been paying attention to this situation, but he'd identified a solid course of action.

"Good thinking. Let's do that. Follow me, kid," Rhineder grunted. "Bring all your weapons online, too. We're gonna be hauling ass."

*****

Chapter Twelve

Night Moves

Jyrall, Larth, and the brothers stared into the open container. "It's not what I expected," Jyrall finally said.

"Nope," agreed Larth. He reached up and stroked the bottom of his chin.

"Maybe…maybe it's behind some of this," Keaton suggested. "I mean, it's a big container."

"It might be," Ricky drawled, "but I'll be danged if it is. See them bars on the bottom? They got sockets on the end of 'em. And they ain't no size I know of. Them's extensions, and they go to the back of that big-ass box. Don't make no sense to put a CASPer on top of them and bend 'em. Mechs are heavy."

"What do you mean?" Jyrall asked.

"Well," Ricky said. "I kin tell what a socket is by just lookin' at it. I know the Human standards and metrics. The Jeha sharvlik sizes, all the Maki standards, including the thirty-thirds. The Zuul stuff has a couple of different systems, 'pending on how old it is, you know."

He bent down and looked at the large sockets. "Hell, I got expanders and retractors, adjustable, and some universal stuff. Ain't shit in my toolbox that'll fit those. Closest thing I have is some Caroon stuff for rock cutters."

He looked closer, pulled a small device from a pocket, and measured the inside diameter with a small laser. He then measured the depth of the socket and shook his head. "I got some stuff that would fit it purty close. I could use a filler iffin I had to and be fine. But I'm tellin' ya right now, I got no idea what these are for."

"We need to unload all the smaller containers, boxes, cases, and crates," Jyrall said, "and open them. That will be the only way to know what everything is. Keaton is right, the Mk 9 could be behind them."

"Maybe it's in pieces and has to be assembled?" Larth suggested.

"If it is, there better be some serious hardware and software in one of those boxes and something to help with the programing and startup," Keaton said. "I'm starting to doubt it's there."

"I got it!" Larth said, snapping his little fingers. "It's tools to set up some kind of assembly to build them. I bet the prototype and other parts are with Gimmold and that damned Nay-Thok."

"Maybe," Ricky said. The word came out slowly, even for him. He scratched the side of his face and left a small smudge. "I'll tack a few welds on the front panel so it don't all go ever' dang where while we go get them sumbitches out near the gate." He turned to get what he needed while Jyrall and Keaton picked up the panel and held it in place.

After it was secure again, Jyrall said, "Prepare for departure. We need to be out near the gate and in position."

"What are we going to do?" Larth asked. "Disable them? Board them? I mean…how are we going to do that? I know this ship has a docking ring, but I doubt they are going to agree to let us dock and make it easy on us."

"I can maneuver the ship and dock with others. Even smaller ships," Keaton said. "But not if they're maneuvering against it. The slightest change in velocity and direction, rotation, or a dozen other things, can prevent it."

"Let me think about it and come up with a plan," Jyrall said.

"Sounds good to me, partner," Larth said. "Because I don't have a clue how we are going to do it."

"Yeah, we'll need a good 'un," Ricky agreed. "I mean, I can hit a gnat in the ass at forty paces with the missiles on this baby, so iffin you want to disable sumthin', you just let me know. I'll bust 'em dead in the ass." He nodded in an attempt to convey his seriousness and skill with the ship's weapon systems.

"He can," Keaton agreed. "He can't fly worth a flip, but he's hell on them weapons."

"Thanks," Ricky said. "I think."

* * *

Strong Arm 64317

Nay-Thok floated in the operations center behind the seats in the front of the large shuttle. Several pincers held two loops to steady him. "Are you certain you hired a Jeha to transport the equipment and not a smuggler who will run off with the credits and the cargo? Some sniveling Zuparti or suspect Bakulu or whatever?"

Gimmold looked back from the co-pilot's seat and said, "Of course, sir. I went through the most reputable source in this sector. I did not contract with a pirate, after all. To have access to the potential jobs listed meant the outfit had to have a good reputation."

"Good?" sneered Nay-Thok. "Since when is anyone who delivers goods, in a manner breaking all sorts of system and galactic laws, while avoiding the fees the various guilds may demand, good?"

The mercenary captain waved a paw in dismissal. "It's all relative. The good smugglers have sort of their own code of honor. There is a fine line between smugglers and outright pirates. It's about how they obtain what they deliver and whether they honor the contract. Granted, the vast majority of the time, the contract is verbal or through messaging, but still."

"Of course, it is, idiot," Nay-Thok snapped, his segments rippling with irritation. "What kind of lawless being would put his mark on a contract to be used as actual evidence by system authorities…or Peacemakers, for that matter."

"Well," Gimmold said, ignoring Nay-Thok's name calling, "if we'd obtained a larger ship, we would have had room to load the container ourselves and wouldn't have had to rely on anyone else delivering it."

Nay-Thok stared at the mercenary for an awkward moment. When the Jivool shifted nervously, he continued, "I'll be sure to let Kr'et'Socae know you demand another ship."

"That's not what I meant," Gimmold said in defense. "I meant we could have loaded the container on the other ship with the security company."

"There was no room," Nay-Thok said, his anger dissipating somewhat. "The extra security members filled the entire hold. I don't think there will be an issue with the ones already stationed there, but it is best to have our own, just in case."

"True." Changing the subject, Gimmold asked, "Won't the gate master suspect something when the ship docks with all the extra security?"

"No," Nay-Thok answered. "Not only does that particular gate serve as a training gate in this sector for future gate controllers, it is often used to familiarize newly contracted security companies. It is the reason it is a large gate, structure-wise, yet run like a small one, with less actual traffic and the need for only solar to charge the power banks."

"No wonder it was chosen," Gimmold said. "Somebody knows what they are doing."

"And he is above us in the scheme of things, to be sure," Nay-Thok agreed. "Now, where is this goods runner of yours?" He looked through the forward ports into the vastness of space, beyond the shimmering gate, toward the planet.

"This ship may have the power to use its internal shunts, but it lacks the power to run decent surveillance systems. We'll know once it's practically on top of us, I am afraid," Gimmold said with a shrug. He looked at the pilot, another Jivool, who nodded in agreement.

* * *

"Hey," Ricky said. "You sure that thang is in operation? It's just a-sittin' there."

"It is," Keaton confirmed. "It's powered up, just not going anywhere fast. It is heading toward the gate on a stable trajectory. They're waiting for us. Well, not us, but the *J-Kithik 908*."

"They think that's us," Larth said. His voice was slightly muffled as he spoke from within his protective suit's helmet. He was in the rear of the ship near the connecting chamber.

"If they are still in place, I must commend you on an admirable job," Jyrall said, from within his own suit. "Not only did you program the transponders to emit yet another signal to match the Jeha we replaced, but you have also managed to send back the readings of a much different ship to their scanning sensors."

"Nothin' to it," Keaton said. "I figured, with that ship, they put all the resources into the power plant and shunts. They wouldn't bother upgrading the programs on their scanners."

"Unless they replaced dang near everything, they couldn't program them any better," Ricky added. "Hell, everyone knows they're junk. They got blind spots. They was junk when they came out of the shipyards, and they're junk now."

Ricky shifted in his seat, trying to get comfortable. The gunner's seat was located in the escape pod and was not often occupied, so it was a little stiff. "These boys ain't gonna know what hit 'em. Especially after I hit 'em."

"We're ready back here," Jyrall said. "Engage when ready."

"Roger, Boss," Keaton said. "We are approaching from the stern at twenty thousand meters, moving slowly. Ricky, it's your ballgame."

"Hell yeah," Ricky confirmed. "I'm on it like fleas on a dog's ass. Y'all watch this."

Ricky ensured he was tracking the exact spot he wanted to hit and launched a missile.

"One awaaay!"

* * *

"What?" Jyrall asked Larth on a private channel. "What in the worlds is he saying? What is a flea, and why would it be on a canine's rectum? I feel like I should be offended."

"I'll explain later," Larth assured him. "It's one of those sayings from where the Human who adopted them was from."

"It would seem I need to learn an entirely new language," Jyrall lamented.

"I'm not saying you're wrong," agreed Larth. "Ricky says the missile will hit the thrusters and cause a system shutdown in the power plant. I sure hope he made sure to disengage the warhead so it only causes kinetic damage and doesn't blow it apart."

"We'll never get our answers if it does," Jyrall said.

"We will know soon, Snarlyface…real soon," Larth said. "And I'm glad. I hate these suits. I only have access to two pistols."

* * *

Strong Arm 64317

The ship lurched and alarms went off in the operations center. Nay-Thok hit the bulkhead nearest him and was stunned. Both Jivool in the pilots' seats were startled but unhurt as they were strapped in.

"What happened?" demanded Grimmold. He reached up and pushed back on Nay-Thok, bumping against him.

"We've been hit," answered the pilot. "We're running on emergency power. The power plant shut down, and the thrusters are showing significant damage. We have a hull breach, though it seems contained to the engine area. If anyone was in there, they're gone. The emergency hatches sealed it off."

"Can you maneuver at all?" asked Grimmold.

"Some of the small thrusters still work. I'm fighting the rotation. It knocked us off track, but we are almost stable now. We're doing little more than drifting."

"Why in the stars did the smuggler fire on us? Why?" asked Grimmold. He looked back at Nay-Thok as he started to regain his senses. "What did you do?"

"I did nothing," Nay-Thok answered slowly. "It was you who set up the meeting out here. You will answer for this."

"Whatever," Grimmold said as he unstrapped. "If we survive, I'll worry about it. As of right now, it looks like we will have boarders. Now move and let me do my job. I may be attempting it by myself if none of the others survived."

Nay-Thok watched him push out of the center, turn, and clutch the back of the unoccupied seat. He twisted back and forth, attempting to rid himself of the dizziness. He reached into a bag strapped to the back of the seat with several of his pincers and checked its contents.

* * *

Jyrall stood with both gloved paws out. He pushed them tight against the bulkheads in the small entry chamber. Larth had his against the hatch to the docking ring, and his back was against the big Besquith's knee.

"I've matched their movement," Keaton said over the frequency they all could hear. "You'll know when we lock on. The magnets on the extended ring should be strong enough; you'll feel it happen.

After that it will take twenty seconds for Ricky's rotating laser on the connection ring to open their hull."

"After it rotates, it should make a nice hole in their cargo area," Ricky added. "Once the camera shows me it is through, I'll wait to a count of three and then open the hatch."

"Wait! Wait," Jyrall said. "Is it one, two, three, then open? Or is it one, two, then open?"

"I don't know," Larth said. "What do you think?"

"I mean, I don't know. I like—"

The ships connected, and they felt the reverberating contact through their boots. A slight vibration rocked the small chamber for the next twenty seconds. Larth stepped forward slightly off Jyrall's knee. Jyrall raised the foot Larth had been pressed against.

"Which one was it?" Larth whispered. "On three or after three?"

"I don't know. Why are you whispering?" Jyrall asked.

"I don't know. Seems like the thing to do."

"Onetwothree!" Ricky shouted into everyone's earpieces. "Go!"

The hatch slid open, revealing the short distance in the connecting tube. A smoky haze filled the area and the cargo hold was visible beyond the glowing edges of the cut hull. Larth pulled his arms in tight as Jyrall kicked out, propelling him toward the hole. Larth shot through, head up, looking for anything that might be in his way as he flew into the shuttle. He passed the floating circle of hull as he moved across the hold.

Several beams hit the hold behind him and left scorch marks as a Jivool fired at him. Surprised by the speed at which he entered, all missed. Larth tucked and rolled, bent his knees to cushion himself, and hit the bulkhead on the far side. As he kicked off, he fired the two flechette pistols in his hands, hitting two of the Jivool. They hung limply. Their magnetic boots kept them in place, although their weapons floated free. A third Jivool fled toward the front of the ship.

Jyrall came through the hole much more carefully than his partner. Though the pressure hadn't changed, he didn't want to risk burning his protective suit. He looked past Larth, who had slowed his momentum by grabbing a dead mercenary by the weapon harness as he flew by, and didn't see the large Sumatozou drawing down on him in the opening to the hold.

Jyrall brought up the short rifle strapped to his chest and fired from the hip. Several rounds stitched their way up the being's chest before it could fire. Clutching at the holes, it released its weapon, its blood floating freely with the rest.

"Hey!" shouted Larth, ducking. "I swear I saw those flechettes whip right past the lens of my helmet! Are you crazy! You didn't even aim!" "

He twisted to see what Jyrall had shot at. "Okay, it was a big target. But still…"

"At least one more went up the passageway," Jyrall said, moving past him. "And we have whoever is in the operations center to contend with, too."

"Gotcha," Larth said, serious again. "You want to kick me down the passageway and see if we can do it again?"

"He could be in any one of the open hatches, waiting for us," Jyrall said. "The ship is not big, and I don't relish being shot by someone lying in wait."

"I got it!" Larth said. "Hold me up near the hull above and throw me. I'll have the angle on him, and he won't expect it."

"You know," Jyrall said as he engaged his magnetic boots, "one of these days, you're going to hit your head when we do something like this."

"I hope not," Larth said as he prepared himself to move quickly. "It might knock some sense into me. Can't have that. I need the conversations."

Jyrall shook his head and gave a mighty heave. Larth moved quickly down the passage and turned slightly, his hand extended. Just as he skimmed off the outer bulkhead, he fired down into an open hatch. He managed to grab the next one to stop himself. His feet slammed against the deck.

"If the pilot didn't know we were here, he knows now," Larth mumbled. "That one hurt."

"Did you get him?" Jyrall asked as he made his way forward.

"Yeah," Larth said. "It was ol' Gimmold himself. He's still wearing an Eye Poker's uniform with his rank on it." He looked up the passage. "Looks like they locked us out of the operations center. We may need to get Ricky."

"Hey, I got a laser or three. What do y'all need?" Ricky asked. The line was still open.

"We need to get through a locked hatch," Jyrall said. "But they may be armed on the other side. Pass one through with any instructions, and we'll figure it out. No sense in putting you in harm's way."

"Aw hell," Ricky complained. "Fine. Y'all get to do all the fun stuff. One of y'all come get it."

"Cover the hatch. I'll get it," Jyrall said.

Larth eased into an alcove and faced the locked hatch. Jyrall made his way back to the open hole. A hand reached out and grabbed his leg. Without thinking, he trained his weapon on it before he could blink. He did not pull the trigger. The Sumatozou yet lived.

He bent to render aid. The being was no longer a threat, therefore he was obligated to aid him. For information if nothing else. He pulled out a sealing bandage and put it over the two worst wounds. They were close together. He took a nanite kit from his thigh pocket.

He switched over to an external speaker. "I can use this on you. You may live. What were you doing here? Why are you with Gimmold? Why the equipment?"

The big Sumatozou stared up at Jyrall. The Peacemaker saw when he made his decision. The being nodded and gestured to his chest. Jyrall inserted the needle and gave the shot. The Sumatozou hissed in even more pain, then whispered. The words came out in a rush, as if they were in a race against time. They were. The nanites were not able to repair all the damage, and the whisper faded as the big being died.

"Damnation," Jyrall said.

"What?" Larth asked. "What are you doing? You went offline. Did you get the laser?"

"Getting it now," Jyrall said, his mind racing, going over what he'd heard and the ramifications.

Several minutes later, he held the laser as he attempted to cut the hatch where Ricky directed. Both flinched when an explosion occurred on the other side of the hatch.

"What was that?" Larth asked. "Keaton?"

"There is a breach in the shuttle," Keaton answered. "It's venting from the operations center. Something must have blown in there."

"It ain't the laser," Ricky said. "I'm sure of it. I'm closing the hatch in the entry chamber so when y'all get into the center it won't cause us an issue."

"Good idea," Jyrall said. "I'm almost through now."

They forced the hatch open and found the operations center a mess. There were several cracks in the front portals, and several pieces of the cushions and fabric from the seats were pulled against them. They did not stop the vacuum of space demanding to be filled. Bits and pieces continued to break off and slide through.

"They're dead," Larth said. "The pilot is still strapped to what's left of his seat. The Jeha, what's left of it, is nasty." He looked closer. "Hey! That's Nay-Thok! I recognize his head."

"It is," Jyrall said. He knew it would be. "He killed himself so he wouldn't be forced to reveal Kr'et'Socae's plans."

"So, what do we do now?" Larth asked.

"We go to the Shaylin System," Jyrall answered. "But we're going to need backup."

"Backup?" Larth asked. "We don't need backup. I back you up. You back me up. We're backup. We're good."

"No, Little Buddy," Jyrall said. "For this, we *really* need backup. Trust me."

* * * * *

Chapter Thirteen

Location: CLASSIFIED

Rest would not come, no matter how still he lay or how he controlled his breathing. His body yearned for activity and rebelled against the constant feeling of captivity. A life on the run seemed hardly a life at all, especially for the leader of a guild. Fully awake now in the dark, early morning, Rsach wiggled up from his bed and rhythmically stretched his segmented body with a series of twists and contortions. Satisfied his body was ready to respond to the rigors of his day, Rsach peered across the small quarters to his slate. After a long moment, he rose and moved across the floor toward the door. Outside were two Lumar guards, Florr and Tramm. They startled when the door opened.

"Guild Master, has something happened?" Florr asked. Of the two, he was far brighter than Tramm, who was easily the strongest Lumar Rsach had ever known.

Rsach chittered. "No. I merely cannot sleep. I'm going outside for a walk."

Florr nodded. "Shall we accompany you?"

"No," Rsach said. "I'm merely going to the agricultural habitat. There are plenty of others guarding the passageways between here and there. Maintain your post."

"Yes, Guild Master," Florr replied. His face twisted in the approximation of a grin. The Lumar knew far more about his guild master than he would ever let on. "We'll remain here and be your eyes."

"Thank you, Florr," Rsach replied with a nod. He glanced across the passageway at a rectangular ventilation grate.

Florr reach over and touched Tramm's bulky shoulder. "Move down the passageway until you can see Peacemaker Jekk at the next junction. Ensure the guild master's passage will be clear."

Tramm immediately plodded down the passageway to Rsach's left. When the big Lumar's back was turned, Rsach stepped across the passageway. Florr held the heavy grate open and allowed Rsach to slip inside.

"Thank you, Florr. I'll return soon."

"Yes, Guild Master."

Rsach moved silently into the ducts and tried not to laugh aloud. He was the master of the Peacemaker Guild, and here he was moving through ductwork toward a private, enclosed space where he could think and plan alone. His quarters were compromised. As was his slate. Everything he'd done, searched for, and acted upon was known by the entity called Counselor. Continued inquiries as to its identity were pointless. The being, whatever or whoever it was, would answer no questions. While Rsach could seemingly do nothing without its knowledge, there were far more troubling developments.

Since Counselor's sudden communication following Force 25's skirmish on Snowmass, several things had moved forward at speeds and complications far exceeding Rsach's comfort level. The development of the Crusader project was merely one area of concern. Whereas the recruiting of Humans, and potentially other races, in an effort to create a lasting peace in the Galactic Union had originally been Rsach's idea, Counselor had pushed hard for newer and more complex weapon systems. Recruitment soared, and the appointment of Crusader Prime, the Human leader of the Crusaders, had taken place without Rsach's involvement.

The decision to organize, train, and deploy the Crusaders had been made by Rsach with the rationale that it would be best for the guild master and the High Council to maintain their isolation. The Crusaders would work quickly to pacify the "hot spots" identified by Peacemaker intelligence with the goal of returning the guild master and the others to Kleve. Rsach's multiple digestive organs disagreed with everything Counselor suggested, but Rsach's arguments fell on deaf ears. Counselor moved forward with the effort, unhindered, and Rsach began to doubt everything around him.

He moved through the ducts and into the transparent domed agricultural habitat. He loved the garden as it reminded him of many of the places of his youth, including Goddannii Two. While he felt a certain amount of pain, and guilt, nearly fifty years on from his first commissioned mission, most of the memory was one framed by regret.

I wish you were here, Golramm. If there was ever a time I needed your brute force advice, it would be now.

Rsach chittered to himself and imagined hearing the legendary Enforcer's voice as if the giant purple Oogar sat next to him under the stars.

You're already doubting Counselor. You're shunning technology. You've put two Lumar on your personal guard because they do not wear pinplants. You trust nothing, and this is a good thing.

"Why is that good?" Rsach whispered aloud.

A Peacemaker should not trust those they do not know until such time as trust has been proved correct, or those they do not know face justice.

Trust. Rsach rolled the word around in his mind for a half hour as he looked at the unfamiliar sky above. As the first tendrils of light touched the eastern horizon, he crept back to the ductwork and made his way to the grate outside his quarters. Once again, Tramm did what Florr asked without question.

There was a certain beauty to the Lumar.

Back in his bed, Rsach allowed himself to rest. A plan was underway in his mind, and he was confident about two things: it would work and those he trusted would understand what they needed to do and do it to the best of their abilities. His satisfaction carried him gently off to sleep for the first real rest he'd had in months.

* * *

Weqq

As they neared the tree line, Rhineder's multifunction display showed three of the enemy skiffs taking up firing positions, while the others continued to move toward the Kin's infantry. The enemy vehicles appeared to be massing their fire somewhere off to his right and not quite in the direction of the infantry. Their mistake.

"They're set up for us," Rhineder called.

Anderson replied quickly, "Coming up on your right. What are they firing at? It's not our folks."

"They don't have eyes on them, yet." For a moment, Rhineder considered their position. The skiffs appeared to be the same design and model as the ones that had beat up Force 25's armor on Victoria Bravo. Their heavily armored and angled fronts would deflect direct fire weapons easily. Actually causing damage to their forward armor was next to impossible. Rhineder grinned to himself. Fortunately, they did have some documented weak spots.

Time for these old dogs to show some new tricks.

"Anderson, get your mortar tubes ready."

"Really?"

"Yes, really," Rhineder grunted. "We're gonna distract them a little bit with some airbursts. Get their vehicle commanders to button up where they can't see as well. Their tops and backsides aren't as protected, so they'll slow down. Maybe even halt in place. We'll have a maneuvering edge."

"Oh, I got it."

Good, I'm glad you got it. Good grief. He really is becoming that guy.

"Three rounds of cluster bombs per salvo. How many rounds you have on board?" Rhineder asked.

"Eighteen anti-personnel and twenty smoke, Nails."

Rhineder started to shake his head and then stopped. "Change that. Two cluster bombs and one smoke per salvo. Get them loaded. We're gonna fire six salvos of three. Let's hope that's enough to draw some of their attention off the infantry."

"Copy, two and one. Loading."

Rhineder activated his mortar tube system and pulled the tube off the mount on the CASPer's left hip. Just to the rear of the tube's mount, he withdrew the first three rounds of ammunition carefully stored there for quick deployment. Using the CASPer's big mechanical hands as daintily as he could, Rhineder dropped three rounds into the tube, raised it, and fired. The rounds arced up through the single canopy jungle and burst above the vicinity of the Cochkala skiffs. His display showed the relative path of the rounds as well as the rough location where First Sergeant Figgle had the infantry waiting. As

Rhineder loaded three more rounds, he adjusted his position to give himself a better opportunity to drop the bomblets directly on top of the skiffs. He noted with quiet satisfaction that Anderson fired almost immediately and dropped his salvo cluster munitions almost on top of the enemy skiffs.

If any of the Cochkala's heads were out of the canopies looking for targets, they've been slapped right upside the head. Isn't that what Ricky would say? Something to that effect?

"Hit them again," Rhineder called. In rapid succession, each of them fired three more rounds and prepared to fire three again. At the completion of the second salvo, it became obvious the skiffs knew where the two CASPers were located, and they turned to bring their direct fire weapons to bear. Rhineder and Anderson, though, had selected a decent firing position behind the ancient, gnarled roots of a large tree. Right on cue, the Cochkala released a massive barrage of direct fire in their direction. Rhineder shifted the position of his CASPer to better use the cover provided by the tree. Neither of the CASPers registered damage from the barrage. He brought up the mortar tube again.

"One more time, Anderson. We've got to keep them busy to allow the infantry to hit."

The additional salvo kept the Cochkala's attention firmly on the two CASPers, which was exactly his intention.

Time for phase two.

"Nails, this is Top. Standby. We're moving forward to an assault position. Provide covering fire."

"Roger, Top. Coming up with a spread of MACs in three... two... one..."

The two CASPers came up firing. Their magnetic accelerator cannons ripped through the jungle in front of them. While he couldn't see the rounds impact in and around the Cochkala skiffs, Rhineder knew from the angle and elevation of his cannon they were having some effect. Due to their position behind the tree, the skiffs could not return fire with any degree of accuracy. Rounds and beamed weapons tore through the foliage around them. Rhineder heard a couple of impacts on the CASPer's exterior, but there was no indication of faults or damage.

"Set!" he heard Figgle call over the company network.

"Down, Anderson."

The two CASPers retreated behind the tree as the Cochkala doubled their rate of fire. Rhineder kept his CASPer absolutely still and watched his MAC tube's temperature gauge. "When temps are green, let me know. We'll pop back up and give them—"

"Proximity warning. Proximity warning."

"What the hell?" Rhineder swung his camera views three hundred and sixty degrees around the CASPer. There was nothing there. The warning system continued to indicate a nearby threat. Rhineder double checked and made sure Anderson was far enough away to fire his MAC. Similar warnings had occurred because of close proximity before, but Anderson was far enough away and in a perfect firing position. He rechecked the settings again and realized they were set for an airborne threat.

"Proximity warning. Proximity warning."

He looked up but couldn't see anything because of the trees above. Rhineder didn't know what it meant, and he also knew the infantry didn't have the same set of sensors he possessed.

"Top this is Nails. Airborne threats inbound."

* * *

Weqq
Blue Ridge Kin Perimeter

From her CASPer's cockpit, Cora studied the displays, looking for the airborne threat. There was none. The two enemy dropships had settled to the jungle floor and offloaded the skiffs. Neither one had lifted off again, and everything she could see via radar was clear. There wasn't a thing in the cloudy skies above them. Cora punched her transmit button as her gut twisted in on itself. Something wasn't right, and her troops were in harm's way. "Conner, run a sensor sweep of the atmosphere. I can't identify any threats."

Conner's voice came back a few seconds later. "Ma'am, I've got four ships inbound from orbit. They're not dropships but something a little bit larger, and they appear more heavily armed. They're squawking Crusader callsigns on approved frequencies. They're tracking toward—" Conner paused. "Ma'am they've fired. They're guiding deployed weapons!"

"How high up are they?"

"Forty-three miles. What the hell is going on?"

Cora's fingers flew over the CASPer's controls. She mashed down with her feet and jumped forward from the perimeter, but not toward her forward troops near the old MinSha science facility. Instead, Cora jumped toward the Crusaders' headquarters.

"Crusaders, this is Colonel McCoy. Cease fire. Cease fire. Your inbound vessels have fired illegally, and my troops are in the area. I say again, my troops are dangerously close!"

Lieutenant Colonel Smith's smug voice came back. "We are supporting your troops by fire, Colonel McCoy. Would you rather we stop firing?"

* * *

Weqq

Blue Ridge Kin Forward

First Sergeant Figgle turned and grabbed the nearest Jivool, Specialist Rynard, and threw him to the ground. Everyone stared. Figgle barked. "Get down on top of them. Do it right now!" As he said it, Figgle lay down atop Rynard and prostrated himself to cover the top half of the Jivool's body. With satisfaction, and more than a hint of pride, Figgle watched the other Goka do the same with the rest of the Jivool, some laying sideways across exposed furry legs. With everyone taken care of, Figgle tucked in his arms and legs and waited for the blast to come. He heard Colonel McCoy saying something about close danger and found himself laughing as if hearing Ricky in his mind.

No shit, Sherlock.

As the multiple detonations fell around them, Figgle continued to laugh while wondering who or what Sherlock might be.

* * *

Weqq

Crusader Command Post

Cora was still moving toward the Crusader command post when the detonations stopped. There was no immediate uptick in enemy fire, which indicated the skiffs had been quelled. While she appreciated that her soldiers might not be directly in harm's way anymore, her concern with the blatant violation of one of the oldest laws in the Galactic Union drove her forward with barely controlled anger. The newest and youngest mercenary company always took the fall for critical mistakes. With the blame typically came a sizable penalty fee. While their coffers were full and the Kin could likely afford such an eventuality, she'd prefer they not separate from any more credits than necessary.

Cora pulled up the Crusaders' radio network and took a deep breath, preparing to give Lieutenant Colonel Smith and whoever else might be listening a sizable piece of her mind. Instead, she heard a smooth Human voice.

"Crusader Five, this is Crusader Prime. Landing your position. Please have Colonel McCoy of the Blue Ridge Kin report to me immediately."

Cora stabbed her transmit button. "You better believe I'll be right there, Crusader Prime. What the fuck do you think you are doing dropping danger close to my troops from above ten miles? Have you lost your mind?"

To her surprise, she actually heard the man laugh. "Colonel McCoy, it's simple. We won this engagement. These mercenaries were sent here to find and kill the TriRusk. Their first rounds of suborbital bombardment hit their cavern complex and demonstrated their intent. The Cochkala landed at a known site, looking for Tri-Rusk. We can therefore assume the Cochkala were landing to gather evidence which they were going to use to track the TriRusk. I have now eliminated their skiffs, and I've targeted their dropships. They've been ordered to fully surrender to me upon my arrival. Likewise, your orders are to report to me. Is that clear?"

Cora's hands balled into fists. Anger seethed through her. This was unlike any situation she'd ever seen before. "I'll report there. You better not try to drop on my forces without my permission again."

Without waiting for a reply, she changed frequencies back to the company net. "Top, Colonel McCoy. What's your status?"

Figgle's voice came back immediately. "We're fine, ma'am. A few minor scrapes and bruises, but we're in good shape."

"How did you manage that?"

He laughed. "Well, we are pretty much indestructible."

"What about the Jivool? Sergeant Gallyind and the others?"

"That's how we got our scrapes and bruises, ma'am. Turns out, if we lie down on top of them, we stop most of the damage."

Cora's mouth dropped open. "You laid down on top of them?"

"Yes, ma'am. They're Kin. You've always said we do what we have to do to protect each other. It seemed like a natural thing to do."

Goka protecting Jivool. Try as she might, Cora couldn't believe it. While they'd said they were kin, and she'd had every reason to believe them when they said so, such a selfless act by a Goka was unheard of. They were truly doing something different.

As were the Crusaders. While Cora appreciated their shoot first and ask questions later mentality, there was a measure of brutality in what they had done. As she watched from her CASPer, the Crusader units poured into the tree line toward the dropships. She wondered what was going on, then realized she did not want to know. But she had to know. If for no other reason than to gather information to make an official report through Jyrall and Larth.

That realization spurred her to action, and Cora moved her CASPer forward toward the dropship location. She max jumped three times and dropped into the artificially cleared area. As she descended, her jump jets fired to cushion her landing, Cora saw Crusaders pulling the Cochkala out of their ship and lining them up single file.

That looks like a firing—

The crack of dozens of hand cannons ended her thought. More than three dozen of the Cochkala fell dead.

Oh, sonuvabitch.

Cora stood frozen for a moment, and her mind raced. As it did, she thought of Colonel Talmore and some of his advice on leadership. She'd never known a mercenary commander more committed to the development of his troops. On more than one occasion, he sat down and individually counseled soldiers regarding their performance and their potential. In one such session, he'd sat down with her. It was after a particularly dangerous mission on Feriduur.

They'd gone up against the Xiq'tal at a small outpost over some disputed territory. While there hadn't been that many of the Xiq'tal, the Ridge Runners had been unable to gain the element of surprise. The goddamned crabs were waiting for them, and they tore the initial units up. Cora and her squad had been the first to recognize the situation, and they pulled back. Talmore sat her down, with a small metal cup of whiskey for each of them, and asked her why.

"It wasn't right, sir."

"What wasn't right, Cora? Your gut? Or what you saw in front of you?"

"It was both."

Talmore shook his head. "You're a mercenary, Cora, and a damned good one. What you saw in front of you was your catalyst for action. You recognized something needed to be done, most certainly. That kind of instinct is second to none, especially for combat leaders. It's the kind of reaction I expect. Your gut is more experienced than you realize. When it says something is wrong, you better damn well listen to it."

Cora turned her CASPer around and jumped toward her infantry's position. Something was indeed *very* wrong. The clenching of her gut was merely a manifestation of her unease. While she recognized that, she also recognized something which surprised her. She wanted First Sergeant Figgle's advice. She couldn't think like a Human mercenary commander anymore. Her forces were overwhelmingly alien. As such, her line of thinking needed adjustment. Cora realized, with more than a measure of shock, that the Crusaders were anything but Peacemakers.

They were something else entirely, and Cora wasn't sure the place for her, or the Blue Ridge Kin, was anywhere near them, regardless of the risk to the TriRusk.

Or anyone else.

*****

Chapter Fourteen

Springton System

"What should I do with their ship?" Keaton asked. "Let it drift, send it toward the star? If I just disconnect, it may end up causing unwanted attention."

"He's right," Jyrall said. "If nothing else, the local authorities will look into it. They will suspect piracy, except nothing is missing."

"Maybe they will think pirates took the cargo," suggested Larth. "That's what they usually want, anyway."

"Unless they want the ship, itself," Keaton said.

"True," Jyrall said.

"Hell, *I* want the ship," Ricky said. "Well, I want the power plant and the shunts and everything else. A ship this size ain't supposed to be able to use shunts."

"What the hell you gonna do with the ship?" Keaton asked.

"First thang I'm gonna do is fix the power plant," Ricky answered. "I done wrecked the thrusters, and it needs new portals in the operations center. Well, not really, you don't *have* to be able to see out, but you know."

Ricky was still in the gunner's seat. He reached up and scratched the side of his face, adding to the smudge already there. He thought out loud. "Coupla new seats. Probably need to replace some panels up there, too. Then there is the hole in the cargo hold. Of course, I have a patch the perfect size for it floatin' in there right now, being as how it was once part of the hull and all."

"No, you dang hillbilly. What are you going to do *with* it? Not what are you going to do *to* it."

"Hell, I don't know," Ricky said. "Use it as a diversion or something. But if we do, I want the shunts first, or at least some of the panels and boards to 'em."

Jyrall listened to the two brothers go back and forth. He kept his helmet on, while Larth took his off and started to get out of his protective suit. He slowly started to grin to himself.

A diversion.

* * *

"Are you sure this will work?" Jyrall asked hours later.

"Yes," Keaton said. "I've run the calculations three times. The powered magnets Ricky beefed up will hold the ship to us. You and Larth put them in the optimum spots. The shuttle is now, for all intents and purposes, part of this ship and, therefore, will travel with us through hyperspace. Our shunts are sufficient to perform the task."

"We're gonna show up in the Krifay System a might bigger than when we left," Ricky added. "Keaton may catch hell landing, but he can do it. Then I can get to workin' on it."

"Are you sure we can do this?" Larth asked.

"We have to," Jyrall answered. "We have no choice. We have to stop them."

"But are they still going to attempt it? Without Nay-Thok, I mean."

"If not him, it would just be another," Jyrall said. "They will have the beings they need in place. Of course they will attempt it. That is why I had Keaton send a message, changing their timeline. I moved it some, but not so much they will suspect anything."

"Well," Larth said, "I sent the message to Kurrang. Let's hope he gets it and figures out a way to get the Kin to Krifay. You're taking a risk changing their orders without talking to Captain Dreel."

Jyrall nodded. "Remember, they weren't ordered. They were asked, and there is a difference. The coded message explaining this to the guild master is ready as well. Only he will understand it; the key is one he made for a one-time use. I don't think it is even written down."

"Once it's sent, that code is burned," Larth said. "One more resource gone. Speaking of which, we're pulling a big resource away from Weqq."

The big Besquith sighed. "I'm positive those at Weqq can complete their task without the Blue Ridge Kin. They may have succeeded in defending it already. I suspect that's the case," Jyrall said as he packed his suit away. "Either way, we need them with us. That, I am sure of."

"We're ready to leave," Keaton said. "Just give me the word."

"The bodies just went out," Ricky said. "I got them jokers headed straight toward the star. Hell, I jettisoned the bags from the vacuum cleaner, too. It was a bitch getting all the droplets up."

"Before we go," Jyrall said, "message your arms dealer, Little Buddy. There are some things we are going to need."

"Yeah?" Larth asked. "Like what?"

"Low velocity rounds that won't puncture hulls," Jyrall said. "More flechette weapons. Low powered laser rifles. Things like that."

"It's big, with multiple outer layers," Larth said. "You sure we need to worry about that?"

"It is best to be safe," Jyrall answered. "The last thing we need is one of us getting hurt because of our lack of precautions."

"Good point," Larth said. "I'll message her."

"So, we're stopping back here after we meet the Kin?" Ricky asked. "What if they don't come?"

"Then we go it alone," Jyrall said. "And yes, we will need to stop here. I expect the Kin to jump in and right back out once we make contact. They will need to stop to assess and resupply."

"This system is close to the Shaylin System," Larth agreed. "Makes sense. Should we just change the message and meet them here?"

"No," Jyrall said. "What Ricky needs to do to fix the shuttle would cause too many questions. On Krifay, we can do what we need to do without interference. We will need the shuttle to make the subterfuge believable."

* * *

Weqq

Cora's hands were a blur as she shut down her CASPer's systems and unbuckled her shoulder straps. She was moving toward the ground even before the CASPer's cockpit had fully opened. Cora climbed out and jumped from the cockpit's lip to the ground below. Leaving the CASPer in a warm shut down wasn't exactly what she wanted to do, but such was her fury at Crusader Prime that she didn't stop to take any other precautions. Instead, she tapped her slate and activated the mech's onboard cameras to record everything around the CASPer and relay it directly to the Blue Ridge Kin's tactical operations center. Satisfied, she stomped into the headquarters and ran immediately into Lieutenant Colonel Smith.

The man looked down at her with a twisted smirk. "Well excuse me, Colonel."

Cora flashed. "Don't start with me, Smith. Where is your Crusader Prime? I'm fixin' to give him a piece of my mind."

"Fixin' to? You must be from the South. I always loved that phrase," said a pleasant voice just to her right. He emerged from the shadows created by the computer banks and storage platforms mounted inside the headquarters. "I'm Crusader Prime. Can I help you?"

"What's your name?"

The older man smiled. His brown hair was streaked with gray, particularly at his temples. His face was tanned and weathered, but his blue eyes twinkled mischievously. "My name is Crusader Prime. Once again, how can I help you?"

"You're trying to tell me you don't have a name?"

"My name is not your concern, Colonel McCoy. You're here because you disagree with our methods. Isn't that right?"

"Disagree? You broke Galactic law! Correct me if I'm wrong, but there aren't many laws on the books across the galaxy but bombing above ten miles altitude is certainly one of the biggest crimes in the books."

"We are Crusaders, and generally, the rules don't apply to us." Prime smiled. He gestured to his command center which was far more technologically advanced than anything Cora could remember seeing in any mercenary company. "Our orders from the guild master are very clear and will not be subverted. Any and all advantages we possess are on the table for our operations galaxy-wide. From here, I can control all the Crusaders on this planet and relay communications to those currently working on missions in other places. We monitor, track, and, when necessary, operate across the galaxy. Our job is simple. A Peacemaker should make peace, not keep it. That is my intent as Crusader Prime."

Cora shook her head. "And you think the rules don't apply to you? Just because you're the Crusaders? That doesn't make any sense. You want to make peace, but you're going to use illegal means to do so?"

Prime laughed. Light danced across the skin of his exposed neck, and it appeared the man wore multiple sets of pinplants. "Oh, Colonel McCoy. You're unfamiliar with the particular gravity of the situation. If we set the rules, we can tweak them to our whims. We can do whatever is needed to accomplish the mission. That mission is to make peace. In this particular case, those Cochkala were landing to set up a staging area to attack and eliminate the TriRusk. That's not something we can allow."

Cora could understand a portion of his reasoning. The TriRusk were vital to rebuilding efforts across the Galactic Union, and to the Peacemaker Guild itself. Her limited interactions with Captain Kurrang proved that, as a species, the TriRusk were far more adept at life in the Galactic Union than most races. She surmised there were a lot of things Humans could learn from them.

But she knew the TriRusk would not approve of the Crusaders' methods. They possessed a strong moral compass, especially when it came to their family—their tribe. For a seemingly passive species, they could certainly wield violence as well as almost any other species. Violence was inevitable, but the Crusaders had taken things to a very different level. Yet their simple act of making the rules whatever they wanted because they were in a position of power did not sit well with her.

"Laws are laws, Mr. Prime."

The man's smile widened almost like a shark's maw. "It's not Mister, Colonel McCoy. It's Crusader Prime."

"Whatever." Cora shook her head and placed her hands on her hips. "I won't be a part of any organization that changes the rules so they win. Where I'm from, that's called cheating."

Prime chuckled. "As we used to say in my mercenary company, win if you can, lose if you must, but always cheat. If you're not winning, you're not cheating hard enough."

Smith and several of the other Crusader controllers burst out laughing. Their attitude, and their blatant disregard for the law, riled her almost to the point of violence. Cora balled her hands into fists and imagined, in a flash, drawing her weapon and killing them where they stood. She couldn't help but think it would be a good thing for the galaxy. Instead, she did nothing.

A Jivool entered the headquarters. She recognized him from their earlier interaction at the landing site. The look on his ursine face was less than pleasant.

"Prime," Enforcer Tok said, "what is the meaning of executing the Cochkala? They'd been defeated, and their full surrender made them non-combatants in the eyes of the law."

Prime turned to the Enforcer with a stone face. "I was just reminding Colonel McCoy here how peace needs to be made, Enforcer. I fully believe you understand that, yes?"

"I do, but not in the way that you have prescribed. This is not how Peacemakers operate, and you know it." Tok's words hung in the still, quiet space for a moment.

All of the mirth drained out of Prime's face. Cora watched blood flow into his neck and face. "Let me tell you both something. I am here, acting on the orders of the guild master himself. What I say goes. I have *carte blanche* to do whatever I want to do. For you, Enforcer, that means the guild master's orders say I have permission to do anything I deem necessary. Whatever it takes. That's exactly what I am prepared to do. We were sent here to stop the Cochkala from attacking the TriRusk, and we did just that. Executing them with impunity sends a further message to the nasty companies of the Mercenary Guild, or whatever's left of it, that we mean business. I am prepared to do the same to any company that gets in my way. Is that clear?"

Enforcer Tok nodded. "It's clear, Crusader Prime."

The man whirled and stared at Cora. An icy ripple of fear tore through her body. His hand came up, and he pointed at her face. "What about you?"

"I understand your position," Cora replied.

"Good, I expect you to recover and refit your forces for the remainder of the day. You will report to me at first light tomorrow to sign your contracts and join the Crusaders."

With that, Prime turned to Smith, and they walked away, leaving Cora and the Jivool Enforcer staring at one another in a mixture of shock and disbelief.

* * *

Outside the Crusader headquarters, Cora was preparing to climb into her CASPer, when the Jivool Enforcer appeared at her side. She looked at him for a second and said, "You can't tell me you agree with this."

The Enforcer grunted. "In a very real way, Colonel McCoy, my paws are tied."

"If you believe that, you've already given in to what they're doing. They broke the law, and you not stopping them has made you complicit. It doesn't matter that they think they can change the law; they can't. Anytime you change the rules of combat to favor one combatant, you're cheating. That's been against the laws of land warfare for the last thousand years, Enforcer Tok."

"I understand your point." The ursid looked down and dragged a foot across the dirt in front of them. "What are you going to do?"

Cora sighed. "I don't know. For the life of me, I can't think of a reason to stay here other than we were ordered to be here." She laughed. "No, it was more like asked. The guild master asked us to be here if an attack manifested. We weren't ordered. We weren't deputized. We were asked to come to this planet and defend the TriRusk. Now, that mission is over, and without a signed contract in my hands, I'm not sure what to do."

"I think it's like you said, you don't have a contract. You weren't deputized. You were *asked,* not hired, to defend Weqq. The objectives of your mission, regardless of the method used by the Crusaders, are complete."

The Jivool turned and walked away. Cora found herself watching him until he was out of sight. Her mind raced. Was he telling her to pack up and leave? Given that no one on the planet had made contact with, much less seen, the TriRusk—were they still on the planet?

What were they doing? Cora believed there was a role her unit was meant to play in whatever the guild master wanted them to do here. Try as she might, she realized letting the situation play out for a few more hours and gaining more intelligence on both the Crusaders and the overall situation might be her best course of action. Prime wanted an answer by sunrise. At that particular moment, Cora didn't know what she was going to say.

But she knew what she was going to do, at least in part.

* * *

Well past dark, and approaching planetary midnight, Cora still hadn't made a decision. She consulted with her officers, her noncommissioned officers, and even most of the company itself. Everyone was aghast at what they had seen. But they also understood their position and what the guild master had asked them to do through Jyrall and Larth. They were ready to move, should it come to that, but Cora wasn't sure, and she'd gone for a walk to clear her mind.

For the longest time, Cora wandered the assembly area before walking to the old MinSha science facility, deep in thought. The jungle was quiet, and the path from the assembly area to the science facility was well lit and well maintained. She didn't sense any danger as she made her way farther in that direction. There were a few Crusader guards present, but they mostly ignored her.

She reached the MinSha science facility and marveled at its dilapidated condition. The time that had passed since Jessica Francis led the MinSha resistance against Reilly's Raiders should have been long enough for it to be repaired. It was obvious the facility was not going to be repaired by anyone anytime soon. The large, square compound still had massive damage. One wall was completely breached and open to the jungle outside. While supplies and armaments had been stacked inside, and construction equipment had been poised to potentially begin work on the facility, nothing had been done in quite some time. The facility was quiet. A few armed guards moved around in the lower interior compound and on the walls above.

Cora decided to climb up on the walls and look out into the dark jungle. She'd been fascinated by the stories and reports of the planet with its strange fauna and flora. She hadn't seen one of the vicious urrtam bird-things while on the planet. She was curious if she'd see anything in the darkness beyond.

Atop the wall, she nodded to one of the Crusader guards who appeared to be listening to some type of entertainment and paid her no mind.

Arms across her chest, Cora stared into the darkness and tried to reason out what her next course of action needed to be. Larth would've told her to shoot their way out. She smiled at the thought and realized, like so many of those in her unit, she loved the little Peacemaker for his fearless approach to life. Yet she found herself leaning toward what she believed Jyrall would say. For such a massive and fearful looking creature, his heart was pure gold. He would've looked at her and told her to do what she felt was right. He would've told her something along the lines of understanding that the mission was always there, but her people and her own conscience came first.

Movement in the jungle caught her eye. In the low light radiating from the security lights on top of the walls, Cora saw an elongated white face poke out from behind a large tree. She recognized it immediately. The TriRusk pointed at her and then back toward the assembly area. A quick look around showed her that the guards weren't paying any particular attention to her. She gestured to herself and then made a walking gesture with her fingers before pointing at the TriRusk. The big head shook from side to side, like a Human's. It pointed at her, tried to do the walking movement with its digits, then pointed back toward the assembly area. Cora understood. Three quick steps took her back to the ladder she'd used to climb to the top of the wall. As she turned to step onto it, she heard a short hooting sound. Cora looked back toward the TriRusk, but it was gone.

She descended the ladder and made her way back toward the well-lit path. Afraid she was rushing and calling attention to herself, she forced herself to stop and re-clasp one of her boots. Her heartbeat accelerated wildly, and a fresh sensation of hope filled her. Maybe there were still answers to be had.

About two hundred meters beyond the science facility, Cora barely saw the blur of a white-furred hand shoot out from behind a tree and snag her arm. It dragged her into the darkness and placed a big digit against her face in a shushing gesture. The alien was filthy and smelled like a wet dog who'd rolled in freshly cut green onions. It reminded her of home.

Cora whispered. "Captain Kurrang, what are you doing here? Where are the rest of the TriRusk?"

He snorted and shook his head. "You remind me of Jessica. Patience, Cora. There are many things in play you don't fully understand right now—the first of which is that all is not what it seems with the Crusaders. I hope you've realized that by now."

"I have. Where are your people? The Cochkala bombed your caverns?"

"There are many caverns on this planet. My family is safe for the time being. Though yours is not." Kurrang studied her for a moment. "What are you doing?"

Cora took a breath and forced emotion out of her voice. Agitation would make her talk louder and faster—two things she couldn't afford to do in close proximity to Crusader guards. "I'm here at the request of the guild master. I don't really know what I'm supposed to do next. Our job was to protect you."

"It was a request and not an order," Kurrang replied with a sigh. "I also do not think it came directly from the guild master himself."

"Then who?"

"That remains to be seen." The TriRusk sat back on his massive haunches and looked at her for a long moment. "You're wondering what to do. Would you consider doing what I tell you? I realize that doesn't strike Humans particularly well—being told what to do—but I can provide you some insight."

Cora felt a smile crawling across her face. "What would you have us do?"

"You strike me as a more than competent leader, Cora McCoy. You know in your heart what you should be doing. You're looking for the validation of someone else to tell you what to do. You don't require anybody's validation. You're a mercenary company commander, and that means you can tell your company to do whatever you want them to do. Damn the consequences."

Cora shrugged. "I'm afraid if I do, the Crusaders are going to come after me. I've seen firsthand what they do to those in their way. They executed the Cochkala they caught today."

Kurrang nodded. "And if you join them? Do you not think they'll turn on you at the earliest opportunity? They can't be trusted,

Cora. You know this. I believe you understand what it is you need to do."

"What's to prevent them from stopping us with force? Placing my troops at unnecessary risk? I'm not sure I can do that."

"Leave that to me. I will ensure you get off this planet. Make sure you do so within the next several hours," Kurrang said. "You are needed elsewhere."

Cora squinted at him. "What do you mean?"

"Go home, Cora McCoy." Kurrang sat up and moved toward the darkness. "I hear the fishing is good on Krifay. Go home and get prepared to fish for something even bigger. Leave these Crusader assholes to me."

"Wait." Cora shook her head. "Did you just call them assholes?"

"I did." Kurrang's maw curled in a grin. "You Humans have such a fascinating language. Now, go, Cora McCoy. Do what has to be done and complete the mission."

Cora took a quick breath and closed her eyes upon hearing him quote their company motto. "Thank you," she said as she opened her eyes.

Kurrang had disappeared. Somehow, the big alien had vanished, leaving only the faint smell of wet dog and green onions on the breeze. Cora checked the pathway for guards and stepped out into the light. Her steps back to the Blue Ridge Kin tactical operations center were light. As was her heart.

* * * * *

Chapter Fifteen

Krifay System

Jyrall closed his eyes and swallowed hard. The nausea faded after a minute or so. He opened them and looked over and saw Keaton watching him intently. He formed a tight smile. Intimidating for his race.

"No, Keaton," Jyrall said. "I will not get sick in your operations center. You can relax."

"What? I—I was just making sure you were all right. I know how you hate the transition back to normal space. That's all," Keaton said. "And, technically, it's your operations center. Me and Ricky are just the crew."

Jyrall shifted in the co-pilot's seat. "It is and it isn't. I prefer to think the ship belongs to all four of us. We are a team."

"The best team," Larth agreed. He and Ricky were floating behind the seats, hanging on to straps, as usual.

"You may not claim the operation's center," Ricky said, "but the repair room and all the tools are dang shore mine. That's what I'm hollering."

All four of them laughed. "Don't know why y'all are laughing," Ricky said, his voice indignant. "I laid claim to all of it. Cain't be no dispute. Appalachian Law…or sumthin'." They laughed even harder.

Ricky said, "I gotta go sketch out a few things to repair the shuttle." He turned, reached for another strap, and left the small center, mumbling, "It's like a dang handshake, is what it is. A done deal, I say."

"I believe he would fight over it," Jyrall said. He shook his big head. "Yes, the tools are his."

"Well, I wouldn't fight him over it," Larth said. "No, thank you. Moving on."

"What?" Jyrall asked. "You? Afraid of a fight?"

"You must pick your battles in this galaxy," Larth said. "I am not fighting a Pushtal who thinks he is a hillbilly from Earth who has been 'done wrong.' Do I look crazy? That is not happening."

"I don't blame you," Keaton said with a grin.

* * *

Weqq

Cora called her leadership team together in the small tactical operations center. When everyone was assembled, she stepped into the center. "Listen up, everyone. There's not much time to do this, so we're going to have to load faster and quieter than we've ever attempted. But we have no choice, and it's not up for a vote.

"We are leaving. Right now. The Crusaders killed a bunch of Cochkala in cold blood, and they've threatened any mercenary company that stands in their way. There's no way in hell we're going to fall in with them. The Kin will not take orders from killers. If we had more combat power, we'd give them the ass whupping they deserve. But, right now, we're going home to Krifay. There's more work for us to do. I'll explain when we get there. I need your best, Kin. Don't leave nothing for these assholes, either. Get our equipment loaded on the dropships. I want us off the ground in an hour. Two max.

"Y'all know what to do. Complete the mission."

* * *

Snapper Isle
Planet Krifay

"It's gonna cost some credit," Ricky said. "I need to hire someone to move the shuttle; it ain't like I can just turn the juice off to the electromagnets and drop it. Then we need to move it into a bay, hire some technicians, maybe a whole crew. They's a company or two right here at the airfield who can do it. But a rush job ain't cheap."

The four of them stood outside the ship looking up at the attached shuttle. Keaton had managed a relatively smooth landing, even after the ship entered the atmosphere of Krifay. The prospect of repairing it well enough for use loomed large.

Keaton ignored his brother and the others as his fingers flew across his slate. "Yes! I knew I was right."

"Right?" Jyrall asked. "About what?"

"Yeah," Larth said. "You can't just announce something cryptic like that and not say what it is."

"That ship," Keaton said as he pointed to an old freighter across the tarmac. "I know that ship."

"Please continue," Jyrall said, now interested.

"It's the *J-Kithik 908*."

Jyrall's eyes widened. "That ship belongs to Ban-Tilk. He said he was leaving the Springton System. What are the odds he came here?"

"Not as high as you think," Keaton said. "It is no secret that runs can be had here. Protein is in high demand throughout the galaxy, and there are those who wish to bypass their system's import laws, food quarantines, and taxes. It is actually a very profitable business. Illegal in many systems, but profitable."

"It is not something we, as candidates, spent a lot of time on at the academy," admitted Jyrall.

"There are crimes…and there are crimes," Larth said. "Like I said, you pick your battles. It's not one Peacemakers have chosen to fight unless a mass sickening or disease occurs."

"True," Jyrall said. "I would not say a blind eye is turned, but it sits low on the priority list. Peacemakers will get to it when they can." The big Besquith winked.

"Nice," Keaton said. "Like when Pops was given a ride home by the sheriff and not arrested for fightin' the man we told you about."

"He beat that feller down with a chunk of fahr wood," Ricky said. "Love that story."

"Precisely," Jyrall said. "Sometimes, the situation dictates, and one must do what is right, even if it is not to the letter of the law."

"You have to love an equalizer," Larth said. "A piece of wood, one…maybe four pistols. Whatever it takes to win, I say."

"Speaking of which, sometimes it takes a smuggler and his crew," Jyrall said. "I think I will seek out Ban-Tilk and gauge his interest in a job." He walked to the exit of the airfield and toward the local town on the island. He called back over his shoulder. "Keaton, will you send me what you can find on this Jeha?"

"If you are thinking what I think you are thinking, it's genius," Larth said. "I'm coming with you." He followed his partner.

"What in tarnation are they talkin' 'bout?" Ricky asked.

"I think they are going to hire that Jeha to play Nay-Thok," Keaton said.

"Oh. Makes sense. Now, what about getting that shuttle down, renting a bay, and everything else?" Ricky asked. "They never said."

"Do it. Spend the credits," Keaton said.

"You shore?"

"Yep. I'm picking this battle. We need that ship."

* * *

"This is the place?" Larth asked. "Doesn't look like it would be a smuggler's pit to me. Then again, the one on Springton is in an unmarked building, so I guess it could be."

"This is the place," Jyrall confirmed. "Keaton said it is. Apparently, there is no true pit here, but beings come to this establishment to learn of potential runs. Here on Krifay, it is not smuggling, it is selling seafood. Once it leaves the system, how it goes or what other systems' laws are being broken is of no concern to them. Hence, no smuggler's pit needed."

"For seafood," Larth corrected. "Who knows what deals are made here for other things?"

"You are correct. But Keaton can find no mention of a pit here in the system. They are not in every system, you know."

"True," Larth conceded. He rubbed his little hands together in anticipation. "Well, let's go in and get a drink and a bite to eat. Maybe we will see Ban-Tilk in here."

"Oh, he is in there, all right," Jyrall said. He turned his small slate toward Larth. On the screen was an image from the security system of the establishment.

"Keaton is good. He is *real* good," Larth said, with a grin.

"Best team ever," Jyrall said, looking down at the Zuparti.

"Hey! That's what I'm supposed to say. Get your own catch phrase."

* * *

"Varkell," Ban-Tilk said. "Yes, you may join us."

"Thank you," Jyrall said and eased into a chair. The table was occupied by the Jeha and two Bakulu. The pair were enjoying a suspicious looking bowl of…something. He could smell it with his sensitive nose and suspected what it was but said nothing.

Larth watched closely but was disappointed when the chair held up. He sighed and sat beside a Bakulu. "What's good here?"

"They serve a wide variety," Ban-Tilk answered, waving several small pincers in a ripple effect to indicate the establishment. "Heavy on the seafood, of course."

"We are having squid puree," one of the Bakulu volunteered. Looking somewhat like large slug-like snails from Earth, Bakulu had a variety of pseudopods capable of performing various tasks. One eye turned toward Larth while the other two remained on his bowl as he spooned the paste into one of his mouths.

"They cook that here?" Larth asked, wrinkling his nose.

"Cook?" asked the other Bakulu. "A decent bowl of squid is not cooked. It is simply pureed."

"Aaannd I won't be having any of that," Larth declared. "That is definitely not a Human recipe."

"I will pass as well," Jyrall said.

"We have to ask for it specifically, with instructions," admitted the first Bakulu. "It reminds us of home."

"As for me, I am enjoying the lobster," Ban-Tilk said. "Though I must admit, I feel a little barbaric and somewhat guilty pulling the meat from its segmented shell."

After Jyrall and Larth took the Jeha's advice and ordered lobster, Ban-Tilk turned to the Besquith and asked, "To what do I owe the pleasure, Varkell? Surely you have not followed us here to Krifay. It does not seem like the kind of place you frequent or offer the type of runs you make."

"Really?" asked Jyrall. "Yet you take jobs here quite often."

"I see you have researched me and my crew," Ban-Tilk said. "Fi-ne, let us admit we dug a little deeper on each other. Speaking of which, you are known as One-Eyed Varkell. Where is your patch? I distinctly remember you wearing one."

The Bakulu directly across from Jyrall narrowed all three eyes and several tentacles eased down to the side of his shell and underneath. He stopped moving when he felt and heard a tap on his shell.

"Pull them back out where we can see them," Larth said. He had a pistol down low, unseen by others in the establishment.

Once the Bakulu did as he was asked, the pistol disappeared. "Let's just enjoy the meal and the conversation," Larth suggested. "We don't have any ill intent toward you three. We can all be civi-lized without threats or weapons."

Ban-Tilk stared at the Bakulu. "What were you thinking, Golund? Really? Here in my favorite restaurant. Varkell and…"

"Call me Switch," Larth suggested.

"...and Switch have made no overt moves toward us," continued Ban-Tilk. "I have told you time and again, we are not that type of outfit."

"My apologies," Golund said. "I get a little nervous."

"He does," agreed the other Bakulu, never once slowing his eating. "Like several others of our extended family."

"Hey, you guys are brothers?" Larth asked. "The other two in our crew are brothers."

"I suppose some races would consider it as such," said the Bakulu. "I am called Traluur, by the way. As I was saying, we are clutchmates of the same season."

"I will explain the eyepatch," Jyrall said. "But first let me ask you a few questions."

The Jeha studied Jyrall for a moment and said, "Very well. Proceed with your questions."

"Why do you slide behind the lines of legality?" Jyrall asked. "You could transfer goods...seafood, within the limits of the law. Why do you not?"

"I could," agreed Ban-Tilk. "But to be honest, there is no thrill in that. I crave adventure. Yes, I—we—could earn a fine living running goods. My ship is large enough to provide a decent profit if we work hard and constantly."

"Constantly," agreed Traluur. "That means no time off to enjoy life, trips home to see family, or having the ability to cover the costs of huge gatherings."

"Wonderful bowls of squid puree when we want," added Golund.

"Ewww," remarked Larth. "But I get what you mean."

"I don't want the same old routes running the same old goods," explained Ban-Tilk. "I want something different. I want to help. Some of the places we take things to really need them. Not just want them, they *need* them. Not every system or planetary government does a good job providing. Some...some even ensure certain races, or groups, of beings get only the bare minimum."

"Sometimes less," Traluur added. "Tyrants."

"I like to provide help. It just feels...right," Ban-Tilk said. "It doesn't always provide good margins of profit." The Jeha rippled his pincers in his race's shrug. "The occasional run of other *things* makes up for it. Like the run from Springton."

"Interesting," Jyrall said. He sat back and folded his arms.

"I know what you are thinking," Ban-Tilk said. "Why do we call ourselves smugglers? I do not care what others think. They need to mind their own business. You, as well, if you think less of me. You said it before, we are in the same line of business, you and I. Probably not. Just occasionally. Now, why the questions, and how is it you require a patch when one can see both of your eyes work fine?"

"One last question," Larth said. "Do you have a job lined up, or are you free to take one?"

"We are in between runs, at the moment," the Jeha said slowly. "Why? Do you have a contract in mind?"

Jyrall reached to the center of the table and grabbed one of the old-fashioned menus. There were several on each table, throwbacks to the owner's home world, Earth. He slipped something into it, leaned toward Ban-Tilk, and opened it slightly. "Let me show you my favorite thing in this menu."

No others in the establishment could see inside the partially closed menu. Ban-Tilk's eyes widened when he saw the open badge holder held tightly against the menu. There was no doubt in his widened eyes. He was looking at a shiny Peacemaker's badge. He flicked his eyes toward Jyrall as the badge and its holder disappeared. "I see."

"What? The desserts?" asked Traluur. "I like pudding myself. Chocolate."

"I'm sure he showed Ban-Tilk what I love, too," Larth said. "The very same thing."

Interrupting the tense moment, though unaware of it, Golund said, "There's Mike. Hi, Mike." He waved a pseudopod at someone who had just walked in the door. "Mike sold me a nice Maki-made auto flechette rifle. A fine Human, that man."

The man they had purchased ammunition and weapons from once before, Mike, walked over and said hello to the group. "Mr. Up, Mr. Face. Good to see you two again. Tell Wally to come by the shop sometime. I have some new items he may be interested in." After some small talk, he mentioned meeting someone for a drink and walked to the other side of the establishment.

"I see you know Mike, as well," Ban-Tilk said. He was no longer worried about being arrested by the two Peacemakers. He was now more curious than ever. "But he doesn't know you two as Varkell and Switch. Perhaps, after this meal, we could reconvene at my ship and talk. Around fewer beings, I mean."

"Yes. Let's," Jyrall said. He gave the waitress a grin when she put a plate with three lobsters piled high in front of him.

"Here you go, mon. De triple lobster special," she said. Her white teeth shone brightly in her dark face. "Dat's a lot of food, you know. You just remember to triple tip, and you can be my favorite customer dis week."

* * *

"Let me get this straight, Peacemaker," Ban-Tilk said. "You want to hire us to take a large shuttle, one with shunts, to the Shaylin System. Specifically, to the stargate there. Dock with it, enter it, and pretend I am a being called Nay-Thok."

"Right," Jyrall said.

"Then you want one of these two to place a small drive in one of the security systems so your crew member can insert a virus to damage their long-range scanning and surveillance system."

"Right," Larth said.

"Then you plan to dock with and board the gate to prevent it from being taken over completely by a group of security specialists who will already be onboard along with the normal security."

"Exactly," Jyrall said.

"Just you four?" Ban-Tilk asked. "To stop a large group from taking over a stargate?"

"No," Jyrall said. "I plan on stopping in Springton and picking up one other. Once I find him."

"One other. Once you find him," the Jeha said. "Wonderful."

"Also, we plan on having an entire merc company with us," Larth added. "We estimate about one hundred security guards on the gate. Maybe a few more."

"You will need more than one company of mercenaries, I would think," Ban-Tilk said. "There are several smaller companies here on Krifay. One that comes to mind and specializes in security is Brentale's Barnstormers. I know Colonel Pete Brentale. He is a good Human. His company made it back here recently, despite the entire galaxy conspiring against Human mercenary companies. They were stuck in a system…from what I was told."

"I may speak to him," Jyrall said. "Thank you for the suggestion."

"Wait," Larth said. "Does that mean you will accept the job?"

"Why, of course," Ban-Tilk said. "To be able to help a pair of Peacemakers? Absolutely. There will be fees, of course. It would appear to be dangerous. And we will need to be deputized. To cover our rear segment, you understand."

"Do we get badges?" asked Golund. "I'm breaking out my Maki rifle."

"I like you," Larth declared.

"When can we expect to initiate this action?" Ban-Tilk asked.

Jyrall smiled. "As soon as our mercenaries arrive. Provided our message has gotten through, that is."

Larth blinked. "That fast?"

Ban-Tilk made the gurgling sound of Jeha laughter.

Jyrall shook his head. "How do you like them apples, Little Buddy?"

*****

Chapter Sixteen

Weqq

For little more than two hours, Kurrang kept himself hidden in the darkness near the MinSha science facility. He crept toward the Crusaders' assembly area when he saw the Blue Ridge Kin loading and preparing their dropships for lift off. As their engines spooled up, he walked out of the darkness onto the wide trail between the facility in the jungle and the assembly area. Within seconds, a surprised guard approached.

"Halt. Who goes there?"

"Captain Kurrang of the Peacemaker Guild with a report for the ears of Crusader Prime only. Lower that weapon, or I will lower you."

The guard, a pimply faced Human much younger than Jessica Francis and her friends, lowered his weapon slowly. "What do you want?"

"I would imagine Crusader Prime would like to speak with me. You will take me to him right now."

The kid reached up to his collar, touched a radio microphone, and reported Kurrang's appearance. He was told to place the missing Peacemaker under armed guard and wait for a quick reaction force from the assembly area to escort them back to headquarters.

Instead, Kurrang slowly started walking down the trail toward the assembly area. If the kid shot him, it would be an unfortunate incident. But he believed the young Human was scared enough to follow along quietly. When the shot didn't come, Kurrang picked up his pace. He heard the young man walking behind him and whispering into his radio.

At the external boundary of the assembly area, two Human CASPers, Mk 7s by their distinctive look, blocked the trail. Between them stood a familiar Jivool. As Kurrang approached, he could see the Enforcer barely concealing a smile.

"Captain Kurrang."

"Enforcer Tok. Well met."

"Well met, Captain. We've been looking for you. I was hoping you'd show soon."

"Take me to Crusader Prime, Enforcer. I would imagine he would like to speak to me."

The Enforcer looked at the mechs to his left and right. "You can disperse. I will escort the captain personally."

One of the Mk 7's external speakers clicked to life. "Enforcer, we have our orders from Crusader Prime."

"And I'm telling you I am taking Captain Kurrang personally to Prime. I do not require your assistance, and I am ordering you to stand down. Are we clear?"

"Yes, Enforcer."

As difficult as the Humans could be, they understood rank and precedence fairly well. They also understood Enforcers could pretty much do anything they needed to in the preservation of their lives and the prosecution of their missions. While the CASPers certainly overmatched the Jivool in arms and capabilities, the pilots themselves could not.

As the CASPers stomped away, Tok approached and waved off the young Human guard. Kurrang started toward the headquarters, and the young Enforcer fell in at his side.

"Interesting time for you to return, Captain," the Enforcer said quietly out of one side of his maw.

Kurrang grunted. "I would imagine. Prime wants me to secure the TriRusk for the Crusaders. That's the only reason you're still here."

"He says our orders are from the guild master."

"And what do you think, Enforcer? Has an Enforcer ever been asked to do what you and your team have been asked to do here? Has an Enforcer ever been told to leave his vehicles in orbit to provide firepower in the event of a rapid escape?"

At that moment, one of the Blue Ridge Kin's dropships lifted off. Kurrang followed it with his eyes for a moment.

"Is that what they're doing? Leaving?" Tok asked. His voice was little more than a whisper, and Kurrang sensed an opportunity.

"Use your brain, Enforcer. You know exactly where they're going. And you know exactly why. Don't you?"

The young Jivool dropped his head slightly and stared at the ground as they walked. "I do, sir."

"Then why are you still here? Why haven't you evacuated?"

"I have a duty. The guild master personally directed us here to assist the Crusaders."

Kurrang turned his head and stared at the Jivool. "Did you receive your orders directly from him? As in physically?"

"No, they came through Stormwatch. That's standard for assignments, is it not?" Tok met his eyes.

"Of course, it is. Stormwatch will tell you if it comes directly from the guild master. You've seen the codes. Did you think to check them? To fully investigate their authenticity?"

"No," Tok replied. "All of our latest communications have been the same."

"I suggest you look a little deeper, Enforcer. I am afraid things are not what they seem. Given the conduct of the Crusaders in this operation, I find it hard to believe you approve of their methods."

"I am concerned," Tok replied slowly. "But my oath says—"

"Your oath is about justice. Your oath is about morality. Your oath is about right and wrong. It's not just about upholding the laws of the Galactic Union. There's only a dozen of them. Any idiot can be hired to protect and uphold those. Just like these idiots"—Kurrang gestured with one large paw at the Crusaders—"feel like they can change them whenever they need to. That's not right, and you know it. I expected more from you, Tok."

They walked in silence toward the Crusaders' headquarters. As they reached the inner perimeter, the second of the Blue Ridge Kin's dropships lifted off and accelerated toward orbit. There was a startling amount of activity in the headquarters. Kurrang wondered how long it was going to take Crusader Prime to mobilize his forces and target them. Or if he had his ships in orbit prepared to attack them, provided they were in a close enough position.

Tok held open the makeshift door of the headquarters, allowing Kurrang inside first. As he stepped inside, all conversation ceased.

"What is the meaning of this?" a Human with white hair on the sides of his head yelled from across the room. He moved toward Kurrang in an instant, with one hand resting on the sidearm holstered on his right thigh. "You can't come in and disrupt this operation. Just where the hell do you think you've been?"

Kurrang sat back on his haunches and stared at the Human for a moment. He didn't recognize the man, but he recognized the type. Crusader Prime was obviously very much in this arrangement, however it had been created, for himself. He loved the power. Yet Kurrang was fairly certain he couldn't carry his feces in his own hands.

"I have seen to the safety of my people. My family is safe, and my mission has been completed."

"Your mission? Well, I'm all ears, Captain Kurrang. When were you going to inform me of your mission?"

"My orders were not given for your approval, Prime. The guild master's orders—"

"Don't tell me about his orders! I am in charge of this operation, and you should've reported to me when we landed. Instead, you've been running around the jungle, doing who knows what. For all I know, you could've sabotaged everything we would lay our hands on."

Kurrang reared up on his hind legs. "Measure your next words carefully, Prime."

"Don't threaten me, Kurrang."

"You have no idea what you're doing or who you're dealing with, Human."

Prime fumed for a moment, saying nothing, but breathing so hard his nostrils flared. Finally, he spun and pointed at combat controllers awaiting his guidance at their consoles. "Contact the *Righteous*. Order her and the fleet to intercept those dropships and the Blue Ridge Kin's vessels immediately. Their orders are to blow them out of the sky."

Kurrang heard the order transmitted. The loudspeaker on the far side of the headquarters clicked to life. "Crusader Prime, this is *Righteous.* We're moving to engage and have a firing solution, but there are two Tangos blocking our path. We've requested they move. There has been no response. I say again, the two Tango corvettes are not broadcasting."

In front of Kurrang, Prime whirled and stepped up to Enforcer Tok. "What in the hell are you playing at?"

Tok shrugged. "I have my orders from the guild master."

"Godsdammit! There is no guild master on this planet. In his absence, you will answer to me." Prime's shriek rang off the headquarters' walls. "Order those corvettes out of the way."

"I'll do no such thing. We are to protect guild partners from aggressive acts," Tok replied. "You cannot turn on partners requested by the guild master without repercussions."

A voice came over the loudspeakers. "*Righteous*, this is *Tango Veritas.* Negative on your request. We will handle this ourselves. The situation must be dealt with. Stand down and clear out."

An evil smile appeared on Prime's face. "Well, if you won't take care of it, Enforcer, your friends will. They understand the chain of command. I'll see to it you're placed under arrest. Insubordination will be punished."

"How?" Kurrang asked. "You'll kill him like you did all those Cochkala?"

Prime's face faltered. "What are you talking about?"

"Don't play innocent, Prime. Whoever you are, you've led a mercenary unit before. You're more than aware of the laws of land warfare. Saying you don't know what happened is the Human definition of bullshit. I watched what you did to them. You've broken more laws than any other being I've ever met. Including Kr'et'Socae. I will see that you answer for what you've done if it's the last thing I do."

"Oh, you will, will you?"

With uncanny speed, Prime drew his pistol and placed it against Kurrang's head. "What's to stop me from blasting your brains all over the inside of this headquarters? Tell me, Kurrang. You and your godsdamned species are so special. Tell me why."

Kurrang turned his head slowly and pressed the barrel against his skull. "I won't stop you, but it's pretty obvious you haven't a clue what's really going on here. But you don't care about that, do you? You love being in charge again. Probably with a much larger budget than you've ever had. You think you're at the top of your food chain, Prime. You are sorely mistaken."

At that moment, Kurrang saw Prime's pupils grow and shrink quickly. His eyelids fluttered and, by all appearances, his eyeballs almost vibrated in their sockets. For several seconds, the Human didn't even appear to breathe. His muscles were almost slack. The pressure of the barrel against Kurrang's head relented. Suddenly, Prime blinked several times and pulled the pistol away from Kurrang's head. "The two of you are under arrest. Crusaders? See to it the Enforcers are separated and deploy the mobile stockade."

Prime stomped back to the console and screamed orders to *Tango Veritas*. A team of six Crusaders approached Kurrang and Tok with their weapons at the ready.

Tok spoke out of the side of his mouth. "I suppose you have a plan?"

"Of course, I do."

* * *

Tango Veritas

"You've seen the video," Zevva buzzed her antennae. "Tok will fill us in on the rest. The first step is to get the Blue Ridge Kin to safety. He promised to fill us in, and he will."

"What about *Righteous* and the other ships?" Kravon asked from the weapons station. Zevva brought the *Tango* around in place as he prepared firing solutions against the Crusader fleet. "You told them we'd handle this."

Zevva chuckled. "We're not doing a damned thing. They'll figure that out eventually, and it should give the Blue Ridge Kin a chance to leave."

Kravon shook his head. "And what happens when they open fire on us?"

"It's not going to come to that."

"They're going to break off," Mratt said. "We're going to thread the needle."

"What makes you so sure?"

Zevva laughed. "Who wants to draw the ire of the Enforcers?"

"*Tango Veritas*, this is *Righteous*. You are ordered to move or be destroyed."

Kravon sighed. "That didn't take long."

"No. Your move, *Righteous*. We have our orders." Zevva replied.

"Do you think that was smart?" Kravon asked.

"I really don't care anymore. This whole thing hasn't sat well with me from the beginning."

"You are ordered to move on the authority of Crusader Prime," *Righteous* squawked.

"We don't take our orders from Crusader Prime. We take our orders from the Prime Enforcer, and our orders are clear. We will not move. Fire on us at your peril."

Mratt called, "*Veritas*, pull up Tok's slate camera; it's still recording."

Zevva studied the screen and reflexively reached for the communications controls. "Tok, are you there?"

There was no response from Tok. Instead, Kravon said, "The feed is coming from his slate, and he's obviously walking with Kurrang. But there's—wait, are those armed guards around them?"

"We'll see about this," Zevva said. She punched the radio controls. "Crusader Prime, this is *Tango Veritas*. Have you placed the Enforcers under arrest?"

"Yes, I have. Now, you will intercept those Human vessels, or the *Righteous* and our other ships will blow you out of the sky. Am I clear?"

"Sorry, Crusader Prime. We will not move."

For a long moment, no one said anything. All eyes were stuck on Tok's slate view. They appeared to be marching him and Captain Kurrang from the Crusader headquarters to some type of temporary stockade. As they watched, the slow and methodical pace suddenly changed with the frenetic swinging of the camera from side to side. In seconds, they realized Tok and Kurrang had attacked their guards and were running away.

"*Veritas*, this is Tok. Do you read me?"

"We've got you, fearless leader. What's the situation?"

"Make sure the Blue Ridge Kin have space to jump."

"We're way ahead of you, Tok," Zevva replied. "Crusader Prime has already threatened to blow us out of the sky. We're going to thread the needle on them."

"I understand. We can't let them take down the Humans. Do what you have to. The situation is worse than you can imagine. Get down here as fast as you can."

"Entropy, you don't want anything easy, do you?"

Tok grinned. His breathing was ragged as they kept up a frenetic pace. "Just do it, otherwise the Crusaders are going to kill more innocents."

"What?" Kravon asked. "What are you talking about?"

"I'm uploading a video file now. If something happens to us, get it to Guild Master Rsach."

Zevva looked at Kravon, who nodded. "We've got the file."

"Oh gods!" Kravon sat back from his console. "They're fucking criminals."

His shocked face stunned Zevva, then just as quickly, motivated her. She called out to the other Tango off her port side. "On me, *Equitas.* Weapons online. Engines to full power in three, two, one…"

* * * * *

Chapter Seventeen

Ricky stepped back and admired the work. "That right there is lined up perfectly." He turned to the three technicians beside him on the lift. "Y'all make that permanent. I'm goin' to check on the operations center." He handed the gauge to the woman and turned to climb down the makeshift ladder hanging from the small platform.

Keaton stood below with his hands on his hips, looking up at the last section of thrusters being attached. He squinted slightly as the bright lights in the bay glared overhead. It was loud, even in the huge building. Rivets were being placed, welders were running, and Humans, as well as several other races, were shouting to be heard as they worked.

When Ricky made it to the ground, Keaton said, "Pops would have said it looks like somebody kicked over an anthill."

"Yep," Ricky agreed. "Except these ants ain't running around all crazy-like. That was a dang good idea you had, adding bonuses for early completion on each assigned project."

He ran his dirty digits through the fur between his ears. "That woman up there with the welder? Hell, she's every bit of fifty years old and can lay a stack of dimes. I ain't never seen anyone draw a bead like she can. She pops it one time with her little hammer, and the whole piece of slag drops off. Dang shore puts me to shame."

Keaton nodded. "I saw. The cargo hull looks like it never had a big-ass hole in it, except for the shiny ring where she grinded it smooth. She's good. Her whole company is good. There is a boy in the operations center reprogramming everything. A boy, I tell ya."

"I saw that. He cain't be more than fourteen years old. He's a little odd, too. I tried talking to him, and he wasn't having it. He just nodded to me and kept rocking back and forth as he stared at the screen and programmin'. His dang fingers were flying."

Keaton nodded. "He's a savant."

"Never heard of them," Ricky said. "Whereabouts they from? Down around Athens? Lotta smart folks in that city, you know."

Keaton laughed. "No, his family ain't from Athens, Georgia. I doubt he's ever been to Earth. He was born right here on Krifay. His last name isn't Savant. It means someone who is a kind of a genius in one or two areas. It's a gift straight from the good Lord. That boy probably already knows more about programming than I will ever learn."

Ricky tilted his head slightly and said, "Well damn."

"Yeah," Keaton agreed. "And you were worried about someone welding better than you."

"Why do ya reckon they are so good…and fast?" Ricky asked.

"Well, near as I can figure, they repair ships and transfer shuttles, refrigeration units, boats, transports, and everything else on this island and several more," Keaton said. "Time is money when you're dealing with perishable goods. Looks like they pulled folks from every one of their other shops and brought 'em here."

"You might be right."

"And," Keaton continued, "it's all work, right here, on the surface of the planet. They couldn't do this in space, or even up there in a shipyard. Right now, they only have to worry about their work—not protective suits, power sources for the suits, recharging, airflow, punctures, or a half dozen other things that can get ya killed up there."

"It does make a difference," agreed Jyrall as he walked up. "Space is an unforgiving environment."

"Yep," Ricky said. "Where's Larth? I wanted to go to Mike's shop and take a look at low velocity rounds and flechette grenades. I figure he'd like to go to."

"He is with Ban-Tilk. Larth is helping him learn the mannerisms of Nay-Thok," Jyrall answered. "You know how he sees every detail at a glance. I study things, but Larth seems to take it all in at once and study it in his mind. It's uncanny."

"Well, he chased that joker for a bit; he ought to know how he moves," Ricky agreed. "It ought to go over good. I mean, all them Jeha look near 'bout the same."

"I will concede the race shares very similar traits with one another, but there are differences," Jyrall said. He gave Ricky a look of disappointment.

"Yeah," Ricky said. "I didn't mean it like that. Hell, folks think Pushtal look the same. Our stripes are different; they's different colored ones, too. I meant, if the security forces never actually saw him in person, they ain't gonna know the difference 'cause video don't convey enough."

Jyrall's attitude changed. "True. But it's better to err on the side of caution. Larth is working with him." He turned to go, stopped, and looked back. "Keaton, are the virus program and the drive ready? They are vital to the success of the plan."

"They are," Keaton said. "I used the stargate simulation files, and I may or may not have hacked into the one here in Krifay. With the information gained, I wrote a good 'un. I am sure it will screw up their scanning capabilities, and they won't even know it."

"Good job. Make two of them. One for each of the Bakulu. We are not sure which will be given the opportunity to plug it in."

Keaton held up two small drives. "Way ahead of ya, Boss. I even made sure the two drives won't cause an issue with each other if both get inserted in different places in the stargate."

Jyrall grinned in approval. His showing of teeth startled a pair of odd, long-legged beings carrying a section of hose. They made a wide berth around the three of them. Jyrall looked down and shook his head.

"Scared the shit out of them," Ricky said, laughing. "That's funny right there. I don't care who you are."

"Speaking of which," Keaton said, "I wonder what race they are?"

"I don't know," Jyrall admitted. "There are thousands of races. One can't know them all. I do know it's not the first time I have startled their kind. It happened in a drinking establishment on our commissioning mission. It was the same reaction."

The big Besquith watched the pair from a distance and shrugged. "I am going to speak to Colonel Brentale. I did some research, and Ban-Tilk is right. The man is honorable, as are his troops."

"Well, good luck, 'cause we need all the help we can get," Ricky said.

* * *

"Colonel Brentale. May I have a moment of your time?" Jyrall asked, as he sat down at the bar with one stool between them. The establishment was empty, save for the two of them. It was far too early in the day for the normal patrons.

"Sure," the man said. "From what Mike tells me, it's why the place is open early, and the bartender is scarce. I took his advice and agreed to the meeting, though the last meeting I had with your kind was…well, let's just say it was rough."

"Mike is a good man," Jyrall said. "Honest in his dealings and discreet beyond measure."

"He is. The bartender left these for us before he went to run errands." Colonel Brentale pushed a bottle of water in front of Jyrall. "Mike and I were in a company together when I first started out. He took a round or two, healed up, and walked away from the mercenary game. Not far away, but he doesn't take contracts anymore."

The mercenary turned his stool to face Jyrall. "So, what would you like to speak about? A contract? I will be honest with you, I'm not in the frame of mind to take on one. The last one was supposed to be easy. It was, except we ended up stranded. It's not the best of times for those of my race and in my profession."

"I am aware," Jyrall said. "And I know of your previous plight. Ban-Tilk told me about it."

Colonel Brentale sat up straighter. "You know Ban-Tilk?"

"Yes," Jyrall said. "He has agreed to the endeavor I am proposing."

"All right, you have my attention," Colonel Brentale said. "Ban-Tilk is how we got back home."

"Now *I* am listening," Jyrall said. "Please continue."

"Well, we're not a big company, you understand. Never have been," the colonel said as he rubbed the side of his face, where the beginning of a beard was evident. "A platoon of mechs, eight including mine, and a platoon of old-fashioned infantry. They're good troops, all of them; it's just that there are only thirty of us."

He took a sip and continued, "It was a simple security job. We deployed and guarded a mine site while exploration was going on. It didn't pan out after the two-month contract, so the renewal option wasn't picked up by the mining company.

"I don't own a ship." He shrugged. "The transport company flaked out on us and didn't come get us. It's a small colony, but I was able to get a message out. I had to be careful how it was worded. Long story short, Mike sent Ban-Tilk to get us."

"Really? He did not mention that," Jyrall said. His estimation of the Jeha was going up rapidly.

"Probably because of the discount he gave us. To be honest, I think he spent more than we paid him to bribe the gate master. I know, beside the bribe, the fees to use the gate were outrageous. Between paying Ban-Tilk and the jump fees, I went into the hole." He grimaced. "It's a good thing I had saved some for a rainy day. Anyway, once we were out of there, I don't think he mentioned the load he was carrying on the next jump."

"That may be why he was on Springton looking for a high paying run," Jyrall thought out loud.

"You do know him," Colonel Brentale said. He gave the Besquith a hard look. "Just who are you?"

Jyrall reached into a hidden pocket and pulled out a small, flat case. He put it on the bar and opened it. The badge caught the light from the nearest display case. "I am Peacemaker Jyrall, Colonel. Well met."

Colonel Brentale reached out his hand, grinned, and said, "Call me Pete."

* * *

Weqq

As they ran east, Kurrang asked Tok, "What does 'thread the needle' mean? Or do I want to know?"

Tok grunted. "One of the ships will make a break for the surface while the other one holds their position and keeps the Crusaders from firing on the Blue Ridge Kin. It's a standard flight operations maneuver. We just don't practice it that much."

"Can you be sure the Crusaders won't fire anyway?"

"No," Tok said. "But the likelihood of it is pretty low. That is assuming, of course, they have a conscience, unlike their leader."

"Are you familiar with the Human word fanatic?" Kurrang asked.

The Jivool nodded. "I am. He certainly fits the bill."

"So, going back to my original question, what does thread the needle really mean, Tok?"

"The Crusader ships and the Tangos are in close proximity, meaning they are probably on the same orbital plane and at a slight difference in speed. Undoubtedly, the Crusaders are going to attempt to catch the Kin. Depending upon how close they are, they could fire, but most likely, they're going to close in for the kill. The Tangos will execute a maneuver and charge straight at them."

"Sorry, Enforcer, but that's not how orbital mechanics works." Kurrang grinned with one side of his mouth.

"I wasn't being disingenuous, Kurrang. What will end up happening is one of the ships will deorbit right in front of the Crusaders. The shock factor of a fast translation and firing of the engines should freeze the other pilots or cause them to take evasive action. It should be enough to slow the Crusaders down and give the Blue Ridge Kin a window to escape."

Kurrang chuckled as they continued to run. "That's a much better explanation, Enforcer. Do the same with the rest of your communications in the future, and you might just make it, young one."

"Is that a compliment?"

"The closest you're going to get for now. If your team gets us off this planet alive, I'll give you another one. That's a promise."

* * *

Tango Veritas

"*Equitas*, are you ready?" Zevva asked.

Mratt replied, "All I have to do is translate the ship, and we're ready to go. I've got a position fix on Tok from his slate. Not seeing much of a ground pursuit at the moment, but the Crusaders have deployed flyers."

Kravon chimed in from his console, "The *Righteous* is closing fast. The other ships are holding back. I wonder why?"

"Like I said," Zevva replied, "they don't want to draw the ire of the Enforcers. If this Crusader experiment goes any more haywire, they realize the Enforcers may be the ones sent to clean up any loose ends. I wouldn't want to be in our crosshairs, would you?"

Kravon laughed. "Not at all. I have weapon solutions on the *Righteous*. I'm ready to fire."

"We're not going to fire unless fired upon. Don't even fully spool up the charge. The whole idea is that we present a threat. If they monitor that threat and they have any shred of common sense remaining, they won't fire either."

"I hope you're right," Kravon said.

Me, too, thought Zevva.

She adjusted her position. For a SleSha, it wasn't pleasant to sit strapped into a multi-species couch. She hoped her gambit was correct. It certainly didn't seem possible the Crusaders would engage two Tango corvettes, but she'd learned not to underestimate Humans. They could be unconscionably brave and incredibly naïve. Yet, if there was a shred of decency in any of them, there would be a moment of hesitation. The critical thing was timing their hesitation so the Blue Ridge Kin could recover their dropships and shunt away.

"Status on those Blue Ridge ships?"

Mratt replied, "They've taken one dropship aboard; working on the second now. Sensors are indicating the first ship, *Kellie's Stand*, is powering up its shunts and preparing to jump."

"Estimated time remaining for the other one?" Zevva asked. She glanced at the mission timer on the pilot's console.

"Sixty seconds," Mratt replied.

"Standby to translate, *Equitas*," Zevva said.

"Roger, *Veritas*. I'm ready."

"Distance to the *Righteous*?" Zevva asked Kravon.

"A hundred kilometers and closing. They're well within our weapons' envelope."

"Hold your fire. I wasn't kidding about that. If they fire anything, target the weaponry and not the ship itself. Tok says to cover the Kin's jump, and that's exactly what we're going to do."

"Understood," Kravon replied.

"*Equitas*, this is *Veritas*. Translate and burn. Thread the needle."

"Translating," Mratt replied. On her central Tri-V screen, Zevva watched the Tango corvette pirouette in place, orienting its nose at the *Righteous* but slightly down toward the planet.

"Burning now."

The Tango's engines came to life, and the corvette immediately moved to close the distance on the *Righteous*, as the Crusaders' ship slowed down and began its descent to the planet.

Now we see if they flinch.

Zevva didn't have to wait long. Despite the obvious trajectory toward the planet, the *Righteous* took evasive action and swung its nose toward space and boosted. Reaction control thrusters along the underside of the ship fired simultaneously. It was enough to break their firing solution.

"The second Blue Ridge Kin vessel has captured its dropship. They're powering up now," Kravon called.

Zevva's eyes were still on the *Equitas* and the scrambling fleet of Crusader ships in its wake. "Let me know when they jump."

"You got it, Boss."

Zevva laughed. "Maybe, one day, I will be the boss."

She glanced at the Tri-V and just happened to see both of the Blue Ridge Kin's ships disappear. "They've jumped."

"Now, what are going to do?" Kravon asked.

"We're going to get our Enforcers off the planet. While we're doing that, you and I have to make sure we don't get destroyed here in orbit."

"So, what are we gonna do?"

"Stay out of their weapons range and elude their pursuit. We'll see how good the Humans are at pin the tail on the donkey."

Kravon laughed for a long moment and then stopped. "What's a donkey?"

* * *

Weqq

Roughly ninety minutes after the orbital engagement, the *Fortissimo*, the shuttle from *Tango Equitas*, set down in a clearing in the jungle more than thirty kilometers from the assembly area. The Crusaders had not bothered to chase them. Perhaps they were tracking them and waiting to deploy their CASPers or flyers, but, overall, it didn't matter to Kurrang. They made it to a safe zone, and the Peacemaker corvette would be capable of getting them out quickly and returning any hostile fire with authority.

"ETA is sixty seconds," Mratt called over the radio to Tok's slate.

"Copy, sixty seconds," the Jivool replied. They'd taken a position in thick foliage along the perimeter of the clearing. In front of them was a veritable sea of long grasses fluttering in a slight, warm breeze.

There was a rustle of movement in the foliage on the far side of the clearing. Several bird-like urrtam suddenly shot up into the air. The carnivorous flyers unsettled him, but their movement was a warning. "Contact," Tok said.

Kurrang shook his head. "It's coming from the wrong direction. Humans can move fast in those mechanical suits, but not that fast. It's something else."

No sooner had the words left Kurrang's mouth, than the familiar form of a TriRusk appeared. The clearing was more than a kilometer wide, and without warning Tok of his intentions, Kurrang broke into a run to cross the distance. He was almost to the other side when the corvette flared for landing and touched down in the middle of the clearing.

The closer he got to the far tree line, the more TriRusk he could see. In the midst of them was the colony leader, Nurr. Kurrang made his way directly to her.

"What are you doing here, Nurr? You should be in the caverns."

"You are right, Kurrang. It is time for us to return. Is there a way to get passage on that ship?"

Kurrang shook his head. "The Tango is not big enough. I can arrange to have someone come get you, but it's going to be at least a fortnight."

Nurr looked pensive for a moment, her lower jaw working from side to side, and, finally, her eyes came back up to his. "That will be acceptable. I worry that our own vessel may be in far too poor condition to do what we need it to do."

Kurrang nodded. "That is a wise concern. I can certainly arrange for the Peacemakers to come get you."

"No," she replied. "Not the Peacemakers. Your Enforcers seem to have a conscience, but I cannot trust the Peacemakers now.

"Not even Jessica Francis?"

"We wouldn't be in this position had she not come along when she did, Kurrang. I'm afraid not," Nurr replied. "These Crusaders have evaporated any trust I had in that guild. I shudder to think of the complications with their continued operations in the Galactic Union. This is why we must return, if for no other reason than to resist the Peacemaker Guild."

"I do not believe my guild is the enemy, Nurr."

"But you cannot be sure, Kurrang. Perhaps, in the next fortnight, you will find some evidence to support your position and assuage my doubts, but, until then, I will not ask the Peacemakers for anything, including protection. They do not bear my trust."

"I understand," he replied with an audible sigh. "I will do my best to prove my guild's behavior remains at the high standard of what it is intended to be."

"You do that, Kurrang. Safe travels." Nurr nodded her elongated head solemnly.

Kurrang answered the gesture in kind. "I will return in a fortnight, Nurr."

She turned away toward the jungle, motioning the other TriRusk he could see back toward another one of their hiding places.

Not wanting to risk engagement or capture, Kurrang turned and ran to the waiting shuttle. He climbed the ramp with a sense of guilt and shame. As guilty as he felt for leaving his people, again, an overwhelming new feeling rose in his chest. He was mad. Disappointed and angry. How could his guild have come to this?

Guild Master Rsach will answer for this.

* * * * *

Chapter Eighteen

Barnstormer's HQ

Snapper Isle

Krifay

Jyrall looked across the warehouse at the equipment belonging to Brentale's Barnstormers. On one wall, plugged into familiar racks, were seven Mk 6 CASPers and a Mk 7. From his limited time around the machines, Jyrall could tell from the indicator lights on the racks that each mech was fully charged.

To his inexperienced eye, they looked to be in good shape. There were no puddles beneath them like a few had when they entered what used to be the ship belonging to Redd's Raiders. Ricky had been livid at the shape those war machines were in. Jyrall remembered what he called them. *A fahr hazard.*

"I see some repairs have been made," Jyrall said. He was referring to the slightly mismatched color of armor on a few of the Mk 6s. "The 7 looks practically new."

"Yeah," Pete agreed. "My cousin Giles bought it and had it shipped to me. I have no idea where he came across it. He has been in another system, mining his claim, for years."

"They are not cheap," remarked Jyrall. "He must have done very well mining."

"After years of struggling, he finally struck it rich," Pete said, with a nod. "Several times before that happened, he contracted with me when times were hard. Ran a squad for me. He was always a little jumpy, but once shit hit the fan, you didn't have to worry about him. He was a good junior NCO."

"You say 'was.' Is he part of your company now?" Jyrall asked. He hoped he wasn't being insensitive. It was possible the colonel's cousin had been killed in action, which was the fate of most Human mercenaries.

"Giles? No. He was always pretty lucky. He took out a merc, one of your kind, on Quainerth…with a knife."

"A knife? That does not sound lucky to me. I am impressed. The man must be a skilled fighter." Jyrall extended the claws on both paws. "A Besquith carries handfuls of blades at all times." He relaxed and flexed his digits several times.

Jyrall paused. "Is that not in the Opulogg System? I am unaware of any conflict there in the past. It is a planet inhabited by a docile race. They avoid any type of conflict, normally."

"It is," Pete said. He reached up and scratched his growing beard. "But you know how it is when you involve credits—well, red diamonds waiting to become credits. Normalcy gets tossed overboard like chum, and the sharks start circling the boat."

"You have a point…and the reference is apt," Jyrall agreed. "As a matter of fact, it is perfect."

"I may be a merc by trade," Pete said, "but deep down, I'll always be that boy on my father's boat on the ocean, hoping to catch the big fish of the trip. Bragging rights among my cousins."

"I love fish," Jyrall said. He looked past the mechs and beyond the racks of weapons and body armor typical of the infantry. In the far corner was a boat, obviously large enough to fish from beyond sight of land. "I have never been fishing, though."

"Maybe, once this all settles down, I can take you," Pete said. "It'll be a good time. Of course, we need to survive the upcoming contract."

"So, you will take the contract?" Jyrall asked. "Excellent."

"Of course, Peacemaker. And not just for the payment you have offered," Pete said. "It's a good cause. Perhaps the only cause right now." Pete shrugged. "I will admit, a large shuttle capable of jumping without the need for a gate and some credit to pay my troops is an outstanding offer and one I would be crazy as hell to turn down. With some modification to its cargo hold, I can squeeze my company in it and never have to worry about being stranded again. If I remove one of the berths, I can even get the gliders in."

"Gliders?" Jyrall asked. He looked back at the equipment.

Colonel Pete Brentale walked over to a shallow locker, opened it, reached in, and pulled out a collapsing wing. It spread open toward him. "Two per locker. Powered hang gliders. They're popular here on Krifay. Well, not powered, but you can imagine seeing them at the beaches and taking off from some of the cliffs."

"Hence the name Barnstormers," Jyrall said, understanding. "My crew members have explained what Humans call a barn. I am aware of the term. How many times have you used them?"

"Well, we have only dropped into a hot zone four times, but we train all the time," Pete said. "It's not cheap hiring a transport company willing to go low enough for us to use them. Maybe I can get the shuttle modified to be a dropship, too. Eight mechs step out of the back, and eighteen troops leap out and pop their wings when it comes time."

"It would be a surprise insertion, if you can cut the power to the gliders," Jyrall said. He motioned to the lockers. "Those are not Human made, and they are not cheap."

"Nope," Pete agreed. "My cousin Giles, again. We only had regular gliders back in the beginning. Then they came upon the Sidar and the Midderalls—flying aliens. But it wasn't as scary as they thought. Especially when they found the gliders. I mean, Humans have messed around with glider designs for like five hundred years. But these? We're not sure where they came from, but they're damned handy."

"So, where is this wealthy cousin of yours?" Jyrall asked.

"I have no clue," Pete confessed. "After his mother died of natural causes, a Peacemaker showed up, and we haven't heard from him since. I like to think he is out there, doing good things. Don't take this wrong, but good things for humanity."

"I do not take it wrong. Let us hope he is. Humanity can use all the help it can get," Jyrall said, with an understanding nod.

"I miss him," Pete admitted. "Even if he was off a little, you know?" He twirled a finger in a circle beside his ear.

"Off?" Jyrall asked as they walked out of the warehouse into the bright light of early afternoon.

"Yeah. The guy believes in myths and rumors. I mean, nothing really crazy, you know, but he thinks Depiks are real. Can you imagine?"

"I can imagine being around someone known to be different, yes," Jyrall said. He was careful with his answer. Some things were not spoken of.

"What kind of time frame are we looking at, Peacemaker?" Pete asked. "I had my XO send out the recall. My troops will start arriving from all over the planet tomorrow. I need to knock the rust off and get 'em up to speed. A stargate is all indoor work…and I mean all. Lately, we've been doing security work. This one will be infiltration and clearing."

"Afterward, it will be a security mission. We will need to hold it against all comers," Jyrall said. "The good thing is you can place your mechs as deterrents in the docking bay and at strategic points within."

"Once we take it, we can damn sure hold it. It's what we do," Pete said, sure of his troops' capabilities.

"Confidence is an admirable trait," Jyrall said, nodding in approval. "The other mercenary company I spoke of will arrive within three days, give or take a few hours." He paused and added, "If they come."

"If?" Pete asked.

"If," confirmed Jyrall. "If they do not, we will adjust the plan. Either way, we must embark then, Colonel."

"Roger that, Peacemaker," Pete said. "I agreed to the terms, and a deal is a deal. What the hell does a man have in this universe if he doesn't have his word? You get the contract ready, and I'll sign."

* * *

"Hey, Snarlyface, look at these," Larth said. He stood with his hands on his hips, looking into a medium-sized box.

"Is it alive? Will it bite?" Jyrall asked. He gave both Larth and Ricky a look that showed he meant business.

"What?" Larth asked. He looked at Ricky. Ricky looked at him. They both started laughing. "No. It is not alive. Ricky scored us a whole box of flechette grenades from Mike."

"Oh, all right, then," Jyrall said, relieved. "Good. They may come in handy in the upcoming fight."

"Oh yeah," Ricky agreed. "I'm 'bout to make a few that will blow on impact."

"You be careful, you greasy fingered hillbilly," Keaton said, as he looked up from the slate he was reading. "One of these days, you're dang Ricky Shit is gonna get a feller hurt."

"Nah," Ricky said, waving him off. He looked at Larth. "Jyrall thought we had another box of crabs. He shore don't like them when they are still alive, does he?"

"Nope," Larth said. He rubbed his hands together and grinned wickedly. "But it gives me an idea. Well, maybe when we get back. There's too much going on now."

"I heard that," Jyrall said as he poked his head back around the corner.

"Heard what?" Larth said, his eyes wide with innocence. "I didn't say anything. You must be hearing voices. Don't be embarrassed, it happens to all of us."

Ricky and Keaton looked at Larth, pursed their lips, and, with widened eyes, slowly shook their heads no.

* * *

Location: CLASSIFIED

A chime from his slate disrupted Guild Master Rsach from his work. With the collapse of the Mercenary Guild, the need for Peacemakers to adjudicate contract disputes had not lessened. In fact, there were seemingly more disputes than ever. Additionally, more of his Peacemakers seemed to be putting themselves in harm's way. The growing conflicts were not limited to the Crusaders and their actions pacifying entire regions of the galaxy.

Across the Union, Peacemakers were continuously being placed in escalating situations. Lives were being lost. As such, his job had never been more important. Yet the chime was one he could not ignore. With a tap on his slate, Rsach secured the doors to his private quarters and engaged the transmission capability. The synthetic, monotone voice of Counselor came through almost immediately.

"Efforts on the planet Weqq have culminated. Captain Kurrang has been apprehended. But the Human mercenary company known as the Blue Ridge Kin have abandoned their post."

Rsach kept his surprise from showing. "I'm sorry, did you say Captain Kurrang has been apprehended?"

"This is what Crusader Prime reports," Counselor said. "He is unwilling to share the details of his mission. He only said he apprehended and then lost Captain Kurrang."

"Crusader Prime does not have the need to know."

"I disagree, Guild Master, and I have informed Crusader Prime about Captain Kurrang's mission. You forget your place. I decide who has the need to know in Crusader operations, Guild Master."

Rsach leaned his segmented body back against the couch. He tried to keep his antennae from bobbing in agitation. "Securing the TriRusk and bringing them back as viable members of the society is not within the Crusaders' mission set. That's why I gave the mission to Captain Kurrang. He alone is responsible for that operation and their repatriation. And what do you mean he lost Captain Kurrang? Explain."

"It does not matter, at least not yet. Captain Kurrang and young Enforcer Tok have apparently eluded capture by the Crusaders and escaped into the jungle."

This is getting worse and worse by the moment.

Rsach maintained his thoughtful ruse. "And what of the Blue Ridge Kin? You said they abandoned their post?"

"It would appear the Humans have issues with our methods. This is contradictory because of the makeup of the Crusaders themselves. I do not understand why some Humans can fall in line quickly while others resist the inevitable."

The inevitable?

"They must have their reasons for abandoning their post. I'm sure they go far beyond disagreement with our methods. The Kin are a hybrid unit. Humans are only part of their complement."

"They are not your concern. I will handle the Blue Ridge Kin."

"And how do you plan to do that? They are a Human mercenary company, operating within the bounds of their guild. They have not been deputized, nor are they active agents of the Crusaders. From a legal perspective, our guild has no control over what they do."

"I said I will take care of it," Counselor replied, but there was a hint of frustration in its synthesized tone. Rsach decided to push against it.

"How? By force? Because, again, that's not what the Crusaders are for. They are not to attack mercenary companies operating within the bounds of their organization."

"I have let the Blue Ridge Kin go. They are Human and will make a mistake. Their folly is inevitable, and when they make that mistake, we will capitalize on it and resolve the situation."

"You sound as if you believe this for all of humanity. Is that true?"

"It is. We will watch them, and Kurrang as well. When the time comes, we will honor the threat they portray."

Rsach bristled. "May I remind you we have three Human Peacemakers? And potentially more entering the academy in the next year. Yes, they are unpredictable, but they have proven steadfast and strong in the performance of their duties."

"You place too much faith in them. We will rectify that situation soon enough."

Gods. You're not rectifying anything if I can help it.

"Then what are your orders?"

"Do not confuse my position of authority with one capable of ordering you to do anything. You have merely agreed. You are bound to deploy the assets of the Peacemaker Guild as I see fit. Do not make me invoke the name of the first Peacemaker again."

The name of the first peacemaker was one of the closest held secrets of the Peacemaker Guild. It was something only guild masters knew and was the equivalent of a master key to certain situations and communications. An entire room on Kleve, locked down well underground, could only be entered by one who knew the name. Yet Counselor was not a prior guild master—of that Rsach was certain. For one thing, all the previous guild masters were dead. True, Counselor's knowledge base contained far more information than he knew as an incoming guild master. Counselor seemed capable of communicating everywhere at once. His hold on intelligence information and communications was unlike anything Rsach had ever seen. For that reason, and his statements about humanity, Rsach realized with a jolt he could no longer trust Counselor.

I should never have trusted him from the beginning.

Counselor continued, "At the earliest opportunity, you will recall the Human Peacemakers."

"That's a bit difficult right now. Lieutenant Francis is separated from duty to assist with the Depik at my personal behest. Peacemaker Sinclair is in deep cover. Peacemaker Rains, from what I understand, has left Force 25, and I have been unable to locate him."

"You misunderstand me, Rsach. Recall them immediately. Order them to meet you soon on Diam at the Acropolis in the Ghumm system. I will determine the precise date at a later time. That will be more than enough time for this gambit to play out."

"And I'm supposed to do what with them?" Rsach asked.

"If I see fit, you will terminate them."

*****

Chapter Nineteen

Blue Ridge
Hyperspace

"We will make transition in ten minutes. Ten minutes, that is," Monty said. "We should let the colonel know. Know, don't you know."

"Roger, I say, roger it is," Stew answered. "I'll send it over the ship's comms. The ship's, of course."

"Of course," Monty agreed.

"The ship's," Stew confirmed, nodding vigorously. The wide floppy brim of his lime green hat waved comically.

Stew, sitting in the co-pilot's seat, reached up and engaged the internal comms. "Blue Ridge Kin, Kin, I say. We will be entering normal space in approximately nine minutes. Nine, don't you know. Please check your uniforms, scarves, hats, and gloves. One must always look their best. The best, I say."

The colorful Miderall looked toward the pilot's seat and saw Monty shake his head no at him, but he continued anyway. "Upon arrival, if we have down time, time, I say. I will be happy to help anyone coordinate their outfit. If you feel you are lacking in appropriate colors, Monty and I have some new cloth. New, you understand."

Monty looked down and shook his head, his large beak moving back and forth. "First Sergeant Figgle is going to kill us. Kill, you remember. You know he said to stop trying to 'froo-froo' his troops. Whatever that may mean. Mean, he is."

Stew waved him off with a flourish of his arm, the bright feathers clashing with the neon-blue ruffled sleeve. He continued speaking into the ship's comms. "Sadly, we don't have much, but perhaps a thin yellow scarf, a scarf, don't you know, to go with a pair of slip-on purple cuffs will make you more appealing to those of refined taste, taste, I say. This has been a message from the operations center. A message, you understand."

"We are a pair of dead Mideralls. Dead," Monty said as he adjusted the image on a screen. "You know we have been instructed to stop giving fashion advice. Advice, that is."

"If they ask for it, it is not the same. The same, you understand," Stew argued.

"Explain that to the first sergeant," Monty said. "Explain, I say. Just because Colonel McCoy has decided to promote the four of us pilots to warrant officers does not mean we outrank him. We do…but we most certainly do not, if you know what I mean. *Do not.*"

"That is what Diamich and Skirith said as well," Stew said, referring to the two SleShas piloting *Kellie's Stand*. He adjusted his hat. "I am so confused by the rank structure, structure, that is. Some ranks are higher than others…but not in reality. Not, I say."

Specialist Conner unstrapped from her station in the rear of the center, put her headset on the console, ensuring the Velcro held, turned, reached for a strap, and eased out the rear hatch.

* * *

Cora looked up at one of the overhead speakers, listened, and grinned. She looked at First Sergeant Figgle, still grinning. The Goka was practically trembling with rage. He kept opening and closing several of his small pincers in anticipation.

"Calm down, Top," Cora said. "You can't kill them; we need them. I will never find pilots as good as they are. The closest two are in the operations center on our other ship."

"But...but..." the First Sergeant stammered.

"You can speak to them," she consoled. "Make sure no one else is around. Since I promoted them to warrants, they actually outrank you. Now, I know the deal, believe me I do, but we can't have the troops witness the...dressing down you are authorized to give them."

"Fine, ma'am," he was finally able to get out. "No killing." He unstrapped from his seat, pushed up and back, and skittered out of the conference room using every surface he could grab in a hurry. They heard him mutter as he went, "I'll choke one out. I'll grab his skinny neck and choke him right out and make the other revive him. That's what I'll do."

"Are you sure it's a good idea to let him go up front now?" Nileah asked. "Top is pissed."

"Aw, he may act that way," May said, "but he won't really hurt them." She paused and asked, "Will he?"

"No," Cora assured her. "He knows we need them. The way we were able to leave Weqq and transition out; that took some extraordinary skill at the controls of both ships. Even with the Enforcers' help, I don't think normal pilots could have managed it. He may scare them half to death, but he won't hurt them. He's the first sergeant; it comes with the territory."

Lisalle laughed. "How fast do you think Specialist Conner will get out of the operations center?"

"Even money says she left before Stew finished speaking," Cora said. She grinned again. "Now, about the message I received."

"Yeah," May said. "I'm confused."

"Kurrang said to drop everything and head to Krifay and be prepared to jump shortly after arrival. He didn't say to where, but I suspect it's important," Cora said. "We will know the answer shortly. Jyrall and Larth are waiting for us."

"Well, we'll be ready," Nileah said. "I got an 'up' from Corporal Rodgett. He says all three are cleared for full duty."

"Already?" May asked. "I knew it was minor stuff on both Goka, but I thought Rynard was hurt more than that."

"He says they are good to go," Nileah said. "Apparently, when you use combat nanites on a through-and-through, it heals purty dang quick. There was no bone damage, and the shrapnel missed any veins or whatever a Jivool has in its shoulder. He says Rynard is good, and Rynard insists he is."

"If it was just a flesh wound, why the nanites?" Lisalle asked. "That's a bit much, and it's not cheap."

"It's better to err on the side of caution," Cora said. "Hell, I agree. Rodgett said he was just guessing with most of it. He has some stuff downloaded on all the races in our company, but firsthand experience is the real teacher, I reckon."

"Maybe we need medics for every race," May suggested.

"I wish," Cora agreed, "but it's not realistic. What do we have, six races within the company now? Who knows how many more we'll gain."

"I can see us growing," Nileah said. "Some more CASPers. I'm sure there are mercs out there looking for a company. They may own their own war machines. Not many, but there have to be some. If there ain't none looking for a unit, maybe we can get those tanks we talked about. It don't matter to me none what race operates 'em, long as they have what it takes to be Kin."

"You and your heavy weapons," May said. "Whoever joins the Kin, and as big as we've become, I just hope we don't lose any."

"That's not realistic, either," Cora said.

The room was silent.

* * *

"Here she comes," Keaton said. "The ship is scheduled to hit the tarmac in four minutes. Looks like she is right on time. I wonder who's piloting the dropship?"

"It is not a Miderall," Jyrall said. "Several of the members of the Kin are qualified to operate the dropships."

"It might be Squarlik," Ricky said. "He's purty good with a stick. We was zipping all around them on Parmick."

"That was the hovercraft," Keaton reminded him. "Not a combat dropship."

"Same thang," Ricky said. "Left, right, fast, go faster. Same concept."

"What about stopping?" Jyrall asked.

"Brakes?" Ricky said, "Pfffft." He waved it off like it was an afterthought.

"Uh, even I know about brakes," Larth said. "I see why Keaton says to never let you drive anything."

Colonel Brentale looked over, his eyes wide. Learning the two brothers had been raised by Humans, with their mannerisms and speech, had been something of a surprise, but finding out one of them had no use for brakes was truly a shock. He glanced over at the staff sergeant standing beside him to see if he was as concerned. The man was grinning and shaking his head.

Keaton leaned close to him and whispered out of the side of his mouth, "Don't let that dang fool drive nuthin'."

Colonel Brentale was unable to answer as the noise from the dropship landing drowned everything out, so he nodded in acknowledgment.

The group waited for the back ramp to lower before walking toward the shuttle. Cora stepped off, followed by Nileah, Lisalle, and May. One more stepped out of the shadows.

"Is that a—" Colonel Brentale started to ask.

"Yes," Jyrall said. "A Goka."

"Interesting," the colonel said.

May broke free of the rest and ran to hug Larth. She gave the brothers and Jyrall a hug, as well. She shocked them when she recognized, squealed, and hugged the staff sergeant. Before anyone could ask why, the others had reached them.

"Cora," Jyrall said. "Allow me to introduce Colonel Brentale. Colonel Brentale, Colonel Cora McCoy."

"Call me Pete." He reached out and gave her a firm handshake. It wasn't the type of macho handshake and hard grip those thinking they had something to prove used. It was the firm handshake of a mercenary recognizing another in their chosen profession as an equal.

"I'm Cora," she said.

"I take it I don't need to introduce Staff Sergeant Jerund," Jyrall said. "Pete said you would recognize him."

"I do," Cora said. "Jimmy-Ray helped us out of a tight spot with our old unit. He's why we were able to leave with our mechs." She stepped over and gave Jimmy-Ray a quick hug.

"You're a colonel now, with your own company, ma'am," Jimmy-Ray said. "You sure you want to be seen hugging a staff sergeant?" He grinned as Nileah moved Cora to the side and took her turn.

"You hush your mouth," Cora said. "Us mountain folk stick together, even if you are from north Georgia."

Both of them moved aside so Lisalle could step up to greet the man who had been the maintenance NCO for their old unit. They knew what might happen. They were right.

Lisalle Jones stepped in front of the man she hadn't gotten to say goodbye to properly on the night they grabbed their gear and left the tattered remains of Talmore's Ridge Runners. They stared at each other.

"I'm sorry, I wasn't able to…" Jimmy-Ray tried to say.

"I know," Lisalle said. "Shhh." She kissed him, then stepped back, not caring who saw it. When they were in the same unit, very few had known about them. "I didn't know if I would ever see you again."

He reached up and brushed her dark hair away from her face. "When my contract ended, I got the hell away from Smith. A few of us did. I don't have no idea where anyone else went. I managed to pay for a ride here on a huge freighter. I figured it was better than trying to get back to Earth where I was a known merc. Cost me dang near every credit I had. Colonel Brentale gave me a contract and a CASPer to pilot."

"It was well worth it," Pete said. "Our CASPers have never been in better shape." He turned to Jimmy-Ray. "You looking to get out of your contract, Jerund? I'd hate it, but I would understand."

"No, sir," Jimmy-Ray said. "Forget the signed contract, I gave you my word. A man's word is worth more than some damn form. I'm a Barnstormer."

Lisalle grinned and punched his arm. "You dang well better not go acting like a flatlander with no honor."

"Besides," the staff sergeant said, "Peacemaker Jyrall says the Blue Ridge Kin are based out of Krifay now, so I'm good. We'll see where it goes."

Cora introduced her leaders to Pete. When she introduced First Sergeant Figgle, he stepped forward and reached out his hand. Pete felt a little awkward shaking hands with a Goka but was put at ease when Figgle said, "How the hell are you, sir?"

"Good, I'm doing good, First Sergeant," Pete said. "Let me introduce you to my sergeant major. Sergeant Major Daniels…"

Several members of the Barnstormers stepped forward, including the officers, to meet the command team of the Kin.

* * *

Jyrall watched the last of Brentale's Barnstormers load into the dropship. He turned to Cora. "It looks like they are ready. Thank you, again, for pretending the shuttle belonged to the

Blue Ridge Kin. The inspection of the power plant and shunts went well."

"Yeah," Cora agreed. "It helps that we used the same company to verify the Barnstormers who certified us. He didn't seem to mind that his company didn't do the actual repairs."

She saw Figgle step off the ramp, patiently waiting for her. "I reckon I need to get going, too. The other dropship should be leaving atmosphere by now. I spoke at length to Staff Sergeant Rhineder. He seemed relieved Colonel Brentele was among the half catching a ride with *Kellie's Stand.* I can't blame him. It's a lot for a career NCO to deal with. I really need to look into contracting actual ship commanders and crew."

"Perhaps, once we accomplish this mission, you will have the opportunity," Jyrall said.

"I hope so. It's not going to be easy, you know," she said. "Taking a stargate with more than its full crew of security? That's a tall order."

"I'd say," Larth said. "That's why we contracted the Barnstormers to help. I'm game for anything, but docking, entering, and preventing a takeover by taking one over? Even I hesitate there."

"We must," Jyrall said. "The Sumatozou on Nay-Thok's ship told me their plan was to infiltrate the gate and kill any security who could not be bribed. He was to take the place of the gate master once the real one was taken out."

"But why?" Cora asked. "Why take over a gate in a dead-end system? A system only used for training?"

"I do not know," Jyrall admitted. "Perhaps they planned to use that particular system to stage another attack on Earth or another system. With complete access to a gate, it would make what they planned that much more secretive."

"It's not like the Cartography Guild isn't already stacking the deck," Larth said. "Do you really think whoever is behind all this needs to take one over?"

"That is the question." Jyrall stroked his chin and replied. "Whatever they plan to do, we will prevent it. An uncontrolled gate is a problem waiting to happen. A gate in the hooves of Kr'et'Socae is a disaster."

"Well," Cora said. She smiled. "Figgle is starting to fidget. Let me get on board before he comes over here and hauls me away. We'll see you in Springton. I sure hope your arms dealer has what we need, Larth."

"They do," Larth said. "They have everything."

* * * * *

Chapter Twenty

300,000 km above Weqq
Tango Veritas

No sooner had the shuttle docked than the two Tango corvettes oriented themselves and burned for higher orbit and departure. The crew powered up the hyperspace shunts and prepared for transition. Kurrang and Tok, as well as the shuttle's pilot, Kravon, disembarked the vehicle and headed for the bridge.

They floated up the main passageway in a loose gaggle. No one spoke. Kurrang wondered if the Crusaders were giving chase. The two corvettes stood virtually no chance against anything larger or better armed. He knew the Enforcers knew their status and their capabilities better than anyone, yet Kurrang was more concerned whether the local gate, located on the far side of Weqq, had managed to send relevant data packages in time for their departure. Intelligence was scant, and he needed to know several critical details, if for no other reason than to calm his roiling stomach.

At the bridge, Tok keyed the hatch open. The SleSha pilot, Zevva, turned in her seat. "Captain Kurrang, well met and welcome aboard."

"Much obliged," Kurrang grunted. "Where can I sit? I need a Stormwatch connection."

"Over here," Tok said, indicating the forward position along the port bulkhead. "Are you looking for something in particular?"

Kurrang pushed off the hatch. "I'll know when I see it."

"That's helpful," Kravon said under his breath.

"Kravon?" Tok asked.

"What? We go down there and rescue the two of you, you let the rest of the TriRusk go, and then he can't even say thank you? Or tell us what he's looking for?"

Silence filled the room. A warning buzzer sounded from the commander's station. "We're being called from the planet. Crusader Prime," Zevva said.

"Don't answer it," Kurrang replied. "As a matter of fact, turn off that communications set entirely."

"But—"

"Do it," Kurrang replied. "Shut it completely down. They are not to be trusted. In person or their data."

"They could send some type of malicious message?" Kravon asked. He immediately shook his head. "Of course, they could. We have to stop thinking they're Peacemakers."

"They're little more than mercenaries," Zevva chittered. "Well-funded and well-equipped ones."

Kurrang snorted. "Young ones?"

He waited until every one of them gave him their attention before continuing.

"They're worse than anything you've ever dealt with in your careers. I am unconvinced the guild master is both fully aware of the situation or has approved the way these units operate. Crusader Prime, whoever he really is, is dangerous. The rest of his staff are barely competent and prone to violence. Their actions do not match up to their stated mission or intent."

"They executed prisoners, following surrender," Tok replied. "That's where things changed for me. For what it's worth, the captain is right. Things here don't make sense."

"So, what are we going to do about it?" Kravon asked. "I understand what you're saying about their conduct. If they really did execute those prisoners—"

"I saw them," Tok said. "Gods help me, I should've stopped them."

Kurrang didn't respond. Sometimes, guilt could be a powerful tool, but it had to be wielded with caution. The young Enforcer showed promise, and while he'd invariably learned a lesson, pouring salt in the wound, to turn a phrase, wasn't going to help. "What matters now," Kurrang said, "is that we get out of here before they can decide to give chase."

"We're still downloading data packets," Zevva replied. "It may be another hour."

Kurrang nodded. "If we have Stormwatch reports, it will be worth the wait."

"I'm not understanding, Captain," Tok said slowly. "What are you looking for?"

"It will be easier to show you." Kurrang harrumphed. "Can you put that station's screen displays on all these stations?"

"Everything except weapons," Zevva said. "I have solutions on the Crusader ships in view. Just in case."

"A worthy preparation." Kurrang half-smiled. There was no appreciable response. Given his earlier run-in with them, alongside Captain Dreel, he'd chosen a semi-violent response to their disrespect. For him to expect them to suddenly understand and appreciate his charm was naïve at best. He rubbed his long chin. "I'm not going to be able to change your impression of me without some reflection, conversation, and a bath. I understand your apprehension toward me. I deserve it, frankly. But make no mistake about this, Enforcers, we don't deserve what the Crusaders bring. This is unlike anything our guild has done in the last two hundred years. I cannot imagine what the catalyst for this action is, but we cannot allow it to stand."

"Stormwatch messages are on the workstation, Captain," Kravon said. "They look pretty standard to me. What are you looking for?"

"A message."

"Beyond the usual coding?"

Kurrang grunted. "Much. In this particular case, there are supplementary reports on administrative status in the reference data, yes?"

All of the young Enforcers nodded, suddenly interested. "We never read it," Tok replied for them. "It's for barracks commanders to request supplies and material."

"Obviously not," Zevva laughed. "Well, it is, but…"

"Precisely," Kurrang replied. "Let me show you."

He floated to the workstation and pulled up the most recent, or what he hoped was the most recent, report. With a glance over his left shoulder, Kurrang saw the others had taken seats and were staring at the report.

"What do you see?" he asked.

"Every barracks makes a report. Never more than a few lines," Tok said.

Kravon added, "Most things are alluded to—like see this report and the like."

"Which are likely valid reports," Zevva commented. She leaned closer to the screen. "The rest appears to be narrative. Casual. Almost conversational."

"Does the order of the messages change?" Tok asked suddenly. "Can they ever change?"

Kurrang smiled, impressed. "No, they remain the same."

"Are you thinking it's a code?" Kravon asked. "That could work. Like certain words from each."

"But just scanning them, there's not a discernable pattern." Zevva buzzed. "We all had cryptography and, if there's a code here, it has to have a key."

"It does," Tok replied. "But it can't be based on the individual letters. Each of the barracks commanders uses their own language in the raw form."

"That doesn't matter," Kravon said. "The translator would work the same for all the messages, wouldn't it?"

"Yes," Zevva replied. "So, it can't be based on individual letters or characters. It has to be words produced by the translator. But in what language?"

Kurrang wanted to laugh. They were close, but yet so far. "Keep going."

"Language, yes, but that could be arranged and agreed upon," Zevva said. "It has to be a pattern. Something that crosses the messages."

"That would mean messages could be edited. I thought barracks commanders outranked just about everyone in the chain of..." Kravon looked up at Kurrang. "This is something between captains, isn't it? A private message center."

Kurrang nodded. "And, to Zevva's point, it is pattern based. And the agreed upon language, in this case, is Human English."

"Why that?" Tok's face screwed in disgust. "Because it's weird?"

"Or just new to the guild?" Kravon asked.

"Because it's the least understood. They speak in colloquialisms and metaphors all the time. I can barely have a conversation with one, even if required." Zevva laughed. She stared at Kurrang. "Which makes it perfect for what you're doing."

"We like to think so," Kurrang replied. "These messages are used by Captain Dreel, primarily. His code for me is 198. Meaning, the first word from the first report, the ninth from the next, the eighth from the third, and then the whole sequence repeats until the message is complete."

All of the Enforcers pored over the messages. Kurrang did the same, and as he read, the light-hearted feeling he'd had melted away to cold fear.

Found primary subject via contract station Karma IV. Moving intercept assistance acquired. Arrive soon.

"Captain Kurrang?" Tok asked. "What does this mean? Who is the subject?"

Kurrang turned around. "This message is the last of the Stormwatch packets?"

"There's nothing else in the hopper. The remaining packets aren't big enough to hold a message," Kravon replied. "This is it, for now."

"The message is five days old," Zevva replied. "Captain Dreel is at Karma IV and he's moving on something, or someone, with backup. Yes?"

Kurrang nodded. "That's correct. But he's moving on Kr'et'Socae. Backup or not, he's in serious danger. Let us hope he decided to wait for us before he moves. How long until we can transition?"

Zevva replied, "We're ready now."

"Tell the *Equitas* what the situation is and have them set course for Karma," Kurrang replied. "If Dreel hasn't made his move, we can assist him and end this all right now."

"And if he has?" Tok asked.

Kurrang frowned. "Then gods help him and whoever he's with. Kr'et'Socae will not go down without blood."

* * *

Springton

"I'm going to need some help," Larth said.

"We can't go with you," Keaton said. "I need to reprogram the shuttle's registration back to its original. Ricky is in the middle of something back there. Ain't no tellin' what it is."

"We are repairing the damage to our mechs," Lisalle answered. "Speaking of which, we need to get back there and test them with the rest of the company."

"The first sergeant has the infantry troops gathering supplies," Cora said. "I have my pilots and the operations center specialists still onboard both ships monitoring incoming traffic to the system."

"Sergeant Squarlik and his guys are back from their supply run," Nileah suggested.

"Already?" Cora asked. "Maybe I should have laterally promoted him from corporal to specialist instead of up to sergeant—a permanent specialist. That guy can scrounge up anything."

"Yeah," Nileah agreed. "Sometimes, I have to make him take it back to our other ship where he got it. He says he only tactically acquires and then relocates things."

"Relocate. Right. I guess it is still within the company, so I can't really bust him for taking things." Cora sighed.

Pete Brentale laughed as if knew exactly the kind of soldier they were talking about. He likely had a couple. They always ran in packs. "I can go. I'll grab a few guys to handle the transport lifts. It's the least I can do since we'll be using the weapons, too."

"Good," Jyrall said. "We have a plan. I will locate the Sumatozou I spoke of. Cora, you ensure your equipment is battle ready. The McCoy brothers will do what they need to do here, and Pete will go with Larth to purchase the weapons and ammunition."

Cora smiled at hearing the McCoy name.

"Pete, take Sergeant Squarlik and his squad with your troops. The more hands…and pincers…the better," she said.

"Will do. Thanks."

The group stepped out from under the shadow of *Blue Ridge*. There, on the tarmac nearby, were *Kellie's Stand*, the large shuttle, and Ban-Tilk's freighter. The Jeha was making his way toward them. Cora waved to Jyrall to let him know she would see what the part-time smuggler needed.

"He's probably letting us know the Barnstormers can move their gear onto his freighter now," she said to Nileah. "Right on schedule."

* * *

Warehouse District

"This is the place," Larth said. "I think the troops can wait out here until they open the big door to move the gear out."

"This building?" Colonel Brentale asked. He read the sign out loud, "*Gatholonik*. I know this company."

"You do?" Larth asked. "You buy weapons from here?"

"Well, I know the clan name," Pete admitted. "Jivool, right? That's about my extent of reading their language. I know Colonel Hyvok Gatholonik, commander of the Slow Killers. I don't buy from here. I buy from him."

"Really?" Larth asked. He put his hands on his hips and looked up at the man. "You buy weapons and equipment from another mercenary company? One that is not even Human? That's crazy, and believe me, I know crazy."

"It's a long story," Pete said. "But I swear it's true. Once, long ago, we came up against each other. There was no fight. We both figured out about the same time we were being played by an Otoo. Anyway, we worked together to get our credits and ensured that Otoo and his company never hired mercenaries again. We've been friends ever since."

"What about stuff for your mechs?" Larth asked.

"Only the rockets," Pete said. "Obviously, I can't get CASPers from him. Every now and then, I get a shipment of pieces—scraps really. Whatever they happen to come across. Staff Sergeant Jerund has been able to use the pieces of armor to make patches."

"Just ships it right to you, huh?" Larth asked.

"No. It comes packed below false bottoms in freezer containers. Mike gets them from the freighters and then to me. There are a few steps involved."

Larth nodded and turned to the troops with them. "Squarlik, don't take anything. All of you wait out here until the bay door opens."

Larth looked at a soldier standing with his hands in the pockets of his fatigues. Compared to the other men in the Barnstormers, his hair was a little long, a millimeter from touching his ears and uncombed. "You. Keep an eye on him."

Pete shook his head. "Haney? Bad choice. Those two could teach each other a few tricks." He turned to an NCO. "Staff Sergeant Wilson, watch them both."

"Roger, sir," the woman said. She glared at Sergeant Squarlik and Specialist Haney.

Larth grinned and reached up to knock. Before he could, the door's locks disengaged. He and Colonel Brentale walked into the warehouse. Inside, Lilnitar was waiting with Wilgith.

"Colonel Brentale!" Wilgith said. "I thought it was you on the screen."

"Lieutenant Wilgith," Pete said. He put out his hand. "I saw the name on the building but didn't think I would see a Slow Killer inside. How are you?"

"I'm good, sir. Let me introduce you to my mate, Lilnitar, Colonel Gatholonik's daughter."

"It is good to meet you. I have heard Hyvok talk of you. Call me Pete."

"He speaks of you often," Lilnitar said. "I am sorry I was not home the time you visited Jawool."

"Looking around, I can see why," Pete said. "A new branch in the clan's business. You must stay busy."

"We are starting to build a list of clients," she said. "I see you know one of my new ones, Switch."

"Swit—Oh, yeah," Pete said, caught off guard by the name she used for the Peacemaker. "I know him."

"Since when does a Human mercenary company deal with notorious smugglers?" she asked. "Are all these weapons for your company? As I recall, you have about thirty mercenaries. I understand having a pistol as a backup, but Switch asked for sixty rifles and forty pistols, with flechette rounds and low power cells for some laser rifles, two cases of flechette grenades, smoke cannisters, and masks."

She paused, looking at them, and said, "The masks can be adjusted for multiple species. Except four of them. He asked for four masks specifically for Maki. You do not have Maki in your company. There is more here than I have been made to know." She crossed her thick arms and waited for an answer. Wilgith stepped up beside his mate.

"Yes!" Larth said, pumping a small fist, surprising the three of them. "Jyrall *always* gets to do this. It's finally *my* turn!"

The Zuparti started to smile, caught himself, and took on a serious look. He stood tall, reached inside his vest to his hidden pocket, and pulled out a small case. He opened it and revealed his badge.

"I am Peacemaker Larth. Well met," he said in his most serious voice. He tried to maintain the look but failed. His grin slowly stretched across his face.

* * *

Downtown

Jyrall walked into the establishment he last saw the sorrowful ex-gate master enter. He had tried four others on the same street before deciding to see if the Sumatozou still preferred the one closest to the Cartography Guild's local offices.

It was nearly empty this time of day. There, in the back, in a large corner booth, sat the being he was looking for. On the table in front of his ample belly were several empty bottles. There were three different types, indicating the Sumatozou didn't really care what he drank as long as he had one in his large hand.

That, or he is not really a drinker.

"Do you mind if I join you?" Jyrall asked. He indicated the other side of the booth.

"Don't care."

Jyrall eased onto the bench and was surprised it didn't shift. The bench had been designed for beings heavier than he was. He found himself pleased, and his look of surprise showed it.

The Sumatozou grunted. "Good seating here. Strong. It's why I prefer it. You pay for it through the drinks, I can assure you."

Jyrall looked at the small menu on the center screen and ordered a drink. "You will burn through your retirement in no time at these rates, my friend."

"Might as well. It's not like I will be adding to it, what little I have." He snorted loudly through both trunks. "The guild took their matching portion back when they exiled me."

"You didn't acquire a sizable portion for yourself through the years?" Jyrall asked.

"Don't you worry about what I acquired. Why all the questions anyway?" He squinted. "I don't know you."

"No. You don't," Jyrall said. The waiter came over with his water. Jyrall waited until he walked away, put a small device on the table, leaned back, and crossed his arms. "But I know of you."

"Why the scrambler?"

Jyrall didn't answer his question. Instead, he continued, "I know of you. I know you were put out of the guild for going against the rules and guidelines on multiple occasions. I know you helped Humans."

"What of it? The cursed guild sent out guidelines to strand them wherever they were, especially the mercenaries. I don't know why; they didn't really give a reason. I just know it was as if they were being hunted." The big being drained his bottle. "It didn't seem right to me, so I let a company leave a system without charging too much. I increased the standard rate, but I did not double it."

He shrugged his huge shoulders and slurred, "It shouldn't have mattered. I was master of a gate in a small system. The few inhabitable planets produced very little in the way of mining. I think it was due to be considered for shut down anyway. Maybe turned into a training and gate storage system like Shaylin."

He picked up his bottle, shook it, put it down and said, "All these years." He sighed. "I gave the guild everything. What did I get for it? Nothing. That's what. It was one awful assignment to the next. Always a system in the middle of nowhere. No traffic to speak of. And the time or two when big military fleets used the system, I was in for training."

He looked longingly at his empty bottle. "When you don't add much to the retirement fund, they don't give you the good assignments. Without a good assignment to begin with, you can't add to the funds. It's a ridiculous cycle, and one I couldn't seem to break free from."

"It does seem unfair."

"Yes. It is. One would think being skilled at one's profession would be enough to move up, not credits earned. I may have been from a long line of gate masters, but that was not why I chose the profession. I chose it for what it was, not for the credits I could earn. To be able to send ships across the vastness of space to far off systems…to places unexplored. Think of it. The science involved. The precision needed at the controls."

He stared off and said quietly, "You know, there are some races who still think it is some type of galactic sorcery. It is science…at its best." He paused. "And art. I was an artist at the controls."

"What is your name?" Jyrall asked.

"Argold. My name is Argold. I am the last in my family. A fourth generation gate master. Well, I was. Now, I am a first-generation failure. For the first time in my life, I am glad I have no family left." He reached for the small slate to order another bottle, something stronger this time.

"Allow me," Jyrall said as he input an order.

A minute later the waiter came over with a small blue bottle. He placed it on the table and bid them good day. Jyrall picked it up and handed it to Argold.

"What is this?" Argold demanded. "System Flush? I don't want to be sober. I want to get more inebriated." He squinted again. "Just who are you?"

Jyrall reached for his inner pocket.

*****

Chapter Twenty-One

Bartertown Spaceport

Karma IV

For two days, Dreel and Millzak kept tabs on all inbound shipments to Karma IV. While Dreel was a somewhat familiar face and was forced to lay low, Millzak was a virtual unknown. Given his extensive experience under cover, he not only blended into the citizenry of Karma, he virtually disappeared. Here, a Lumar was either a security guard, an out of work merc, or a faceless worker. No one saw him as a serious threat, much less a Peacemaker.

Dreel was only able to follow Millzak's moves using Karma's extensive closed-circuit television system, prearranged communications, and the oldest form of communication known— they were able to pass each other handwritten notes through a network of accomplices. Some of them were completely innocent except for having been in the wrong place at the right time. Using other GalNet message systems was out of the question. When Millzak asked him why, he'd shrugged.

"The time to trust has passed, Millzak."

Given his training and experience, defeating facial recognition systems was fairly easy for Peacemaker Millzak. So, they'd arranged for several different visual cues. The presence of Lumar on Karma wasn't all that unexpected, though with the recent troubles in the

Mercenary Guild, the familiar pits were often devoid of them. While there were plenty of Lumar mercenaries, Karma IV was not one of the places you would normally find them. Certainly, there were a few hundred at any given time, and those numbers were enough to guarantee his anonymity. Given his current disguise, using one crutch under his lower left shoulder and simulating a catastrophic leg injury, it was easy to follow Millzak. Yet he brilliantly decided to do something about his appearance. Temporary tattoos swirled around his head and face. He looked positively menacing. It was a brilliant and cunning play.

Gaining actual intelligence on Kr'et'Socae's moves and contacts on the planet was difficult, but they'd been able to ascertain several key facts. Their subject was currently not on the planet. It was believed he would be arriving soon to intercept the cargo Barlung had told Nikki Sinclair about weeks before. She was still on Parmick, investigating the goings-on there and looking for answers.

Barlung's initial testimony said Kr'et'Socae would be coming. When he did, there would be some indication of an inbound ship. Given there were hundreds, if not thousands, of inbound ships to Karma every day, they identified certain landing pads where illicit shipments might come in and who might take those payments. One of the most unique sites for this conduct was on the same spur of the landing facilities as the Peacemaker's entry point.

Make the gauntlet work against us. Brilliant.

Based on their communications plan, he'd seen Millzak making his way from normal areas toward the landing facility. Dreel understood this meant one of two things. First, that Millzak had some type of intelligence that might pin down the actual facility Kr'et'Socae and his entourage used and whomever they manipulated in the performance of their duties. Credits tended to talk. Given recent history, plenty of people on Karma would do almost anything to secure funds. The second thing, and the one that most worried him, was that Kr'et'Socae and his cargo had already arrived, and they would need to work quickly.

As he watched Millzak make the turn toward the landing facilities, Dreel stood and moved out of their interim office. The old mercenary unit headquarters served as a valid clandestine command post. Located in the main hub, it was not very far from the landing facilities. He knew that, at a casual walking pace, not trying to call any more attention to himself than normal, he could make it to the gauntlet within a couple minutes at most. Ensuring his weapons were in place, Dreel pulled on the dark blue Peacemaker vest, pushed through the door, and stepped into the main passageway beyond.

He caught up to Millzak just inside the entrance of the gauntlet. As they'd arranged, he made his way forward at a brisk pace so he could take up a position at the Peacemaker checkpoint. Since his arrival and shock that the checkpoint was unmanned, Dreel had ordered Peacemakers to again stand watch. As he walked up to the checkpoint, a young Altar stood and tapped one claw against its breast.

"Captain Dreel. Is there something wrong?"

Dreel tried to appear relaxed. He waved the young Peacemaker back to his seat. "Checking on some inbound cargo with sketchy manifests, that's all. I'm not here to bother you in the performance of your duties."

"Certainly, sir." The Altar lowered itself back into its seat. "Please let me know if you require any assistance."

"Stand or fall," Dreel said.

"Stand or fall, sir."

Halfway down the second portion of the corridor, Dreel stopped and ducked to one side. He appeared to be wrestling with his gear vest and then using his slate. He knew the ruse wasn't a good one, but he'd been careful to do the same thing on his many journeys around the station's facilities for the last several days. Anyone who'd been following him would notice a familiar pattern to his movements. Hopefully, it would be enough to divert unnecessary attention from his pursuit.

Millzak limped past him and turned left down the sub-corridor toward the landing pads designated 96 through 100. After a moment, Dreel followed. At the entrance to landing pad 99, Millzak waited, and, as Dreel approached, Millzak tapped his slate. The plan was to cut all video feeds and overpower the security protocols in the landing pad itself. The Lumar's eyes came up to his, and there was a touch of a smile on his thick face. All was ready.

They ducked inside the outer door into an alcove immediately inside the bay. Such spaces were reserved for customs and similar registrations. It was obvious there were no officials present to perform such inspections. Beyond the hatch to the landing pad, they could hear a shuttle's engines spooling down.

"It's here," Millzak said. "No credible report of Kr'et'Socae being here, but his target has arrived. I thought this might be our only chance to get close and take a look at it."

"That depends on who's on the other side of that door to meet the shuttle."

Millzak nodded. "I have closed-circuit security footage on my slate, but I don't recognize any of the players. There are four visible.

I've been monitoring them for thirty minutes. I have seen no other signatures."

"Are they all Equiri?"

"No, sir. None of them are Equiri," Millzak replied. "It's a spread. Maki, Zuparti, SleSha, and MinSha. I'm worried our target's network is far deeper than we suspect."

"Anything else?"

"There may be at least one Peacemaker on the other side of that wall."

"Who?" Dreel growled.

"I believe the MinSha is Rehnah."

"How is she out of prison? I thought her sentence was a decade?"

"Good question. I cannot be certain it's her. I checked the prison system manifest but did not see her listed." Millzak shrugged. "I imagine we'll get to the bottom of that after we get a chance to observe the cargo. I'm pretty certain we can bring her in for questioning at the very least."

Dreel shook his head. "If we do that, it throws off the entire operation. Let's let this play out as long as we can."

"There are four targets on the other side of the wall, which doesn't count anyone who may be on the shuttle," Millzak said. "Are you ready?"

Dreel nodded and withdrew his large hand cannons from their holsters. With one in each fist, he nodded toward the door. "Let's hope they play nice, then. Two versus five is still in our favor."

Millzak drew his own weapon but did not reply. For a moment, Dreel sensed apprehension, but there were no outward signs of it in the elder Lumar's movements. He was ready. Fighting against the aliens on the other side in a hand-to-hand situation would not benefit them, hence the drawn weapons.

"Activate the door," Dreel said. "I'll go first. You've got the blind spots, standard deployment."

Millzak nodded and moved to the door controls. "Ready. In three, two, one..."

The door opened, and swirling wind from the shuttle's exhaust ripped through the small space. Dreel stepped through the open hatch with his weapons outstretched and centered on the four individuals just to his right and about ten meters ahead. Movement to his left caught his attention. Dreel turned his head slightly and found a Zuparti crouched out of sight, pointing a rifle past him, into the space they'd just emerged from. Millzak was clearly in its sights.

At the same time, a weapon pressed against the side of Dreel's head. Under his fury, Dreel fought to keep from recoiling as a deep, gravelly voice laughed in his ear. "Captain Dreel, I've been expecting you."

Weapons still in hand, Dreel did not turn his head. Instead, he spoke through gritted teeth and out the side of his mouth. "Kr'et'Socae."

"You're exceptionally easy to track, Captain. One would think the Prime Enforcer would be better skilled at disappearing, especially in familiar places. Your accomplice, now he has talent enough to be a Peacemaker, even disabled as he appears. But he's just a Lumar. A good one, yes, but the two of you can't affect what's underway now."

Dreel kept his weapons on the four onlookers to his front. "What's to stop me from opening fire? I can certainly take out a couple of your people."

Kr'et'Socae laughed. It sounded like an earthquake. "You'll get three or four rounds off at most. You might take one out, but you're not a good enough shot, Dreel. You never were. I, on the other hoof, have a cannon pressed against your skull, and there's nothing to stop me from splattering your brains across this landing pad."

"What are you up to, Kr'et'Socae?"

"Another asinine Peacemaker trait. Ask questions with your slate running so you can gather recordings of the subject without the need for any other type of involvement. It's a shame barristers are no longer needed in the Galactic Union. Though you would've made a terrible one, Dreel. Keep me talking. Give yourself time to think of something else to extend your play. It's not about waiting for reinforcements, either. The Peacemakers here are quite removed from what you think they should be. They've realized all things are possible for the right price."

"What's to say there's not more of us coming? That the guild master is aware of your plans and is ready to spring on you at a moment's notice?"

"I know that's not the truth." Kr'et'Socae leaned closer. "It's a ploy to keep me from killing you and your accomplice."

Dreel sneered. "Rains was right, you won't do your own dirty work. You've become a true psychopath, haven't you?"

"And now the anger ploy. Pitiful. I think this has gone far enough." Kr'et'Socae's voice showed irritation. With a gun to his head, it was as much of a lifeline as Dreel could take advantage of.

Dreel turned his head abruptly to the right to look the Equiri in his face. The older being's dark eyes burned. There were the first touches of white in his coat, especially at his ears and on the broad slope of his nose. Age was becoming a factor. Youth and skill could be used. He needed only to turn the correct phrase and elicit the response. "What would your mentor say, Kr'et'Socae?"

"Hr'ent Golramm is dead. And so are you."

"Yet here I stand. Enforcer Prime, no less. Which you could have been had you chosen a different path. Followed the rules of engagement. Stood with honor."

Kr'et'Socae growled. "My path was chosen for me by your guild master. I was nothing but a sacrificial pawn in his game. He underestimated my abilities and my resolve, Dreel. And like you, he'll pay for that mistake. Honor isn't the measure of a being. Strength is."

"You think you're better than me? Stronger than me?" Dreel asked, letting a hint of a smile cross his maw.

"I know I am. And your ploy to trick me into a physical confrontation is a weak attempt to divert my attention, Enforcer. Let me assure you of the endgame." The Equiri's left ear flicked.

A shot rang out from Dreel's left. It was close enough that he felt the heat, but there was no explosion of pain. He turned his head further to the left, pressing it hard against the hand cannon in Kr'et'Socae's grip, and saw Millzak sprawl backward awkwardly. The upper chest wound did not appear to be mortal, but he was down for the count and losing blood.

Millzak's eyes flashed with a defiant glare, which Dreel returned. The Lumar stayed down.

Dreel swiped backward with his right hand and dove forward quickly. Kr'et'Socae squeezed the trigger, and the blast was close enough to singe the hair on the back of Dreel's neck, but the round did not strike him. Dreel was already moving with a vicious left hook aimed for the side of Kr'et'Socae's long face. His fist never made it. As he exploded up from his hasty crouch and swung, sharp pain drove down between his shoulder blades. The impact drove the air from his lungs. His arms refused to operate. Breathing hurt. Every movement sent a tendril of fire through his limbs.

Dreel froze and stared down at his chest. A long, dark blade had run him through. He grasped at air, trying to snatch the blade out of his back. Through the pain he gasped, "You continue to dishonor Peacemakers, Kr'et'Socae."

"You have dishonored yourselves. Purity will be established. As your Peacemakers fail, willing parties will take up the mantle and return the guild to what it should have been all along. I will have my revenge in the sweetest manner—perched upon the very seat of authority Rsach used to betray me. We are already well underway."

Dreel grunted. "All of this? For the guild master's chair?"

"No. All of this is for me." Kr'et'Socae's muscular arms spread wide. "I will take it all, and the Peacemaker Guild will be the extension of my rage."

"Peacemakers… are not meant to rule." Dreel staggered. The pain was unbearable, but he would not fall. Anger kept him upright, staring into the disgraced Enforcer's face.

Kr'et'Socae laughed. "A long-spoken fallacy, Dreel. To think I thought better of you."

The Equiri brought up his hand cannon and placed it in Dreel's face. Dreel edged closer. Fate may have sealed his destiny, but weapons of doubt served well. "You're nothing, Kr'et'Socae, and you continue to underestimate our guild. Hr'ent was right about you. You were a mistake."

Kr'et'Socae hit him. Dreel never saw it coming. He reeled and came back up with his fists ready. The Equiri laughed.

"I certainly overestimated you, Enforcer Prime. Speaking of mistakes, let's rectify one right now, shall we?" Kr'et'Socae re-centered the handcannon on Dreel, then stepped forward to press the barrel against his head.

"Fuck you!" Dreel spat frothy blood across the deck and lashed out. There was a flash and an instant of heat…then nothing.

* * *

Kr'et'Socae holstered his hand cannon and turned to the entourage around him. "Prepare the crate for shipment. Locate Dreel's launch and commandeer it. Pay whomever whatever they want, but secure that ship. Ensure the crate is loaded and the ship is fueled. I am leaving immediately."

Millzak heard the Maki ask, "What about the Lumar?"

"Old and decrepit," Kr'et'Socae snickered. "I fear nothing from it or its kind. It is no Peacemaker. I don't care what you do, just make sure it's never found."

The MinSha appeared in his view. Millzak easily saw it wasn't Rehnah, but the mantis-like being stared down at him for a good thirty seconds. "We'll dress that wound. I have an idea for who might take this big, dumb thing off our hands on the cheap. Once Kr'et'Socae departs with the dead Enforcer's body and ship, I know just what to do."

* * * * *

Chapter Twenty-Two

Location: CLASSIFIED

The now nightly sojourn through the ventilation system's duct to the agricultural habitat invigorated Guild Master Rsach. Whether it was the idea of doing something operational, in the very minimal sense of the term, or doing something akin to sneaking out of one's nest as an adolescent, he enjoyed it far more than he should have. There was a sense of adventure, to be sure, but with every occurrence, Rsach decided the feeling was not adventure, but freedom.

How quickly we lose sight of what we have until it's gone.

The time spent in the flora of the habitat gave him much needed relaxation and focus, albeit only for the relatively short time he spent there. Since ascending to the guild master's position, his life away from the guild had ceased to exist. While he'd mated, as every Jeha did, his connection to his offspring was nowhere near paternal. Other species, particularly the MinSha, developed an affinity for their matriarchy, but the Jeha simply nested, reproduced, and went their own way. His own way had been the Peacemaker Academy. During his first year, a couple of upperclassmen pulled him and a few others aside and explained to them that successfully passing the academy was all about "playing the game."

"Do what they want. Nothing more. When the spotlight is on you, give your best. When it's not, don't. Take care of yourself and your close friends. Screw everyone else."

He'd taken their advice to heart and soared up the informal popularity rankings within the academy. Life had been easy. The spotlight was easy to detect, and he certainly excelled when the time came, but far too often, he refused to give his best for others. Eventually, it caught up with him. His first mission to Godannii 2 resulted in several of his friends dying on their first mission as Peacemakers. The only reason he'd made it out alive was the one being he'd ridiculed the most relentlessly. Hr'ent Golramm didn't have to care about Rsach, and likely shouldn't have, but he understood something about being a Peacemaker that Rsach and the others did not.

The spotlight is always on, and it's always pointed at everyone else. We measure up in how we show up for them, not ourselves.

Sitting alone in the darkness of the habitat, Rsach stared up through the clear ceiling panels at the alien sky.

Damn you, Golramm. You're still kicking my ass from beyond the grave.

And I deserve it.

I have been wrong about many things. Haven't I?

Hr'ent didn't answer, as usual. Rsach laughed. "But I can still do things right, old friend. As long as I do them right when they matter."

Sleep had not come, as was often the case during his self-imposed exile. The daily mechanics of the guild were enough to keep him busy, yet his brain worked double the time and effort to stay ahead of Counselor. Doing so was next to impossible, and Rsach believed he knew why—yet he would not say or think it in an effort to keep it untrue. The truth would destroy the guild, though in many ways, those seeds appeared to have been sown *by* Counselor.

The Crusader program had grown quickly and begun to exceed its operational guidance. Under normal circumstances, the High Council would have met and assessed the situation, presented recommendations, and then implemented those necessary to accomplish the mission. The High Council hadn't met in more than six hundred days. Counselor took care of all the particulars when it came to the Crusaders, only bringing news to Rsach sporadically. Too often, he'd had to figure things out from one-sided and closed conversations.

Earlier that day, Counselor had chimed in during Rsach's scheduled time to handle things for his eyes only. Rsach had answered, per the mandate of communications between them, and immediately feared the worst.

"Guild Master, there are personnel actions you must address in your priority folder."

Rsach said nothing but directed his slate through the appropriate file structure and found the aforementioned folder. At the top was a designation order extending the position of Enforcer Prime to an Oogar named Talus. Rsach's antennae bounced in shock and agitation.

"What is the meaning of this? Captain Dreel continues to perform his mission, Counselor. He has done nothing worthy of demotion or relief for cause."

"Of course not, Guild Master. I have reviewed many of the Guild's policies and procedures and find the lack of contingency planning abhorrent. This is one example of my effort to address those concerns."

Rsach chittered. "I understand, but Talus is not an Enforcer I would consider for this position. As a matter of fact, he's not even on my list of three potential replacements."

"I've reviewed performance appraisals, mission reports, conduct analysis, and more than sixty other statistical factors. I believe he is the most qualified candidate. He is the contingency replacement for the Enforcer Prime."

"Entropy he is!" Rsach snapped. "I am the guild master, Counselor. I choose the personnel for the Guild's leadership. I appreciate your analysis, but statistics are far from the measure of a being when leadership, service, integrity, and courage are required."

Counselor chimed off without a response. In the immediate silence, Rsach's stomachs flipped over one another. Actions were being prepared in the event of the loss of guild leadership, which meant Counselor either expected casualties in coming conflicts or was making a play to lead the guild.

Not on my watch.

With his fresh anger, Rsach realized both purpose and folly. Purpose told him it was time to assert himself in the leadership of the guild in a way he hadn't done before. Counselor's machinations were clearly, in Rsach's mind, building the Crusaders as a way to subvert not only mercenary forces, but governments and even the Peacemakers themselves. The folly amounted to the burden of proof. Rsach had none. His gut feelings were never going to be enough to confront Counselor, but his comments about Humans, the creation of the Crusaders, and these "helpful" assumptions all pointed to something nefarious, and that could not stand.

A faint rustle of leaves caught his attention. With the lack of any appreciable breeze in the habitat, such movement might have frightened him, but it did not.

"Come out, my friend. The time has come, and we must act."

The ripple of quintessence widened enough that a pair of yellow eyes, almost glowing in the low light of the habitat, appeared. The Depik's mouth opened, revealing sharp teeth, but it was not a threat.

"How can I be of assistance, Guild Master?"

Rsach warmed in recognition. "Thrast of the Crashing Storm. These last few months have treated you well. I am thankful you have been here watching over my antennae, so to speak. Your abilities are without comparison. Never a clue or a sign of your presence. I am impressed beyond measure."

"Honored Guild Master, at our negotiation, my pledge to protect you, given your actions to protect us, was clear. I am here to do whatever I can to assist you. Including stand against your opponents, external to your guild and internal." Thrast crossed the longish grass and settled onto his back legs.

"You feel the same way about this?"

"Leading your guild is a burden you must bear alone, Honored Rsach. My feelings, as it were, align with yours. I stand ready to assist, as I promised."

Rsach sat quietly for a moment. The totally black Depik sat in the grass a meter or so away and stared at him. Starlight caught the ripples of his fur as his tail swept from side to side rhythmically.

"We are about to fight a war on two fronts," Rsach said. "Two different enemies—one who wants control and the other who wants chaos and destruction. I am afraid we must prepare for both concurrently. I am concerned about this development, but I wonder about my power to do anything."

"You know you must address the closest, most tangible target," Thrast said. "Your concern over the disappearance of James Francis is merited. You believe he knows something about this coming war and at least one of its proponents."

"I do. His cache sites prove it." Rsach's voice was little more than a whisper. "If I am right about where he is, and they are holding him against his will; finding him is the least of our concerns. Many will be lost."

"Yet you already have a plan in motion." Thrast chuckled. "Have faith, Guild Master."

"My ability to have faith is the same as my ability to remain connected and in control of the situation without Counselor's attention. I am severely lacking in both faith and control right now. Which is why I need your help. To get a message through."

Thrast was quiet for a moment and perfectly still. "To whom?"

"Jessica Francis."

"An interesting choice," Thrast said. "She and Azho have paired and such a bond is for life. I can get a message to her, Guild Master."

"Even my entire plan?" Rsach replied.

"Of course," Thrast purred. "That you would trust her, and us, to relay the message gives us hope for the future."

"If we don't pull this off, I'm not sure how much future any of us have," Rsach replied. "When can you send the message?"

"Let's begin, Guild Master. Welcome to our shared future."

* * *

Springton

The feeling of eyes following his every move was something Jyrall couldn't ignore any longer. Since returning to Krifay, he'd spent more time staring into shadows and using his senses to detect something his brain repeatedly told him was not there. He felt it on this planet, too. Even as they prepared for the mission, and everything seemed ready, the big Peacemaker could not shake the feeling. He'd taken a moment to slip away from the others to clear his head using Peacemaker breathing techniques. A vacant hangar seemed the perfect place for him to meditate and get ready for the final phase of the mission.

He stood in the middle of the empty hangar, listening to the air handling units moving the atmosphere. Scents of lubrication products, spent fuel, and various species filled his sensitive nose, and while almost overpowering, Jyrall filtered them out. Eyes closed, chest rising and falling, he was two parts into the first movement when a powerful scent he'd never detected before rose around him.

His eyes snapped open, and his jaw followed. In front of him, sitting on the deck with a bemused smirk on her face, was a Depik. From his coursework, he knew of them but had never seen one with his own eyes. Shock became reaction, and he reached for his pistol.

"Stop, Peacemaker. I am not here to harm you."

Jyrall settled the weapon in its holster and released his grip. Studying the curious creature with her fur of mottled darker and lighter greys and her light blue-grey eyes, Jyrall realized the cause of his feelings, and his unease, sat in front of him. "You've followed us since Krifay."

The Depik chuckled. "Longer than that, Peacemaker Jyrall. Nikki Sinclair wasn't the only ally you acquired at Parmick."

"You were there?" Jyrall shook his head. "Following us?"

"Not implicitly." The Depik raised a paw to her face and brushed her lower jaw. "My… travels took me there. I merely arrived a few hours before the attack on the mine took place. Watching you reveal yourself, badge and all, in the compound, was thrilling entertainment."

Jyrall almost chuckled but ony allowed his maw to curl under on one side. "Much appreciated. Theater was never my specialty. Why follow us?"

"You sell yourself short, One-Eyed Varkell, but I digress. You ask a reasonable question. Let us begin our conversation again. I am Tsan." The Depik slow-blinked at him. "You are Peacemaker Jyrall."

"Well met." Jyrall nodded. He wondered about decorum and decided to lower himself to the deck and sit with the Depik. In most cases, he did such a thing to put the other at ease regarding his size. In this particular case, he knew the Depik was a more than worthy opponent. He sat as a sign of respect. "Why are you here?"

"I am here because of your guild master."

"Guild Master Rsach wanted us followed?" Jyrall scowled. "Impossible. His orders were—"

The Depik raised a paw and pointed a clawed digit at him. "Hear me, Peacemaker. There were no orders. Even one as honorable and respected as Rsach understands he cannot order the Depik. We are here at his request. There are not many of us anymore, but we were asked to stay close to the Peacemakers. For our mutual protection."

Jyrall nodded. "Our guild directives are clear. We are to support you in any way necessary should you make yourselves known to us. Is that why you're here? Now? Is there something you need?"

"No," Tsan replied. "I am here with a message from Guild Master Rsach."

"He could have simply sent a Stormwatch."

The Depik slow-blinked. "No, he couldn't. Very many things in your guild are not what they appear, Jyrall. He is concerned there are those close to him who are attempting to undermine his leadership and the guild itself. Standard communications, especially for your mission, are to be greatly filtered to protect yourselves, and others, from those who wish to do you harm."

"What?" Jyrall shook. "Who are these…beings?"

"Why did you pause just then?" Tsan replied. "It was a curious action."

Jyrall's brow furrowed and then he understood. He laughed. "I almost called them a definitively Human term."

"Which one? Isn't their language unique?"

"Assholes."

Tsan chuckled. "We do not know who these *assholes* are. At least, I am unaware. What I do know is that I am to continue supporting you, and you are now aware of my presence. Our negotiation with the guild master is clear in this case."

"I agree," Jyrall nodded. "What is the message?"

"The message originated from Guild Master Rsach, but it comes from Peacemaker Francis," Tsan replied. "She is quite *emphatic* for a Human."

"That she is," Jyrall said. "At least from what I have heard. I've never had an actual conversation with her. I saw her, many times, at a distance, during the academy. What has she sent?"

"Peacemaker Francis is unique," Tsan said. "She is half of a bonded pair. She and the hunter Azho have done great work to restore our species, but there is more work to be done. There are three parts to her message.

"First, while your plans and intent must remain the same, the result must be different. The Shaylin System contains a depot of unused, ready to be initialized and operated, stargates. With Guild Master Rsach's direction, you are to steal an uninitialized one and deliver it to a consolidation point for operations. Once you have the gate, I will provide the coordinates for your destination. Given its highly secure nature, we cannot risk anyone knowing about it should your effort fail.

"Second, once you deliver it to the forward point, where it will remain guarded by your forces, I'll be in touch again. We're going to use this gate for a highly dangerous mission, and you, Peacemaker Larth, and your allies will play a critical role. But there are intermediate steps we must negotiate together in order to be successful.

"Lastly, consider all messages from the guild to be suspect. Even those with the proper marks and codes may be untruthful. I recommend you discontinue regular use of Stormwatch other than for information and intelligence gathering. We must limit our secure communications like this because of the risk to the Depik and to each other. And, in case you're wondering about the authenticity of this message, Director Aarrtraa did not believe Larth voluntarily left his contraband. The director was not amused and says you owe him a bottle of Jl'al in payment. Good luck, Jyrall. Stand or fall."

Jyrall blinked and laughed. "Aarrtraa figured it out, huh?"

"I am glad you laughed." Tsan ran one paw over the side of her face. "If you hadn't, I was instructed to kill you as an impostor."

"What?"

Tsan chuckled. "I understand it refers to something called a…prank?"

Jyrall smiled. "One I thought was untraceable. I guess I was wrong."

"Nothing is untraceable."

"Says a Depik." Jyrall tilted his head to one side. "Without the message, you would have remained in the shadows, yes?"

"Make no mistake, Peacemaker, I will return to the shadows following our conversation. Your friends cannot know I am here."

"I do not wish to keep things from my friends." Jyrall's maw worked from side to side. "Larth, especially, will want the message verified. As well as the source."

Tsan was silent for a moment. "You may tell him, as it does not break the negotiation with your guild master. No one else must know. You've merely received a verifiable mission from the guild master. Is that agreeable to you, Peacemaker?"

Jyrall thought for a moment. Working with a Depik was a topic he'd never learned at the academy. The common perception of the felinoids hinged on the fact that seeing them meant it was too late to save oneself.

"It is agreeable, Tsan," Jyrall said. "How often are you…in contact with others?"

"When it is necessary, Peacemaker. As your mission is vital, I will remain where I can be of assistance should the need arise. But

Peacemaker Francis is correct; we must limit this approach as much as possible."

"Do I call upon you if I need assistance?"

Tsan laughed. "No, Peacemaker. If you need me, you have far greater worries."

*****

Chapter Twenty-Three

Springton

Jyrall stood in front of the group. They were nearly centered between all the ships on the tarmac. Behind the huge Peacemaker were the two Blue Ridge Kin ships, now registered as *Z-9006* and *Z-9008*. On the other side of the group were the freighters *Synchronicity* and *Synchronicity II*. Off to the side was the large shuttle *Strong Arm 64317*. Keaton had put in the work to change the identifications for the mission.

"All right," Jyrall said, his voice carrying so those in the back of the formations could hear him clearly. "The plan is finalized. You have all been briefed. Any last-minute changes, should they occur, will be conveyed by your leaders." Cora and Pete nodded, both standing in front of their troops. On their right, Larth stood in front of Ban-Tilk, his crew, the ex-gate master Argold, and Ricky and Keaton.

He paced a short distance back and forth, thinking. All eyes remained on him. He stopped, remembering he was out front. Working with his partner and their small crew was much different than leading two mercenary companies, not to mention Ban-Tilk, his crew, and the Sumatozou Argold.

Several nodded. The senior leaders let him know he was on the right track. The troops needed to know they were led with competence. Both companies had the utmost respect for their own leadership but knew another was in command. This last formation would help ease their minds, though most would never have mentioned it, not that First Sergeant Figgle or Sergeant Major Daniels would have tolerated it for a second. Professional soldiers understood leadership sometimes meant following other leaders than their own.

Of late, he and First Sergeant Figgle had spoken of some of the things the Goka had learned while studying Human militaries. In particular was an old NCO Creed. Jyrall agreed with it. One thing stuck out when planning this operation. *I will communicate consistently with my soldiers and never leave them uninformed.*

"I will not make light of what we are about to attempt—no, let me rephrase that, what we are about to accomplish. There are those who wish to take this gate and hold it. In doing so, they will be able to continue their goal of crushing humanity and, believe me when I say, they will not stop there. They have a foothold already. We've got to tear them loose."

He paused a second to allow the hoots and cheers to die down. "Ban-Tilk will arrive first. He and his crew will insert the program Keaton devised. They will be expecting the other four ships as part of their plans. They will not be able to scan them properly. Continue to study the layout of the station while we are en route. When your ships dock, the faster we gain control means less chance of casualties.

"I will not stand before you and say there will be none. That would be a lie. I will not lie to you. You are all volunteers. Those of you contracted as mercenaries knew the possible cost when you made your mark. You others were given the option to walk away. None of you hesitated. Thank you for that.

"Speaking of walking, the station will have gravity close to what you are used to with its rotation. Argold tells me it should not be an issue.

"Now, back to the plan. When we dock, the frigates will be on the far side, with the smaller ships in the middle. Argold tells me the docking bays are not far apart. We will not all be able to dock in one. Depending on the resistance, we may go with one of the contingency plans. If we must go to the CASPer plan…pilots, be aware of the damage your weapons may cause to the station. We do not want a hull breach. Remember those not sealed into mechs. Friendly fire of any type is unacceptable, including losses to the vacuum of space."

The infantry platoon members in both companies gave the mech pilots sideways glances. The mech pilots looked nervous. First Sergeant Figgle glared at the backs of their heads from his spot behind the Kin. He had two sets of pincers on what would have been hips on other races. The sergeant major gave him a thumbs up and grinned.

"The Kin will fan out to the right of their docking bay, and the Barnstormers will move to the left. Take out all security and clear rooms as you go. We do not want any surprises later. Larth and I will get Argold to the operations center. The ship's security consists of a company of Blevin. You all know Blevin are not true mercenaries. They have the training and capabilities of mercs, but they do not have to follow the rules and guidelines of such. Do not underestimate them. They are skilled and ruthless. If it is not safe to take prisoners, make sure you eliminate them."

He paused before continuing. "But, if they surrender, you must treat them as mercs. Secure them and render aid. Just because they do not adhere to the regulations does not mean we will not.

"We should receive updates on the station's defenses as soon as we emerge in system. The battle is planned, and we feel we have accounted for any contingencies. You know how it goes. Be prepared to shift to them or to a new one altogether. No plan remains fully intact five minutes after contact with the enemy."

* * *

Synchronicity

Jyrall tightened his harness and mentally prepared himself for the jump. Keaton glanced over and continued adjusting the controls before he initiated the hyperspace shunts. Ricky and Larth hung from straps behind them, like usual.

"Before we do this, I feel I must inform you of a change in the plans," Jyrall said.

"What?" Larth asked. "What change? We go in, we take the station, and Colonel Brentale and his troops keep it for us. His idea of talking to the Jivool he knows and hiring their company to defend it with his after the mission was brilliant. Once we have it, it will be damn near impossible to take back."

"Especially if we actually take it," Jyrall agreed.

"That's what I said. Take it," Larth insisted.

"Exactly," Jyrall agreed.

"I don't mean to interrupt," Ricky said. 'But what in tha hell are you two arguin' about? You're both sayin' the same dang thing."

"But with different meanings," Keaton observed. He looked over at Jyrall. "Am I right?"

"You are," Jyrall answered. "How did you know?"

"It finally dawned on me what that crate is full of, back in the hold," Keaton said. He took a deep breath and sighed.

"What?" Ricky asked. "Tools?"

"Yeah," Larth agreed. "Tools."

"Not just any tools," Keaton said. "Gate maintenance tools. And a little more."

"That's it!" Ricky said. "Those extensions would reach into the connectors of a gate. The pieces are prebuilt and put together in place. Wait…what do you mean a little *more* than maintenance?" He squinted and stared at his brother.

"We are going to take the gate," Jyrall said.

"That's what I said!" Larth exclaimed. "We are—oh shit. You mean we really *are* going to *take it*? Where are we taking it?"

"I don't know yet," Jyrall admitted. "The information will be forthcoming."

"Well, I'll be a sumbitch," Ricky said. "I can probably figure out the main points to disassemble a gate, but who the hell we gonna get to put it back together?"

"Don't look at me," Argold said from the entry hatch to the ship's operations center. "I can operate one like no other. I'll stake my reputation on it. But—but I have no knowledge of more than normal operator-level maintenance."

All eyes turned to Ricky. "Shit," he said. "Argold, can you help me find manuals or instructions or something? Hellfahr, this ain't good."

"With Keaton's help, I am sure we can find them," the Sumatozou said.

"We will need them," Keaton said. "I can use the simulated gate files and the ones I jacked from the local gate, here in the system, but

I can't initialize a gate. Not without the core programming. We can use some of the pieces from the ones in storage, but we need the working gate. As much of it as possible." He paused, smiled, and continued, "I guess we're gonna see what that greasy fingered brother of mine can do with the tools."

"I see that dang grin on your face, Keaton," Ricky said. "For that, I'm telling Jyrall why you named the ships *Synchronicity*."

"Why?" Jyrall asked. "It does seem…different. What is the meaning?"

"It's one of his favorite albums from Pop's collection," Ricky answered.

"A musical album? By who?" Jyrall asked.

Keaton grinned sheepishly. "By The Police."

Larth nearly lost his grip laughing. "The Police? That's hilarious. We're undercover with ship names telling them all who we are! I love it!"

Argold backed away from the hatch, the look on his face showing he was clearly wondering if he had made a mistake joining the mission. Ricky shook his head and showed his teeth. Jyrall stared at them with big eyes.

* * *

Shaylin System

Heavy Shuttle *Strong Arm 64317*

The shuttle *Strong Arm 64317* approached the stargate's docking bay. Traluur was operating the ship with three different appendages, one of which was rotating through the different outside views from visual sensors built into the hull.

"Why must you do that?" Golund asked. "What you see on the outside of this ship will not help you operate it. The sensors are all that are needed."

"I am making sure there are no surprises waiting for us," answered Traluur. "Backing into the docking bay is disconcerting when I can only see out the front portals, and we don't want anyone to notice they are new. It's bad enough I have to match the gate's rotation and do this. Stop co-pilot seat operating. What we are attempting is very dangerous."

"You have a point," Golund said. "That freighter dock is decent sized. The new sensors show it has offensive and defensive weapons it did not come out of the shipyards with. Whatever security company Nay-Thok hired knows their business. What do we do if that ship uses their sensors to scan the others following us?"

Ban-Tilk pulled his segmented body up across the back of both of the Bakalu's seats. Ricky and the Makis had removed the seats designed for humanoids and put in ones to accommodate them. Ricky had not been happy about swapping the seats after he had just finished overseeing the repairs to the operations center.

"It looks like it is powered down to the bare minimum," Ban-Tilk said. "Perhaps every member is on board the gate."

The communications center crackled, and a translated voice asked, "*Strong Arm 64317*, why are you coming into the landing bay aft first?"

Before either of the Bakulu could answer, Ban-Tilk grabbed a maneuvering strap with two lower pincers, stretched out, and answered the call himself. "Who is this?" he demanded. "If I decide I have the time to seek you out, there will be a discussion about questioning one who holds your company's contract. Tell your commander I want to speak to him as soon as the bay is pressurized. I expect no delay."

After a tense moment, the voice answered back, "Yes sir. The commander will be waiting."

Ban-Tilk's body visibly relaxed. He swung himself back to his position between the two straps behind the seats. "I think that is what this Nay-Thok would have said. From all accounts, he was not a pleasant Jeha."

"You convinced me," Golund said. "From the information Keaton was able to retrieve, all communication with the security company has been through messages, so maybe this will work after all."

"Remember, these are Blevin we are dealing with," Ban-Tilk said. "Peacemaker Jyrall says they have dealt with some in the past. This security company, here under the guise of training to work other gates, does not adhere to the rules mercenary companies must follow. They are not members of the guild."

"They are just hired guns," Traluur said. "I would not be surprised to find they have already taken care of the small security unit assigned to this gate."

"They outnumber the Blue Ridge Kin. Of that we are certain," Ban-Tilk said. "*You* just be certain you can get the drive Keaton gave you into a port, while Golund and I deal with the commander. Without it, we will have major issues."

* * *

Ban-Tilk undulated down the ramp into the bay. He was followed by both Bakulu, as they moved slower. Standing a short distance away was a large Blevin. He was a head taller than Colonel Brentale, so Ban-Tilk decided he was a little over two meters. Taller than most Humans, but not as large as Peacemaker Jyrall.

A flechette rifle hung on a strap under one arm and a pistol was strapped to his thigh. Slightly behind the Blevin were two more. Neither were as tall as the commander, but both wore body armor and carried similar weapons.

"Captain Ravgart, you would do well to speak to whoever is operating your communications," Ban-Tilk said before the commander could speak.

"My apologies, Honored Nay-Thok," Ravgart said. "But it was not one of my own. More than half of the security team on the gate now works for me, and they are learning my way of doing things. It will not happen again."

"If he works for you now, he *is* one of your own," Ban-tilk countered. "Do not make excuses. Tell me, is everything in order?"

Realizing the one he thought of as Nay-Thok was correct, the commander was happy to change the subject. "Yes, sir. The security team put up a small fight when they realized we were not here for training purposes. The ones who failed to see things my way died. Half signed on."

"What of the gate master?" Ban-Tilk asked.

"Like you advised, we left him in his quarters," Ravgart said. "He never stirred. I looked in on him, and he just laid there, staring up, with a strange look in his eyes. If I didn't know any better, I'd say his pinplants are malfunctioning. I've seen it before, but that time, the

HecSha with them died. Served him right for getting another set of the damned things. Two should have been enough for any being."

"You won't see any in my head," Ban-Tilk said. "I prefer to think for myself."

"I like the advantage of having my one, but I refuse to spend the credits on more," Ravgart said. "Foolish, if you ask me. My pilots and technicians can do their jobs with one pinplant in their heads. The communication is fast enough.

"Speaking of which, my pilot needs to plug in. There are messages waiting for me, and there is an issue with the shuttle's communications system. It is why I have not forwarded you more information."

"I wondered about that," Ravgart said. He shrugged. "Still, the credits cleared into my account, so I followed my last instructions. There is a communications center up the passage to the right. We go left to the conference room."

"Good." Ban-Tilk waved several pincers, indicating that Traluur should go right. None of the Blevin gave him a second glance as they led the way to the conference room. "The ships with the equipment will be entering the system within hours. There was no room on my shuttle. I will give you their identification. You do have someone operating security, do you not?"

"Yes, sir. We are in full control."

"Good," Ban-Tilk said. "A small fleet follows me. They will dock, and we will have a final meeting before they deploy to help defend the entry points."

"A fleet? How many ships?

"Two frigates and two freighters. You do not think I would show up with a true fleet of warships, do you?

"No, sir. I only asked to let my controllers know. Will you have one of yours transfer the information? My ship is on standby, if needed. It can be crewed and undocked in a half hour. The pilots are in the gate's operations center, helping run surveillance."

"Good," Ban-Tilk said. He rippled his pincers in appreciation. "There are plans for this system. It would not do for unknowns to approach without the proper clearance. The last thing we need is Peacemakers, or whoever, sticking their trunks, eyestalks, snouts, or whatever into our business."

"I agree," Ravgart said. "It is why I brought one hundred and fifty soldiers with me."

"One hundred and fifty?" Ban-Tilk asked, stopping in his tracks and staring at the captain.

"Plus the fifteen who contracted with me these last few weeks," Ravgart replied. "One can't be too careful these days."

* * * * *

Chapter Twenty-Four

Emergence Point
Shaylin System

Synchronicity emerged flawlessly, but Jyrall wasn't looking. Every transition was at night behind his closed eyes. The disorientation was far too great to try and see anything as it happened. His stomach flipped and rolled inverted, and then his equilibrium matched the movements. As fast as they came on, the symptoms faded, except for a lingering foul taste in his mouth. The freighter oriented toward the gate and boosted its engines. At the controls, Keaton double-checked the navigation information for a proper, if fast and efficient, burn across to the gate for holding. At their best speed, they'd make the gate in roughly sixteen hours.

He turned to Jyrall, who sat frowning in the seat to his right. "You okay, man?"

Jyrall nodded. "Transition always gets me. But I do think it's getting easier, the more I have to do it."

"You're finally getting your space legs." Keaton laughed.

Jyrall shook his head. "I am not growing legs. A Besquith cannot not grow—"

Keaton raised his paws and waved them. "No, no. It's a term. You heard the term sea legs on Krifay, right?"

"No," Jyrall said. He turned and gazed at Keaton for a moment. "But I understand the phenomenon. You're discussing adaptation to the sensations of hyperspace transition like sailors becoming accustomed to the movement of the sea."

"Precisely," Keaton replied, with a toothy smile. "Anyway, we're sixteen hours from the gate. You might as well get some rest."

Jyrall nodded and turned to stare at the system beyond. The gate reflected light as if it were a magnitude 4.0 star. Its unwavering beacon held steady at the opposite LaGrange point. "How long until they contact us?"

Keaton shrugged. "Give it a couple of minutes, tops. But, if Ban-Tilk has convinced them he really is Nay-Thok, there's a pretty good chance we won't hear from 'em until we're on final approach."

"That would be pleasant," Jyrall commented with a sigh. "How long until the others emerge?"

Keaton pointed at the central Tri-V on his station. "Four minutes and ten seconds for *Synchronicity II*. The others are spaced out a minute or so after that. Gives them enough time to boost away from the point and follow us. We'll hold up a bit so they can join us, and we can all move in together."

Jyrall grunted and released his shoulder restraints. He pushed gently on the control panel and swung his big frame up and out of the seat. After a transition from hyperspace, he never had trouble returning to microgravity. The constant freefall of long-duration space travel was almost a welcome sensation. For a being his size, moving around in gravity was hard, and freefall gave him a chance to relax and, if only in his mind, fly.

"I'm going to check in on Larth and Ricky. They've been quiet for the last several hours, and it…worries me."

Keaton laughed and looked over his shoulder to make eye contact with Jyrall. "They were working on Frank and Stein again. Larth said they were refining their targeting systems."

"He said that?" Jyrall snorted. "More like he's bought into Ricky Shit and is fueling the fire."

"Them two's like fire and gasoline for sure, Peacemaker." Keaton laughed. "I'm sure it's nothing to worry about. Unless they've got live rounds loaded again."

Jyrall's frown deepened. The last time Ricky and Larth had tested the two autonomous drones, they'd gone ahead and loaded the ammunition magazines. Both of the systems engaged their targeting systems and auto-engaged the loading mechanism, charging the cannons. Jyrall had never seen Larth or Ricky move as fast as they had to shut down the drones. After it was over, and the drones and their cannons were safed and cleared, they laughed. In the few minutes it took to shut down the drones, clear their weapons, and safe their onboard systems, there hadn't been much laughter.

"They've assured me the dummy rounds are the only ones available during testing." Jyrall grinned. "Let's hope the rounds aren't the only dummies in the weapons room."

Keaton howled with laughter. "Oh, hell no! No bet, Jyrall. No bet."

* * *

As he approached the weapons bay, the sheer silence of the passageway shocked Jyrall. Usually, Larth and Ricky bantered like pups on a playground and listened to a variety of Human music. As Ricky described it, there were two kinds: country and western. Jyrall wasn't sure that was an accurate representation of Human music, because Keaton listened to other types, but Ricky often said a bunch of things that were as manufactured and crazy as his mechanical miracles. Today, everything was silent. Had a light not been on in the space, Jyrall might have assumed the two of them were resting or cooking in the galley.

He grasped the open hatchway to stop his momentum and peered inside. The larger Pushtal sat atop the drone Stein peering down over the smaller Zuparti. Larth mumbled something, and Ricky reached down with his paws on either side of the Peacemaker's head.

"I done told you to stop, Larth."

Larth grumbled. "I have stopped. The damned bolt's not moving. It's frozen or stripped or both. Hell, I can't get it to move."

Jyrall pulled himself more around the hatch edge. "Something the matter?"

Ricky didn't move his paws; instead, he looked up and grinned. "Looks pretty funny, I bet."

"You have no idea."

"Screw you, Snarlyface." Larth grunted. He could see the Zuparti's arms flexing and trying, in vain, to move something deep within the attack drone. There was a snap and thud inside the machine. "Ow! Shit that hurts!"

Ricky kept grinning at Jyrall. "You mind grabbing the first aid kit?"

"Not at all." Jyrall propelled himself into the space, turned to the wall-mounted lockers, and opened the one labeled "Medical Supplies." A small red pouch with a zipper around its entire width sat inside, underneath restraints. "This one?"

"That'll do," Ricky replied, shaking his head. "Just put the darned thing back up there, too."

Jyrall turned and grinned as Larth removed his hands from the machine, revealing three bandages around his tiny digits.

"What are you grinning at?" Larth frowned and reached for the pack.

"You guys were being quiet. I had to come check on you to be sure everything was okay." Jyrall handed over the pack. Larth was bleeding from a small cut. He quickly grabbed an antibacterial cream and bandaged the cut before reaching back into the machine.

"We found a problem." Larth shook his head. "Took us about five minutes to fix Frank over there, but we've been trying to budge this last bolt for an hour."

Jyrall glanced around the workspace. "You don't have that forty double-d liquid anymore?"

Ricky and Larth erupted in laughter. Larth hunched even closer to Stein's open maintenance hatch, his small body shaking with laughter.

Ricky rubbed his forearm across his eyes in between guffaws. "You...mean...you mean WD-40?"

"That's it," Jyrall said. The two continued laughing. Jyrall flushed and turned for the hatch. He saw the bulb of fluid floating in one corner and quickly retrieved it. He threw it at Ricky's head and missed. The bulb bounced off the far wall.

Larth grunted in his laughter and exclaimed, "Hey, I got it!"

They high-fived each other, and Jyrall couldn't help smiling. During their time together, they'd really become a team. More than that, they'd become friends. Even in their good-natured ribbing, he saw that they respected him and his leadership. Whether they were on an actual mission or not, they protected each other, even while they laughed. Sometimes, laughter was exactly what the group needed, even at Jyrall's expense. He'd known what the lubricant really was. He ducked out of the hatchway and made his way forward.

"Thanks, Snarlyface!" Larth called after him. "How long until we dock at the gate?"

"Sixteen hours," Jyrall replied over his shoulder. "I'm going to get some rest. You two should do the same. It's your turn to make dinner, too, Little Buddy."

"Oh, don't you worry. I've got something special planned. Hell, even Argold might like it."

Jyrall smiled and changed his path. He'd also look in on their Sumatozou passenger and make sure he hadn't found Ricky and Keaton's stash of liquor. The plan required a qualified gate master to not only shut down the gate and prepare it for transport, but also to restart the damned thing on the far side. Of course, if they didn't find the manuals Ricky needed, it wouldn't work anyway.

Have faith, pup.

Jyrall smiled at the voice of Captain Dreel, his mentor and emerging friend, in his mind. There was much to be said for faith and patience. For the next fifteen hours and fifty minutes, all he could do was eat and prepare for the mission ahead.

* * *

Synchronicity II

Colonel Brentale glanced at the small timer counting down in the main screen's corner. "Two hours until docking procedure. Have we been contacted by the gate yet?"

Specialist Haney turned his head and faced his commander. "No, sir. I've spoken with the other three ships, and they haven't been contacted either, other than with the prerecorded message about there being one hundred and fifty security company members we received from Ban-Tilk. I guess the plan worked." The perpetual specialist shrugged as if it were no big deal. "That Jeha must have fooled them into thinking he was that other guy."

The colonel shook his head. Specialist Haney always behaved as if nothing bothered him. Everything was just…whatever. Haney was one of those soldiers who preferred to stay in his current rank. Did he have the skills and knowledge to move up? Easily. But the specialist always found a way to stay in just enough trouble to keep it from happening.

Colonel Brentale had not been surprised in the slightest to find out the specialist could pilot the freighter with skill. Need someone to operate a crew-served weapon? Haney. Operate a powered hang glider like it was part of him? Haney. Drive an armored sled like he stole it? Haney. Accommodate a rare part to take something off deadline status? Haney. Get in a huge barroom brawl over scantily clad females of multiple races and win his part of said fight against several opponents and make his way back to the unit without a credit left to his name? Haney.

"Keep me updated."

"Roger, sir," Haney replied.

Colonel Brentale made his way back to the hold where his troops were preparing for the docking and assault. As he glanced around the busy hold, he appreciated the no-nonsense attitude among his troops. This was a serious undertaking, and they would be ready.

* * *

Blue Ridge

"How're we looking, Top?" Cora asked.

"We are as ready as we are going to be, ma'am," First Sergeant Figgle answered. "Everyone is familiar with the flechette weapons and the use of their masks. The troops know the plan and the contingencies. The officers have all the mech pilots ready to be regular infantry."

"Good," Cora said. "What do we hear from *Kellie's Stand*?"

"Nails has it under control," Figgle confirmed. "He says they are up."

"I don't doubt it," Cora replied. "I hate that I have to have you and the officers here with me to plan and always have to leave the other ship and half of the troops with him, but he does a good job."

"I agree," Figgle said. "It pains me to say this, because I hate to lose a good NCO—no, a great NCO—but maybe you should consider—"

"Promoting him to an officer?" Cora finished. "Believe me, I have been considering it."

Figgle did his best to nod, a movement that was difficult for his race. He and his commander were on the same page with this one. Nails might not be...but that was something to consider another time. Right now, they had to prepare to take a gate.

* * *

Stargate

"All four ships are on their final approach. Turnovers and deceleration are complete, sir," the operations control said.

"Good," Captain Ravgart said. "Once they are docked, I will inform Nay-Thok. His orders are not to disturb him or his pilots until those he hired are on station."

"Sir," the control said, "I am picking up some strange readings."

"What do you mean?" Ravgart asked.

"It's probably nothing, but one of the freighter's holds is emanating multiple sources of power. I can see them in *Synchronicity II*. This system is not very good. I have been tweaking it with some of my own programming, so I have only now noticed it. I cannot tell the source."

Captain Ravgart waved one of his six fingered hands in dismissal. "It's probably some of the specialty equipment we were told to expect. I would imagine much of it is powered. Powerful equipment, powerful enough to show on the sensors through their hull, means large equipment. Send a platoon to the berth in the bay. They can help move the equipment. Operate the lifters or whatever."

"Yes, sir."

"Besides, the men need something to do. Idle fingers and all that," Ravgart said.

* * *

Synchronicity

"Jyrall!" Keaton called out over his shoulder. "We have an issue!"

Jyrall turned back to the operations center. "What? Have they powered up their ship?"

"No, but I detect a lot of bodies outside the berth for our other freighter. More than twenty," Keaton said. "I was able to get into the gate's security system, but no video yet. I don't know what they suspect, but it is something."

"Get me an encrypted channel direct to Pete, Nails, and Cora," Jyrall said as he moved toward the comms.

Larth looked at Ricky. "Fire up Frank and Stein and a couple of those drones. This may go really bad, really fast."

"I'm on that shit, right now," Ricky said as he moved down the passageway.

Larth glanced back to Jyrall and saw his friend raise the microphone to his mouth. "Listen up, everyone. Here's what we're gonna do..."

* * * * *

Chapter Twenty-Five

Blue Ridge

Cora froze at her station on the bridge. They'd been able to tap into the station's closed-circuit television network, and they watched the crowd of security forces gather outside of their ship and around *Synchronicity II*. As much as she wanted to open the hatches and let the Kin bring hellfire and damnation onto the station's hired guns, she waited.

She owed Jyrall that much, even if she didn't like his plan one bit.

Jyrall's last transmission to them worried her immensely. "We're going to open our holds first. We have no reason to think Ban-Tilk's mission has failed, so we're sticking to the plan. Argold and I will disembark the ship. If we're still a go, they'll welcome us and stand down. I don't expect that. I really expect them to do one of two things: either they will shoot at us where we stand—which will bring every ounce of Ricky Shit this ship can bring to bear on them—or they will capture us for questioning. Either way, we'll have to fight our way in. If things go south, Cora, it's in your hands."

Let's pray they don't go south.

Even as she thought it, Cora knew the likely outcome. Ban-Tilk would have to be a world class actor to pull off his charade. Cora seriously doubted his abilities. Of course, Jyrall would have already thought of that. Taking Argold with him was a smart play. If anything, they could ascertain the situation with the hired guards and provide some type of warning to the others. He expected a fight, that was certain, but he'd hoped for a peaceful resolution, whether by ruse or by sheer luck.

We ain't got much luck left in the tank.

"Ma'am?" It was Figgle from the main cargo hold. "We're standing by. Permission to unlock the door?"

"Negative." She shook her head as if he could see her. "Wait for Peacemaker Jyrall's signal."

"There's a signal?" May asked behind her. "I mean, if they run back into the ship, I suppose that means we attack, right?"

"Hush, May," Lisalle called. "We have to see what happens and hope all hell doesn't break loose out there."

Cora didn't reply. There was no question in her mind about what was going to happen next. Beyond that, though, she had to believe in the plan and in Jyrall. She cared for the big Besquith. Of all her friends, she had the most unique connection to him. Losing him, she realized, would hurt far deeper than she would have imagined.

As Jyrall and Argold appeared in the hatch of *Synchronicity*, no one in the security forces moved. Their weapons were at the ready. The large door slid open and more of the armed troops poured into the bay. Argold's hands suddenly shot up into the air.

Jyrall's massive paws followed.

Oh, shit. Here we go.

* * *

Synchronicity

"That's far enough, Varkell," one of the Blevin security said. Jyrall couldn't pick out the voice from the crowd. "Get all limbs where we can see them. Reach for a weapon, and you'll die right now. I just received word there are some strange readings coming from your ships. I don't like it, and I don't like you. I read your file, and I am not taking any chances. I want to know more."

They've certainly honored the threat.

Argold raised his hands as if he'd been shot in the ass by a dart. Jyrall raised his hands more laconically, staring holes into the nearest Blevin who would make eye contact with him.

"Where is Nay-Thok?" Jyrall growled. "We have orders to report to him and no one else."

"Shut your mouth, Besquith," a particularly stocky Blevin snapped in return. Jyrall turned his gaze to the being's leathery face.

"Are you strong enough to close it?"

"Another word, and we'll open fire." The Blevin motioned for the squad nearest to them to close in. "Tell your ships to surrender and prepare to be boarded."

"I will do no such thing," Jyrall replied. "Either we see Nay-Thok or whoever your commander is. I will speak to no one else."

"So be it," the Blevin replied. "Take them to Captain Ravgart."

Ravgart. The Blevin head of security.

Ban-Tilk has either failed or is dead.

Jyrall took a breath and placed both of his paws on top of his head, giving a clear signal to the other ships.

The Blevin walked them toward the hatchway into the station's deeper passages. Jyrall knew it was a matter of time before the Kin, and his partner, opened a can of whup-ass on the gate security. He smiled to himself and studied the half dozen Blevin around him, looking for his first target.

* * *

Kellie's Stand

Nails Rhineder saw the Peacemaker's subtle signal and leapt up from the bridge controls and made for the cargo hold. He knew everyone in a CASPer had seen the feed relayed to their internal multifunction screens. They were all locked and loaded, ready to burst out of the hold, breathing fire. If he didn't get down there first, they'd scatter on their own excitement and stupidity.

He weaved through the CASPers and climbed aboard his mech, sliding backward into the cockpit and activating the powered armor from feel and memory. Decades of mercenary work had given him both the skill and experience to effectively wield it.

He tugged on his comms headset and sent a message. "Listen up, Kin. CASPers, you're on me. When I move out, you select a target. If they start firing, light their asses up. You with me?"

There was a collective cheer on the radio frequency, but he wasn't paying any attention to it. Before the cockpit even fully closed, he walked the CASPer toward the door.

"Make a hole! Make a hole!"

A pathway opened, and he stepped up to the very edge of the hatch. His radio clicked. Colonel McCoy's voice came over the frequency. "All right, Kin. Up and at 'em. Follow the plan and stay in your lanes. Let's go get our friend. Move out!"

* * *

Blue Ridge/Synchronicity

"Sirs," Specialist Conner said, "get ready. Once the last of the troops are out, the colonel said to make sure they are clear of the berth and to shut the emergency departure hatch. It will give me enough time to get on board and seal the ship before the berth depressurizes and you undock."

"Ready," Monty said. "We are ready, indeed, I say, indeed that is."

"I will then bring up the weapons systems," Stew added. "Systems, don't you know."

"Right. We will still have the benefit of some gravity, which will let me move fast enough to get back in here in time to launch missiles into their weapons targeting systems," Conner said. "You two make sure that when we pull out, you get this thing oriented so they have a little time until impact. We cannot let them use that ship to attack us…or the gate after we take it."

"Roger, that," Monty said as he brought up several smaller screens on the main display. "Roger, that is." The colorful Miderall paused and straightened the floppy brim on his hat. "I say, I am still to meet this Roger fellow, meet, you understand."

"I worry we leave the commander with nowhere to retreat to. Retreat, don't you know," Stew said. "Once that bay's emergency hatch closes, their back is against it, back that is."

"I know," Specialist Conner said, but she had her orders. "I know."

* * *

Synchronicity II

"Shit!" Colonel Brentale said. "Looks like we go with the CASPer plan right out of the gate. Lock 'em down."

His hatch locked shut, and he engaged his comms. "Sergeant Major, we will lead out of the ship; have the grunts use us for cover as they move. You know the deal."

Sergeant Major Daniels touched the pad on the inside of his wrist and answered, "Roger, sir. We knew it was a possibility. We will go with the CASPer Arrow. We will have three-man fire teams behind every mech. Well, except for Haney. Once he puts the ship in lockdown, he will catch up."

"Hey!" Staff Sergeant Wilson said over the command net.

"Three-man…three-women," Sergeant Major Daniels said. "You know what I mean."

"I know, Sergeant Major," she answered, with a chuckle. "I just thought I would give you some shit."

"We are about to be in plenty," the colonel said. "Let us, at least, get out of this before you and the ladies give us more. Well, not me. I didn't say it."

"Thanks a lot, sir," Daniels said.

"Dropping the ramp now," a voice interrupted.

"Roger, Jerund," Colonel Brentale said. He moved his Mk 7 to lead his troops into the station.

* * *

Docking Bay

Lieutenant Pynilk stared at the closed ramps of the two ships near him. Captain Ravgart had sent him and his platoon down to help unload, but it didn't feel right to him. He knew what was in Varkell's file and didn't trust him. Something about the big Besquith seemed off. From the moment he'd walked out of the hatch, Varkell had scanned the area as if taking in every bit of information he could. As a youngling, Pynilk had seen others up close who did the same thing. While Varkell was casual in his appearance and mannerisms, there was no escaping his actions and the twisting sensation Pynilk felt in his stomach. A long time before, he'd seen a squad of Peacemakers quell a dispute between two rivals. They'd come off their ship, in their blue clothing and silver pointed badges, with the same eyes. His gut hadn't lied, but Pynilk wondered if he had made the right decision.

Nay-Thok didn't want the Peacemakers here. He didn't want anyone he couldn't trust here. Yet, Varkell has to be a Peacemaker.

He has to be.

Now that the Besquith and the Sumatozou were around the bend and out of his sight, he was a little nervous. Ravgart might get angry at what he'd done. He'd just put the smuggler under arrest for no real reason besides his gut. The last thing he wanted to do was embarrass his commander in front of Nay-Thok…again.

"Well?" one of his troops asked.

"Well, what!" he shouted.

"Do we force them to open up or—"

He shot the sergeant a look that silenced him. He had raised his comm to his mouth to call Ravgart when the ramps slammed to the deck of the berth. Eight huge mechs stomped out, and the soldiers following each one opened up with flechette rifles. Five of his soldiers went down while others scrambled for cover behind containers and support columns.

The mechs moved closer while the rest of his platoon fought back. Pynilk screamed into his comms, "Sir! It was a set up! We are under attack!"

"What?" Ravgart's voice demanded. "By whom? Did you just arrest Varkell?"

"There are troops in all four ships. They have those damned CASPers! And from what I can see, two big drones on tracks. They—"

He never finished his report. A MAC round from the lead machine tore through the crates he was sheltered behind and cut him in half. The carefully aimed round stopped midway through the next big stack of metal boxes.

* * *

Gate Operations Center

"Curse that Jeha!" Ravgart shouted. He threw the comm in his hand against the bulkhead, shattering it. He turned to the nearest console and the one operating it. "Maximum alert. You get everyone moving to the docking bays. Have them take the crew served. Now!"

"Crew served sir?" the sergeant asked. "But they—"

"I know they are not for shipboard use! Idiot!" Ravgart said. He stepped over and looked down. "We either take a chance with a hull breach, or we lose the station. We don't have much of a choice.

While the troops gather, enact the 'bots. They may give us some time."

"Sir? Where are you—"

Ravgart snarled, "I'm going after Nay-Thok. Send a squad to meet me. And hold Varkell and that damned Sumatozou in the reception bay. Push the 'bots there. Whatever he's trying, they'll come for him, and we'll trap them inside."

The sergeant opened a small box on the console and pushed the button. All over the gate, automatic defense drones and systems came to life. The sergeant shrugged. His job was to turn them on, not control them. Whatever program they followed was beyond him. He reached for the comms as the commander ran out of the room.

* * *

Cora walked her CASPer into the bay behind May and Lisalle. The urge to bring up her weapons and fire was almost overwhelming, given the proximity of the fight. She held back. May and Lisalle engaged targets and protected her movements so she could get eyes on the situation and do what leaders needed to do. The Blevin security teams had fallen back to shipping containers stacked along the bay's internal wall. Based on their rate of fire, slow and methodical, they were well trained and attempting to ration their ammunition until support could arrive.

Not if we can help it.

"Brentale," she called over the CASPers comms, "once you can, move your guys into the passageway and press toward the command center."

"Copy, Cora," Brentale replied. "We've got a ton of automated defense robots and drones engaging us. We'll get through them. They're filing in from the passageway."

Cora swept her eyes around the bay and saw the first of the small, aerial drones swarm through the open hatch. She pressed her comms button as May and Lisalle moved further out of the ship and into the bay. She hesitated, but she did not follow them. "Ricky? You seeing this?"

"Reckon they're being controlled from the station's comm network. Keaton is trying to find a way in to shut 'em down, but he says it's gonna be a minute."

"Give me Frank and Stein," Cora replied. "Have them clear the aerial targets. That'll be enough for us to keep moving."

"Ten-four, good buddy," Ricky yelped. Cora thought she heard Ricky say "Ow" and something she couldn't make out until Keaton's voice rang in her ears.

"I'm also tracking Jyrall. They're getting him out of the fight," Keaton said. "That means they think he's leading the troops and don't know our capabilities."

"Get me a location fix, Keaton. As soon as we stomp all over the security forces and their drones, we're going after Jyrall," Cora said. She changed frequencies quickly. "Larth? You ready, honey?"

"You know I hate being called that, right? I'm not that sweet, and honey is really sticky, and—"

"Larth!" Cora's voice rose, but her tone remained casual. "You ready or not, Peacemaker?"

"This is the kind of thing I signed up for, Cora."

* * *

Jyrall used the hidden camera in his eyepatch to closely observe the squad of Blevin surrounding them. Argold simply moved beside him at the guards' urging. When the time was right, Jyrall hoped he could count on the big Sumatozou. If not, he hoped the ex-gate master would be smart enough to stay out of his way and the fire from the guards' weapons while he took them out. He was pretty sure he would be able to.

Ban-Tilk and his two pilots appeared from around the bend up ahead. The three of them were alone. Jyrall cocked his head in question. Perhaps the ruse had worked. *Did I give the signal too soon?*

"What is the meaning of this?" Ban-Tilk asked, his voice rising in volume.

"Sir, I—" the squad leader stammered. His hand reached toward his ear. Jyrall saw the unmistakable small glow of light from a pinplant. All six of the guards' demeanors changed. Their eyes tried to roll upward and an under lid nictated open and shut rapidly.

Pinplants!

Jyrall grabbed the nearest guard as his weapon came up. He slammed him into the next one, and they both went down hard against the bulkhead. From the corner of his patched eye, to his delight, he saw Argold bounce another's head into the same bulkhead with a mighty right cross. Given the size of the gate operator's meaty fist, that soldier would never move again.

With a side kick to the chest, Jyrall pinned another guard against the other side of the passageway with his foot. As the soldier scrambled to bring his weapon to bear, Jyrall flipped the small hidden blade from his sleeve and sank it in the Blevin's throat.

Before Jyrall could turn his attention to the remaining two guards, he heard the loud sound of a flechette rifle on auto. He flinched, expecting the worse. For him, for Argold, or even for Ban-Tilk and the two Bakulu. Bodies dropped.

Jyrall grinned when he realized Golund held the rifle he had purchased from Mike in two of his pseudopods. Ban-Tilk was crouched behind Traluur's shell. Traluur slowly extended an eyestalk to see if it was clear. He ducked it back inside when Golund's rifle barked again.

Jyrall spun and saw the two guards he had stunned go down. Argold's eyes were wide. Jyrall nodded once in approval.

"I now know why Larth likes you so much, Golund," Jyrall said. "Ban-Tilk? Are you hurt?"

"Only in that my nascent acting career appears to be over before it began. I was just warming up to the megalomaniacal crime boss," the Jeha chittered. He rose from behind Traluur. "I am fine, Peacemaker. What's next?"

"Get their weapons and lock down this compartment. Then we take the gate."

* * *

Weqq

In the sweltering heat, Crusader Prime stood fuming under the artificial shade created by a communications tower. For seven days, Crusader units had swarmed the jungles on each of Weqq's four continents looking for any and all signs of the elusive TriRusk. For their troubles, they'd received two deaths due to unprovoked attacks from the local fauna, sixty-two injuries from the same, and the loss of three Mk 8 CASPers. After sweeping, sensing, and prodding each of the continents, they were no closer to identifying the location of the TriRusk. Despite this turn of events, Crusader

Prime smiled. Command was good and proper—exactly where he should be.

"Sir?" Lieutenant Colonel Smith called behind him.

Instead of turning to engage his executive officer, Prime leaned against the tower. "What is it, Smith?"

"Your private slate has been buzzing with notifications for the last hour. I took the liberty of checking the screen and—"

Prime whirled on his executive officer. "And you what?"

"Who is Counselor?" Smith asked. "Is that an office under the guild master?"

"Did you see any of the messages?" Prime stepped in the other man's direction.

"No, sir," Smith said, taking a frightened step back. "I was making sure there wasn't an emergency notification being sent through the wrong channels. It's…it's happened before."

Prime stopped and allowed a smile to form. "You're right, Smith. A good observation on your part."

"Thank you, sir."

"However," Prime said, more from his throat. The effect of the near growl did exactly what he wanted it to do; it restoked the younger man's abject fear. "If you, or anyone else, ever reads a message on that slate without my express permission, I will kill you where you stand. Am I clear?"

Smith swallowed. "Yes, sir."

Prime walked up to the man and slapped him on the shoulder. "Prepare the units for departure. I expect we're about to be redeployed on a far more useful mission."

He didn't wait for a response. The fear he detected in the young, former mercenary almost aroused Prime. Small unit leadership hadn't always been easy. He'd been a mercenary commander, once, but it seemed incredibly distant. Almost fuzzy. Being a Crusader, he'd known, was his calling. His true purpose. Yet the breadth of his operations far exceeded anything he'd commanded before, through fifteen years of victories…and losses.

Entering the dark, cooler command post, Prime hesitated. The darkness brought a slashing, visceral image of a feral Oogar almost on top of his vantage point. Prime shivered involuntarily. The memory, he knew, was real and had most certainly happened to him. Yet he couldn't place it. Sometimes, there were other faces. Occasionally, snippets of words and radio transmissions. The total sense of it was shock and panic.

And then shame.

With the next blink of his eyes, the image and the emotions dissipated, leaving a disconnected feeling. He shook this away with a flutter of both hands, stretching and airing out his palms, before clenching his fists and relaxing them. His eyes adjusted to the dark quickly, and he confirmed none of his staff were watching him. They were intent on their consoles and diligently doing the jobs he'd personally selected them to perform. His core staff of five never spoke unless spoken to. They worked silently, soundlessly, save for the tapping of console keys. Their given names and their prior careers were information he eschewed. For him, they were his archangels, and he'd named them so for the odd times he'd had to call on them.

Prime moved silently to his console and sat down. The specially made chair connected instantly to his pinplants. At the moment of connection, a burst of white noise hammered his eyes, and the screens of the entire command post darkened. Primary power failed. Secondary generators kicked in and then sputtered quiet.

Counselor's digitized voice filled his ears. "Let me be exceedingly clear, Prime. When I call for you, you are not to be on your private time. You serve at my discretion and my desire. Further failures will cause reevaluation of my choice. Am I clear?"

Prime found his tongue. "Yes, Counselor."

"Have you found the TriRusk?"

"No," Prime answered. "We continue to search on two continents. We have suffered losses and casualties—"

"Which I care nothing about. Your soldiers and supplies are plentiful," Counselor snapped. "Human lives are inconsequential to the cause, Prime. You must find the TriRusk. They have not left the planet. Wherever they are, you must find them. Until you do, you are to remain on Weqq. Am I clear?"

"Yes, Counselor."

"Excellent, Prime. You are an adequate commander. Contact me when you find them, and do not ignore my communications again."

The connection terminated and, instantly, the power returned. Surrounded by the whine of terminals spooling up to return to operations, Prime sat and fumed. The TriRusk might never be found. But if he did find them, and Counselor ordered it, he would enjoy slaughtering all of the damned things.

"Crusader Prime?" one of his archangels asked. "We have reports of fresh tracks on the far western continent. Shall we engage the search drones?"

Prime smiled to himself. The far western continent didn't surprise him. "Send in the first battalion. Have them on station within the next twelve hours. Full space deployment is authorized. Prepare the *Herald* for orbital bombardment. If they do not surrender, they'll die for galactic peace and prosperity."

"As it will be recorded," the archangels chimed in one toneless voice.

Prime's smile widened. *They'll pay. These abominations should never have returned to the guild. It's all her fault.*

A voice from his past, both soft and cold, said. "You are no commander."

We'll see, dear. Won't we?

* * *

Enforcer Landing Pad

Peacemaker Headquarters

Karma IV

Given the nature of their mission and the need for operational security of the highest levels, the Peacemaker Guild's Headquarters on Karma limited transport traffic to Enforcer and Blue Flight vessels. All other ships and operations connected to the main reception hub at Bartertown and then ferried official business via one of the more standard modes of transportation available. As *Tango Veritas*' shuttle flared for landing, Kurrang stood at the main hatch with his long face pressed against the small porthole. He'd last been to Karma more than one hundred and fifty Earth years before, and, as he'd expected, much appeared to have changed.

The Enforcer landing pad was three times its original size and capable of receiving multiple shuttles while maintaining room for no less than two Blue Flights at any given time. One Blue Flight always remained on the pad, per standard operating procedure. Given the state of operations, he'd expected to see another in place, but its pad lay empty. In its place appeared to be maintenance racks for the powered armor Humans called CASPers.

The Crusaders have infiltrated even these private spaces. This must end now.

Kurrang reached for a communications panel mounted to the right of the door and slapped the connection button for the bridge. "Tok? Are you seeing this?"

"Looks like Crusaders." The Jivool growled. "I don't like it, sir."

"Me either." Kurrang chewed on his tongue for a moment. "Have you established short final with approach?"

"Negative. We're coming around the opposite side of the pattern now. They'll contact us in about thirty seconds."

Kurrang tapped his digits on the hatch. "Zevva? Where is Dreel's ship?"

"It's gone, sir. The official manifest says his shuttle departed two days ago."

Entropy.

"Where was it docked? What bay at Bartertown?"

"It wasn't at Bartertown," Zevva replied. "His shuttle's final departure was from an outlying pad near Zutone. It left Pad 85 and was marked as official business."

"Then we start at Pad 85. Tok, declare an emergency and divert to Bartertown."

"What's my emergency?" Tok replied. "Approach is calling us, and all of my systems are showing green. They won't believe us."

Kurrang grinned. "Declare a chemical spill. You have a TriRusk on board, and it suffered a glandular imbalance and spoiled your main cargo hold."

"A what?" Tok replied.

"Trust me, Tok." Kurrang allowed himself to grin. "They haven't seen a TriRusk here in a hundred years or more, and I'm guessing their emergency action procedures will reflect the last time this happened. They diverted a Blue Flight then; they'll have no problem letting you go now."

"Sir?" Zevva asked. "Not to speak out against your plan, but if the Crusaders are here, they already know you are aboard. What's to stop them from coming after us?"

"Good question," Kurrang conceded. "We'll save that scenario for another time. Tok, disregard all radio traffic and boost out like you're going to orbit. Once you're past their radar, declare an emergency and descend like you're falling out of a tree. Get below sensor height and then double back toward Zutone. We'll land there."

"That's on the restricted access list, sir," Zevva replied and then laughed. "No Peacemakers or deputized agents officially allowed."

"The Crusaders won't be there, either," Tok agreed. "Copy, sir. Everybody, hang on. We've got one shot at this."

Kurrang moved quickly back toward the bridge so he could strap himself in. When he reached the hatch, he glanced at Zevva. "Pull Stormwatch, if you can. I want to know what's going on—at least as much as we can determine."

"What do you mean?"

"The Crusaders being at the Enforcer pad isn't a mistake or a case of nowhere to put them. We have to believe the entire guild is compromised." Kurrang strapped into his seat. "We're going outside the established laws to do what we have to do."

"Save Captain Dreel?" Kravon asked. The Caroon had been quiet the entire time. "Or save the galaxy?"

"Likely both." Kurrang grunted. "This is where I'm supposed to ask if you want to walk away."

Tok laughed. "And this is where we say something overly dramatic and stay. We're with you, sir."

Kurrang nodded, and a smile crossed his maw. "We do this together, then."

"*Shuttle Veritas*, this is Crusader Approach. You are cleared for short final."

Kurrang shook his head. "Maintain course and speed."

"Yes, sir," Tok replied.

"Anybody think it's weird they said Crusader Approach? Where are the Enforcers?" Kravon asked. "Have they been disbanded?"

"Unlikely. Either they've been assimilated into the Crusader effort, or they've abandoned their posts," Kurrang replied. "I'd like to think the latter, but I doubt they've seen the truth."

"I can fix that," Zevva said. "I only need thirty seconds to broadcast Tok's video to every Peacemaker slate on the planet."

Kurrang shook his head. "Not yet. Let's see what they do when we disobey their instructions. Put the ball in their court and ascertain their next move."

"Sounds good to me," Tok replied. "Ready to accelerate for orbit on your order, Captain Kurrang."

As they passed over the outer marker and did not turn for the landing pad, the approach controller called again. This time, there was no denying their real intention. "*Shuttle Veritas*, you are directed to land and surrender. Move immediately to the pad, or you will be shot down."

"I'd like to see them try," Zevva laughed.

"Let's go, Tok. Make it look convincing."

Tok grinned. "Boosting."

Acceleration slammed Kurrang into the seat. He'd not pulled any serious G-forces in years, but he felt no adverse effects. Unlike Tok and Kravon, Zevva would also have little issue with the rapid acceleration. Kurrang turned his head, a motion which would make Tok and Kravon pass out, and looked at her.

"Zevva. Push me Stormwatch when you have it."

"On the way."

Kurrang powered up a Tri-V and studied the most recent dispatch. There were several troubling entries, both in the codes he knew and in openly reported updates from several regional barracks commanders. As troubling as the updates were, there were two unaccountable notations. One was about a young Zuparti Peacemaker named Zetchek overseeing a dispute involving the Dream World Consortium on Arduna.

We may have to look into that.

The other notation struck him as odd. He didn't know the Peacemaker mentioned, but a full Lumar Peacemaker was a very rare occurrence.

<<Peacemaker Millzak. Last seen on Karma. Four days, no report.>>

That's where we begin.

*****

Chapter Twenty-Six

The ramp on the Peacemaker's ship slammed to the deck, and Frank and Stein rolled out on their tracks. Larth glanced at Ricky and asked, "Are you all right?"

"Yeah," Ricky said, shaking his hand. He took off the insulated gloves and threw them aside. "I got that connector back on the rotation gearbox. Had to wear them dang gloves 'cause there weren't time to kill the power. It got a piece of a finger and nipped me. Should be good now."

"Good, get them in the fight," Larth said. He drew his pistols from his hip holsters. "I gotta go meet Jyrall. He probably already took out those guards. If I don't catch up, there won't be anyone left to shoot." He ducked behind the nearest crate as the battle raged ahead and slipped out of sight.

Ricky stepped behind Stein as it followed Frank. Up ahead, the CASPers of the Blue Ridge Kin led the fight on this side of the bay and into the passageways. They were engaging a host of drones, flying back and forth, firing lasers. Parts of each mech's armor were scorched and burnt. An occasional piece was missing.

Below them, closer to the deck and around crates, the infantry soldiers led by First Sergeant Figgle fought another battle with the security forces. Ricky saw a Jivool go down but was too far away to see who it was. He nodded in satisfaction as the four Maki each grabbed a limb and started dragging the downed trooper to cover behind a long, low crate. In the distance, he noticed the few mechs of the Barnstormers and other troops attempting to fight through and move into the passageways.

"Ricky!' Cora called out over the command net. "Any time now would be good. These drones are slowly picking us apart. They are everywhere."

"I'm on it, Cora," Ricky said, as his fingers flew over his slate. "I gotta program them to track and hit flying drones…There!"

The side-by-side hatches on top of Frank opened and the fifties came up. Right behind them, the mast with the antenna followed suit and began rotating. The weapons opened up with a loud, continuous roar, and drones began shattering and dropping. The barrels moved in unison, left right, up, down, tracking the targets. Ricky turned to Stein's controls.

"Good job, Ricky," Cora shouted. "We've been picking them off but missing most of our shots. Now, what can you do about them ones coming down the passage?"

Ricky pulled up Stein's optics on the small slate in his hands. "I see 'em. Dang if they don't look like little tanks." He saw one fire, and one of the Mk 4s toppled over, a leg blown off. "Oh shit, they shoot like one, too!"

His fingers flew as he input the commands. The rack with the missile launcher came up out of Stein, and the missiles began launching off. The knee-high miniature tanks began taking hits. Members of the Kin who were not engaged shouted encouragement. After a few seconds, they put their masks on to protect themselves from the acrid smoke from the damaged machines and the battle itself.

Ricky coughed and reached for his own mask as the last of the missiles emptied from the rack. Stein's front panel opened, and the two .45 caliber guns came up, both built from old tommy guns. Ricky ducked his head to put his mask on when they opened up.

"Ricky! Ricky! Stop th—" May called out. Her voice cut out mid-word.

Ricky looked up, and time seemed to slow. The two guns were at strange angles, as if the gears hadn't rotated all the way. Both were emptying their drums into the back of May's CASper. At such close range, pieces of armor were chipping, breaking, and flying off. Out of the corner of his eye, he saw the thrusters ignite as Cora dove toward May's machine and tackled it. The remaining rounds hit the nearest bulkhead and ricocheted everywhere.

His mask forgotten, Ricky scrambled to get past the two machines. He noticed a piece of glove stuck in Stein's rotation gear as he went by the smoking weapon. The sounds of the fight eased off as the Kin took out the rest of the guards in their area.

Cora was out of her mech. It was now upright, while May's was down on its back. Ricky helped Cora open the cockpit with the emergency release. "May! May!" he shouted as they worked.

Once it was open, Cora undid the straps, and Ricky reached in to pull May from the machine. Some of the smoke from inside cleared, and he saw May grimace when they moved her. "Dammit! Easy! Easy!" May said. "My shoulder is on fire."

"Shit," Cora said. "Looks like you have some shrapnel from your mech in it. It's long and it's deep. Maybe to the bone. Medic!"

"May, I am so sorry," Ricky said. His voice trembled. "I'm so fuckin' sorry!"

"Not your fault, honey," May said. "Shit happens." She grimaced again. "Hey, Frank and Stein took out all the drones so our troops could take care of the security guards. Listen, the fighting has stopped."

"Yeah, but..." Ricky started to say. The words wouldn't come. He swallowed and shook his head; images of what could have happened threatened to take over reality.

He was interrupted by a call from Larth over the command net. "Hey, I'm out of the area, but they got a call out. You guys can expect reinforcements. Probably the other hundred or so guards, would be my guess."

* * *

Colonel Brentale stopped his mech at the edge of the passageway. The direction they needed to go was not conducive for machines the size of CASPers. "Sergeant Major, looks like we'll have to dismount and join you."

"Sounds good, sir," Sergeant Major Daniels said. "We can use you down here. From what I can tell, that group up ahead is getting reinforcements. It looks like it's going to be an old-fashioned, man-on-man fight through these passages."

"Hey!" Staff Sergeant Wilson said. "You just keep digging deeper, Sergeant Major."

"I know, I know!"

"Seriously, sir," the sergeant major continued. "We're down five troops. Doc said it didn't look like any would be fatalities, but they are out of the fight for sure. He's back behind that double stack of crates with them."

"Shit!" Brentale exclaimed. "All right, pilots. Back 'em against the bulkhead, dismount, and lock them down. We go on foot from here."

Once they were reformed and in squads, Colonel Brentale looked around. "Has anyone seen Haney?"

"Not yet, sir," Staff Sergeant Wilson said. "He was supposed to lock the ship down and catch up. I hope he's not down somewhere behind us."

* * *

Docking Berth, *Blue Ridge*

Specialist Conner slammed her palm on the emergency panel in the berth, turned, and ran toward the ramp on the *Blue Ridge*. Behind her, a wide section of bulkhead slid toward the deck to seal it from the rest of the bay and the gate itself. She ran up the rising ramp and raced toward the operations center, feeling the vibrations of the ship as it started to undock.

"Weapons systems online, online, that is," Stew called out.

Conner felt the gravity fade away as the ship undocked and moved away from the spinning station. She slid into the weapons seat and strapped in. "Launcher one and two locked on. Swing us out a little, sir. I don't want any debris to hit us."

"We are seconds from a safe distance, Specialist. Seconds, don't you know."

"Just in time," Stew added. "Time, I say. That ship is powering up now, as in, now."

"Firing one and two!" Specialist Conner called out. The XT-88 anti-radiation missiles leapt from their launchers. "Bringing the main laser on target. Ten seconds to fully powered."

"System shows a direct hit on their targeting array, direct, I say," Stew said. "They will still be maneuverable. They may try and put some distance between us and attempt repairs. Repairs, that is, don't you know."

"No, they won't," Specialist Conner said. She brushed a wisp of red hair out of her face. "Those bastards ain't going anywhere with their thrusters destroyed." She hit the panel, and a steady beam of laser fire burned into the thrusters before the enemy ship could fully get underway.

* * *

Cargo Bay

Larth glanced around the last row of containers. He did his best to ignore the battle raging behind and to the side of him. Up ahead, he saw three Blevin security guards. One was screaming into his comms for backup.

"Shit. They got more coming this way. I better get while the getting is good," Larth said to himself.

"I know. Don't rush me," he answered himself with a laugh.

With both hands extended, Larth ran at the surprised guards, firing both pistols. He slid to a stop among the bodies, just as both slides locked back. He glanced left and right to see if he had been noticed as he reloaded. He checked his small handheld device to make sure the shortcut he had planned would still work, shrugged, and ran down the small passageway to his right.

"I'm coming, Snarlyface! Don't kill them all before I get there," he called out as he ran.

After a few moments, he giggled. "Me, too!"

* * *

Golund secured the compartment, locking the dead and injured Blevin away from the fight. While doing so, he secured their weapons. Jyrall watched the Bakulu's fluid grace and deadly precision with a sense of awe and gratitude. They could have done far worse in choosing partners for this mission.

"We're set, Peacemaker," Golund said. "What's next?"

Jyrall didn't immediately reply. He walked several meters down the passageway toward the main gate control area and promenade level. The enhanced audio sensor built into his eyepatch detected subsonic vibrations coming from the floor. The intensity of the vibrations appeared to be getting stronger, meaning someone, or many someones, were coming. There was no question who they would be and what their mission was. Reinforcing the security forces meant more of the Kin and Barnstormers would die. Jyrall would not stand for that, and he realized what he and the others had to do.

Now, we honor the threat.

He turned to the others and surveyed their space. The compartment entryway diverged from the main passageway at a ninety-degree angle. With the right amount of firepower, they could hold the position and wait for reinforcements.

"We're going to defend here."

"Righteous." Golund looked quickly around the space. "Threats arriving?"

"Any second."

"We'll be ready for them." He turned to Traluur. "Grab some of those weapons."

"How will we fire them?" Traluur asked. He had a valid point. The Blevin weapons were awkward and unsophisticated.

Golund chittered. "We'll find a way. I'm on the corner. Traluur, get behind me. Peacemaker Jyrall? You stand over us. I think you'll be able to see just fine."

Ban-Tilk cradled a Blevin weapon in several sets of pincers. "I'll back you up. But what if they'll listen to reason."

"Reason?" Jyrall whirled to face the Jeha. "You're wanting another chance?"

"Technically, I haven't worn out my old one. Put your weapon to my head and hold me out in the passageway. You might, at least, stop them and provide some easy targets."

Jyrall grinned. "Excellent idea, Ban-Tilk."

"I do try, Peacemaker."

"Traluur and Golund, grab a weapon and take cover. Ban-Tilk? You ready for your close-up?"

"My…what?"

"Forget it." Jyrall shook his head.

I've been watching too many old Human movies. Damn you, Larth.

Ban-Tilk moved closer. "I hear them coming, Peacemaker."

Jyrall made eye contact with Golund. "Don't fire unless I'm fired upon. If that happens, hit them with everything we can muster. No quarter."

"Now you're talking," Golund replied. He settled against the corner of the junction, with his weapon at the ready. He held two more magazines in other appendages, ready for use.

"I'm ready when you are, Peacemaker. Just grab lower than my neck, and I'll be fine," Ban-Tilk said. "At least, I think I'll be fine."

Jyrall wanted to laugh, but he heard the Blevin in the passageway. He reached out with his right arm, grasped Ban-Tilk as requested, and held him off the ground and around the corner of the junction.

"That's far enough!" Jyrall roared. "What is the meaning of this? You have been infiltrated. This is not Nay-Thok at all. What are you playing at, Captain Ravgart?"

Ban-Tilk squirmed and sighed but said nothing. His antennae sagged, and Jyrall knew he'd have questions to answer once this affair was done.

Sometimes, an unwinnable situation can be turned around merely by attempting the impossible.

From their silence, Jyrall sensed confusion. They had not opened fire, so he carefully peered around the corner. There were at least twelve Blevin. He could not make out the captain, and all of them stood mute, wondering what had happened.

"Firing positions," a voice called. The Blevin snapped into two rows, with the front row kneeling like something out of a Napoleonic battle painting. As they did, he caught sight of their leader standing behind them. "Varkell? What are you talking about? Let go of Nay-Thok and surrender yourself and those Humans in the docking bays. There's been some type of misunderstanding."

"Misunderstanding?" Jyrall growled. He shook Ban-Tilk with his raised arm. "This is not Nay-Thok. You have been infiltrated. My arrest proves it. We had an arrangement."

"Arrangements change." Ravgart raised his weapon and fired once. Jyrall pulled Ban-Tilk back toward the protection of the corner bulkhead, but he wasn't fast enough. The round tore off one of Ban-Tilk's upper pincers.

"Gaaaahhh!" the Jeha squealed.

Golund and Traluur opened up on the Blevin, and Jyrall gently lowered Ban-Tilk to the ground. The two Bakulu pilots worked in concert with one another to rake the main passageway with weapons fire.

"You okay?"

Ban-Tilk breathed heavily. "It hurts."

Jyrall nodded. "Stay down. We'll handle this."

He quickly looked over the wound. Ban-Tilk would lose the pincer, which he'd likely embrace because it would give him an experienced, tough look amongst his peers. There was a lot of fluid and blood around the wound, but from his xeno-anatomy courses at the academy, he triaged the wound as superficial but messy. Given that, he could go about his business. Drawing his hand cannon, Jyrall returned to the corner as Golund finished a long burst of fire. Jyrall extended his arm and waited. Two Blevin appeared, coming up to fire, and both saw him in the same instant.

Jyrall fired twice and dropped them.

As he turned back to the corner and safety, he heard Ravgart yell, "Cease fire! Cease fire!"

They waited for a long moment, breathing hard in the smoky, acrid air of the passageway. Golund quickly reloaded his weapons and prodded Traluur to do the same.

"Varkell!"

Jyrall snorted but did not emerge from behind the bulkhead. "What is it, Ravgart?"

"Your last chance to surrender. You have thirty seconds to come out with your limbs where we can see them."

Options whirled in Jyrall's head. He could play the tactical situation a number of ways. The first option was to surrender and allow the Blevin security team to capture them. They'd undoubtedly take him and his friends deeper into the gate for safekeeping. The chance they would slip up and make a mistake securing him or the others was almost certain. What he didn't know was how committed Ravgart was to their mission. Mercenaries were easy to distract with more credits. Paid security forces, however, tended to have other motivations to maintain their station during combat. Figuring out what motivation Ravgart clung to would take time they didn't have.

Which left two options: fight the Blevin or attempt to blindside them again.

Jyrall holstered his pistol and reached into his tactical vest. Withdrawing the slim black case never failed to center his thoughts. With a deep breath, he held out the case around the corner and let it fall open.

"Captain Ravgart, my name is Peacemaker Jyrall. On the authority of the Peacemaker Guild, you are ordered to stand down your security forces and prepare for investigation."

There was a laugh from the corridor. "On what grounds? And, Varkell, impersonating a Peacemaker is a very serious crime. You should be ashamed of yourself."

Jyrall edged out into the hallway but stayed close to the corner bulkhead. "This is no ruse, Ravgart. Stand down, and the forces in the cargo hold will do the same."

"They're Humans. They're not going to stop until they ruin this gate and everything else they touch." Ravgart shook his head in disgust and brought his weapon up again. "Ten seconds, Varkell."

"My name is Jyrall, and I *am* a Peacemaker. If you will not stand down, we have no choice but to honor the threat you provide and take you down."

Ravgart laughed. "I don't think so, Varkell. You're just a smuggler, and smugglers always run."

In a millisecond, Jyrall knew Ravgart was about to fire, so he jumped back behind the bulkhead. The shot, meant for Jyrall's chest, impacted his Peacemaker badge and flung it down the main passageway toward the cargo bays. It would have to wait.

Jyrall drew his weapon and looked down at Golund. "That went well, yes?"

Golund chuckled and hefted his weapon. "Not as well as this is going to go, Peacemaker."

As the Bakulu fired a burst down the passageway, Jyrall activated his personal comms through the eyepatch.

"Larth? You there, Little Buddy?"

"What is it?" His partner was breathing hard. "I'm a bit busy trying to get out of the cargo bay. These fuckers are everywhere. Where are you?"

"Pinned down off the main passageway. There's twenty Blevin blocking our way. I've got Ban-Tilk and the others with me. Going to need your assistance."

"Good thing I'm on my way there in a hurry, Snarlyface," Larth called. *"Meep-meep!"*

* * * * *

Chapter Twenty-Seven

Shaylin Gate

First Sergeant Figgle made his way back to Cora. "Ma'am, they have pulled sections of bulkhead out of another large area into the passageway. Nail's and his squad have point. Once we round that corner, it's a straight shot for an easy hundred of your Human yards. They have cover. We will be exposed as we try to get to them."

"Can we smoke 'em out, Top?" Cora asked. She put her hand on the mask at her side.

"No. Those fuckers have masks, too."

"What about a few grenade launchers?" Lisalle asked. She had her first aid pouch in her hand. "We could fire the flechette grenade launchers."

"I was looking at that," Nileah said. She shook her head and hissed as Lisalle tightened the bandage on her forearm. "Near as I can figure, we can't fire 'em with enough angle to go the distance. Them damn things will hit the ceiling and come down fast and just go sliding."

The comms crackled in everyone's earpieces. They were all on the unit command frequency. "Colonel McCoy, Nails."

"What do you have for me, Nails?" Cora answered.

"Ma'am, we have a problem. The group ahead just received reinforcements. Not a lot of them. Looks like about five more joined them. With some gear."

"What does that give them now?" Cora asked. "Maybe thirty up there?"

"No, ma'am," answered the gray-haired NCO. "Anderson tells me twenty just peeled off and went down another passage. The problem is, the ten who remained behind just finished setting up a crew-served system. It's hard to tell what it is. The small drone Anderson sent over the first barricade just got knocked out of commission. It was the last one my squad had. Anyway, it looks like the Piltak Zen 3200."

"Shit."

"Yes, ma'am."

First Sergeant Figgle tried to squint. It was the closest he could come to a questioning expression on a Human face. "What type of system is that?"

"Jivool. That damn thing spits out more rounds than seeds at a watermelon eatin' contest," Lisalle answered. "Bad business."

"It makes some Ricky Shit seem tame," Cora said. "A long time ago, several of them took our old battalion down to little more than a company. I can't believe they're going to risk a possible hull breach. Those rounds may go through a bulkhead…or two."

"What do we do?" Nileah asked. "We can't just sit here."

Cora thought for a moment. "We really need a CASPer. Maybe, with a few MAC rounds, we can get through and take out that weapon."

"There are sections between us and the bay where a mech is too tall," First Sergeant Figgle countered. "One won't make it here."

"There is no other choice," Cora said. "I will go back and get mine. I'll crawl her if I have to, but I'll be back."

"You're not going alone," Figgle said. His tone invited no argument. "Squarlik! Take your squad and go with the commander. If anything happens to her, I'll cut you out of your hide."

* * *

Colonel Brentale switched frequencies and called Cora. "Cora, Pete."

"How's it going on your side, Pete?" Cora asked. She sounded winded.

"Not good. We're pinned down. They have some system on a tripod throwing slugs like there's no end to them. We can't break cover. It's a stalemate."

"How many are you facing?" Cora asked.

"Looks like about thirty," Pete answered. "We have a handful of wounded and a couple of casualties."

"We're facing the same Jivool system," Cora said. "Except we don't have any cover like you do. I'm on my way back to mount up and bring a CASPer down on them. Can you do the same?"

"No can do," Pete answered. "Where they are makes it impossible. They will gun us down from behind. Sounds like you have your own problems. We'll get it figured out. Keep your head down."

"You do the same," Cora said. "Out here."

"Not good, sir?" Staff Sergeant Wilson asked. She wiped the blood off her hands again. There wasn't much left, but she kept wiping them. Over and over.

"No," he admitted. He looked over at Sergeant Major Daniel's body. The bandages had done little to stop the flow of blood on wounds too great for the nanites used to save him. "They are facing the same thing." He switched back to their internal frequency.

"Sir," Staff Sergeant Jerund called.

Colonel Brentale took a deep breath and answered his comms. "Anything new up there, Jerund?"

"Yes, sir. Looks like they're unpacking two more boxes. Might be more of those damned drones. I—hold on sir, I have Specialist Haney on my squad net. Wait one, over."

Brentale looked toward Staff Sergeant Wilson. "Haney? I thought we lost him. We haven't heard from him since he was supposed to lock down the ship."

"It's Haney, sir. Who the hell knows what he has been up to?" Wilson answered.

The comms crackled to life. "Sir," Sergeant Jerund said, "Haney says he's coming…and he's coming in hot."

"Hot? What do you mean, he's coming in hot? What the hell—" Colonel Brentale started to ask. He didn't get to finish his sentence.

The unmistakable roar of the thrusters on a powered glider echoed through the long passage behind them. He saw occasional sparks as the sound grew louder. Haney, operating one of the unit's gliders, shot overhead, the edges of the wings scraping one side of the passage and then the other. His boots raked over the stacked-up cover Wilson was behind, and she ducked even lower when the top box fell.

The Blevin crew on the tripod-mounted weapon hesitated, as though they could not believe what they were seeing. By the time the gunner swiveled the barrels upward, Haney was overhead. He released the first belt of flechette grenades from a hand gripping the controls. He dropped the other belt on the group of bunched-up Blevin he careened over after edging against the side of the passage.

Loosening the second grip had cost him the control he barely maintained at that speed in the tight confines, and the glider glanced against a bulkhead hard enough to snap a strut and send him sliding down the passageway beyond the guards. The first belt of grenades went off, killing the weapon's crew and four others. The weapon was in pieces. The next belt was more devastating to the remaining troops, as the darts ricocheted off the bulkheads and containers they were using as cover.

Staff Sergeant Jerund and his squad raced ahead to the first of the Blevin's cover and dispatched the remaining guards. Most were already wounded beyond fighting back. He didn't give them a chance.

"There's something wrong with that guy," Staff Sergeant Wilson said.

"Just be glad he's on our side," Brentale replied. "A damned glider in a stargate." He shook his head. "Send someone to help untangle him from the glider."

"You think he lived through that crash, sir?" the staff sergeant asked. She was serious.

"I know good and well he did. Hell, he probably doesn't even have a scratch, knowing him."

"That, or he is so banged up, you'll wonder how he's walking. Like that one bar fight," Wilson suggested.

"True. But he'll be walking."

* * *

Corporal Bweenkit eased his head around the corner to check if it was clear. For most of the way back toward the bay and the CASPers, Sergeant Squarlik and his squad had scrambled to keep up with their running commander. Squarlik had insisted she wait before rounding this next corner. He had spotted one of the flying drones up ahead. When it zipped out of sight, he called a halt.

Several shots were fired from the next passage, and Bweenkit fell back, a small trench burned along the side of his head. It had gone through the hard outer layer of armor to the flesh below. It wasn't a killing hit, but he would lose sight in his eye. Squarlik slapped a hard bandage on it, specifically designed for the Goka; the adhesives held it tight against the wound.

Bweenkit hissed in pain. "There are at least twenty of them. They are unboxing more drones."

Cora brought up the frequency to reach Keaton directly. "Keaton, we really need these drones taken out of commission. It's about to get really bad."

"I've been working on it, Cora," Keaton answered. "I found the frequency they're all operating under. The thing is, it was triple encrypted."

"Triple?" Cora asked. "That's a lot, right?"

"Yeah," Keaton answered. "The first two, I got through easy enough once I figured out the maker. The last, I am just now breaking and…There! I'm shutting down control to all the drones. Cora, that last was like something I have never seen. I had to chase it as it adapted to my attempts. It's like something I would set up. Anyway, the first two were really interesting. Those drones were made and programmed by the Science Guild."

"The Science Guild?" Cora asked. "Make sure you let Jyrall know."

"Calling him next," Keaton agreed.

Cora turned to Sergeant Squarlik. "Keep them occupied. I'm going back to that last side passage to make my way around them. They won't have the drones to see me doing it, now."

"Ma'am, the first sergeant will have my hide if we let you out of our sight," Squarlik said.

"I'll deal with Top, Sergeant," Cora said. "You just keep them occupied."

"Yes, ma'am."

As shots rang out behind her, Cora made her way through the small passage. After two turns, she checked her slate and headed toward the bay. She stepped into the area where she'd left her CASPer and climbed in. The cockpit of her CASPer, nicknamed Lucille by her father, felt comfortable to her. She left the area, went about fifty yards, rounded a bend, and slowly raised her machine's hands. No less than fifty Blevin were staging for an attack.

One with leadership markings on his uniform stepped toward her. He stopped abruptly as his body quivered and his eyes rolled back. Cora saw the small light glowing on his pinplant. He shuddered one last time and focused on her. Even in her mech, the odds were not good. She dropped the CASPer's arms and fired.

Minutes later, it was all over.

"Remove her from that machine and take her weapons. Take her to the control station," the lieutenant said. "We will avoid the main corridors and use the customs bay. Let's move."

* * *

Above Karma IV

Tango Veritas

The shuttle continued upward under thrust. Kurrang saw a notification on the Tri-V to his right, and he selected the message. As he read, he chewed on the side of his mouth. His hasty plan hadn't survived enemy contact, after all. A few taps on his console confirmed his suspicions, both for his ship and for their sister ship in orbit. There wasn't much time now.

"Change in plans, Tok," Kurrang said. "Continue to orbit. Zevva? Get in touch with *Tango Equitas*. Have them de-orbit and check the hangar at Zutone. The Crusaders have put out a warrant for our arrest and a bounty to local mercenary forces."

Tok chuckled. "I guess that confirms we are public enemy number one, right?"

"Something like that," Kurrang grunted. "Zevva? Kravon? How much have you been able to get from Stormwatch and other sources?"

"Not as much as I'd like," Zevva replied. "I have footage of Dreel and a Lumar moving down the gauntlet at the main spaceport. I don't know exactly where they went. The security feeds in that area are incomplete. Data uploads are really slow for some reason."

"Which doesn't sound accidental at all," Kravon added. "The Crusaders have labeled us rogue Enforcers. That comes with a kill-on-sight justification."

Thank you so much, Kr'et'Socae. Kurrang shook his head. *Think. You have to find a way out of this for everyone.*

"Zevva, can the *Equitas* get to Zutone before the Crusaders?"

"It's a tight window, sir," Zevva buzzed. "I'll have line of sight with them in five seconds. They're hailing us. Putting you through."

"*Veritas*, this is *Equitas*. What's your status?" the Tango's lead pilot, Mratt, growled over the frequency.

Kurrang cleared his throat. "*Equitas*, we have a situation. We're going to separate. I need you to jump to Krifay and ensure your tail is clear. Once you've done that, I need you back here in deep cover. The passage of time can't be helped, but it's too dangerous to have you deorbit and rush in there now—it's likely a trap. When you return, you're looking for the captain, a Lumar Peacemaker named Millzak, or anything else we can use."

"Copy, sir. Are you tracking the bulletin and bounty declarations?" the Sidar Cha-Myt's higher-pitched voice asked.

"We are, *Equitas*. We probably caused it. The Crusaders are already here, at least a few battalions of them. They've taken up a position at the Enforcer landing pads. We have to assume they've infiltrated not only the guild, but our very own brothers and sisters."

"Entropy," Mratt said.

"Can't be helped," Kurrang replied. "You have your orders."

"I have to say, sir, I don't like the sound of this," the unmistakable voice of an Oogar, in this case Tavarra, spoke slowly into the radio. "This could be a trap."

"A minimum of two weeks should let the situation develop enough for you to move without being seen. Krifay is far enough out that nobody should be looking for you, and there's a friend of a friend there—drop the name Jyrall. He's a—"

The ship's power plants dropped offline as did its engines. Backup systems failed to immediately engage. Darkness and silence filled the spacecraft.

"Zevva?"

"I've got nothing, sir. That data packet we downloaded was the last traffic I saw before we went dark."

"Tok?"

There was no response for a moment. Kurrang turned and saw the Jivool furiously tapping his controls. "We're in a ballistic arc. We're going to reenter, and if we don't get this thing under control, we're going to burn up. We've got about twelve minutes to figure out what's happened and restart our power plants."

"Oh, gods!" Kravon said. Kurrang spun and saw the Enforcer pointing out the window. "There was an explosion about where the *Equitas* should be."

"Securing all comms and exterior sensors," Tok reported. "Power plants on standby."

"Starting auxiliary systems," Zevva called. A few seconds later, she said, "I've got nothing. This never happens. The whole system can't go down in flight like this. The flight control systems are Jeha designed and are supposedly secure against everything short of—"

The speaker above Kurrang clicked to life.

"Captain Kurrang, Enforcers Tok, Kravon, and Zevva. Your mission has ended," the toneless, disembodied voice said. "Sacrifices are necessary to move the galaxy forward. Your names will be duly inscribed in Memorial Hall, despite your behavior. Appearances need to be maintained, for now."

"Who is this?" Kurrang demanded. "Who are you and what have you done to this ship?"

"*Equitas* and *Veritas* have been decommissioned. You and your Enforcers are a liability to the guild and must be executed."

"Like hell." Kurrang unbuckled himself. "Zevva, with me! We can bypass—"

Kurrang's ears popped violently, and the air around him tore away. The Tango's emergency escape hatch had blown. There were no warning klaxons in the dead ship. Kurrang clutched at his seat but could not hold on. He tumbled violently into the hatchway, slamming his ribcage painfully. He struggled to dig his claws against the metal. Debris of all type careened out of the hatch and caused his grip to weaken. Cold seeped through every exposed pore in his skin.

With a slash, he whipped an arm through the hatch to gain any type of purchase on the nearby equipment. He failed and tumbled into space. There was nothing to breathe in the mind-numbing cold. Eyes jammed shut, his body tearing itself apart from the inside, Kurrang saw a flash behind his closed eyes and then felt the pressure wave when the Tango detonated a few milliseconds later.

He thought of his daughter, Maarg, under a clear sky, surrounded by the green fields of their home. The sun was bright and warm. Wind ruffled his fur. They laughed and played together. All was right in his world.

And then there was nothing.

*****

Chapter Twenty-Eight

Shaylin Gate

"Cora. Come in, Cora," Nileah said again. She turned to Lisalle. "Nothing. It's like she dropped off the net completely."

"Can you reach Squarlik, ma'am?" First Sergeant Figgle asked.

Nileah switched frequencies and dropped down to one the Sergeant would be monitoring to keep up with his squad. "Sergeant Squarlik, Captain Sevier."

"Squarlik here," answered the Goka sergeant. "What can I do for you, ma'am?"

"Do you have eyes on the commander?" Nileah asked.

There was a pause before the answer came back. "No, ma'am. Not at this time."

"Explain."

"It better be a good one," Figgle added. He had switched to the same frequency.

"She had us lay down cover fire while she slipped back and took another route. Those we were engaged with have backed off and slipped away. We are just waiting for her to get here with her war machine."

Figgle looked at his company's executive officer. "I'm going to tear one of his pincers off and beat him to death with it. I swear I will."

"Not now you won't," Nileah said. "Lord-a mercy this ain't good. Let me think."

After a moment, Nileah switched frequencies yet again. "Ricky…Ricky!"

"I'm here. I'm with the Maki and the wounded. May is resting," Ricky answered.

"I need you up here with us," Nileah said. "And bring those two drones you've been working on. The ones with the grenades attached."

"What?" Ricky asked. "I—I don't want to leave May. She may need something. A drink or whatever."

"I need you and those drones up here. *Now*," Nileah said, a little more forceful.

"Nileah, I can't. Besides, we can't trust those things. We can't trust anything I work on. It all turns to shit. Keaton was right. Some of my Ricky Shit got someone hurt. May is hurt. Coulda killed her. Hell, we all coulda died on a jump with the shunts the ship used to have."

Nileah looked at Lisalle, concern in her eyes. Lisalle nodded encouragement for her to go on. Nileah took a deep breath to calm herself.

"Ricky, listen to me." Her voice was more like herself. "You turn a good wrench. Cora believes it. I believe it. We have to find a way to get past the weapon set up in the passage ahead. We have to find Cora. I think she's been captured. We need you. She needs you. Your family needs you."

There were a few seconds of silence.

"I'm coming."

* * *

Ricky ran as fast as he could while carrying two drones. One was heavier than the other, which made it even more difficult. He rounded a bend and slid to a stop. Up ahead, several weapons were pointed at him from behind some crates. He turned to duck into an opening.

"Hold fire," a voice rang out. "Hold fire."

Ricky turned back. "Squarlik?"

"The XO told us to meet up with you and bring you to her," Sergeant Squarlik said, standing. He tried to wink, but only squinted. He shifted the .50 caliber sniper rifle strapped on his back. Even when the mission dictated the flechette rifle in his pincers, he wasn't going anywhere without it.

He turned to his squad. "Grab those drones and let's move out. Whatever you do, don't drop them. I can guarantee they are some kind of Ricky Shit."

Ten minutes later, they slid to a stop behind the piece of bulkhead beside Nileah, Lisalle, and Sergeant Bailey.

"I'm here," Ricky said between deep breaths. He noticed her bandaged forearm. "What's the plan?"

"I need you to fly those drones over that gun emplacement and drop those grenades," Nileah answered.

"How far is it?" Ricky asked. He peeked over the cover. "All I see is a bulkhead."

"It's around the corner and wide open," Sergeant Bailey explained. She had a bandage on her thigh. A dark bandage. "See Top up there with Nails?"

"Yeah, I see 'em," Ricky said. "I can do it from here. Nobody needs to expose themself and get their dang head blown off."

"What if they shoot them down?" Lisalle asked.

"Shit," Nileah said. "I didn't think about that. You got any ideas, Ricky?"

Ricky turned to Squarlik. "Get up there and get a good firing position. You track these drones with that long shooter. If either one of them starts acting squirrely, you shoot the drone. Not the grenades."

"Got it," Squarlik said. "Squirrely. Shoot the drones." He turned to move forward and stopped. "Figgle is up there. This is not good."

"Nope," agreed Sergeant Bailey. "He just might kill you himself."

Resigned, Squarlik placed his flechette rifle against the bulkhead, took his sniper rifle off his back, and moved up to the corner. When the first sergeant started to speak, he held up two pincers. "I'm on a mission for the XO. I'm looking for squirrels. Whatever they are."

Figgle stared at him with an open mouth as the sergeant settled into a good prone position. He waited for Ricky to let him know when he could roll over so his weapon would be pointed toward the enemy.

Ricky powered up both drones and let them hover beside him. He reached for his comm. "Keaton, you got me?"

"I hear you," his brother answered.

"You still have all the drones offline?"

"Yeah," Keaton said. "But I have to keep changing my program. Someone is rewriting theirs faster than I can, but they are reacting to what I do, so I am a step ahead for now."

"I need you to let him gain control for just a minute," Ricky said.

"What?" Keaton asked. "You're crazier than a cornered racoon. I can't do that."

"I have to send my two drones over," Ricky explained. "If you let theirs power up and get airborne a little, them sumbitches might not notice mine until the dang things are right on top of 'em."

"I can give you thirty seconds," Keaton said. "That's all. Any more and I'm hacking and programming from scratch. I can set my next bit of code with a timer. Hell, maybe it'll screw with whoever is on the other end of these things."

"I can get it done in thirty," Ricky said. "Count it down."

"In three, two, one, now!" Keaton said.

Both drones shot up and away from Ricky. He used the cameras the lead drone had for guidance and had the other follow right behind. As they whipped around the corner, he shouted at Squarlik. "Now!"

Squarlik rolled once, exposing himself, as he tracked the lead drone with his scope. He ignored the movement beyond them, as some of the drones that had flown earlier powered up and started hovering. He shifted slightly and could see the Blevin stir behind their barricades. They had noticed the movement of the small tanks and drones behind them and were not looking his way.

As Ricky's drones flew over the first piece of cover, the enemy drones started falling toward the deck. They slowed and stopped above the gun emplacement. Squarlik was waiting for Ricky to let him know what to do, when he noticed the closest drone shift to the left and right erratically.

Squarlik took a breath and let half out. He had started to slowly squeeze the trigger, when he heard Ricky shout in the distance, "Theirs are down, but I'm losing mine! The grenades won't release! Someone is overriding them. Squarlik..."

The .50 caliber round hit the drone dead in the middle and shattered it. The bottom piece dropped with the three grenades attached. When they hit the deck, all three blew. Just before they exploded, the second round clipped the smaller drone. It careened into the closest bulkhead, and the two grenades it carried blew. Devastation and darts flew everywhere.

Squarlik shifted his aim again and shot the first head to appear over the barricades further back. "The gun is down, Top!" he shouted.

The Kin poured around the corner, firing as they went. The onslaught kept the remaining guards pinned down until they could toss their grenades. That part of the battle didn't last long.

* * *

Jyrall struggled to contain his rising anger. The Blevin were formidable opponents, and they'd taken a good position to hold him and his small group for as long as they had ammunition. Something had gone wrong in the first phases of the operation; that much was clear. The CASPers should have already cleared the passageways and taken any real fight deeper into the gate. The passageway they'd maneuvered through was quiet all the way back toward the cargo bay. He rolled his broad back off the wall and fired down the corridor. Two Blevin went down. Seemingly, another four took their place.

"We've got to press forward," he grunted.

Golund peered up at him. "Unless there is a possibility of distraction, the only way is to charge straight at them and hope surprise is enough to break their defense."

"That's not an option," Jyrall replied. He glanced at Ban-Tilk's wounded pincer and shook his head. "We hold here. Larth will get here in time. Cycle your weapons and fire only enough to keep the Blevin in place."

"Yes, Peacemaker," Golund replied. He turned to Traluur. "We alternate firing positions. Maintain good trigger discipline. Find actual targets. We aren't trying to get lucky."

"We're putting them down," Traluur replied. He turned to the corner of the bulkhead and did just that.

Jyrall tapped his eyepiece. "Cora? Cora, are you there?"

There wasn't a response. He tried again.

Keaton answered, "Jyrall, we've got Science Guild drones kicking our asses in here. Well, trying to, anyway. There's millions of 'em according to the manifest for the gate. I'm hoping most of them are still in crates."

"We'll investigate that later. Where's Cora?"

"We don't know," Keaton replied. "She got separated from Sergeant Squarlik. Her CASPer's beacon has been disabled, too. We can't talk to her or see where she's at."

She's been taken hostage.

Jyrall's hands clenched on his pistols until he felt a rush of heat through his chest. Teeth bared in near rage, he tapped the button again. "Get me a position fix on Cora, Keaton. I don't care what you have to do. Break encryptions and anything else you can, short of burning it all down. Find Cora for me."

"You got it," Keaton replied.

Jyrall changed frequencies. "Larth? Where you at?"

"On…my…way." The Zuparti was breathing hard. Given his frame, Jyrall couldn't help but imagine his partner resembling the frantic cartoons the Pushtal brothers watched almost every day. Well, he and Larth watched them, too. In fact, they rarely missed them as part of their morning routines. Jyrall blinked several times to clear his mind.

The sound of constant laser fire around him changed abruptly. A heavier, more thumping cannon opened fire down the passageway. Impacts at the corner bulkhead showered them with sparks and debris. At the same time, more conventional rounds ricocheted through the passageway. One screamed as it tumbled off the wall across from Jyrall and Golund. A split second later, Argold screeched.

"Gahhh!" the Sumatozou yelped. One large hand clapped over his upper left chest. Rich red blood flowed out from behind Argold's massive hand. "They've shot me!"

Traluur was already moving in his direction. Jyrall took the Bakulu's position behind and over Golund. Waiting for the inevitable pause, as he'd been taught at the academy, Jyrall reloaded both hand cannons.

"How is he?" he asked Traluur.

"Pretty decent hit. I don't know Sumatozou anatomy, Peacemaker. But this much blood scares me."

"Well, that makes me feel better," Argold trumpeted.

Jyrall snorted. There was a pause. It was brief, but certain. His instructors, especially Dreel, told him most pauses were no more than a few seconds. Each side was waiting to see if they could catch someone rising from their position to fire. The key was to be in position and pick an enemy off when they emerged. Jyrall stepped in the passageway with both fully loaded cannons pointed toward the Blevin. As the first popped up, he opened fire. Before he'd pulled the triggers two times each, the passageway filled with more Blevin. Realizing his position was deteriorating by the millisecond, Jyrall tried to duck back to the safety of the corner bulkhead and—

"Yeeeeeehaaaaaawwwww!"

Larth appeared behind the Blevin, with both of his pistols firing. The Zuparti's hands were a blur as he fired every round, holstered those two, crossed his arms, and grabbed the pistols from inside his vest. When they were empty, he reloaded, his hands still moving fast, empty magazines dropping to the deck. Blevin fell as they tried to turn and engage the new threat. Jyrall brought his cannons up and supported his partner.

"Way to go, Little Buddy!" Jyrall grinned as their shots knocked down the Blevin in a matter of seconds. His training kicked in, and Jyrall moved through the passageway to observe the carnage and, if necessary, secure any survivors.

There were none.

"Golund? With me." Jyrall called over his shoulder. The Bakulu moved quickly after him, cradling a weapon and systematically moving to each Blevin and firing a single round into their heads. Jyrall gaped.

Golund grunted. "Blevin have hard heads sometimes, Peacemaker. I don't take chances."

"Noted." Jyrall turned and saw Larth holstering his pistol. The Zuparti's sly grin was infectious. "It's about time you got here."

Larth shook his head, and his smile faded. "They're putting up a better fight in and near the docking bays. It's a shit show."

"Where's Cora?"

Larth shrugged. "My guess is they've taken her hostage."

Jyrall growled. "I have the same feeling. Keaton is going to find her and let me know where she is. Then, I'm going after her and—"

"This isn't because you have feelings for her or anything, is it?" Larth asked, crossing his arms for emphasis.

"What?" Jyrall blinked. "What are you talking about?"

"I mean, you're a Besquith, and she's Human. The sheer physics of a relationship between you two are impossible. I doubt even Ricky could come up with a way you two could—"

"No!" Jyrall said loudly enough to cause Larth to flinch backward. "She's my friend. Outside of you, Cora McCoy is the best friend I've ever had. I'm going after her because I cannot bear to lose her and because her people need her. We are friends, Larth. Simply friends, but the kind you want having your six every time you're under fire. *That's* why I'm going after her."

Larth visibly relaxed. "Okay. Okay, Snarlyface. I'm sorry. I thought you two were getting busy or something."

"Busy? We're always busy. What are you talking about?"

"Nothing." Larth grinned. "I'll take Ban-Tilk and the others back toward the Kin. Maybe we can take out the Blevin there like we just did here."

Jyrall nodded. "Good idea, but they're staying put. Argold's hit. We don't think it's bad, but we don't know his anatomy very well. They'll wait for a medic from the Kin. You're going after the gate master."

"The gate master?" Larth shook his head. "You want me going after him because I'm small and can get close to him."

"That," Jyrall grinned, "and because you're the best in the business. Right now, we don't know where Ravgart is. He may be in the control center, too. Get close and take him down."

Larth flexed his digits. "Deal."

"Jyrall?" a voice said over their communications links. "I've got Cora's location. Same deck as you, but a couple hundred meters away. Sending guidance to your eyepatch."

"Copy that." Jyrall held out his fist to Larth, who bumped his against it. "No mercy, Little Buddy."

Larth nodded. "You get those assholes before they hurt Cora."

"Fuckin' A."

* * *

Larth peeked around the corner. The corridor was clear. It had been clear all the way to the gate's heart of control. He looked down at the device in his palm. It glowed green, letting him know the closest security cameras were not working, if those inside the operations center were even looking outside their closed hatch.

He spoke quietly, "Hey, Keaton, I know you're busy, but can you tell me how many bodies are in the control center?"

Keaton's voice came back, "Well, hell yeah, I'm busy. Whoever they have programming for them is the best I've ever seen. Hell, the best I ever heard of." After a moment, Keaton said, "I count five thermal images. They're fuzzy. You must have the jammer on you. Its range is interfering with the cameras inside the center. One of them is big, another is real big. Sumatozou sized."

"Thanks," Larth said. "You wouldn't be able to give me a layout of their positions, would you?"

"Oh shit!" Keaton exclaimed. "I gotta go. This guy is trying some shit that might work. Shoot whoever looks like he is working overtime on a 'puter when you get in."

The call ended.

"Damn," Larth said to himself. "I guess I go in sight unseen."

"First, I gotta hack the hatch controls."

"I'm trying. Give me a minute, will you."

"Shhhh," Larth said. He giggled.

Using his knife, Larth pried the cover off the control switch. He studied the small wires and the circuit board. Several hacking techniques came to mind from his training. His small slate had built-in programs and patches he could use.

Larth glanced to his left and right, without moving his head. He put his knife away and drew his pistols. He stood to the side of the hatch, his back to the control panel. He slammed his elbow into the delicate insides.

There were sparks, and the door slid open. Larth spun, took the room in in an instant, and shot three Blevin, sitting at consoles, in their heads. He stepped in with both pistols raised. A large Blevin, wearing a captain's rank, had his pistol in his hand and aimed it at Larth. Neither spoke. As they stared each other down, Larth noticed the gate master seated at his console, eyes rolled back, showing white.

Larth stepped to the side, shuffling his feet. The Blevin followed suit, matching his movements, and like Larth's two, his barrel never wavered.

"Ravgart, I presume," Larth said.

"Maybe," Ravgart said. "Doesn't matter. You won't be alive to find out."

Larth grinned. "Really? You think you can squeeze your trigger before I squeeze both of mine? Is it me, or did those six shots when I double tapped your cronies sound like one long explosion of a single round?"

"Auto pistols," Ravgart said. His eyes darted down and back up as he tried to verify the type of weapons in Larth's small hands.

"Auto?" Larth dismissed. "Please. That was six trigger pulls."

They continued to circle each other slowly.

"I have fast hands," Larth explained. "You'll find out if I decide to take you out with them. A couple lefts, a right for good measure. That's all I'd need take to take your big ass down."

Ravgart paused in disbelief. "What? I am twice your size. I have been hit by others bigger than me, and they could not best me. It would be no match."

"Says you," Larth countered. "I don't think you are brave enough to find out, so I guess we will just shoot each other and see what happens." He raised his pistols slightly.

"A fight," Ravgart said. "Between a Blevin and a Zuparti?" He started grinning.

"Up to you," Larth said, his voice sounding bored.

"I suppose, next, you will tell me you are a Peacemaker, too?" Ravgart asked.

Larth shrugged. "There may be something inside my vest for you to see."

"You lie, like Varkell," Ravgart said. "But if you would prefer to die by my fists, I can accommodate you."

Larth paused, studying the Blevin commander. After a moment, he raised the barrels of both pistols. He bent slowly and placed them softly on the deck and took a step forward. He was taking a chance the Blevin wouldn't decide to shoot him now that his hands were empty. Blevin were arrogant assholes, according to the Peacemaker Academy's instructors.

Ravgart grinned and shook his big head. He tipped his own pistol upward and tossed it onto a seat at an empty console whose previous occupant was dead beside it on the deck. He interlaced all twelve of his fingers and cracked his knuckles. He rolled his neck and stepped forward, shrugging his shoulders like a prize fighter of any number of races across the galaxy.

Larth crossed his arms and pulled his two backup pistols from their hidden holsters under his arms. Three shots rang out. Two from his left gun and one more, for good measure, from his right. Ravgart dropped with three holes in his forehead.

Larth stepped across the room to his body and looked down. "Did you see what was in my vest, or was it too fast for you? Two lefts and a right, in case you're wondering." He shook his head. "Me against you? A Zuparti fighting a big-ass Blevin? I don't damn think so. Do I look crazy?"

* * * * *

Chapter Twenty-Nine

Springton Gate
Operations Center

"Hey, Keaton," Larth said. "Are you there?" He eyed his pistol for scratches and put it in his hip holster to match the other.

"Kinda busy here…still," Keaton answered. "But I have a second."

"Are you still trying to stop their programmer?" Larth asked. "I killed all three of the ones at consoles. Nobody is doing anything in here."

"Did you kill everybody?" Keaton asked. "Like, as in *everybody*?"

"Well, no. The gate master is still alive. He is just sitting there with his eyes rolled back," Larth answered. "It's kinda creepy. Like some of those old movies you showed me. The zombie stuff."

"What?" Keaton asked. "Can you check his pinplant? Do you see it? Is it glowing?"

"Yeah, I see them," Larth said. "All three are glowing."

"Three?" Keaton asked. "He has three? Shit. I need to call Jyrall. The programing is coming from somewhere other than this gate, and I think I know how their forces know where ours are ahead of time."

"What should I do?" Larth asked. "Shoot him and go help Jyrall?"

"I would wait and see what Jyrall thinks," Keaton suggested. "But you're the Peacemaker."

"True," Larth said. "But you know 'puters, and signals, and data, and all that type of stuff. I'm not gonna be the one to ignore the expert. I think I will wait but be ready to kill him."

* * *

Zeha

Ten minutes past local sunrise, the *Victory Twelve* flared over the landing pad near the queen's quarters and touched down. When Lieutenant Colonel Tirr keyed the controls for both hangar bays to open and then the main passenger door, he hadn't expected the crowd outside. He heard and felt their excited hypersonic communications through his antennae. In the host of data, he recognized Keshell, the queen's chief of staff, was present in the crowd. Queen Taal, herself, appeared to be on the way.

Pushing through the ship's shutdown checklist, Tirr couldn't help chittering to himself. The long procedures would have been much easier had he not asked Jessica to remove the copy of Lucille, her near-AI assistant, from the ship. While Lucille's capabilities far exceeded his own, or that of the MinSha warriors he'd ferried as security and support for his investigation, having her along could have caused problems. As much as he would have enjoyed the ease of navigation and control her presence would have created, her autonomous data connection history threatened to disclose what he might find. In this particular case, his findings were inconclusive and troubling.

He heard the scratching of MinSha claws on the *Victory Twelve*'s decking. The return of gravity, welcome and frustrating, kept anyone from sneaking up the passageway. He turned his head to see Sezza, the squad leader, peering through the hatch at him.

"Are you coming, sir? The queen is approaching."

"I am," Tirr said and pointed at one of the Tri-Vs with a foreclaw. "Humans require far too many switches and controls to fly these things."

Sezza chittered. "I think you've done a commendable job with the ship, sir. You trained four others to fly it as well. Some warriors could not do something similar with such success."

Tirr paused but did not look at Sezza. While he held a higher rank, the highest of any MinSha male he'd ever known, to be compared with a warrior was unheard of and the highest of compliments. He turned his head slowly toward her. "I don't know what to say, Sezza."

"There is nothing to say, sir. You've already done far more than words." Sezza's antennae waggled in amusement. "But you don't want to be late for the queen. I can handle the shutdown procedures."

Tirr waved her off. "I have two more items. Make that one."

"Are you certain?"

Tirr finished the power plant shutdown sequence and set the ship's computer to standby. He rose up to his legs and felt the pull of gravity. Flexing his joints, Tirr unfolded his body out of the commander's console and stood on the deck. Sezza towered over him, as all MinSha warriors did, but her demeanor was anything but threatening. She tapped her thorax with a foreclaw.

"It has been an honor to serve with you, Colonel Tirr," she said. Her antennae relaxed in total respect which made Tirr's nervous system tingle in pride.

"The honor was mine, Sezza," Tirr replied. "I think it's time we report to Honored Queen Taal. Don't you?"

Sezza looked over her shoulder at the poster of the University of Georgia on Earth Jessica Francis had taped to the wall a long time ago. Tirr turned and followed her gaze.

"I'd like to see Earth someday," she said.

"As would I. I'd like to think there are more friends to be made there," Tirr said. "Let's not keep the queen waiting."

They walked off the ship together. A warrior and a male officer in the highest standing. The crowd outside was easily more than a hundred MinSha, and the reverberations from their antennae almost overwhelmed Tirr. He'd never seen anything like it, save for the processionals of the queen during the mating season. As he scanned the crowd, Tirr saw the Honored Queen, her chief of staff, and her latest chosen consort. The sight of the latter set his anxiety to rest. He would likely survive the day if the queen were pleased with his report.

That, he decided, was an iffy proposition.

They made their way down the main ramp and approached the queen. Sezza paused and let Tirr advance first, as was protocol. Tirr walked to within five paces, knelt on one front leg, and bowed his head.

"Honored Queen Taal, I greet you."

"Rise, Lieutenant Colonel Tirr," Taal replied. "You are recognized and welcomed home."

Sezza repeated the ritual with one additional sentence. "Honored Queen Taal, I greet you. My squad of eight returns without casualties."

"Rise, Lieutenant Sezza. You are recognized and welcomed home."

The buzzing of the air around them, with the exuberant silent communications from their antennae, washed over them. The chief of staff, Keshell, approached and placed a foreclaw on Tirr's shoulder. "Welcome home, Tirr. The queen very much wants to hear your report."

Tirr nodded. "My gratitude, Keshell. I will report to the queen whenever she wishes. I am at her service."

"You misunderstand, Tirr. She wants to know. Now."

Tirr looked up at the queen's impassive face and realized the crowd, and their silent communication, created a field of noise effective enough to jam and disrupt any type of surveillance equipment. As the crowd trilled, he stepped closer to the queen, far closer than even a consort usually reached. Had he not been familiar with her pheromones, the effects would have blinded him. With professional aplomb, Tirr brought his eyes to hers and spoke slowly.

"Honored Queen, we have identified test samples from numerous Dream World Consortium sites. They match closest to a most unlikely source." Tirr clenched and unclenched his maw. "On Snowmass, with Force 25, I secured a sample from the tank of a Wrogul in their employ. The water originated from the planet Azure and is closest to certain areas of Krifay in its chemical composition. It matches closely enough to our samples from the water sources on Cruxton Prime, Tilgh-23, Lake Pryce, and Earth."

"What do your instincts say, Tirr?" Taal asked, her voice low.

"There aren't many Wrogul, and they've never been very interested in other places, but it could be a legitimate colonization exercise," Tirr replied.

"Do you believe that supposition?"

"No," Tirr confided. "The Dream World Consortium is duplicitous. I believe something else is at play, my queen. I do not know what it is, but I believe our allies in the Peacemaker Guild need to know. I believe such a warning is best heard by their council from your governance."

Taal was silent for a moment, her antennae vibrating. She looked down at him. "There are things happening across the galaxy, things reported by other hives and regencies which I cannot ignore. I do not trust the Peacemaker Guild fully, nor will any of our forces. I do, however, trust Jessica Francis, as I know you do. She must know what you've found. I fear we have only one recourse once you do."

Tirr nodded. "We must prepare for war, Your Majesty."

"We will prepare the garrison, and you will lead them, *Colonel* Tirr. When Jessica calls, we must be ready to assist. I fear the consequences if we do not."

* * *

Weqq

After six coordinated logistics jumps, two full battalions of Crusaders descended upon the unnamed western continent. Following fresh footprints and other signs, they followed the TriRusk to a region of exposed rock formations within the deep jungle. Sensor sweeps indicated an immense cavern system under the rock, but no viable entrance had been found. Determined to get inside, Crusader Prime ordered mass landings to establish a beachhead and search, on foot, for the entrance. No sooner had they made camp and found space for their maintenance racks, than the attacks began.

For twenty-six hours, many of Prime's forces could not exit their CASPers because of the damned bird-things. The rest of the units were trapped onboard their shuttles and dropships as the black things swarmed across the sky and blotted out the light. Even at night, they'd been able to make no progress as the bird-things and other creatures harassed them at all hours. Standing on the bridge of his shuttle, Prime clenched his fists and pressed them into his hips. Every move he attempted, the fauna of the planet rose against it.

He'd gathered the eight CASPers that had managed to deploy into a squad. None of the pilots held a leadership position. With eight motivated pilots all trying to lead, nothing of any consequence had happened.

And now, they were pinned down, unable to see more than a few meters, and had no telemetry information being relayed from the landed Crusader ships. What he had were systems not designed to penetrate the thick blanket of living organisms swarming over them and the surrounding area.

"I want eyes on them," Prime ordered his archangels. "Where are they?"

"Security systems appear compromised. I have a vague thermal outline on Tri-V two, Prime."

"Clear off the damned birds again." Prime turned to his weapons specialist. "Fire the scatters on pods three and four."

"Pods three and four firing," the specialist answered. There was no report of weapons fire from outside.

"Fire pods three and four!"

"Commands sent and acknowledged." The man frowned. "Command failure, sir. We have to assume those things have severed our linkages."

"Verify that," Prime barked.

"Without eyes out there, we can't—"

"Send a drone."

"We have no more drones to send. All have been compromised," his executive officer said softly.

A warning buzzer sounded. On his Tri-V, Prime saw the status for two of the stranded CASPers drop from yellow to red.

Prime fumed. "Get them on the radio. Get a status report."

"Ammunition is out on two CASPers. They're starting to take damage from bird strikes."

A third CASPer blinked red. A few seconds later, one went black.

A hiss of static burst over the bridge speakers. Prime heard Sergeant Edwards call, "…zzzzzz…Crusader Prime…taking heavy damage. Moving on panic azimuth toward landing site alpha. Please advise."

Prime stepped over to his console and stabbed the transmit button. "Recall beacons are activated, Edwards. Follow those."

"Negative…zzzzzzzz… all onboard instruments are compromised. Using the compass ring to navigate in the blind. Continuing to follow 095 to you."

"You should have been here by now." Prime looked up at his archangels. "Get them on the scope. I want to see them."

"There's too much interference—"

"Find them!" Prime roared.

But it was no use. In the space of two minutes, three more CASPers went black. The normally silent archangels chattered back and forth, their tempers rising. No one could find the missing CASPers. Prime dialed what video sensors he could to an azimuth of 275 to watch for them. There was nothing but a swirling black mass of birds. The radio was dead, and there was nothing they could do. Within another three minutes, all the CASPers' signals were offline.

"Goddammit!" Prime sat heavily in his seat and rubbed his face. His mission was clear and yet impossible. He looked up at the expectant face of his executive officer.

"Orders, sir?"

"What's our status? How much did we unload before this shitstorm?"

Smith consulted his slate. "Twelve CASPers and their maintenance racks. Two CASPers recovered. Both Mk 7s. Eight Mk 8s lost."

"I know that," Prime growled. "We have two CASPers unaccounted for? But we have their pilots?"

"Affirmative. The first two out the door emplaced their racks and mounted the CASPers before moving back. We have multiple crates of ammunition and weapons on the ground, as well. I can get a full inventory from Chief Potter."

Prime shook his head and rubbed the two-day growth of stubble on his chin. Through his pinplants, he could access the same data twice as fast. Instead of worrying about the losses, he worked through his problem set. They'd obviously found the TriRusk, but there were several questions remaining. First, how did they move from their previous location to a whole new continent? There was evidence of others having been on the ground at the MinSha station, but they'd covered their tracks fairly well.

Could Captain Kurrang have led them? Perhaps even convinced the Enforcers to help him shuttle them?

Their sensors and planetary assets would have detected such activity. The TriRusk had either moved on their own, by foot and by sea, or by an unfound and undetectable conveyance. Given the mounting defense—and that was exactly what it was—being put on by the local fauna, there was no way they were going to find the TriRusk or figure out how they'd jumped to a separate continent without more losses—both men and material.

Fuck this. There are only two hundred and something of these things. How important can they really be?

He touched the console, keying the communications systems to all Crusaders in their party, at the original landing site, and in orbit.

"All Crusaders, this is Prime. Recall. I say again, recall. All stations report ready status. I want us off this godforsaken planet in thirty minutes. Leave everything two Humans can't carry behind. Special compensation bonuses in play for every minute faster than thirty minutes." Prime paused, and a wicked smile crossed his face. "*Deliverance*, establish a R&S ring around the planet. I want to know the minute anything resembling a TriRusk appears planetside. Ensure all platforms are armed with kinetic rounds only. Acknowledge."

"Crusader Prime, *Deliverance*. It will be as you direct. R&S platforms being prepared now. Over."

"Excellent." Prime looked up at Smith. "What are you looking at and why are we not already launching?"

"We're leaving all this gear? And everything at the main site, too?"

Prime nodded. "Combat losses. We're missing out on a whole galaxy of opportunities sitting here chasing ghosts. If they show up again, we'll kill them."

"What about Counselor?" Smith asked.

Prime smiled. "Leave that to me."

* * *

Shaylin Gate

Hangar Bay

Rhineder moved his CASPer to what limited cover there was in the hangar bay and reloaded his hand cannons. His magnetic accelerator cannon was running hotter than he liked, and the process of reloading, while smooth and fast for the experienced NCO, gave it some time to bleed heat and be ready for the next run.

"Nails!"

"What is it, Anderson?"

"The drones are swarming again," the kid replied. "You wanted to know."

Rhineder curled one side of his mouth up. He had indeed wanted to know when the flying drones reconstituted in a tight swarm. From what they'd observed, the drones gathered pending a concerted attack. They still left a few dozen out of the swarm to continue the harassment of targets, and likely to relay possible targeting information to the rest, but the bulk of the drones in his docking bay formed a cloud almost exactly in the center. It swirled counterclockwise like a gray-black hurricane. Damned if it didn't look ominous.

And stupid.

At least, Keaton seemed to have stopped the miniature tanks from powering up again. That allowed his group to get back to the mechs and mount up. The flying drones were a whole different beast.

"Anderson? Have your squad ready. We're gonna lob some K-bombs together."

"Copy, Nails."

Rhineder depressed his transmit button. "Listen up, Kin. First squad, keep your base of fire on the drones not part of the central cloud. Second and Third squads, ready K-bombs, launchers aimed for the center. Let's break up their little party."

First squad tore into the outside drones. Their fire was heavy and accurate; even the mech missing part of its lower leg was able to stay on target from a prone position.

"Now!" Rhineder called. He came up with his K-bomb launcher and lobbed six quick shots toward the center of the cloud. Around him, other CASPers did the same. A few actually used their mechs' arms to throw the grenades. While not as accurate, or distanced, as a launcher, the effects were still impressive. Dozens of bombs exploded in near unison. Rhineder heard the Kin around him celebrate. He remained quiet.

As the smoke cleared, the damned things continued to swarm and swirl. Then, as one, they rocketed toward his position.

* * * * *

Chapter Thirty

Shaylin Gate

Main Passageway

Jyrall ran deeper into the gate. Navigation icons flashed in his eyepatch, guiding him toward Cora's CASPer. For the briefest moment, he wondered if there was a way to incorporate the eyepatch into his traditional Peacemaker uniform. As much of a hinderance as he'd first believed it to be, he'd become quite attached to it over time. The Peacemakers often wore combat goggles and eye protection capable of similar performance, but the one-eyed visage was—

Stop it. Focus, pup.

Cora's signal gained strength as he ran. Leaving Ban-Tilk with the Bakulu pilots to guard Argold hadn't been an easy choice, but speed was far more important with Cora in danger.

"Jyrall?" The voice was Keaton's. "How close are you?"

He glanced at the indicator. "Two hundred meters. I'll be there in half a minute."

"No, stop!"

Jyrall skidded to a halt, pulling his hand cannons from their holsters at the same time. "What's wrong? Where's the threat?"

"Look, I don't have much time. Something's really screwing with about every system I've got. It's messing with the security forces, too."

"The pinplants?" He'd been listening to Larth and the others as he ran.

"Yeah. I've never seen anything like it. I can't find a local source either. It's not in the mainframe or anything like that."

Jyrall took a deep breath and settled himself from the run. "Have you checked the antennae? What they're receiving? There might be a—"

"Oh, shit! I've got a primary antenna pulling down—shit, what's a thousand petabytes? Isn't it—oh, hell! Forget it. I've got a source on the exterior of the gate."

"Target it."

There wasn't an immediate response. "Umm, we've got *Blue Ridge* out there now. I'm not sure I want Monty and Stew firing at anything, Peacemaker."

Jyrall snorted. He had to agree. "Can't be helped. Tell them to focus on the job and that First Sergeant Figgle will be the least of their problems if they screw this up."

"Copy."

"When the antenna blows, look for secondary connections. See if you can find out how everything's being manipulated," Jyrall replied. "Keep all of your eyes open and attack viciously. Stay ahead of it if you can."

"I'm tryin', Jyrall."

"I know you are and—"

A piercing Human scream came from down the passageway. There was no doubt it was Cora.

"She's in danger. I'm going in, Keaton. Do what must be done!"

Jyrall didn't wait for a response. Cannons in hand, he sprinted down the passageway. Rounding a corner, he saw the customs inspection bay open. Inside, there were at least thirty, if not fifty, Blevin huddled in a circle. He saw Cora's CASPer, open and heavily damaged, on one side of the room. Around it were a dozen or more bodies.

She didn't go down without a fight.

There was a sickening smack from the bay, an unmistakable sound of a weapon on bare flesh. He heard Cora exclaim in pain. Fists clutching his pistols, Jyrall forced himself to wait. Fifty Blevin wouldn't exactly be a fair fight…for them. But if they were being controlled and directed by someone else, they had an advantage.

Come on. Come on, you damned overstuffed peacocks. Burn down the house.

* * *

Blue Ridge

The entire ship reverberated when the landing struts locked onto the drifting, spinning enemy frigate. The sound made Specialist Conner flinch. She breathed a sigh of relief and sat back against her seat. She reached up and loosened the harness holding her in place.

"I say, I say, that is. Excellent piloting. Piloting, don't you know," Stew said. "You have managed to lock on their ship as if we were catching a ride to exit a system on a much larger ship. Ship, that is."

"Thank you. Thank you, indeed," Monty said. He straightened the ruffles on his sleeve. "You may take over and back it into the slot it occupied. Occupied, to be sure. I am quite sure you will display the same light touch. Touch, that is."

"Hopefully, they can manage to dock it," Conner said. "Don't give them more than one chance. If they can't manage it with their maneuvering thrusters, then they can get ready to be boarded the old-fashioned way. They know the deal."

"Their pilot has assured us there will be no aggressive actions on their part. On their part, I say," Monty said.

"I know what he said, sir. I also know what could happen…and it's not going to happen. Mr. Stew, you wait until we get word from the colonel before we help dock that ship. I'm sure she'll have a ring of CASPers waiting when they drop the ramp. If they decide to come out fighting, it won't be a long fight."

"Yes, Specialist," Stew replied. He leaned over and whispered to Monty. "Does she secretly outrank us, even though we officially outrank her? Officially, that is."

Monty whispered back, "She is an E-4, and, as such, is part of a secret brother and sisterhood dating back to the 1980s on Earth. Earth, don't you know. We have no idea where she stands in that hierarchy. Many of the lower enlisted defer to her, and the NCOs tend to leave her alone to do her job. Her job, you understand."

Stew glanced back to see if Specialist Conner was listening or could hear them with her headset on. "Military rank can be so confusing. Actual rank, perceived rank, positions of authority regardless of rank. Regardless, I say." He lowered his voice even more. "And then there are the super-secret organizations that can make or break a unit. I heard that, over in the Barnstormers, they have a Specialist Haney who is a Made Man. Whatever that means. A Made Man."

Specialist Conner smiled inside. *Even those of other races are learning of the E-4 Mafia. I wonder what they will think when they learn warrant officers have their own idiosyncrasies and secrets. Like: where the hell do they go during the duty day when they are not flying or in their shops? And why don't they have to strictly adhere to the grooming regulations?*

She was shaken from her thoughts when the comms crackled to life. "*Blue Ridge, Night Moves.*"

Conner quickly answered, "Go for *Blue Ridge.*"

"Conner, it's Keaton. Listen, someone is communicating with the gate from elsewhere. It's why I'm fighting a running battle to keep all the drones from activating."

"Roger, I have been following a lot of the communication traffic about the drones," Conner said. "What do you need us to do?"

"Peacemaker Jyrall wants you to destroy the antenna arrays and any receiving dishes on the outer hull of the stargate. I can't guide you. I can't spare the time as I try to counter this guy. He is getting the upper hand, and when he regains full control, there will be so many drones active, our folks won't stand a chance."

"Roger that, we're on it. Out here," Specialist Conner said.

Monty and Stew were looking at her, waiting to hear what the conversation was about. "We have orders to destroy the antennae and receivers on the gate. We have to stop a signal from getting in. The survival of every one of our troops on that gate depends on it."

Monty reached up and threw a switch and turned off the powerful electromagnetic struts. The ship moved away from the disabled one. With a deft touch, Monty was able to leave the ship at a near standstill. What little movement remained would not take it far, and it could be retrieved as easily the next time. It definitely was not spinning like before. Conner changed frequencies and informed its pilot to sit tight and not do anything stupid.

"Sirs," Conner said, "I need you to get us close so we can use the sensors and the video feed to find them. It's going to take all your skills. If I fire a missile, it has to hit the protruding gear and not the hull itself. Same goes for the lasers, both the main laser and the smaller two. As a precaution, I am dialing down the main one."

"Got it," Monty said. "Move the ship into positions where whatever we intend to fire on is ridge lined."

"Damn," Conner said. She was impressed. "Where did you learn the term ridge lined?"

"We sat in on a class Nails was giving on terrain," Stew answered. "He said to never have your ass on a ridge line, or you will become an easy target. I think he was talking specifically to Anderson."

Conner smiled and said, "I can believe that. Anyway, yes. We want emptiness behind whatever we target. I have a big set up on my sensors now. Let's get into position, and I'll hit it with Launcher One."

Less than two minutes later, the missile impacted and blew apart several protruding pieces on the hull of the stargate. Monty kept the ship moving slowly as they allowed the sensors to scan.

"There is one," Stew said. "I can disable it with one of the smaller lasers. The small one." He engaged the weapon and did just that.

"What is that?" Monty asked. He indicated the view on the main screen. "Looks like some sort of receiving dish. My turn. My turn, don't you know." He engaged the other laser.

Specialist Conner grinned. She found another impressive-sized array. She directed Monty into the right coordinates and verified the flight path and beyond. She hit the panel. "Two on the way!"

They circled the entire stargate. Conner did not find any more of the larger pieces protruding, but Monty and Stew did. They kept the two smaller lasers busy. Conner noticed they were getting reckless with their shots, and a few of the targets had been questionable. It was getting kind of dicey up front.

"There's one," Stew said. "Another one, I say." He fired the laser.

"There you are. Don't hide," Monty exclaimed. "Hide. It's a hider!" He engaged it.

The two of them shot several more, caught up in the act.

"Sirs," Conner said, realizing there was an issue.

"Ho-ho, I see you," Stew shouted. "Zap! Zap, I say."

"Sirs."

"And another," Monty said. "Not anymore. Zip! Zip on you. Hey, perhaps we can burn a nice pattern on the hull. Checkers, maybe. Checkers, that is."

"Sirs!"

"Hey!" Stew exclaimed. "Look. An outer hull service bot. A bot, that is. It moves. It's a mover!"

"Shoot it! Shoot it, I say," Monty yelled.

Stew obliged with a cackle.

"SIRS!" Conner screamed.

The two of them froze and turned slowly to face her. "Yes, Specialist?" Monty asked.

"That poor bot was doing what it was programmed to do. Work on the hull. It was not one of the drones. You two melted it into slag. I'm locking out the weapons controls from the pilot consoles. I hope you're both happy."

Monty and Stew looked up and around. Everywhere but at her.

"Now, there are no more receiving or sending antennae on that hull. Take us back to the frigate and lock on while I call to see if it worked and if we need to do anything else." She paused and said, "If we do, I am operating all weapons. *All*, don't you know."

* * *

Docking Bay

The swirling mass of bots looked like the head of a giant drill as it spun and came straight at Staff Sergeant Rhineder and his platoon. He glanced at his readings, relieved to see them back in the green.

"All squads, pour everything you have into them. Everything!" he ordered.

The fire from the three squads would have been impressive in anyone's eyes. Drones shattered and burst into flames as the hand cannon and MAC rounds tore into them. Many of the shots went through drones and destroyed others. The ones in the front fired back, their shots peeling armor from the older war machines. The Mk 4s had an impressive amount of armor, but even they could only take so much before the inner workings and the pilots themselves would be exposed to the firepower of the endless drones.

The tip of the swirling mass was destroyed, but those behind kept coming. Rhineder could see his levels in the orange and climbing. He knew everyone would be experiencing the same thing. *Not good. This is not good at all.*

Suddenly, the tight formation of drones broke apart. Many didn't pull out of the swirling flight path and crashed into the bulkheads, ceiling, and floor. Their shots were erratic, no longer aimed at the mechs engaging them. Drones began engaging other drones as if the tracking and aiming sensors were receiving no guidance.

Rhineder seized the opportunity. "First Squad, time your shots. Control your rate of fire. Second Squad, reload. Let 'em cool. Third squad, get rid of the rest of your K-bombs, then reload. And make sure somebody covers Anderson. They're gonna notice his mech lying there eventually."

He observed First Squad take deliberately steady shots as the large grenades flew past him. He watched his own readings drop into the green as he reloaded. Well, except for the armor on his right shoulder. It was good for only a couple more direct hits. "All right, people. Some are dropping to the deck, but there are a lot left. Let's take the rest out and rejoin our Kin."

He heard the Pushtal he could understand calling over the radio, "Kin! Targets are down! Engage! Engage!"

* * *

Passageway

Jyrall didn't need to hear the radio traffic to know it was time to move. Almost as one, the Blevin twitched and stumbled. Some rubbed their pinplants and others rubbed their bleary eyes. Two turned toward him, stared for a second, and then charged. Roaring like nothing Jyrall had ever heard and twisting their faces into grotesque masks of rage, there was no doubt about their intentions.

Jyrall met them with his cannons.

The first two went down quickly. As the rest turned toward him, Jyrall held his ground and dropped another two. And then another two. The Blevin didn't slow down. He aimed faster, fired faster, and missed more than a few shots. Both pistols were expended within a millisecond of each other, and Jyrall realized only Larth would have been fast enough to reload in this situation. Instead, he holstered his pistols and withdrew his large knife from its sheath on the underside of his vest. Gripping the hilt so the blade pointed down in his left hand, Jyrall entered the fray with a grin on his wide maw.

The time is going to come, pup, where you have to let go. Your restraint is admirable and well-meant. It does you honor as a Peacemaker and as a Besquith. But make no mistake, we both know your rage is there, simmering just under the surface. You hold it back because you fear it will overcome you fully. You misunderstand it, and you will continue to do so until placed in a situation where you must realize it.

Realize it!

Dreel's words flashed through his head as he came up with his fists at the first Blevin to reach him. A slash of the knife took one down. A heavy right hook staggered another, and his slash of the knife finished the work. Every nerve ending fired. His weapons, both knife and fist, worked in concert with one another. Strength flooded every fiber of his being.

Jyrall roared and cut loose.

* * *

Gate Operations Center

Larth watched the big gate master twitch in his seat. His head rolled, and he closed his eyes. Slowly, the Sumatozou reached up and held his head as if he had the worst headache of his life. After a couple of deep breaths, he opened his eyes and looked around. They widened as he focused on Larth standing there. Then he noticed the bodies in the center, one of which was still slumped over a console.

"Who are you?" the gate master asked. He stood, perhaps too fast, then sat back down. He slowly stood a second time. "What is the meaning of this?"

The gate master took a shaky step toward Larth and raised his hands threateningly. Larth's hand shot into his vest, and he pulled out…his badge.

"I am Peacemaker Larth," he said. "You will comply with any and all instructions as of right this very instant. I have some questions for you. *Sit down.*"

The big Sumatozou backed up a step and sat down slowly. "I don't know what is happening. Everything is a blank. I do remember my gate receiving new security members. After that…nothing. Certainly, I will comply, Peacemaker. I hope I can answer your questions. And, perhaps, you would be so kind as to answer some of mine."

* * *

Customs Bay

Pain blurred Cora's vision. While the Blevin had used their open hands when they hit her, they'd done enough damage. Her head rang with pain, and her left eye was swollen almost shut. She tasted the coppery tinge of blood on her lips. Her left arm ached where they'd dragged her out of the CASPer's cockpit and thrown her to her knees. She'd expected them to be furious about the attack, but the torture surprised her. They wanted to know intricate details about the Kin. They'd asked about Weqq.

Where were the TriRusk? The way some of the Blevin looked, they had no idea what their squad leader was talking about. His eyes…his eyes had been rolled up in his head during his interrogation. When she didn't answer, he'd slapped her. Hard.

After the second time, she'd lost count.

On her knees, leaning forward on her right arm, Cora watched blood drip from her face and splatter on the cold decking. The drops fell in slow motion. She breathed hard through her mouth and closed her good eye.

Come on, Kin.

Come on.

Her unspoken prayers ceased at an earth-shattering roar from the passageway. Cora turned her aching head and looked through the curtain of disheveled dark hair hanging around her face. Around her, the Blevin turned as one and ran toward the roar. In the midst of the Blevin, slashing and snarling, was Jyrall. The mighty Besquith ripped a path through the Blevin. As fast as they'd charged into battle, some stopped and tried to back away.

Jyrall kept coming.

A half-dozen Blevin turned tail and ran back toward Cora. There was nothing she could do to stop them, but she started to crawl toward her CASPer. When the retreating Blevin didn't stop to pick her up, she raised her head again. Jyrall stood in the passageway, with blood dripping down his arms. His head swiveled and checked his surroundings. The look on his face was feral, like a mighty wolf on the hunt. Then, as he looked at her, the look vanished. He wiped his knife on his arm and sheathed it as he ran toward her.

"Cora!"

She tried to say something, but her limbs gave out, and she sprawled on the cold floor. It felt so nice and she was so…tired. The urge to close her eyes grew stronger.

Rest…just for a second.

"Cora!" Jyrall roared. She watched him skid and slide to a stop and reach down for her. His strong hands easily picked her up and turned her over. He swept her hair out of her face. "Cora! Cora, stay with me."

She opened her eyes and tried to smile, but it hurt too much. Her lips worked, but all she managed to say was, "Hey."

"Stay with me, Cora," Jyrall said to her and then she heard his voice change and rise. "Kin! Kin, this is Peacemaker Jyrall. I need a medic, right fucking now!"

* * * * *

Chapter Thirty-One

Customs Bay

A voice came from Jyrall's blindside before he caught the Depik's scent. "Peacemaker, let me in. She won't survive until a medic arrives. I've brought nanites with me."

Jyrall whipped his head to his left. His eyepatch, for all its advantages, hadn't picked up the Depik's arrival. "Tsan?"

"Yes." The Depik approached with an easy grace. "Now, please. Lay her down and let me in. She's badly injured."

Jyrall did as the Depik requested. "What can I do?"

"Raise her legs. I do not want her in shock while the nanites work," Tsan said. The Depik's eyes scanned Cora from head to toe as she reached into a pouch and withdrew two very Human syringes.

"Where did you get those?" Jyrall asked.

"The Human aid station," Tsan replied. "I like to be prepared."

Jyrall moved to Cora's right side and sat on the floor, pulling her legs over his knee. Almost immediately, the color returned to her face. She moaned, and her non-swollen eye fluttered open.

"Jyrall?"

"I'm here, Cora."

She strained her neck, raising her head off the floor, and stared at him. Her eyes flashed to the Depik and back to him. "Jyrall? Is that—?"

"I'll explain later," he replied.

"Lie still, Colonel McCoy," Tsan said. "And, yes, we'll explain later."

"Okayyy." Cora set her head back down on the deck and closed her eyes as Tsan administered the first shot. Tsan's eyes met Jyrall's.

"Remember our conversation? About security being near a Peacemaker?"

"I do," Jyrall replied. "You've decided to come out in the open because of that?"

Tsan finished the first shot and prepared the second. Her eyes were not on him. "I have my reasons, Peacemaker. Your fighting ability notwithstanding, which is impressive, your dedication to friends and confidants impresses me. I believe it's in both of our best interests that I emerge. I believe I can trust you and these Humans."

Jyrall nodded as he studied Cora's face. "The Humans have a phrase, at least these Humans do. It's a colloquialism from their part of North America. When they like you, they call you 'good people.' From everything I have seen, these are 'good people.' Even the Goka."

"So I've noticed," Tsan replied and administered the second shot. "This shot has a mild sedative. We'll need to get Colonel McCoy back to one of the ships for observation and to let the nanites work. She'll be out of danger in a few hours."

Behind Cora's CASPer, a door opened. Jyrall drew one of his hand cannons and aimed it in that direction. Tsan glanced that way and shook her head. "You can put your weapon down, Peacemaker. Two CASPers are approaching."

Sure enough, Jyrall heard them a half-second later. "Your senses are more acute than we were taught at the academy."

"Not everything is best learned in a school, Peacemaker."

"Would you consider calling me Jyrall?"

Tsan slow-blinked. "I would be honored, Jyrall. Well met."

Jyrall grinned. "Well met, friend."

Two Mk 7 CASPers bounced into the bay and stopped. One cockpit opened, and Jyrall saw Lisalle Jones undoing her shoulder straps. Before he could stop her, the young woman dismounted her mech and ran to them. Eyes wide, she pointed at Tsan.

"Jyrall?"

He nodded at the Depik. "Lisalle, this is Tsan. Yes, she is a Depik. You didn't see her. We need to get Cora back to one of the ships to let the nanites work. Can you help us?"

Lisalle kept staring at Tsan.

"Captain Jones?" Tsan asked. "Can you get Cora back to a ship?"

"Holy shit," Lisalle said. She blinked and shook her head. "I'm sorry. Yeah. Sure. I'll get her moved back."

"There will be time to talk later," Tsan said. "Right now, take care of your commander so Jyrall and I can ensure the gate is secured."

There was an edge to the Depik's voice which Lisalle recognized. "Yes, ma'am. We're on it."

"Who's in the other CASPer? Captain Sevier?" Tsan asked.

"Yes, ma'am," Lisalle replied.

"Not a word of my appearance beyond you officers, is that clear?"

Lisalle's head bobbed up and down. "Yes, ma'am."

Tsan turned to Jyrall. "Pick her up, Jyrall. Captain Jones? Get your CASPer. Jyrall will put her in your arms—it's the fastest way to get her back to the ship. I'd suggest you get Staff Sergeant Rhineder to link up with Captain Sevier in the main passageway, too. They'll be able to detain the rest of the Blevin."

Lisalle's eyes were wide, but she nodded. "Got it."

As the young woman ran back to her CASPer, Jyrall scooped Cora up into his arms. She looked up at him.

"Jyrall?"

"Yes, Cora?"

"Thank you," she said. "For being my friend."

Jyrall chuckled. "I have no better title, Cora McCoy, except to say you are my pack sister. For a Besquith, there is no greater endearment. Let's get you back to the ship."

He made his way to Lisalle's CASPer and passed Cora over. The two CASPers made their way back toward the landing bays. Jyrall watched them go for a long moment before turning back to Tsan. The Depik sat, watching him intently.

"You're right, Jyrall," Tsan said.

"About what?"

"They are *good people.*" Tsan stood. "Now, let's go make sure Larth doesn't kill anybody else and secure the station. Once that's done, the real work can begin."

"Moving the gate."

"Yes, that, but also, we need to talk about pinplants." Tsan licked one paw. "I've never seen anything like what the Blevin did. But I'm thinking Cora has, on Weqq. Once we get back to Krifay, all the Kin with pinplants will need them removed or disabled."

"Why?"

"They're being manipulated, Jyrall," Tsan replied. "But I don't know by whom, and that scares me."

* * *

Docking Bay

Colonel Brentale stood with First Sergeant Figgle, Staff Sergeant Wilson, and Staff Sergeant Rhineder. "It looks like Colonel McCoy is going to be all right. She's beat up pretty bad, but it's not life threatening now."

He took in the entire bay with his gaze. "What I need is the status of both units. Compile a list of KIA and wounded and indicate if the soldier is out of action or can still be utilized. We all lost someone we know. I get that, but we have to keep the troops occupied, or morale is going to plummet. Right now, they are pumped about winning the battle. Jyrall says we are to take advantage of it, and I agree."

"The numbers aren't good, sir," Staff Sergeant Wilson said. "We lost both officers, Sergeant Major Daniels, and seven of the troops. That crew served gun tore us apart. That's fully thirty percent of the Barnstormers. Not to mention the six wounded. Oh, and Haney broke his arm."

"Dammit," Brentale said. "First Sergeant?"

First Sergeant Figgle reached up and wiped his face with a pincer. "Sir, the Kin lost six. Three Humans, a Jivool, and two Goka. We have nine wounded, including the Ol' Lady, Captain Sevier, and Captain Bolton."

Figgle glared over toward the Kin, gathered together, cleaning weapons, eating rations, and drinking water. He continued. "Sergeant Bailey is a damn hard head and didn't let on how bad her wound was. The medic realized it in time, though, and she'll survive."

Figgle blew out a sound of frustration. "Corporal Bweenkit lost an eye and is running around with the patch Jyrall gave him. Some dumbass taught him to say 'arrrr, I be a pirate' in Human. He won't stop saying it. When I find out which fuck-winkle did it, I intend to PT him half to death. I don't care if he is one of the walking wounded."

"It might have been a she," Staff Sergeant Wilson suggested. She tried to suppress a grin.

"Male, female. Doesn't matter. I got something for their ha-ha funny ass," Figgle said. "Wait, you think it was Specialist Conner? Fuck. I hope not. Her and Squarlik get me the stuff that's hard to find. Damn."

"Speaking of hard to find," Keaton said, as he and his brother walked over, "Jyrall says you need to keep the troops busy, and we have just the thing."

"Yeah?" Colonel Brentale asked. "Do tell."

"We want the gear," Ricky said.

"What gear?" Staff Sergeant Rhineder asked.

"All of it, sir," Ricky answered.

"Hey," Rhineder said. "I'm not a 'sir.' I work for a living."

"Sorry, Staff Sergeant," Ricky said.

He hid his grin. "Anyway, gather the weapons and stack 'em in crates. Most of those are for the Kin and Barnstormers. Pack up any ammo, grenades, knives, good helmets, armor, everything. What your units can't use, you can sell or trade. Hell, grab it all. A damn utility belt if it's good. Fill up the holds of the ships. We'll have 'em make a run or two if we need to offload while we grab more shit."

"More shit?" First Sergeant Figgle asked.

"Yep," Keaton answered. "We want a bunch of them drones. Both kinds. Any comms gear they used. All the good shit. There are plenty that were not destroyed, they just quit working. Fill up the Blevin ship, too. We'll lock on and bring it back with us."

"We're going to be taking this dang thing apart," Ricky said. "It needs to be pretty much empty."

"Empty?" Specialist Haney asked as he walked up. "Really?"

"All of it," Ricky confirmed. He looked at the cast on Haney's arm. "Laser or a chunk of lead? Well, not lead, but you know what I mean."

"Neither," Haney admitted. "Crashed my glider."

"Oh," Ricky said. He started to turn away and stopped. "Wait, did you say you crashed your glider?"

"Yeah," Haney answered. He brushed his longer-than-regulation hair off his forehead with his good hand. "Wrecked, flipped, skidded a ways...you know, crashed." He shrugged.

Ricky turned to his brother. "And I thought Peacemaker Larth took risks. That's crazy. Flying a dang glider through these corridors. Hayy-yel Naw. Not me."

"Haney Shit may be worse than Ricky Shit," Keaton admitted.

Colonel Brentale said, "The cargo skiffs are in the loading bay. The troops can use them. Might as well get started now that we've accounted for and gathered the downed troops and have them in cold storage."

"Well all right," Specialist Haney said. "Time to pillage and plunder." The look in his eyes made those around him nervous. He was in his element now. He walked off and turned down a passage and disappeared out of sight.

"Pillage and plunder?" First Sergeant Figgle asked. "Nails?"

"More pirate terms, Top," Staff Sergeant Rhineder answered.

Bweenkit, still feeling good from the painkillers the medic had kept him on, stood and said, "Arrrr, I be a pirate." It was loud enough for all to hear.

First Sergeant whipped his head around and said, "That son of a bitch. He taught Bweenkit to say that shit. Asshole. Where did he go?"

"Good luck. You won't find him," Staff Sergeant Wilson said. She shook her head. "It's like he is on an appointment when we are back in garrison."

"Hmmph," Figgle said. "Hey, where is Squarlik?"

* * *

Gate Control Center

Larth turned to the door and put his arms on his midsection like the Humans did. "It's about time, Snarlyface!" His eyes dropped down from Jyrall's smiling face to the Depik at his side.

"Holy shit!"

Tsan purred. "It's nice to meet you, too, Peacemaker Larth. Well met. My name is Tsan."

Larth's mouth dropped open. His brain fuzzed over, and his inner voices, every last one of them, struggled to find words.

Jyrall stage whispered, "The proper response is 'Well met, Tsan.'"

Larth blinked and glanced up at Jyrall. "Kiss my—"

Jyrall raised a clawed digit. "Don't disrespect our new friend."

Larth clamped his mouth shut and sighed. "Well met, Tsan. Would you mind if I kicked my partner's ass now?"

"I would. Very much so," Tsan replied and nodded to the Sumatozou. "Who have we here?"

"Gate Master Fingelda," Larth said. "He's still recovering from the shock of all this. The disconnection of his pinplants from whatever signal they were getting from the antenna seems to have really disoriented him."

"I can imagine," Jyrall replied. "I've never seen anything like the Blevin swarming me. It was like they didn't care about the consequences. They tortured Cora, too."

"They what?" Larth whirled toward the unresponsive Sumatozou and then back to Jyrall. "You better have fucked them up, Snarlyface."

"He did," Tsan replied. "The great question is how this happened and who could be behind it. Pinplants are a galactically accepted device for many species. Someone able to exert control over pinplants would be able to drastically affect entire populations."

"And guilds," Jyrall said.

Larth's brow scrunched in confusion. "But most of the Humans in the Kin have pinplants. Not Cora and her officers—her old commander didn't like them—but many of the rest."

Jyrall nodded. "They weren't targeted or affected. We'll see if there was an attempt. I had Keaton monitor everything around the station he could see or sense when we took out the antenna complexes. Forensic examination may take some time, and we, unfortunately, don't have much."

Tsan pranced up to the Sumatozou and sniffed. "He appears to have dropped into a catatonic state. We may have to move him to one of the ships for the jump to Tambu."

"Tambu?" Larth asked. "Where the hell is that?"

The Depik turned to him. "It's coreward. Jessica Francis is consolidating assets there now. We will use this gate to move additional supplies for the rescue of her father from a planet named Uluru."

"I've never heard of that, either," Jyrall commented.

"Uluru is in the forbidden arm of the galaxy, and Jessica's father is there. His condition and status are unknown, but we fear the worst," Tsan replied. "If Jessica is correct, both the Science Guild and the Cartography Guild are not pleased with him. Specifically, they may be after something he has."

"And they're willing to take him hostage?" Jyrall asked. "This sounds like they've set a trap for Peacemaker Francis, and we're all going to fall into it."

"Perhaps." Tsan shrugged. "But knowing Jessica, and her allies, the ability to make powerful, lasting friendships is critical to the success of this mission. Whether you realize it or not, you've followed her model with the recruitment of the Kin. You have Goka, Jivool, and Humans working together. Jessica has befriended a MinSha queen. And through all of this, the Depik have realized we must align ourselves with new allies we trust to have our…backs…when the time comes."

Larth squinted at her. "How long have you been watching us? Jyrall and I specifically?"

"I've followed you since Parmick. I was tracking down information on the Veetanho, but it turned out that my target was actually the Science Guild. After great consideration, I've revealed myself to you. I believe we can work together and—"

"Holy shit!" a new voice called from the open hatch. Jyrall whirled and saw Colonel Brentale standing there with his mouth hanging open. "That's—that's a—"

"A Depik," Jyrall finished. "Pete, this is Tsan. Tsan, this is Colonel Brentale of the Barnstormers. His company will secure the gate at Tambu."

"Tambu?" Brentale asked. "Where is that?"

"We'll brief you," Larth said. "It's a long story."

Brentale's eyes were locked solely on Tsan. "Yeah. Okay."

"Colonel Brentale, hear me well," Tsan said. "When you emerge at Tambu, start talking on all Human frequencies. Ask for a man named Bull. Your code word is *resurgens.* When he asks why you are there, tell him Jessica sent you. Do you understand?"

Brentale nodded. "Bull. *Resurgens.* Jessica sent us."

"Pete?" Jyrall asked softly. The Human's eyes turned to the big Besquith. "You didn't see a thing here."

"I what?"

"You didn't see a thing," Jyrall said and nodded at Tsan.

"No…no, I suppose I didn't see anything." Brentale smiled. "Not a thing."

"That's right," Larth grinned. "But on the bright side, your cousin isn't crazy. I mean, I know crazy."

"No." Brentale nodded. "Not at all. I came up here to tell you the gate is secure. We're getting casualty counts now."

"And Argold?" Jyrall asked.

"Superficial wound. Turns out Sumatozou's are bleeders when hit in the right spot. Argold's fine. He's getting patched up now," Brentale said.

"Good," Jyrall said. He turned to look at Larth. "You'd better find Ricky and Keaton before they tear this place to shreds. We need a plan to disassemble this thing and get it ready to jump. Tambu has got to be at least five transitions away."

"Gotta make sure we have everything when we leave. I got you," Larth replied. "Pete, once you've got everything secured, let's grab a few of the drones for Ricky to dissect. They belong to the Science Guild, and something tells me we ain't seen the last of them."

Brentale nodded and tossed a salute before glancing one last time at Tsan. "Got it. Keaton already asked for a lot of them. I'll get them up here the minute I see them."

"Tell First Sergeant Figgle they have an hour to scrounge what they can," Jyrall said.

"They've already started." Brentale laughed as he turned down the accessway. "In an hour, there might not be anything left of this gate."

The colonel's departure gave them a moment of silence. Larth startled. Tsan was gone.

"Damn, she's like a ninja! Poof! She's gone."

"You get used to it," Jyrall said. "What is a ninja? Never mind…more Earth shows. That's twice she's done it to me." He shrugged. "She told me she was heading to the Merc Guild, but that we may see her again."

"Well, damn." Larth rocked back on his heels. "Are we going straight to Timbuktu?"

"It's Tambu, and no. We're taking the Kin back to Krifay. The Barnstormers and Slow Killers will provide security while Ricky and Keaton work with Argold and Fingelda to get the gate working again."

Both of their slates chimed. Larth glanced at the message and looked up at Jyrall. "A big meeting with the guild master soon, huh?"

"Given what our…friend relayed? Gosh, that doesn't sound suspicious at all," Jyrall said. "When it happens, we'll take the Kin with us as deputized agents. Something tells me we might need them."

"You've seen too many movies," Larth said. Jyrall didn't reply. Instead, the big Besquith smiled at him with his "I got you" smile. "What?"

"Nothing."

"Don't give me that crap." Larth raised a digit and pointed at his partner. "You don't smile like that unless you're thinking something funny."

"Well, it's more like a question," Jyrall said.

"Then spit it out. What's wrong with you?"

"Did you really just say 'ain't?'" Jyrall's grin widened.

Larth thought for a moment and realized his partner was right. He smiled slowly, laughing as he did. "Well, shit fahr."

The two Peacemakers dissolved into laughter.

*****

Chapter Thirty-Two

Shaylin Stargate

Ricky looked around at the tools scattered in front of him. They weren't really scattered. They were together by usage. "All right. This is gonna be a bitch."

He looked at the Maki waiting on instructions. "You four get started in the control center. We have the files to let us know how to disassemble the gate components. Cora has six pilots and their CASPers to do the stuff on the outside. A couple of them are Barnstormers. I'm going out with them. I shore hope they have as delicate a touch as she says they do. We're gonna need the strength of them big-ass machines to turn some of the bolts. It's a good thing these things were designed to be taken apart and moved."

Corporal Kylont nodded. "You handle the big things. We will get the small stuff. How soon before help arrives?"

"They's s'posed to be a whole team of technicians coming with the ships. They dropped off full cargo hulls. Hell, and some of the berths too. We'll get it done. Shit takes time."

"Ban-Tilk and his crew delivered the old gate master to another system. Not Springton," Ricky said. "He says he is retiring. Seems like a good enough feller. He read through the message traffic Keaton set up and thinks his replacement is Argold. He got a bonus to not speak of what happened here. Larth and Jyrall trust him not to talk. As long as he waits a few weeks, it won't matter none."

Ricky pointed a thumb in the direction the four Maki needed to go. "Argold is in the center. He's moving around a little better now. He's waiting on y'all. Let's do this shit."

* * *

Krifay

Cora watched her troops as they worked on their personal gear. They were sitting in the warehouse in squads as they worked. There were a few new faces. Through Mike's contacts, several good prospects had been recommended. She and First Sergeant Figgle had interviewed a few and found some experienced mercs. Two came with their own CASPers. They were both Mk 6s, but they used much the same technology as the 7s, including the missiles.

Even those recovering from wounds were working with their fellow Kin. Like all units, tales were told and embellished, some were teased, while others were serious in the conversations.

First Sergeant Figgle moved among them, checking weapons and gear. He had a word for everyone. Encouragement, a name, a threat, all the things that endeared him to his Kin. The first sergeant looked down and shook his head when a flash of color walked through the big open door. All four of the pilots had completed their systems checks and were coming in to service the pistols Cora had issued to them. The two SleSha, Top could handle. The Mideralls tested his patience like no others.

"Come on over, sirs," Figgle said. "Sit with Headquarters Platoon. Specialist Conner will give you some instruction on the safety and handling of those flechette pistols. You better listen to her or so help me…"

Cora laughed and turned to her officers. "Looks like Top has them under control. Let's find a room and go over the upcoming mission."

"Are we really going to meet with Guild Master Rsach?" May asked, once they were settled in a room off the larger area of the warehouse.

"Yep," Cora answered. "He has requested a meeting of the Peacemakers, and we are to attend as well."

"That's not something we can say no to. Not that we would," Nileah added.

"Hell no, we wouldn't," Cora said. "We're going to Diam, in the Ghumm system."

"When will we meet up with the Barnstormers?" Lisalle asked.

"Not sure. Probably after," Cora answered. "You'll see your honey soon enough. Jimmy-Ray has his hands full, working on their gear. They will provide long-term security while the gate is rebuilt and put in place."

Lisalle smiled but didn't say anything.

"Them and the Slow Killers," Lieutenant Rhineder said. "Through the years, I've heard of them. They have a good reputation."

"Pete swears by them," Cora said. "They did provide us with weapons and ammo. When I met their commander, I knew right away he was good people."

May giggled. "I wondered if you were gonna say anything, Nails."

Rhineder shrugged. "It's my first meeting with the command as an officer. I'm not sure what I'm supposed to do or say."

"Just be yourself, Nails," Cora said. "I think you will be just fine. I'm just glad you accepted the promotion and didn't fight me about it."

Rhineder grinned and ran his hand over his gray flattop. "You really didn't leave me any choice, ma'am. You called me out front, and Specialist Conner read 'Attention to Orders.'" He shook his head. "I stress training, discipline, and improving on soldier skills to the troops. To get better…to get promoted. I couldn't *not* lead by example. I just couldn't…And you know that."

Cora smiled sweetly. "When the fight's on, you use whatever you need to win. A weapon, a piece of dang firewood, or even knowledge learned through observation."

"Duly noted, ma'am," Lieutenant Rhineder said. "Duly noted."

* * *

After the meeting, Cora stepped outside the warehouse and looked across the tarmac. Jyrall waved to her from beside *Night Moves.* She saw the flash of orange and black as Keaton moved up the ramp and back into it. She walked over to see what Jyrall wanted.

"Hey," Cora said. "Whatcha doing?"

"Hey, yourself," Jyrall said, with a toothy grin.

"You actually said that with a slight drawl," Cora teased. "Next thing you know, you'll be saying y'all like Larth does."

"Is that a bad thing?" Jyrall asked, as he draped an arm over her shoulders and turned her toward the warehouse opposite the one her company used.

"I don't reckon," Cora said. "I kinda like it."

Jyrall laughed. "Come on, sister. Come with me to check on Ricky. He has been quiet and out of sight all day. It makes me nervous."

"Well, he has all my technicians with him. I ain't seen those Maki all day, either," Cora said as they walked.

"Keaton tells me the new contracted crew are with him as well," Jyrall said.

They walked out of the bright Krifay sunshine into the bay and paused to let their eyes adjust. Larth, standing near the open bay door, walked over to join them. Jyrall glanced at him and then back to the interior of the warehouse.

"What's he doing?" Jyrall asked.

"It's the Ricky-ist Shit I ever seen him do," Larth admitted. "Ever."

Concerned, Jyrall took long strides toward the waist-high table covered in printed diagrams and several upright slates. Ricky held a large blueprint in his hands and conversed with the same Jeha who had inspected their ships. They were so deep in conversation, Jyrall hated to interrupt.

He waited a moment and took in the rest of the open area. Frank and Stein were parked in a corner and looked pristine. They had been repaired and painted. CASPers were backed into their racks. Most had new armor patches, and all were plugged in, charging, and receiving diagnostic upgrades, including the Mk 4s. One had a shiny lower leg. The four Maki were scrambling all over two older model Mk 6 CASPers, excited in their work.

Covering a portion of the floor was an obvious section of the gate. It was enormous, yet Jyrall knew it was a very small piece. Several other Jeha were looking at part of it. Jyrall knew the rest of it was floating in stacked storage out in the system, away from all traffic and guarded by the repaired frigate *Daniels*, the newest addition to the Barnstormers' budding fleet, and two of the Slow Killers' ships.

Larth and Cora caught up with Jyrall just as Ricky looked up and realized they were all there. "Hey, Boss, what's up?" Ricky asked.

"What's all this?" Jyrall asked, indicating the large table.

"Manuals, diagrams, instructions," Ricky answered.

"See!" Larth exclaimed. "The Ricky-ist Shit ever."

"What, exactly, are you doing, cousin?" Cora asked.

"He's *reading* the directions," Jyrall said. The Jeha beside him nodded comically.

"You mean to tell me, you're actually reading the directions?" Cora asked.

"When the time comes, I ain't gonna be the one to mess things up," Ricky said.

"See! What did I tell you?" Larth exclaimed. "That's the Ricky-ist thing he ever did."

Cora stepped over and put her hand on his shoulder. "We believe in you, Ricky." She glanced at Jyrall and Larth. They nodded in affirmation. "You turn a good wrench."

"I ain't gonna let anyone down again, cousin. Especially kin."

* * *

Weqq

The Crusaders were gone. By the look of it, they'd been gone several weeks, if not months. Fresh growth had sprouted up between maintenance racks and pallets of abandoned supplies where they'd made their camp. The scavenged hull of the *Satisfaction*, now almost two years into its purgatory stranded on the surface, sat rusting off to one side of the wide marsh. The dropship call-sign *Mako 13* lowered its ramp, and a Mk 8 CASPer, fresh from the Intergalactic Haulers' stash on Snowmass, stomped toward the ground. After moving a hundred meters away from the ship and surveying the surrounding area, it lowered its weapons.

"There's nothing here," Araceli Cignes called. "I think it's safe to—"

Maarg was already moving. With her powerful legs, the young TriRusk bounded into the marsh toward what had been the Crusaders' headquarters. She didn't look back, but she knew the Misfits were deploying for security. Instead of tapping her headset to turn them off, she listened to them, and it settled her raging emotions.

"Homer, you take the far left. Keep your eyes on the tree line," Quin'taa growled. "I've got the right side."

"This would be easier with more bodies," Homer growled.

She heard Quin'taa chuckle. "No more than five or six of us. That's what the boss said from the beginning—when she bought into our little idea."

"I know, but it's just that it would be—"

"Guys!" Araceli said. "Let's cut the chatter and be here to support Maarg, okay?"

The frequency quieted immediately. As much as she enjoyed their chatter as a distraction from her own emotions, she appreciated Araceli's gesture. Maarg was quite fond of the young Human CASPer pilot, and they'd started the process of becoming friends. Her concern for Maarg made the TriRusk's heart swell, even among the frightful pain.

Her father was gone. She'd felt his death. When her mother passed, Maarg had been far too young to understand the intensity of the connection of the TriRusk to their young. Given her genetics, and the burden of her albinism, her pain far exceeded what other TriRusk felt from the death of a parent. Her *mallen*, the physical manifestation of the feeling, had been intense cold. While on Snowmass, she'd been cold almost all the time. As the *mallen* fell upon her, Maarg had shivered so violently, she'd been taken to the infirmary for emergency warming. It was there, under the bright lights of the medical station, that she'd realized what had happened. Her ears had popped hard enough to bleed. The air in her lungs felt like it had been sucked away. The cold permeated every cell and then it all vanished.

Her father, Kurrang, was dead.

There was nothing official in any documentation from the Peacemaker Guild that she could find. No news reports on GalNet that discussed the death of a TriRusk which should have been news considering their recent re-emergence in the Galactic Union. Instead, there was silence.

Knowing her father had been here, their home, before his death was enough that Maarg asked Tara Mason for permission to visit. Her commander had only one requirement—that she take the Misfits for security. Maarg was grateful for their company during the transition and now. As she approached some of the last ground her father walked, anguish gripped her heart, and her memories of him suddenly filled her mind. The warmth of the sun on her broad back reminded her of playing with her father in the wide clearings of the nearby jungles.

She stopped and raised her long face to the sun. Behind her eyelids, explosions of color framed her memories and slowly lifted the weight off her heart. He'd had a long, full life and they'd shared so many things. He'd prepared her for this moment from the time after her mother passed away.

You'll have to move on. Find your place in the universe and make it yours. Nothing can be assumed. Everything must be worked for—diligently. Do that and you will succeed, dear one.

I miss you, Father.

And I will honor you.

"Hey guys?" Homer called. "I've got fresh tracks over here. Tri-Rusk."

Maarg opened her eyes and turned toward Homer's position. She sniffed the air deeply. "Not too fresh," she replied. "How many?"

"Maybe two or three at the most," Homer replied. "Looks like they've been checking out all these materials and supplies. There's a ton of stuff over here."

"I see a few CASPer maintenance racks we could grab."

"No," Quin'taa replied. "Tara said not to grab anything here. There's no telling if it's been sabotaged."

"Huh, yeah," Homer replied. "Nothing's been messed with—just looks like they've taken stock of it."

"We don't have need for any of this equipment or their supplies," Maarg replied. "The colony here won't mess with it."

"How can you be so sure?" Araceli asked.

Maarg snorted and turned to look at the approaching CASPer. "Because it's just not something we…do."

In the distance, near the *Satisfaction*'s hull, she saw a group of four TriRusk making their way toward her. She sensed something was different, then she realized their scents were covered, and they appeared to be carrying weapons. Not the spears and other tools Nurr mandated they use, but actual weaponry. The leader, a big male she thought could be Ghar, raised his right paw.

Is everything okay?

If she raised her right paw, they would attack. Maarg raised her left paw. The four TriRusk continued to march toward her. Maarg met them halfway, in the midst of what had been the Crusaders' supply point.

Ghar seemed happy to see her and just as suddenly sad. "We fear for your father, Maarg."

"Father has found his way to the clearing. The sun is bright and warm," Maarg replied.

Ghar stepped up to her and placed his paws on her shoulders. After a moment, he pressed his forehead to hers. "Your father will be greatly missed."

"Thank you, Ghar."

The big male released her shoulders and stepped back. "Things are very different now. We have decided to protect our planet. Your father wanted us to return to the Galactic Union. Nurr has decided we will pursue that path. Our first step, though, is our own security."

Maarg nodded. "We have many allies, Ghar."

"We have recognized that, but we've also recognized we have many enemies." Ghar gestured. "These Crusaders. They worry us."

"You're not alone," Maarg replied.

"We worry they aren't alone."

Maarg squinted at him. "What do you mean?"

"Come," Ghar said. They walked fifty meters to a pile of abandoned supply crates. Maarg read them quickly and saw they were supposedly full of rations, medical supplies, and tools. Ghar pointed at them. "See? They are not alone."

Maarg followed his gesture and saw what he meant. Hidden by the thick grass, the last line of external information caused her to suck in a surprised gasp.

"Lemieux's Marauders." She looked up at Ghar. "Oh, shit."

# # # # #

About Kevin Ikenberry

Kevin's head has been in the clouds since he was old enough to read. Ask him and he'll tell you that he still wants to be an astronaut. A retired Army officer, Kevin has a diverse background in space and space science education. A former manager of the world-renowned U.S. Space Camp program in Huntsville, Alabama and a former executive of two Challenger Learning Centers, Kevin works with space every day and lives in Colorado with his family.

Kevin's bestselling debut science fiction novel, ***Sleeper Protocol***, was released by Red Adept Publishing in January 2016 and was a Finalist for the 2017 Colorado Book Award. Publisher's Weekly called it "an emotionally powerful debut." The sequel, ***Vendetta Protocol***, is due for release in September 2017. His military science fiction novel ***Runs In The Family*** was released by Strigidae Publishing in January 2016.

Kevin is an Active Member of the Science Fiction Writers of America and he is member of Pikes Peak Writers and the Rocky Mountain Fiction Writers. He is an alumna of the Superstars Writing Seminar.

*****

About Kevin Steverson

Kevin Steverson is a retired veteran of the U.S. Army. He is a published songwriter as well as an author. He lives in the northeast Georgia foothills where he continues to refuse to shave ever again. Trim…maybe. Shave…never! When he is not on the road as a Tour Manager he can be found at home writing in one fashion or another.

*****

The following is an

Excerpt from Book One of the Salvage Title Trilogy:

Salvage Title

Kevin Steverson

Available Now from Theogony Books

eBook, Paperback, and Audio Book

Excerpt from "Salvage Title:"

The first thing Clip did was get power to the door and the access panel. Two of his power cells did the trick once he had them wired to the container. He then pulled out his slate and connected it. It lit up, and his fingers flew across it. It took him a few minutes to establish a link, then he programmed it to search for the combination to the access panel.

"Is it from a human ship?" Harmon asked, curious.

"I don't think so, but it doesn't matter; ones and zeros are still ones and zeros when it comes to computers. It's universal. I mean, there are some things you have to know to get other races' computers to run right, but it's not that hard," Clip said.

Harmon shook his head. *Riiigghht,* he thought. He knew better. Clip's intelligence test results were completely off the charts. Clip opted to go to work at Rinto's right after secondary school because there was nothing for him to learn at the colleges and universities on either Tretra or Joth. He could have received academic scholarships for advanced degrees on a number of nearby systems. He could have even gone all the way to Earth and attended the University of Georgia if he wanted. The problem was getting there. The schools would have provided free tuition if he could just have paid to get there.

Secondary school had been rough on Clip. He was a small guy that made excellent grades without trying. It would have been worse if Harmon hadn't let everyone know that Clip was his brother. They lived in the same foster center, so it was mostly true. The first day of school, Harmon had laid down the law—if you messed with Clip, you messed up.

At the age of fourteen, he beat three seniors senseless for attempting to put Clip in a trash container. One of them was a Yalteen, a member of a race of large humanoids from two systems over. It wasn't a fair fight—they should have brought more people with them. Harmon hated bullies.

After the suspension ended, the school's Warball coach came to see him. He started that season as a freshman and worked on using it to earn a scholarship to the academy. By the time he graduated, he was six feet two inches with two hundred and twenty pounds of muscle. He got the scholarship and a shot at going into space. It was the longest time he'd ever spent away from his foster brother, but he couldn't turn it down.

Clip stayed on Joth and went to work for Rinto. He figured it was a job that would get him access to all kinds of technical stuff, servos, motors, and maybe even some alien computers. The first week he was there, he tweaked the equipment and increased the plant's recycled steel production by 12 percent. Rinto was eternally grateful, as it put him solidly into the profit column instead of toeing the line between profit and loss. When Harmon came back to the planet after the academy, Rinto hired him on the spot on Clip's recommendation. After he saw Harmon operate the grappler and got to know him, he was glad he did.

A steady beeping brought Harmon back to the present. Clip's program had succeeded in unlocking the container. "Right on!" Clip exclaimed. He was always using expressions hundreds or more years out of style. "Let's see what we have; I hope this one isn't empty, too." Last month they'd come across a smaller vault, but it had been empty.

Harmon stepped up and wedged his hands into the small opening the door had made when it disengaged the locks. There wasn't enough power in the small cells Clip used to open it any further. He put his weight into it, and the door opened enough for them to get inside. Before they went in, Harmon placed a piece of pipe in the doorway so it couldn't close and lock on them, baking them alive before anyone realized they were missing.

Daylight shone in through the doorway, and they both froze in place; the weapons vault was full.

*****

Get "Salvage Title" now at:
https://www.amazon.com/dp/B07H8Q3HBV.

Find out more about Kevin Steverson and "Salvage Title" at:
http://chriskennedypublishing.com/.

*****

The following is an

Excerpt from Super-Sync:

Super-Sync

Kevin Ikenberry

Now Available from Theogony Books

eBook and Paperback

Excerpt from "Super-Sync:"

The subspace radio chimed an hour later, just as Lew put aside the holonovel with dissatisfaction. There was no such thing as "happily ever after," no matter how many books she read. No one was going to carry her off into the sunset. Lew reached for the radio controls and felt the thuds of Tyler's boots on the deck in the passageway below. He burst onto the bridge and vaulted into his chair.

He looked at Lew. "Identify the transmission."

Lew fingered the controls and read off the diagnostic information, "Standard Ku band transmission from Earth. Origin point known through Houston nexus. Encryption is solid Johnson Analytics with the proper keys."

Tyler grinned. "Boss."

Lew nodded and smiled as well. "Appears so."

Their mysterious benefactor hadn't called them in more than six months, but every time he'd employed them, the take had been impressive. How he was able to garner the contracts he had bordered on magic. Lew thought the man sounded like some kind of Texas oil baron. Despite the technology, his calls were always voice-only, and there was never any interaction between them and whoever he represented.

Whatever he contracted them to acquire was delivered to a private, automated hangar on Luna. The robotic ground crew would unload *Remnant* and send them on their way again. Anonymous cash transfers always appeared in their accounts by the time *Remnant* returned to lunar orbit. The first mission had earned Tyler's company over a million Euros. The following missions were even more lucrative.

Their benefactor went by a call sign, and they talked in codes meant only for their own ears. It should have been a red flag, but the money was too damned good to pass up. A call from him could *not* go unanswered.

Tyler punched a few buttons on his console, and a drawling voice boomed through the speakers, "*Remnant*, this is Boss. Are you receiving?" The transmission ended with a chiming tone that dated back to the early days of spaceflight. The clear delineation of conversation allowed Tyler to answer.

"Boss, this is *Remnant*. Nice to hear from you. How can we be of service?"

A few seconds passed. "Tyler, it's good to hear your voice. I understand you're on a contract flight from our friend in India."

"That's affirm, Boss."

"Roger, you've got a shadow. Are you aware of that?"

Tyler's face darkened. "Roger, Boss. We're aware of the bogey."

By definition, a bogey was an unknown contact with unknown intentions. Should the situation turn bad, the radar blip would become a bandit. Lew checked the telemetry from the unknown ship. There was no change in direction or speed. It was still gaining on them.

"*Remnant*, the trailing vehicle is not your concern. I have a change in mission for you."

Tyler shook his head. "Negative, Boss. I have a contract."

"*Remnant*, I bought out that contract. The shadow on your tail is the *Rio Bravo*, under contract by me to get Telstar Six Twelve. You're going high super-sync."

*****

Get "Super-Sync" now at: https://www.amazon.com/dp/B07PGS545X.

Find out more about Kevin Ikenberry and "Super-Sync" at: https://chriskennedypublishing.com.

*****

Made in the USA
Columbia, SC
13 May 2021

37904698R00226